BESPOKEN

A Nightangel and Daydreamer Novel

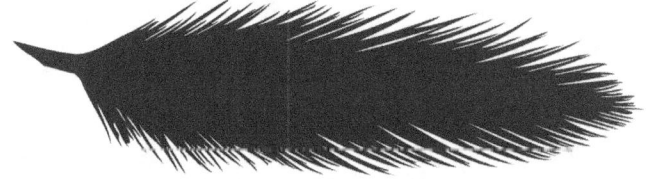

Marie Michelle Coleman

SUBURBAN ISLAND PUBLISHING

Dedication

This book is dedicated to my dad, whose love of reading helped set me on my path as a writer.

Acknowledgements

A special thanks to my family for their constant encouragement—you are my greatest blessing in life; my best friend, Linda, for her patience in reading more early drafts than should be legally allowed; my wonderful friend and mentor, Ron, for making sure I never dropped the ball; my mom, for her steadfast confidence in me; my editor, Erin, for her insight and honesty; and fellow blogger, Christopher, for his enduring faith in my ability to write this book. I'd also like to give a big thanks to my beta readers: E.J., Jackson, Josh, Karen, Ron, and Susan.

Definition: night-an-gel

noun

1. A preternatural entity with both angelic and vampiric aspects to its nature.
2. A winged vampire with angelic powers; a vampiric angel.
3. A supernatural creature superior to humans in power, part angel and part vampire; can be originally mortal in nature.
4. An angelic being often confined to the night, requiring blood to survive; a type of vampire.
5. An overlord, or controlling presence, in the vampire or paranormal community.
6. A protector or guardian.

   - Synonyms: bloodangel

≪ CHAPTER ONE ≫

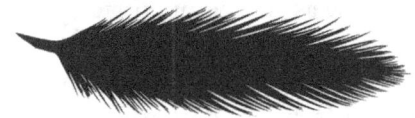

CASEY SLOANE WAS BALANCED on the curb of a busy downtown intersection like a particularly delicate snowflake impatient to be swept into the heart of the storm. At the height of rush hour, Washington, D.C. was emptying out for the night with all the precision of a routine emergency evacuation drill. Patches of weary conversation floated above the low grumble of the bumper-to-bumper traffic. The damp air was spiked with exhaust fumes and the flash of brake lights stained the street neon red. This was not the time of day to jaywalk, or Casey would have done it. In her experience, rush hour drivers were a dangerous lot.

Instead, she tightened the scarf around her neck with fingers already growing stiff from the cold and waited for the light to change. She was tired and hungry. Now, she was freezing as well. For an instant, she wished she could go home, throw dinner into the microwave, and watch one of the shows stacking up on her DVR instead of just saying she'd get to it. The thought floated away like one of the puffs of white air that formed in front of her face each time she breathed out. There would be none of that home sweet home stuff. Not for hours yet. She was an associate attorney at one of the large law firms nesting like fierce birds of prey in the office buildings that lined the streets and avenues of Northwest D.C. Going home was not an option. It didn't matter. She had nothing to go home to that could not wait. She lived alone and liked it that way.

Snug houses tucked away in suburbia such as the modest red brick house she called home were welcoming enough after a busy day but did not require undue attention. Her mind was most often on her job, so that worked out well for both her and the house. To work long hours and survive the stresses and hardships inherent in the life of an associate in a leading Washington, D.C. law firm without complaint was a basic rite of passage. She meant to be a partner and that required sacrifice. She was a good attorney. That went without saying. That was not enough. She must work long past weary during the workweek and give away her weekends and holidays to the firm without comment or protest. Tossing aside any real personal life was an essential ingredient to success. And so, she did it. The climb to partnership was too competitive to do otherwise. She was not the only associate attorney who hungered for a partnership at the prestigious Phillips & Row. A few would make the cut. She planned to be among those. This escape from her desk was limited to a quick break for food, semi-fresh air, and the illusion of freedom.

Casey retrieved her cell phone from the depths of her coat and speed-dialed Ricki. "So, what was it today—day in court, or paperwork and client meetings?"

"All of the above. Some of my clients need their heads examined, or maybe I do for taking them on."

Ricki was her best friend and the most badass attorney she knew. A solo practitioner, she managed to juggle a diverse portfolio of clients requiring her services for everything from divorce and employment cases, to matters springing from the kind of poor life choices that always require legal counsel in the end. She was not afraid of anybody or anything except rampant stupidity and any extended potential for a little peace and quiet.

"Rethinking attorney-client privilege?"

"Rethinking my career path. Don't ever take a divorce case. One of my clients tried to take the law into her own hands today. I can't blame her. Her soon-to-be ex crossed the line. It's a given he's a liar and a cheat. That's why she's divorcing him. His real mistake was holding out on providing her the court-ordered cash she has coming to her."

"Your clients are so much more interesting than mine. What did she do?"

"Oh, nothing much. Just chased him around a parking lot in her car this morning—the one he's trying to take from her. The guy was on foot and carrying a venti triple shot latte. He spilled it all over his pants and a fine pair of Italian shoes. I understand he ordered it extra hot. Karma is a bitch."

"Everybody survived the incident?"

"You worry too much about people who don't deserve it. The guy went in and bought another coffee. My client will be taking the metro for a while until she simmers down. She's also signed up for yoga classes. The check arrived this afternoon and it looks like the car is hers. I think all will be well. Unless she skips the yoga or he keeps ordering his coffee ready to scald."

Casey thought this was another example of how it was almost always a bad idea to indulge in the phrase, "Make mine extra hot."

"He needed one of those stopper things you stick into the top of the cup to keep the coffee from sloshing all over your hand while you carry it."

"True, but you have to know to ask for one."

"Did you notice they hide those things behind the counter like they are made of gold? They figure some kid will poke one in their eye and the parents will sue."

"If the kid isn't blinded forever, it's the perfect scenario. Kid learns lesson. Parents get college fund started."

"And, if it's a local occurrence, you might get a new client."

"Yeah. I look forward to taking on that case. You're not calling to cancel our dinner this week, are you? There will be hell to pay if you try to put it off again." Ricki loved to say things like that. A good argument was better than a day at the spa, the way she looked at it. Got the blood pumping, mind working, discharged any stress build up, and resolved the problem at hand.

"No need to stress," Casey assured her. "Your dinner plans are safe with me."

"They had better be. I'm not switching things around again due to the unreasonable demands of Pilfer and Woe."

"It's Phillips and Row. And that's what you have to call it when I make partner there. Which I will. And no worries. We're on. Go back to your happy life of chaos and mayhem."

"And you enjoy the major law firm associate angst factor. That place is going to turn up on the news any day now as the newest black hole to be discovered by modern science."

A new set of evacuees had joined Casey curbside. *Crap.* She had missed the light.

"Will do." Casey disconnected and shoved the phone back in her pocket.

She swallowed a mouthful of winter air as if she was popping a decadent chocolate into her mouth and studied the darkness descending over the city. She thought about slipping into a quick daydream but she did not allow herself that secret pleasure. She had too much to do tonight to tumble into dreams that would tempt her to stay well beyond what time she had to spare. She closed her mind to the idea and a tiny sigh escaped her lips.

Her gaze skipped across the street, past the light, to the crowd of people waiting to cross. She sucked in her breath as her eyes landed on Gabriel. It didn't just look like him. It was him. She knew because he lifted his eyes in a quick glance of the most intimate recognition and the hint of what she took to be a consoling smile leapt to the red, familiar curve of his mouth as the shock registered on her face.

Red—his lips were red. Just like in the dreams. Red against pale. The forbidden and the irresistible were all held within the calm curve of that smile.

There was one problem. Gabriel, with or without that killer smile, should not be there.

The light changed. She wanted to run away from him and toward him at the same time. She was not sure what might be most sensible, or worse, which of the two she was most inclined to do. She had never been so close to danger. Not in the real world anyway. She checked her surroundings to make sure she had not drifted into the center of some insistent daydream that held less ordinary things.

This was no dream.

Everything around her was as it should be except for the inexplicable vision standing across from her. She was leaning toward running like hell rather than moving to meet him but her feet did not seem under her command. A thrill of fear coursed through her; a sense of confusion overrode it. The look Gabriel gave her tumbled her emotions.

His smile was definitely consoling. She wished it were not. He knew her too well. *He has a lot of nerve to show such deep understanding when he is something that could not be explained at all*, Casey thought. She was still staring into his eyes with as much bravery, or at least bravado, as she could manage. She would have preferred he taunt her with his presence than seek to comfort. Then she could have dismissed him as an unfortunate figment of her imagination brought about by the combined effects of overwork, too much caffeine, and long-term sleep deprivation. A sort of residual haunting. Perfectly harmless. Quite forgivable.

The walk signal flashed an electric command across the avenue. *Walk. Walk. Walk.* She did not. Instead, she stood frozen as people pressed past her into the crosswalk. She was waiting for his approach, wrapped in a haze of hope and dread that was violet-sweet and nauseating. She was dizzy with it. She looked down at the pavement to try to regain her equilibrium. She was afraid to look up again and find herself face to face with him. She was terrified she might have to stare into those siren-song eyes and those smiling lips would part to speak her name—like in the other place, like so many times before.

That was impossible. *Impossible.*

She raised her head to prove the truth of it. Gabriel could not be there. Gabriel could not be anywhere. He existed in the daydreams—and no place else.

But he was very present. He had not moved from the spot where she had first glimpsed him. The smile was gone and those red lips had faded to something approximating a normal shade. He was staring back at her; inviting her next action, waiting with great interest to see what it would be. The Don't Walk sign flashed a neon warning. Casey remained where she stood.

The light turned yellow. He turned his collar up against the cold, although Casey imagined something like Gabriel would be immune to the winter wind. He stepped back into the crowd. He was leaving.

She could beat the light. She could race across the street before the stream of rush hour traffic began again. But she stayed put and stared after him, her heart pounding away, while a sea of intruding headlights flooded between them and he lost himself in the deepening night.

Off in the distance, the icy streaks of crimson painting the horizon melted away like Gabriel's lips had faded to pale. The light straight across the way changed. And changed. And changed again. But Casey did not cross.

Red. Green. Yellow. Red. Green. Yellow. Red.

Always, Casey thought. *Always*. Red.

≪ CHAPTER TWO ≫

CASEY HAD BEEN BROODING over the dangers of a vivid imagination—specifically hers—since seeing Gabriel two nights before. His presence had disturbed her but his attitude had caused her the greater concern. He thought he had every right to be there. He thought she should not be so surprised to see him. Staring into the certainty his eyes always held with regard to her was bad enough in the comparative safety of a secret daydream, but it was quite a different thing when experienced in person. A sickening wave of anxiety grew within her as she recalled the look on his face as their eyes had first met. A little tendril of longing twined around that anxious feeling and made it something else altogether as she imagined when she might next stumble upon him. It felt like eager anticipation when it should be dread.

This was stupid.

She did not have anything to anticipate or dread. She would not stumble upon him. She would not overexcite herself about his sudden arrival or the possibility of his continued presence because he had not arrived. He could not hop on a train or catch the next flight to D.C. That was not the way it worked. He could not be anywhere she was right now so to have seen him was impossible. She had been mistaken because it was dark. That was all.

Casey scanned the street for an empty taxi. She could not quite accept her own arguments. He certainly seemed to have arrived. And without much trouble either. She hated the way her mind switched back and forth between reluctant belief and desperate disbelief. It made her feel a little crazy. And crazy was not a good option for up-and-coming attorneys in the town in which she made her living. Although now that she was thinking on it, maybe it was the ideal state of being for attaining the elusive state of partnership.

She should never have paid him the slightest notice to start. That had been her first mistake. She kept daydreaming about him too because she could not stop herself from thinking of him once they had met. That compounded the error. Now there was trouble and Gabriel was at the center of it. There was no use pretending the night before last had not happened. He had stared into her face with a proprietary intensity she could not help recognizing. His smile said he saw her as his in the same way as he always saw her to be his. That hungering smile was like a dart shot straight through to her heart, for Casey feared there was some truth to his assumption—even in this place where he should not be, could not be—and she did not want to think it, or at least, admit it.

His arrival, even if it were imagined, forced her to begin reconsidering what she thought she knew in the world, as if everything she took for granted must be examined and revalidated. She did not like to think what seeing Gabriel could mean. It would switch up things in a way she dare not consider, in all likelihood, forever. She would prefer to believe he was just a favorite resident of her daydreams who—if it was necessary to get all technical about it—might be seen without being seen at all. That would be so much easier. Besides, it made much more sense—given whom and what he was, given whom and what she was. But then, that smile he had bestowed upon her was nothing if not real and just the tiniest bit demanding. It had an edge of impatience to it as it faded from his face and he melted back into the night that had brought him to her. Its meaning—his meaning—terrified and beguiled in one stroke.

She squinted, looking up and down the block. She was checking for him. She could not stop herself. She stepped into the street and flung her hand up high as she spotted an empty cab.

She might have lapsed into a state of general confusion but there was one thing she did know with a certainty. She did not want to glimpse Gabriel walking around in her world for any reason whatsoever. It should be a simple enough thing to wish for and receive. Yet now, everywhere she went, she dreaded coming upon him. She feared having to face that intimidating red smile. The way it faded from his lips before it faded from his eyes made her shiver with desire to watch it land on her again and again.

Bad idea.

Was he following her right now? Had he been following her for days or weeks—or from a time before she had first come upon him in the whispering green field of a daydream?

Now she was being paranoid. Nobody was following her and if someone was, she did not care—they could follow away. They were going to get bored fast. She waved her hand higher. She wanted to jump into a cab so she could hide away from whatever might be watching that she did not believe was there but still might be anyway. An empty taxi shot across three lanes of traffic and lurched to a stop beside her. She threw a backwards glance over her shoulder as she got in. No Gabriel, just a predictable six o'clock street in Washington, D.C. Nothing special. Casey sighed in relief and rattled off an address to the driver. The radio was set to the standard NPR drone D.C. cab drivers so often favored. She made no request for him to turn the blaring commentary down. It protected her from any conversation and kept her free to sink into her own version of All Things Considered.

Watching the city slide by, she asked herself why it would be a surprise to find Gabriel roaming about in a place that lit up like a fairytale kingdom each night. A city full of granite and marble monuments rising from long velvet stretches of emerald green or shimmering alongside still pools of water edged in white stone was a fitting backdrop for him. It made as much sense as anything else that he should be wandering its streets. He would like this place. Perhaps he believed he had been invited by her in a hundred different ways she had not even realized would be taken in such a light.

She thought she had been so careful, too. She never said anything to him out loud in the dreams that would reveal the depth of her feelings for him. She was smart enough to realize, even done in a whisper, such an admission would be unwise—for who knew to what it might lead? At the minimum, it would create another level of expectation between them. Casey felt the danger of such an outcome and the breath rushed from her parted lips as if yanked out of her.

When it came to Gabriel, following the rules was not always easy. Given recent events, it was clear she had not been careful after all. The bottom line was she had never expected to see him in her city, or for that matter, on Planet Earth. Dreamland was okay. Anywhere else was much too close for comfort. She had settled into a pattern of seeing him in her daydreams each day without fail. This behavior wasn't safe, it was smug. Her mistake was his invitation.

She would admit, if pressed, sometimes she wanted more. She wanted him there with her on this side of things for a few minutes—alright, maybe a little longer than that. She wanted to see a flesh-and-blood Gabriel instead of the Gabriel who walked in the lilac-skied daydreams she spun in her mind with alarming regularity. She had tried, on occasion, to see if she could make him materialize in front of her by sheer force of will. She would lie on her bed, and summoning all her powers of concentration, squeeze her eyes shut and try to feel some inkling of his presence beside her. No shadowy, half-world Gabriel ever appeared. No big surprise there. She could not say in those moments whether she was relieved or disappointed. He was not there. If she wanted him, she must find him in that other place. She would have to do without him in the cold light of her day-to-day life. That's the way it was. It made sense. So she would get up and get back to reality. She still had him in her dreams. That was something, after all.

But she had never considered finding him in this place. Not ever. Not even on those few occasions when she had wanted more and tried to wish him into being there with her. Not until that frozen moment on the curb with the wind gusting against her body like it had sprung from the wings of an impatient angel and nothing but the small distance of the avenue between them. Maybe she had never perceived him clearly until that moment.

Now, she could not release that image from her mind. How he stood so sure and peaceful, shooting that superheated smile her way. How he had turned up his collar and gone again without a backward look. That's the way she knew who he was, what he was. Knew for sure. In her heart of hearts. It was Gabriel—even if he walked the landscape without wings. He had not looked back. Nightangels never did. They moved forward with confidence—certain of every action they took.

And that Gabriel was a nightangel of great and glorious aspect and nature could not be denied. She knew this without a doubt. She knew it

9

firsthand, but in a way that made it seem a reasonable thing for him to be when it was anything but that. After all, she was well acquainted with this nightangel. Every daydream she had was about him in the end. Casey's stomach lurched. She did not want to believe. She would not believe. She would prefer to think she was crazy.

She paid the taxi driver and climbed the trio of shallow steps that led up to the Madison Building. Two hours of solitude within the walls of the Library of Congress and dinner with Ricki afterward was what she needed to clear her head.

Maybe she would tell Ricki about Gabriel. Maybe Ricki would think she was crazy and tell her so. It would almost be a relief. Maybe she had been working too hard. Maybe she was having a nervous breakdown or a bad reaction to workplace stress. A few stern words from Ricki would put everything back in place again. If anyone could see her through a nervous collapse or impose a stress management regime geared to shutting down a nightangel, that person would be Ricki.

Even a nervous breakdown was starting to sound like a pretty good alternative to having Gabriel dogging her steps. However, she had no time for breakdowns. She hoped a few hours of concentrating in a practical manner on the topic of Gabriel, and the sorts of things that must be considered alongside of him, would push the potential for craziness right out of her brain and replace it with a reasoned response. She had set a deadline for this research project and lawyers live for deadlines, especially self-imposed ones.

She took the elevator up to the second floor and pushed through the painted steel doors that opened into the reading room as though fleeing into a sanctuary. Here, she could think without interruption and bypass inquiries by coworkers while still feeling assured she was not alone in the world. The presence of other researchers made her feel safe in a way she did not feel when by herself now—even when in her own house behind locked doors.

The prior night had been a sleepless, worrisome affair, as had been the night before that. She could not deal with many more of them and stay sharp. She had already committed a terrible oversight with regard to filing a routine court document and it had not gone unnoticed. She blushed with shame when she recalled the angry words the managing partner had heaped on her when he found out about her error. Ed Johnson didn't forgive and he didn't forget but he had let her walk out of his office with the case still safely hers. Some people would call that a miracle. Casey knew it was just a lucky break. Ed had some reason to leave her caseload as it stood. She accepted her reprieve at face value without imbuing it with any special meaning.

There could be no more mistakes. She had to prove to herself that everything was okay, that she was okay, and push the daydream back into the place it belonged. She could not continue to be distracted and exhausted by something that could not be happening. She had to take care of this now.

She found an empty table to one side of the reading room and laid her briefcase down on it. She tossed her coat across the chair beside her and put her handbag on the seat. She slid into the hard chair and a weight of fear and confusion lifted from her shoulders. She could figure this out. She just needed to calm down.

Casey loved the hushed intimacy of a library—fancy or simple. The no-nonsense quality to this reading room was what she craved at the moment. Books, workspaces, technology, and the subtle buzz of activity created a soothing oasis of relative quiet. She was glad she had come, glad for the serviceable tranquility of the brightly lit reading room. She had a weakness for libraries that went beyond what she felt for her other secret escapes—coffee shops with web access, and the expensive aisles of the bookstores that dotted the landscape around her office and littered the shopping areas of her neighborhood. She had spent the last part of her afternoon sitting in front of her computer in her associate-sized office and she was happy to be free of such overt confinement. Some days, the beige walls of her office pressed in on her and she was glad for the airshaft window that gave her the barest hint of the world outside.

She put work out of her mind. This was not about work. This was about Gabriel and figuring out what the hell she was dealing with—be it nightangel or nothing a good night's sleep and a tighter rein on her imagination would not fix. She had some ideas that went beyond standard web searches. She was familiar with a few reading rooms at the Library of Congress and she wanted to use this one as a quiet place to read some articles and review a list of titles she had identified as worth a look. She drew the folder with her printouts from her briefcase and began flipping through them. Nothing was quite on point but maybe she could find something buried there—some clue or hint that would help her start to understand what was going on. If he'd just been something simpler—werewolf, standard-issue vampire, elfin prince—this would be easier. Casey settled into her chair and pulled a pen from her bag. She was going to figure this out, starting now.

The after-work crowd filtered in. The rustle of paper, coughing and throat-clearing, and shifting of bodies in uncomfortable chairs echoed through the room. None of it broke her concentration. She began marking up the list; crossing things out, identifying sources worth a closer look. She shuffled through the articles, making an occasional check mark to the side of a line. The list wasn't much to start with and now that she was going through it in detail, any hope of answers stemming from the books and articles included there seemed remote. She was going to have to dig deeper or let it go. She was leaning toward letting it go. She tossed the pen aside and stretched. Researching the possible reasons she might have seen a nightangel hanging around a cold D.C. street as though there was nothing he'd rather be doing was not going well. Somehow, that made her feel better, made the answer more clear. She had no problem to solve because there was no nightangel.

That was just as well, Casey thought, because it was seven forty-five and she had to meet Ricki outside the building by eight—angel or not. Casey allowed herself to indulge in a small sense of accomplishment for the evening's work as she prepared to leave. It had not yielded much but she had taken some action and it had cleared her mind. She had things more in hand then when she walked through the doors of the Library a few hours before.

She flipped the pages she had been working with back into a stack and tapped them straight on the table before returning them to the folder. She was going to file these away with her groundless fears of daydreams run amok under C for Crazy. Yes, she was feeling much better now. There was nothing like the ambience of a proper library and sitting motionless in a straight-backed chair for hours to give a person perspective.

Too bad the hairs on the back of her neck were standing up like in one of those ghost hunting shows she made sure to DVR every week. She found herself scanning the reading room for Gabriel. She was going to be so annoyed if he damaged her state of denial before she was even out the door. It would be just like a nightangel to puncture the oasis of nose-in-a-book calm Casey had induced within herself by turning up to prove her wrong.

Her glance skipped across the reading room. There he was. In plain sight and yet obscured until he chose to reveal himself. *How did he do that?* She should have seen anyway. The nightangel without the beating armor of his wings was still the nightangel. She knew him well enough, winged or not. She should have noticed him, damn it.

A whole evening of stress management via research was going up in smoke and it was hard for Casey not to resent it. *Maybe on top of getting my head checked, I should get my eyes checked too*, Casey thought, squinting across the room as if she could squeeze the nightangel back into the dreams by the force of one outraged look.

◄ CHAPTER THREE ►

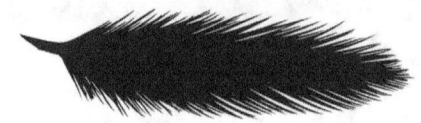

CASEY GATHERED GABRIEL WAS not one to put too much store in outraged looks. He was sitting on the far side of the room near the exit. He looked downright comfortable there. She was certain it was his doing she had not seen what was right in front of her, but she still blamed herself for not being more observant. Overlooking a nightangel was pretty damn hard, no matter how that angel came to you.

One thing was for sure, she saw him now. And he saw her, too. He was leaning back in his seat with his left arm flung over the chair back beside him, his right hand laid flat on top of an open book. He was assessing her with eyes the color of a midnight forest shot through with sharp shards of moonlight. Falling into them was easy. She should know. She had made a habit out of letting him yank her close with a look that held her teetering on the edge of all sorts of dangerous things. But that was there. Not here. There is a difference between stumbling upon someone like Gabriel in a daydream interlude and spying him right before you in the ordinary course of real life. The real-life Gabriel was bound to be more trouble. And Casey did not want any trouble with residents of alternate universes, supernatural entities up to who knew what, or men of any sort who wanted too much from her for any reason right now. Maybe later in life, when she was regretting all her missed opportunities and trying to make up for lost time. Maybe then she would be ready to dive into those evergreen eyes and do some skinny-dipping. For now, she was keeping her clothes on and putting up guardrails around that deep water.

She wanted the angel back where he belonged—in the daydream. She needed her daydreams, but in order for them to work the right way, it was essential he was happily ensconced in the dreams and nowhere else. He was ruining everything, sitting there staring at her like that. He looked so real, so happy to see her. She had some news for him—she was not happy to see him.

If she could just find a way to stuff him back in the dream, then all would be well. They could go on and pretend this ill-considered incident never occurred. He could stay put in the dream and Casey could fall into it forever.

She should never have dreamed that first daydream so unlike all the ones that came before. This entire problem had begun there. But she had not seen it coming. She had daydreamed her way through everyday life for as long as she could remember and nothing like Gabriel had ever occurred before. That was why she should have turned away when she saw him striding across the green field gone still under a lilac sky empty of every cloud it had held a moment earlier. He was something so different from everything that had come before it should have made her stop and think. Instead, it fired her curiosity and overrode her good sense. She wanted to understand what sort of creature had emerged within the landscape of her daydream to command her attention. She was mesmerized by the way his heavy wings furled and unfurled as he approached her; how he spoke her name through scarlet lips as if it was going to be his favorite prayer. Finding him so set on befriending her, hearing that voice spinning around her in a storm of ceaseless desire while the world outside paid her little notice in comparison, made his immediate regard all the more intriguing. It buried every rational thought and hesitation beneath its certainty. She wanted to know him better. She wanted him to stay. And he had.

She set aside the logical concerns about encouraging such a thing as Gabriel because after all, it was just a dream and he was the best thing she had ever found within it. He would come with or without her invitation and she would look for him to arrive at every moment he was not beside her. What was wrong with that? That was the power a good daydream held when woven by a dreamer who had a talent for it.

15

The problem was, Gabriel was right in front of her and she was not in the midst of a daydream. There he sat, meeting her glance without seeming to take her displeasure to heart. It did not look as if he meant to leave. Her eyes slid away from his at this realization and her frustration deepened. He should not have come. His being there was annoying to her. Casey felt she could upgrade annoying to terrifying given another minute or so. Her glance fluttered toward his again and her heart began to pound at the way her mind filled in the blanks his presence presented to her. She did not want him there. She could not have him there.

And still, the angel sat quiet, waiting upon her to come to him within the plain walls of a library reading room as he had so often waited for her to take his hand at the edge of the garden path that led between the ruby roses; overcome with a breathless eagerness to hear the beguiling words he would speak to her when they were alone together—the roses scenting each syllable he spoke until she was dizzy with it. She could smell the roses now, as if the garden was pushing up behind her and if she turned, she would see it there. She tightened her hands around the edge of the table to ground herself in the ordinary landscape in which she stood and closed her eyes until the shadow of the dream receded. When she opened them again, any hopes she had for his immediate disappearance were disappointed. Gabriel was still there.

His gaze had intensified and the power of it threatened to strip away what courage she had left to marshal. To see this unnatural creature moving through the world on his own steam, without a hint of the dream about him, was beyond eerie. How had he done it—arrived from the beyond as if they had already agreed on it and she was awaiting him like a smitten schoolgirl? And did he have to look so smug about it if seeing him there did make her feel a little star-struck? *And wasn't that just like an angel?* Her anger comforted her. She turned her eyes down. She would not acknowledge him with another look. She shoved her papers back into her briefcase.

To hell with nightangels met in gardens who think they can turn up in the hard light of the real world to an eager welcome. She almost toppled her chair as she pushed up from her seat. Her pen rolled to the ground. She left it where it lay. She slammed her briefcase shut. The man two tables away gave her a look between annoyance and curiosity and went back to his reading. He did not glance up again.

She grabbed her briefcase and purse, tossed her coat over her arm, and made for the door. He had put himself between her and the way out. Maybe he would melt away as she came closer. *Not likely. Not likely.* Casey's heart sunk.

Navigating the length of the room in the spotlight of his gaze had many of the same unfortunate characteristics as walking the plank. She could not shield herself from the heat of his scrutiny as she made her way toward the door. The quiet, self-absorbed attitude of the researchers left in the library accentuated the relative emptiness of the place. No one lifted their head as she walked by. No one looked up. Not one person stirred in their seat. *Why was that? Why was that?* She was sure from the throbbing silence surrounding her that for all intents and purposes, she was alone with Gabriel. She meant to go rushing straight past but she was mesmerized by his closeness, his boldness, and her own reaction to him.

She stopped short to one side of the table at which he had stationed himself—careful to stay out of his reach. Her breath came in sharp, rapid gulps. The relaxed posture of his athletic body, the loose cropped curls that fell dark against his fair skin, the sculpted strength of his hands, the undeniable invitation extended in his look—she took it in with one disbelieving glance. She wanted to sigh out loud for the pleasure of seeing him right there in front of her as though it was where he had always belonged.

In the dreams, he dressed as befitted an angelic prince—a great lord of some far away and indiscriminate age of romance and chivalry made fierce and powerful under the weight of glinting wings that shone like daggered slices of the firmament. Within the walls of this Library of Congress reading room, he looked like something else altogether. He was the perfect contemporary man. He might have stepped out of a high-end magazine ad for men's clothing—oozing a mixture of masculinity and casual, effortless good looks. His clothes were modern and understated. He was dressed in jeans and a black wool sweater. His boots looked new and expensive. The solid weight of a gold watch glinted on his wrist. A leather coat was tossed over the chair beside him. Everything about him was natural, comfortable, and true.

The irrefutable proof of Gabriel's existence outside the realm of her dreams had parked itself along the path she must take to make her escape. Casey could not stop from standing in stunned silence before him instead of passing him by and rushing out the door. He had the face of a renegade angel. He was jarringly beautiful. As much as she wanted to

17

rebel against the idea, she was positive he was as alive and real as she was.

Now that this had been established, she succumbed to gawking at him as if she had stumbled upon her biggest celeb crush and could not believe who she was seeing. She looked him over; her eyes lingered on the fine curve of his hand resting with casual grace on the open book before him. He flipped it shut and her eyes flew back to his face. She found herself caught in his gaze again. Just as in the dreams, it was a pleasant and inescapable imprisonment she did not seek but did not want to end. He leaned forward. She stepped back a pace in answer, trying to stare him down and take him in at the same time. Even if she was fleeing him in her heart already, she was not willing to end this meeting between them yet.

His mouth tilted up into one of those assuming smiles he gave her when he thought he was a step or two ahead of her in the game. Casey frowned at him with greater resolution. The fine corners of his mouth softened. He pushed out the chair across from where he sat with one deft kick of his foot, as if he did not wish to break the spell that had been wrought between them by speaking the first word. He was giving her an invitation to sit down across from him and begin a conversation. He wanted her words first. They were always what he wanted. His smile said he believed she might take him up on his unspoken invitation if given encouragement. The encouragement came from a sweetening of that look of his that was always her eventual downfall, and the slightest nod he made toward the chair on which he wanted her to sit.

His small confident action could not be ignored. Casey resented the hell out of him for making it. She considered taking the seat he offered, though. The prospect of a few minutes of speech with her nightangel was tempting. He was so near. He was so willing to give her this audience. If she reached out, she could touch him. Not like in the dream. That didn't count. This would be the real thing. A thrill curled up her spine. Casey stared at the toe of his boot for a long moment—considering—before her eyes traveled back to his face again. She had made up her mind. She did not think it was the decision Gabriel would be expecting. She forced herself to look away and lurched forward past the last few worktables and through the heavy doors.

She had no idea where the steps were. She had never used them. She did not have time to wander down empty corridors in a desperate attempt to find them now. She raced to the elevator and punched the

18

down button instead. Her attention was riveted on the double doors leading out of the library. They did not open. The angel remained within.

"Come on." She slammed the palm of her hand against the down button and held it there. "Come on. Damn it. Open."

He could walk out at any second. She would be standing there by herself. No elevator. Cornered. He would make her talk to him. She would say something stupid. Then he would smile at her. Those deadly sweet smiles of his should be outlawed.

Why didn't he come, then? She did not understand his motivation. Given his sudden and persistent pursuit of her, why did he allow her to go? Why did he wait when he was someone who, she imagined, did not need to wait for anything? His pursuit of her was calculated to obtain her immediate attention and, if she knew anything about nightangels intent on a goal, which she did, that was just a hint of what was to come. What that indefinable something Gabriel required from her was, she could not say. She could not fathom what he could want with her. She did not care at the moment. All she could think of was escape.

The elevator chime sounded. The down light flashed round and white in front of her. The elevator doors slid open with a soft, metal sigh. She stepped across the threshold. She still expected him to rush at her through the closing doors. She prayed for the doors to slam tight against that possibility. She did not let out her breath until they had. She was safe inside a brass cocoon. The shadow of her image was repeated in the burnished gold of the elevator compartment like so many secret sepia-toned sisters rallying around her.

"Girl power," Casey said to her reflections like a whistle in the dark, wishing she could bring her brassy entourage with her. The elevator stopped with a bounce. The sisterhood parted to reveal the first floor and the path of her retreat. She took it without pause.

The staccato click of her heels on the stone floor rang through the wide, deserted lobby. The guard was all that stood between her and the long range of glass doors that led outside. She looked up to the concourse and straight into Gabriel's face. She wasn't surprised. He had let her catch her breath. He was not done. She figured that was going to be the case.

He stood above them, brazen, his hands gripping the curved edge of the rigid ebony wave of railing that ran the full length of the overlook. As before, he was without wings. Where were they? She loved the wings and thought it somehow unkind that he arrived without them. If he had shown himself to her all in wings, she might have sat down and had that conversation with him. Something about those wings made her knees shake, her heart race, and her willpower falter.

The guard cleared his throat, waiting for her to show him what was inside the briefcase. Casey glanced back up at Gabriel. His lips curved into the same insufferable smile he seemed so fond of bestowing on her since his arrival.

There will be no more of that, Casey thought. She lowered her eyes and opened her briefcase. While the security guard poked through its contents, she stole another glance up. He was still smiling. She flipped him the bird. "Smile about this," she said with her eyes. His smile hardened and then disappeared. She turned back to the guard, almost glad she had done it. She wasn't one for flipping people off. Maybe that was a little too much girl power. She didn't like to be rude—even to an emboldened fantasy—but he was pissing her off and scaring the shit out of her in turns.

She thought maybe she should be a bit more concerned at the speed at which his smile had disappeared and the set of his lips just before it was gone. In the present circumstance, Gabriel not smiling was feeling a whole lot worse than she had banked on. She could not do much about that now. She gave a dismissive toss of her head and did not look his way again. *Go ahead. Stand there. You don't scare me*. Like that was true.

Casey turned her attention to the guard as if that would hurry him along. He did not look at her. He did not look above them. He gestured toward her purse instead like maybe searching it would quell his boredom. *Do I look like the type to rip pages out of books and shove them in my bag?* She wanted to scream. Instead, she put her energy into not glancing back toward the nightangel. She knew he was still observing her. She imagined he was smiling again. This delay in her flight from him was sure to amuse Gabriel. She could not even run away from him with any sense that she had overcome the moment as much as been swept up by it. If this were a B-grade horror film, she'd already be a goner. She pulled her purse open to display the typical jumble of keys, makeup, wallet, phone, and change. The guard nodded for her to pass.

She did not look back, even though she was desperate to do so. She fled. Once outside, she turned and stood trembling in the cold, clear air at the top of the steps. Now, she would look back. Now, she must look

20

back. But there was nothing, no one. He had not followed her. She knew if she traveled back into the lobby and retraced her steps to the reading room, he would no longer be there. He was already gone from this place. She sighed. Nightangel: 1. Girl Power: 0.

Casey gave a parting glance to the massive frieze above the entrance to the library. A metallic burst of stars and planets spilling from a cascade of open books into the gray night sky like the frenzied flood of thoughts spinning out of control in her head, a small universe of bright things exploding into being.

Just so, she thought. *Just so.*

She had no illusions. She had not escaped him. He had let her go because it suited him to do so. He had stepped aside and allowed her to run. He had yielded up the evening—a concession to her astonishment and evident fear. How much longer did she have before he refused her any more such concessions? Weeks? Days? Hours?

Casey lifted her head a fraction higher. "Okay, have it your way. Game on," she said.

Too bad the only games she knew how to play were of the classic board variety.

≪ CHAPTER FOUR ≫

R ICKI'S CAR WAS IDLING at the curb. Casey tore down the steps and flung herself into the passenger seat. A moment later, they were speeding away. She was glad she knew Ricki. Ricki was girl power epitomized and magnified, and she could drive like a bat out of hell. Normally, that was not good. Tonight, it was Casey's happiest thought. She wanted to put as much distance as possible between her and the angel in the library.

"Hi." Ricki's hazel eyes darted across the car to meet hers.

"Hi." Casey tried to smile. She could not. She looked away instead.

"What's the matter with you?"

"Nothing." Saying the word "nothing" to Ricki was risky. It invited a remorseless interrogation and the possibility of spilling your guts at a much deeper level than if you had just answered the question in the first place.

Ricki shot a curious look her way and Casey felt it best to pretend to answer the question. "I'm fine." The shadow of Gabriel's red lips curving into a hint of a smile flashed before her as she spoke this lie. He would never have believed her. Casey waited to see whether Ricki would. Another flash of green streetlight, bright against the dark night, moved across their faces and opened the road before them. Casey held her breath.

Ricki scrutinized her friend in a glance. Casey gave Ricki her best why-are-you-looking-at-me-like-that stare, and Ricki's eyes slid back to the road. "You'll catch cold, running around like that with no coat on. It's freezing out." She cranked up the heat and then the music.

Thank goodness for small mercies. Casey sank back into her seat, grateful for the chance to ponder her troubles, the core of which could be summarized in one word—Gabriel. She had never faced such a serious, unpredictable, inescapable sort of trouble in her life. She was certain she had egged that trouble on tonight with her small show of rebellion. The tiny victory she had won through that one moment of overt insolence was sure to be a hollow one. A nightangel liked a show of spirit well enough but never appreciated disrespect in any form. Flipping someone off, especially if that someone was a nightangel, would be difficult to position as just an over-enthusiastic expression of a momentary opinion and she did not believe Gabriel would think anything so silly.

Game on, my ass, Casey thought as she recalled the way the smile had disappeared from his face. She loved and despised the power of that smile. She clutched her coat against her.

The more she thought about Gabriel, the more she could not think of any way to place seeing him in a light that would make it even a somewhat good thing. And not seeing Gabriel, and thinking she had? Well, it would solve the immediate Gabriel-walking-around-trying-to-talk-to-her problem but it would kick open the Casey-is-going-crazy door in a big time way. She did not like the idea of being crazy. She was sure it would cramp her style and deep six her career. Maybe she could learn to ignore Gabriel when he turned up. She did not see how that would help much. He was not the sort of creature who would tolerate being ignored for long; she would be willing to bet he wouldn't last five minutes.

Casey did not remember how they got to the restaurant—not crossing the river, not cruising down the short stretch of interstate to the parkway, not driving past her own neighborhood, not passing Ricki's red brick condo building. The brilliant neon sign for the restaurant looming ahead of them pierced her thoughts. *This was not going to work.* She could not go in and face Ricki across a table with nothing but a basket of bread and a glass of wine to distract her from her fears and Ricki from her curiosity. Ricki would have the truth out of her before the pasta was ordered. Casey was finding she had a sudden aversion to pasta for dinner. She thought she had a can of tomato soup at home, and an empty house did not ask uncomfortable questions.

What Casey wanted to do was the exact thing she had done with Gabriel earlier in the evening. Escape without having to say a damn word. She had done it with the nightangel and he had let her go. She suspected he was just being a good sport. She doubted Ricki would be so obliging. She wondered what she could say that could provide her a graceful exit from this awkward evening and she was coming up with nothing. Ricki was going to be pissed. Casey hated when that happened.

Ricki pulled into the parking lot. She brought the car to a sharp stop one row from the back of the lot. She snapped off the music and began to gather up her keys and bag.

Casey took a quick breath and put some extra steel in her voice. "I can't stay."

"You're kidding." Ricki was already frowning. "Why? We've been planning this all week. I'm starving. We're right here."

Casey knew better than to give a complicated answer. She had learned the fewer facts you gave Ricki to pick apart, the better. "I have to go home."

Ricki opened her mouth to speak.

"And I'd rather not explain why right now."

"No. Explain. I'd like to know what would cause you to bail on your best friend at the last minute. That's not right—especially when there's pasta and red wine involved." Ricki gave her a hard, measured look. "What's this about?"

"Hard day, that's all. I'm wiped out."

Ricki was remarkably unmoved. "Not impressed with the explanation so far."

"I'd be terrible company tonight. I'm doing you a favor."

"A favor would be you getting out of this cold car and into that warm restaurant with me before they close up for the night."

"I wish I could do that but I can't. I think I may be coming down with something."

Casey said this last part as if the possibility cheered her up somehow. *Maybe it was some kind of brain fever that caused hallucinations. That would be good.*

"You don't look sick," Ricki countered, as if she was talking to a kid trying to skip school by faking a stomachache. "Although, something is wrong. Don't look at me like you have no idea what the hell I'm talking about."

Casey was never good at lying—she was a ridiculously good girl for

24

someone who chose the law as her profession—and she liked straight shooting with her friends. Yet, here she was lying her ass off, or at least trying to, and not having much success for all her effort.

Ricki continued on in a manner that said she was absolving her friend of any offense stemming for this attempt to keep something intriguing from her and she would have her answers anyway, so no harm done. "So what if you're not good company. Do you think I've never seen you in a bad mood? The requirement for tolerating each other's bad moods is in Chapter One of the Basic Rules of Friendship Handbook."

Forget the can of tomato soup. Casey longed to sink into a deep, numbing sleep with no friend to face, no answers to give—not even to herself. What she did not want to do was pretend everything was normal and there was no presumptuous nightangel ranging loose in the city tonight with her name on his lips.

She was well aware Ricki was not going to stop pushing unless she pushed back. They had not been friends since the first week of law school for nothing. Ricki always sought to get her way. She wasn't selfish; she was just determined to prevail because of her unshakable opinion that she knew best.

The friendship rules were going to get some testing tonight.

"Sorry. I just can't. Not tonight. Let's go. Next time, it'll be my treat."

"Stay now and I'll treat. I'm craving their lobster ravioli in that pink sauce," Ricki replied, as if that trumped any reason Casey could have for not going in. "I've been starving myself all day so I could eat it."

The ravioli was amazing. Casey was beginning to think Ricki was more hungry than offended. She'd get her some as takeout if she didn't have to answer questions while they waited for it but she knew that would never happen. Ricki was not going to see any lobster ravioli in pink sauce at the moment no matter how much she craved it. "I gotta go."

"You could tell me what's going on, you know. How bad can it be?"

Pretty bad. Pretty damn bad. Casey fumbled around in her brain for some reason to explain her behavior. Why not tell Ricki the truth—or part of it? "I missed a filing deadline."

Ricki relaxed against the back of her seat and the annoyance drained from her face. "Nice going, Case. How the hell did you manage to do that?"

Diplomacy was not Ricki's strong suit but she was right. "I'm an idiot."

"No, you're not. What happened?"

"I've had a lot on my mind. It slipped through the cracks."

"Slipped through the cracks?" Ricki said with disbelief. "You'd better get yourself together, Case. Whatever is going on can't be as important as your career. I hope you didn't take that go-have-some-fun-once-in-a-while advice I gave you last month too much to heart." She gave Casey's arm a poke. "Hey, could it be? Is there hope for your love life after all? This isn't over some guy, is it?"

Casey did not answer. Ricki assessed her and then tossed the idea aside. "I know it isn't. You'd have told me. Well, whatever the reason, make sure it doesn't happen again. The firm of Filet 'Em and Go isn't exactly the forgiving type."

"It's Phillips and Row. And you can stop the lecture. It won't happen again. It can't. Ed almost had my head on a platter. If it ever happens again, I'm sure it will be my ass."

"I wouldn't be surprised. Edward Johnson is a managing partner at one of the top 100 law firms in the country and he didn't get that way by being a real nice guy."

"No kidding. I was fortunate to be assigned to the case by Ed in the first place."

"What about the client? How did they take it?"

Ricki was not very good at comforting the troubled soul even when her intentions lay in that direction. "Not well. Then that jerk, Derek Rider, made sure it did the rounds of the office. Mr. I'm-Going-To-Be-a-Partner-or-Bust couldn't contain his joy at my error. He thinks the case should be his and maybe now it might come his way."

"But it hasn't. Damn, Case. I'm amazed Ed didn't pull you off the case and pack you off on an extended document production somewhere dreary and soul-numbing."

"A local Siberia with a windowless chamber stacked to the ceiling with boxes of documents and one chair and a table in the center of it?"

"Or Siberia proper. I'm sure he could arrange it." Ricki laid her head back against the gray leather headrest. "Sorry you got yelled at."

"Me too. It was pretty humiliating."

"Well, it stinks you had to deal with that but it's in the past now and the good news is you're still on the case. That's the most important thing."

"And Derek's not. That's equally important."

"Good point." Ricki turned to face her. "I think you're lucky—very lucky. Just remember that luck can run out. Even yours, Case."

Casey nodded her agreement and congratulated herself on flying under Ricki's radar when her friend turned to focus curious hazel eyes on her with renewed interest. "You know, it's not like you to drop the ball."

Casey cringed. "It was just a stupid mistake."

"Don't give me that. There's more to it. Fess up."

Casey was beginning to wish they were in the restaurant after all. That way she might have a chance to scurry into the restroom and climb out a back window or rush off to take an emergency call that would allow her to disappear into the night before Ricki noticed she was gone.

"You know you're going to tell me in the end. So do it and stop wasting time."

Maybe she should. If there was one thing Casey understood about her friend, it was that she was just hitting her stride. Besides, she had seen a nightangel without wings on a windy D.C. street corner, and then again tonight in the middle of a library reading room; each time looking interested in her and nothing else. The nightangel seeking her out when he should be locked in her daydreams was just not right. She had better tell something to someone and soon.

"It's not like me. It's not like me at all." The traitorous thought slipped out as the wet sting of barely-restrained tears pricked the corners of her eyes. Breathing the words out loud was difficult. She was ashamed of what she was saying, as if all of this was unfolding as a result of some secret flaw in her mind or character. "I think I'm cracking up."

Ricki patted her hand. Two fat tears ran down Casey's cheeks and fell into her lap one after the other. "I'm sorry, Ricki." She rubbed the tears into the fabric of her skirt as though that would erase them.

"What do you have to be sorry about? Look at that stupid line. I'm not in the mood to wait around. Let's pick something up at the store and eat at my place."

A minute later they had pulled into the grocery store parking lot and Ricki was taking charge. "How about some wine and cheese? You like that. Besides, you need a drink. And I'll get some of those little crackers. You know—the kind with the sesame seeds on them. You always like those. I don't know why. They make me gag. I'll get a box of those."

Casey wiped at the tears that clung to her face. She tried to smile.

"You'd better wait in the car. You always look like crap once you start crying."

"Wow. Thanks."

"It's my obligation as your friend to tell you these things. Just sit there, alright?" She was already out of the car.

"Hey, Ricki."

"Yeah?" She stuck her head down to look at Casey. Her hair was a shiny, golden flutter in the backlight. Her breath hung white and feathery on the air. She was waiting. "Well, what?"

Casey shuddered. The wind that rushed over Ricki's shoulders and raced through the car held the subtle trace of a voice within it. "Casey. Casey. Casey." Now she was hearing voices harbored in random gusts of wind. Maybe it was a good idea to have wine and cheese in the security of Ricki's condo and shut herself away from everything that sought to haunt her—even if it was only for a few short hours and it was all just in her head anyway. "Get some chocolate—any kind of chocolate."

"Sure, Case. Whatever you want." She began to straighten.

"Ricki. Ricki, wait." She did not want to be alone.

Ricki bent again. The wind dropped. Ricki's voice filled the void. "What? I'm freezing my ass off out here. I'll be right back."

Casey doubted it. Ricki tended to wander in stores. "Remember, I'm out here. Try not to be forever."

"I'll hurry. Promise." She slammed the door, locking it.

Sure. Casey hugged herself and waited for Ricki to return. She would have liked to rest her head on the dashboard and close everything out but she was afraid if she did, when she lifted her head again she would find herself face to face with her angel. She could not take that chance and so she gazed through the bright glare of the grocery store windows instead.

Where the heck was Ricki? What was the holdup? Picking up *everything she needed and hadn't gotten around to buying for the last week while she was in there— that's what.* "Come on, Ricki. Get out here."

As if on command, Ricki stepped through the set of automatic doors and headed across the lot—well dressed, silky-haired, model-sleek—a brown bag in either arm. Everything was going to be okay. Ricki was striding toward the car like a rescuer appearing out of the mist in the nick of time—and she had groceries. Casey leaned over and unlocked the door. *Maybe everything really would be okay.* She hugged the unlikely idea close as they headed out of the parking lot.

∞ ∞ ∞

By the time they were standing side by side listening to the quiet hum of the elevator that would take them to the fifth floor and Ricki's one bedroom plus den condo, Casey had managed to salvage some small vestige of her composure. The doors opened. Ricki marched down the hall. Casey trailed a few steps behind. Ricki thrust the two grocery bags into Casey's arms, juggling her purse and briefcase as she unlocked the door. She pushed it open and tugged Casey in by the arm. The door closed behind them. The deadbolt clicked into place. She relaxed.

Here in these rooms was a temporary refuge. Ricki would ask her to stay. Casey would take her up on it. The sofa was a mix of hard and soft, like an uncomfortable gray cloud that had landed in Ricki's living room by mistake—but it was better than the prospect of her own bed. Maybe Gabriel knew where she lived, maybe he would be waiting for her in the dark, looming silence of this particular evening, maybe he would not be so easy to put off after all. These were maybes—sturdy, threatening, very possible maybes. And she respected them for what they were. Well, she would let him wait. He could haunt her doorstep all night. She was not going to turn up. No maybe about it.

Ricki walked past Casey into the living room and continued switching on lamps, each on its own dimmer, until the space was suffused with warm light. She turned the stereo on and down. The mellow music drifting through the apartment was the final touch that made the place spring to life as she moved through it. Ricki set the mood by sound and light as it struck her at the moment, and solitude was something she rarely craved. Tonight, judging from the West Coast jazz and the fact that every light bulb in the room was in use and turned up to the maximum, she was striving for bright and upbeat. Casey was strangely reassured. No way would the nightangel show up here. The heavy-handed use of lighting and steady stream of breezy jazz would probably screw with any radar he had honed in on her.

Casey stood clutching the bags, while Ricki buzzed around the room.

"It'll be okay." She had caught Ricki's notice again. "Believe me. It can't be that bad. It never is. It just feels that way right now. Here. Give me those bags."

Casey followed Ricki into the stark white kitchen. The only warmth in the room came from the lipstick red appliances on the straight shot of white granite counter—a microwave, a blender, and an espresso machine. After a recent trip to New Orleans, Ricki began calling them the holy trinity. Casey loitered in the door; watching Ricki pad around the kitchen in bare feet, listening to the reassuring slam of cabinet doors and the clink of glass on glass.

Ricki opened the wine and poured out two glasses before grabbing a serving bowl and dumping an entire bag of miniature chocolate bars into it. "First things, first." If there was one thing Ricki understood, it was Casey's longstanding chocolate requirements. Tonight was an old-school choice, comfort chocolate. She tossed one of the miniature bars to Casey—special dark chocolate, Casey's favorite.

Casey crossed the room to take the glass Ricki held out to her. Her friend had poured her a big glass. She planned to drink the whole damn thing and then have another.

Ricki had set out brie, a creamy herb and garlic circle, and a port wine cheese ball. Ricki made a cracker for each of them. Brie for Casey. Creamy herb for herself. "Are you going to tell me?"

"I don't know. I feel better now anyway. False alarm." Casey gave a weak laugh.

"Don't start with me, Case. Just tell me right now. What's wrong?"

"I don't know how to explain what's wrong." She nibbled at the edges of her cracker.

"Well, try."

"It's too weird."

"How weird can it be?"

"Bad cable sci-fi fantasy movie weird."

"Oooh. I like the sound of that. It has potential."

Casey took a big sip of her wine and frowned at Ricki.

"Are there zombies? Please tell me this doesn't have anything to do with zombies."

That's what she got for watching the zombie movie marathon with Ricki last time they went to Ocean City and wound up stuck inside because of the rain. Next time the clouds rolled in during an OC visit, they were turning off the TV and going to the Outlet Malls in Rehoboth.

"Don't say it's mutant spiders. I hate those things."

Ricki did not understand. Not at all. Casey picked up her cracker and bit into the rich cheese but all its creamy goodness didn't make her feel any better.

"The problem's not with aliens, right? That would be so passé."

Casey sliced into the port wine cheese and pressed a thick lump of it on a cracker. The knife made a loud clink as it hit the edge of the china plate. "I know you think this is funny but I'm freaking out here."

"About what?" Ricki tried to maintain an air of concern for Casey while eying the plate for damage at the same time.

Casey twisted the ring that circled her right ring finger. The light danced across it as if it was littered with diamonds and yet it was a simple golden span of delicate roses and leaves. It reminded her of the lush garden pathways in her dreams that so often led to the nightangel. Now, under the harsh kitchen lights its sparkle reassured her. "About being crazy. I hope I'm not going crazy, Ricki."

"Case, I've known you for a long time. You're not crazy."

"How do you know? You haven't heard what I have to say yet. It's bad enough I think I may be nuts. I'm not sure I want you thinking so too."

Ricki gave her the look. The one that said she was reaching her limit on patience. "I won't think you're crazy. I promise. Now, spit it out."

"Alright but don't say I didn't warn you." The source of all her current difficulties may not be easy to explain but it was simple to pinpoint. If only it were as easy to make go away. "His name is Gabriel."

Ricki's lips pressed together and then curved into a wicked smile.

≪ CHAPTER FIVE ≫

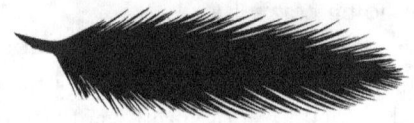

"GABRIEL." RICKI'S EYES BRIGHTENED as if she had heard enough to guess at the rest. "Nice name."

"It's an angel's name." *And that was too much information*, Casey rebuked herself.

"I know. Everyone knows that. He turns up in the Bible somewhere." Ricki's voice trailed off.

"The Annunciation, maybe?" Casey prompted her.

"Oh, right. The Annunciation. Was that Gabriel?"

"Yes." Casey found it hard not to roll her eyes. How Ricki could be so smart about some things and yet know so little about others was beyond her. She supposed it was that Ricki tended to skepticism and dismissed everything but hard facts and what she could see for herself. Ricki would never have a problem like Gabriel crop up in life. It just wasn't reasonable. "Gabriel was a special angel. He was an archangel; an angel of revelation."

"So let me get this straight. You've got a problem with an angel of the biblical sort named Gabriel."

"No. Of course not. You're not listening to me."

"Oh, I'm sorry—an archangel. I know—there's some kind of difference."

"First, he's not *the* Angel Gabriel."

"That's a relief."

"Second, if you want to get technical, yes, I think there is a difference between an angel and an archangel."

"I thought that's what you'd say. Go ahead. Explain."

Casey sighed. "Fine. Archangels are angels but not every angel is an archangel. As I understand it, archangels are a rank above regular angels and there are others above the archangels. The archangels and angels; they're the closest to mankind."

"You ought to be more upwardly mobile, Case. What comes above an archangel?"

"You're still not listening."

"Sure I am. You've got a problem with a garden-variety angel or archangel; goes by the name of Gabriel."

"Not quite."

"What? Gabriel's not a garden-variety angel or archangel?"

"Not exactly." Casey did not know how to clarify her statement without diving deeper into the secrets of nightangels and that was something she did not want to do. Anyway, there was less she knew about such unaccountable things than she did not know. Nightangels were unfathomable most of the time. She could not find any Nightangel 101 books to which she could refer for additional information. She had looked—really looked. She knew nothing about any of it but Ricki was waiting for a response. Casey sucked in a deep calming breath and blew it out again with a hiss like it was steam instead of air. Sometimes it was difficult to be patient with Ricki when she turned a conversation upside down for no particular reason at all except to see what shaking things up would yield. "Look, here's the bottom line. I've got a problem and his name is Gabriel. Why are you giving me that look?"

"I can't believe this is all over some guy."

"He's not some guy." Gabriel was no more some guy than a hurricane was a summer shower. "He doesn't even exist. At least not here. And I'm starting to see him everywhere."

Ricki cocked her head like a clever bird about to catch a worm. "If he doesn't exist, how can you see him?"

"You tell me."

The cinnamon starbursts at the center of Ricki's widening eyes grew more distinct. "Are you sure you're seeing him?"

"Yes. I'm sure." Ricki's gaze scoured her for some nuance of

33

expression or body language that might reveal something held back. She liked to know everything and was good at discovering what was left untold in a glance.

She seemed satisfied to let the discussion continue along these lines. "Well, he must have come from somewhere then."

"He did."

"Where then? Out of thin air?"

Ricki had no idea how close she was to the truth of it. Casey was certain she was going to hate that she was on the right track when what Casey was trying to tell her sunk in. Being wrong about something wasn't always bad. Casey would love to be wrong about Gabriel—open her eyes and find herself waking from a bad dream and closing them again with the express purpose of falling into a daydream that led her to a safer, more contained version of Gabriel.

"Maybe. I don't know." Casey glanced at Ricki as if she could weigh out her tolerance for stories about nightangels named Gabriel and daydreams thick with blood-red roses through a single look but she was not as good at such things as her friend. She was going to tell her the truth—at least some of it—and see how Ricki took it. "He's a figment of my imagination."

"You're losing me."

"A daydream. Even you must daydream sometimes."

"Never. I'm strictly reality-driven. Even if I did, I don't think I'd be daydreaming about someone who doesn't exist. And that's what it sounds like you're doing."

"I have a good imagination. Sue me."

"I'd be tempted to do it if it would get your mind off this nonsense. Why would you waste your time daydreaming? Don't you have enough to do?" She was starting to look more like a storm cloud than a concerned friend.

"It's just once in a while." *Okay, maybe a little more. Did Ricki need to know that? No, she did not.* "Don't judge. Daydreaming is a recognized form of stress reduction."

"And how is that working out for you?" Ricki was trying hard not to judge her but Casey could see she was losing the battle.

Casey pictured Gabriel sitting in the library like a lion lying in wait for his little lamb. What did it matter what Ricki thought when Gabriel was out there somewhere longing to either consume her with one fierce

34

glance or befriend her forever with the merest smile. Either way was trouble. "Okay. Not well right now. But it *was* working fine."

"Sure it was. Thinking about some made-up guy worked so well it caused you to miss an important deadline."

"Yes. About that. The thing is—I think he might be real now."

"So he wasn't real and now he is? Case, I have some news for you—that can't happen. Alright, so you have a good imagination. Lots of people do. That doesn't make dreams come true." Ricki favored her with the kind of reassuring smile a parent gives to a child who needs the effects of a bad dream soothed away before everyone can go back to bed.

Ricki had a lot to learn about settling down the over-imaginative if she thought a few sensible words, spoken in a calm voice, were going to do the trick. "What does make dreams come true then? I'd like to know because something from my dreams has been turning up all over the place—specifically, Gabriel. And he seems very alive and present to me."

"What do you mean—you saw him tonight?"

"I saw him at the library."

"Fine. Let's say you did see him there. What did he want? Did you talk to him?"

"No." She regretted not seeing that perfect bow of a mouth open to say something to her that did not begin and end in a daydream. "I took off."

"I don't know why you didn't stay and solve the big mystery. I would have." Ricki thought she was braver than Casey. Maybe she was. Then again, maybe she wasn't. Ricki had never seen Gabriel in fierce wings riding down from the great forest that darkened the edge of her dreams. She had not stood small and alone at the edge of the murmuring field of green that stretched below the gardens as he raced across the distance between them like an arrow shot from a crossbow flies toward its mark. She had never faced that flurry of power as it came near and settled its sights upon her. She had never been caught up and held fast by such a thing; clinging tight to that which carried her off in a roaring flutter to the deeper dream. But Casey had. Casey figured that made her plenty brave; braver than Ricki would ever know. In that moment within the library, being pulled closer and closer to the angel by his powerful gaze, there had been no choice but to flee. He could read her like a book. In the dreams that could charm; in this world it worried her. What had she told him in those few moments they had been together without a word exchanged between them? The very thought of what the answer could be had freed her from his glance and set her racing off.

"But it really doesn't matter whether you stood there and talked to him or not. It couldn't have been him, Case. You told me yourself, the guy doesn't exist."

"He does now. It was Gabriel."

Ricki's eyes narrowed but she let Casey go on without disputing her statement.

"He's not just a make-believe person in a dream. I don't even remember thinking him up. He simply arrived one day. And anyway, he's more a creature or being than anything else."

"You mean like a garden-variety angel or something?" Ricki raised one perfect eyebrow in a way that spoke volumes in the courtroom.

Casey's throat tightened around the words that formed her answer. "Not quite."

"But kind of? You said he wasn't an angel." Ricki's hands were on her hips now.

"Well, you keep saying 'angel' like fluffy clouds and harps are involved."

"What other kind of angels are there but the fluffy cloud and harp sort?"

"There's the kind he is."

"Which is what kind, exactly?" She stood taller, as if steeling herself to hear bad news.

"He's a nightangel." *Yup, bad news.*

"A what?" Ricki sputtered, averse to the idea of any sort of angel being involved. Casey could not blame her. She felt the same way about it.

"A nightangel." Saying it the second time was no easier. "He's not some angel with a halo. He's this vampire with wings."

"So now he's a vampire—with wings?" That was all Ricki had to hear. She threw back her head and, lifting her hair up so it could spill through her fingers like a waterfall of gold, let out a hoot. "Ms. Sloane. I would never have thought it of you. It's always the quiet ones. My. My. A vampire? With wings? That sounds a wee bit wicked. I would never have pictured you conjuring up some supernatural bad boy to moon over in your spare time."

"He's not bad or wicked. He's…perfect—in every way."

"Fine. He's just dreamy, I'm sure. But given he's a vampire, and vampires don't exist, you have to admit he can't be here no matter how perfect he is."

36

Casey would have argued the point, seeing as how she had experienced him walking around firsthand in the heart of the nation's capital just hours earlier, but Ricki anticipated her.

"Someone would have noticed him walking around. Wings are a big giveaway something unusual is going down. There'd be a video. It would go viral. But there's nothing, is there?"

"He didn't have his wings."

"What? Did he forget them?" Ricki was shaking her head with relief-tinged amusement.

"He didn't have any damn wings, Ricki. I don't know what happened to his wings. Maybe he doesn't see the need for them here. But it doesn't matter. I would know him anywhere, with or without those wings. You don't confuse someone like Gabriel with anybody else. There's no one else like him in the world—or the dreams."

Ricki lifted her eyes heavenward as if praying for patience but kept quiet.

"And now that he's here instead of there, I don't think he's going away anytime soon. He's going to keep following me around until something more happens. I just don't know what the something more is he's after." *And maybe I don't have to know if I can avoid him until he gets tired of chasing after me, or realizes I'm not worth all this trouble anyway, and goes away again.* How many nights would Ricki allow her to sleep on her sofa? More to the point, how many nights could she tolerate sleeping there, before coming to terms with the fact that the success rate for dodging a vampire prince, with or without wings, would always have to be a big, fat zero. She knew very well already Gabriel would not start something he did not mean to see to the end. *I'm so totally screwed.*

She wished she were better at accepting defeat but she liked her way as much as Ricki did. "How long can I camp out on your couch before you kick me out?"

"For as long as you can afford the chiropractic visits. My sofa is hell on backs."

"Thanks. I appreciate it." A great weight lifted from her shoulders at the promise of a safe haven from Gabriel, even if it was just a temporary delay of the inevitable. Gabriel was inevitable. He was a damn nightangel, after all. But Casey was stubborn with a capital S. Just because she was constrained by all the limitations of being a regular person living in the regular world and did not have, nor had ever had, a set of wings of even the sorriest sort to her name in the dreams or anywhere else, did not mean she had to make this easy for him.

Besides, she had coverage in her health plan for a certain number of chiropractic visits per year. Why let them go to waste?

"Not so fast. There's one more part to the deal. You have to tell me everything about your dreams." Ricki was considering what Casey's gorgeous, winged vampire looked like. The fact that he could be categorized at best as either a stalker angel or dangerous blood-drinker was of no significance when considered in light of his hotness potential. The wings earned him some extra points in Ricki's assessment and she had not even seen them. *Imagine if she had*, Casey thought.

Casey opened her mouth to protest.

"Or you can't stay." Ricki smiled and continued to stare at her with wide, curious eyes. "I want all the details." She was more interested in the story about to unfold than the possibility of pursuing nightangels wandering around D.C. looking to connect with Casey. In a heartbeat, she had knocked him down on the threat meter from possible sexual predator to probable sexual fantasy worth hearing more about. She was silent, waiting for Casey to begin.

"Fine. What do you want to know?" Casey inquired, tearing the wrapper off another piece of chocolate.

"Tell me about this vampire, or nightangel, or whatever he is, first. I have to admit, he does sound pretty hot."

Hearing her friend use the word "nightangel" had been a shock. It felt as if she was crossing a line she should not cross. She was going to cross it anyway. She was going to take the chance that talking to Ricki about the nightangel Gabriel would do her some good; that Ricki would know what to do next. Besides, she was not the one who had crossed the line first—Gabriel had done it.

Casey shrugged.

"What's he look like? Let's start there."

She glanced at the artwork hanging on the wall across from them—a large numbered and signed black-and-white landscape. Compared with the landscape of her dreams, even before she factored in the nightangel moving through it, it was ordinary. "He's handsome."

Ricki clicked her tongue. "Is that it? Of course, he's handsome. That goes without saying. A little more description would be nice."

"He has brown hair."

"Wow. I can picture him now."

"It's in these beautiful dark, loose curls."

Ricki frowned at her. "Okay. Really nice, dark-brown hair. And what about his eyes?"

Casey thought about how his eyes held the shadowed lure of the forest within them. How she wanted to get lost in them, let him find her there and take her deeper. "They're really pretty." Every word she said felt like a betrayal. She was glad those really pretty eyes were not fastened on her now.

"That's it? A good-looking guy with really nice, dark-brown hair and really pretty eyes?"

"Well, for your information, his eyes are—they're melting."

"Hey, you could be describing a puppy dog here."

Casey crossed her arms. "More like an I-could-eat-you-for-dinner-if-I-wanted-to-lion."

"And what color are the savage beast's eyes? Black-as-night, amber yellow? Come on, Case. This is like pulling teeth."

"They're dark green." Ricki was expecting more. "Like a forest at dusk."

Ricki shook her head. "A forest at dusk. I had to ask. Forget the poetic descriptions. Give me something else besides eye and hair color."

Casey struggled to think of something else. "He's taller than I am."

"This is pitiful. Elaborate. You're giving me nothing."

"He's muscular but not in a bulging biceps kind of way. He's fit and he doesn't have to strip off his shirt for you to tell it." Not that she would have complained about him doing that. She indulged herself in a momentary mental picture of a magnificent, inexplicably shirtless Gabriel and smiled.

"That's it? Fit guy, taller than you, dark hair, eyes the color of some forest? What about fangs?"

"When you look into his face, it's hard to notice anything but the way he smiles at you. But once in a while," she faltered, picking her words, "you can see a sharpness behind it."

"So what's he say to you when he's smiling that sharp, white smile?"

"Everything I need to hear. It's the way he says things as much as what he says anyway. He has a voice like a song you can't get out of your mind. It hangs in the air and follows you around long after he's done talking. If I could download it and stick it on my iPod, it's all I'd ever want to play."

"Sounds like a Class A sweet-talking vampire—more bark than bite," she teased. "He does bite though, doesn't he?" Ricki asked, as if she would be surprised indeed if Casey's vampire did not hunger for his love's red blood to flow beneath those garnet-hard lips of his at every turn.

Casey imagined that kiss and then erased the possibility of it happening from her mind. "No. At least, he hasn't bitten me yet. It's not like in the movies, you know."

"How should I know? You're the one hanging out with vampires. I don't understand. Aren't you worth biting? Doesn't he lust for your blood? What would hold him back from doing what must be natural? He sounds like a sorry sort of vampire if he can't make you his willing victim."

"He's not sorry, he's patient and understanding. Besides, you can't make someone willing. I think that's what he wants—me to be willing and to tell him so. He wants me to tell him I love him. But I can't tell him that. Who knows where that would lead? There's way more to it than he's letting on. So I don't know what the natural progression would be once things got started in that direction. Sometimes, I wish I could be brave and do it no matter what the consequences."

"Excuse me, but could you beam yourself back to Earth, please. There are no consequences. You could say, 'I love you'; he could bite your neck and drink your blood over and over and it wouldn't make a bit of difference. It wouldn't be happening because it's a daydream."

Casey was sure Ricki was wrong. Something would be happening, something that would expand into the real world and draw her in, holding her captive forever. Her words would bind her to him in ways she did not wish to contemplate.

"He's just a vampire you thought up to keep you company in your happy place. Some sexually-charged cardboard character you concocted. He's mind-candy and you've been overindulging. I guess I can see how that could happen. Now, it's time to put away the sweets."

Mental fluff? Mind candy? Gabriel? And Ricki thought *she* should get real. "It's not my 'happy place'. It's not some stupid game and he's not some pawn I move around on a board at my whim."

"Well, isn't it a little like a game—an amusing mental game you are playing with yourself? And it is your dream, so of course he's a piece you move around in it however you like. Your problem is you always take things too seriously. Even in these daydreams it sounds as though you worry too much."

"I do not worry too much," Casey said, knowing Gabriel would agree with Ricki.

"Take the biting—why not let him do it? I'm a little disappointed about the biting. Half the fun of the vampire is in the bite. That's always the best part in the movies. You're not letting your bad boy be bad enough. Are you sure he's a vampire?"

"Yes. I'm certain about that."

"Why call him a nightangel then?"

"That's what he calls himself and I believe him. He does have a set of kick-ass wings."

"I'm sure," Ricki purred. "Especially when you're snuggled up together under them."

Casey longed for the haven of Gabriel's wings with a hunger that sprung to life in a hidden corner of her heart like a campfire she couldn't stomp out no matter how hard she tried. Those embers were always ready to explode into flame. All she had to do was think of him. The angel holding her so close. Everything so peaceful. "No, it's not like that," she protested, stomping down the flames again extra hard. She needed a fire marshal for her heart.

"Whatever." Ricki loved to think everything boiled down to sexual attraction between a man and a woman, even if it was in a daydream and the man was a winged vampire. "But a vampire can't be an angel even if he has wings for some reason."

Ricki had no imagination.

❮ CHAPTER SIX ❯

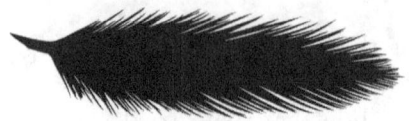

"I TOLD YOU, HE'S not that kind of angel."

"Doesn't matter what kind of angel you call him, he can't be both things at once. One is good and one is bad. Everyone knows that."

"He can be both. And he is."

Ricki rolled her eyes to express her utter disregard for the angelic qualities of something that had been tagged as a vampire.

Casey did not take it to heart. Ricki could roll her eyes all she wanted but it didn't mean a thing except that she did not know crap about angels, or vampires, or what a proper daydream could deliver. Casey did know something about that, and it made her smile with such serenity at her friend that the condescending grin faded from Ricki's lips.

"Vampires don't have to be bad. That's a stereotype. You don't know anything about it but I do. And I'll tell you this, Gabriel is good."

"He can't be." Ricki was matter-of-fact. "He can't be good. And he can't be an angel, or archangel, or any kind of angel at all. You can't say he's an angel because it suits you to call him that and think that's all it takes to make him one. It isn't. Not if he's a damned vampire. Then he's a blood-drinking bad boy and nothing else. Appealing—yes. But good—no."

"Suddenly you're an expert on paranormal beings? Who says there can't be something between angel and vampire? Who says that something can't be as good as you or I?"

"Okay. For arguments sake, let's say there are angels and vampires tearing around the city. Let's say they got mixed up in some sort of supernatural blender and the result is this half-vampire, half-angel creature you're describing. That doesn't mean it isn't something a thousand times worse than the stock variety of either half of the equation."

"Well, it doesn't matter what you think because you don't know him and I do. If you met him, you'd see he was good." She could not fathom why she felt compelled to defend Gabriel when a few minutes before she was scared to death of him.

"If he's so good, then why are you so afraid of seeing him here?" Ricki had her there.

"And given he's a figment of your imagination, meeting him isn't going to be possible, is it? Considering where it's landed you, I'd pass anyway."

Ricki wasn't getting it. Casey was ready to shrug and let it go when Ricki cast aside the whole good-or-bad argument and changed the topic with a flash of mischief in her eyes. "So, what do you do—you and Gabriel—in these dreams of yours? What do you do with a vampire that looks like an angel, but isn't? I bet I know because you're blushing." Ricki smiled at her in a way that made Casey want to sink into the ground.

"This is not some stupid sexual fantasy. The daydreams are way more than that."

"I'm sure. But most of the time, it's sexual, no matter what you say."

"No, it's not and that's how I want it to stay, too. You don't know much about angels or vampires of any sort or you wouldn't be so flippant about this. Do you think it would be like mortal sex? Do you think it would be that simple?"

Ricki looked to be considering the difference between mortal-to-mortal sex and mortal-to-nightangel sex and getting no answers. Casey, however, had thought about it quite a lot, as Gabriel seemed hell-bent on having more from her than friendship infused with an intoxicating dose of heavy-duty flirtation. She had concluded it was a bad idea to take it any further but she could not help considering it anyway; wondering what it would be like.

"It wouldn't be like mortal sex. Once you did it, everything would be different forever. Your life would never be your own again. There'd be no turning back. Because they don't turn back. Angels don't turn back.

So you see, it would be dangerous. Even in a dream."

Astonishment flashed across her friend's face at Casey's adamant assertions.

In fact, Gabriel had already tugged her miles past flirtation but why ruin everything by admitting it. Casey thought about the kisses Gabriel could bestow and how easy it would be to lose herself within his wings forever for just one more of them. Okay, sometimes it was about sex, but there was no need to admit it to Ricki.

"We're just friends and that's all there is to it."

Ricki did not look impressed. "You know what your problem is?" She stopped pacing the kitchen tiles to jab a finger in Casey's general direction. "You have an overactive imagination."

"Well, I'd say it was a bad case then, because Gabriel is walking around the city tonight and he's looking pretty self-sufficient."

Ricki shook her head as if she still could not believe Casey was thinking about such impossibilities when she ought to be doing sensible things like working her ass off and having dinner with people when she said she was. "He can't be here. He only exists in your daydreams. He's probably there right now, hanging out in some castle chamber, trying to sort out his conflicted nature." Casey could almost see the light bulb going on over Ricki's head. "Oh my God, there has to be a castle there or how could he hold you captive—a prisoner to his every whim."

Casey struggled to contain her annoyance. *Where was a mind-erasing ray gun when you needed it?* She would use it on Ricki in a heartbeat if it would stop her from pursuing this new line of questioning.

"Wait. I know. Is it one like in a fairytale? You love that stuff. You couldn't stay away. All the better to lure you within to have his way with you. Wicked angels with castles must at least do that—lure you in and bolt the door behind you—or why dream about them at all?"

"He is not wicked. He doesn't lure me there or lock me anywhere. I've never seen the inside of it."

"There is a castle. I knew it," Ricki crowed.

Damn. If she had that ray gun she'd flip it to the use-your-head setting and turn it on herself.

"Yes, okay. There's a castle." Why deny the truth? At the core of the dream, sitting on some prime daydream real estate, was a spectacular castle. It belonged to her nightangel prince; *of course it did.* He had asked for it right away. She had agreed he could have it and there it was—

44

before she had the time to think about the proper sort of castle to create for him. His castle had sprung up in a shaded corner of her sprawling gardens as if it had always been there, looking over the landscape of her dreams. The castle was the angel's down to the last stone, not hers; his seat of power within her secret kingdom.

What a foolish thing to do—giving him such a thing. And yet, she did not regret the deed. Her gift, even if the design and placement were all his, was a basic act of hospitality. Since he had made it clear he was not going anywhere, he might as well make himself at home. Besides, it pleased him and pleasing the nightangel felt good.

The truth was she couldn't get enough of him from the very start and the angel could not settle his gaze on her without desire flashing in his evergreen eyes. It was the coolest thing that had ever happened in her life—him longing for her and her longing for him from the first moment of his arrival—even if Ricki did not believe he existed. It didn't matter because he *was*—at some level. And that could not be disputed. Besides, Gabriel was *her* vampire prince, with or without the wings, and there was such a thing as loyalty. However she looked at it, he was the best, most spectacular thing she had ever experienced in her life. Ricki could smile but before this was done, Casey was pretty damn sure her friend was going to suffer a pang of jealousy that she did not have a nightangel of her own.

"What I don't understand is why you don't know the way to the castle bedchamber by heart. As far as I can tell, he may be a bad sort of angel but he's not a very good sort of vampire. Talk about missed opportunities. I don't know who I'm more disappointed in—you or him."

I do, Casey thought. *If you looked into the radiant face of the nightangel, you'd say me.*

"You've got a castle with some angel-slash-vampire—though he can't be both—in residence. He's loitering around there like some overly virtuous prince in a private fairytale who ought to be kicked out of the story for not stepping up to the plate. I mean, he doesn't even have the nerve to invite you in and put the bite on you when he ought to be all about it." Ricki was too busy criticizing the nightangel she did not believe existed to notice Casey's face was paling. "Well, what good is that? Why even daydream? Why bother with vampires pretending to be angels if they won't do what they're supposed to do?"

And what would that be? What is it they are supposed to do?

45

"Well? No answer?"

Bite me came to mind but she remained silent. She was thinking of the nightangel. It did not take more than a moment in his presence to know Gabriel was not the sort of being who would be shoved into the constrictive mental cubbyhole Ricki had constructed for supernatural creatures as she envisioned them. Casey had no answer for questions that held so little understanding. "No."

Ricki, encouraged by this concession, warmed to the topic. "Look at where it's gotten you. Missing work deadlines and who knows what else. All because you've been over-indulging in a ridiculous daydream. The daily grind isn't that bad. Some of us thrive on it. You need to stay put in the moment like everyone else."

Her smile had a self-righteous curve to it that tempted Casey to stop listening to everything she would say next. "It's not that easy. I like to daydream," Casey stated, smiling right back at her.

"No, you like to daydream about this make-believe person, Gabriel. And by the way, yes, it is that easy. I've pinpointed the source of all your trouble and I know how to fix things." Sensible Ricki. It figured she would know—or think she did. Either way, it would have to do.

"How? Go ahead. Tell me." Casey was willing to consider any solution Ricki could devise if it would remove Gabriel from the picture.

"My advice usually costs money. So before I give it for free, I need to have your promise you'll follow it. Will you?"

Casey figured she'd better do something even if it resulted in Ricki favoring her with another smug smile. Let her smile. Easier to deal with her smiles than the nightangel's; she never knew where those might lead. She had not come up with one decent idea yet for getting rid of a stalking daydream that had the audacity to cross from one dimension into another. She was running out of time for thinking up more when Gabriel seemed to be hot on her heels everywhere she turned. She'd have to swallow her pride on the off chance Ricki had devised a nightangel antidote that would do the trick. "Yes."

Ricki took a turn around the kitchen, pausing for maximum effect in the curved archway that led into the living room, so she was framed in the backlight like a movie heroine about to recite the best lines in the film. "Okay then. Here's my advice. Stop it. Just stop it. Don't daydream. Forget Gabriel. He's a fragment of a daydream, a fantasy. Don't think about him anymore and poof—no more Gabriel, the angel-vampire guy.

46

Your worries will become more mundane and manageable in a snap."

"That's it?" Casey felt as if she might begin to cry again.

"That's all there is. Simple, huh?" The smile Casey dreaded appeared.

For all that Gabriel had scared her to death not too many hours before, she was resistant to Ricki's suggestion. Even if something that simple could work, she did not want to do it. She wanted him to recede into the safe world of her dreams without any argument so she could pretend this had never happened and carry on with the status quo. She could not imagine the dreams without her nightangel or life without recourse to her daydreams.

Ricki added some further encouragement upon registering Casey's mood. "Reality is not that bad, you know. Sometimes it's boring, but you can count on it."

"That's your advice?"

"Yes." Ricki came back to sit against the edge of the kitchen table. "It is and it's good advice, too."

"It's not going to work. You're forgetting one key point: I'm not in control here. He is. He's the one who turned up without notice or invitation. He's the one who has been following me around. The problem isn't that I'm thinking about him. The problem is that he's thinking about me."

"Case, he can't think about you. You can only think about him. You made him up—out of thin air. You told me so yourself. He's just a habitual thought that needs to be erased. How hard can it be? I bet it will be much easier than that time you gave up diet cola for a month just because I said you wouldn't be able to do it."

Bad example. That was a month from hell. And Gabriel was much more than a fizzy can of no-cal soda pop.

"You can do it. You can do anything you set your mind to do. Determination is your middle name." Ricki had adopted a soothing, positive tone. She might have been talking a suicide down from a high ledge. Casey was not deceived. She was well aware that, like the potential suicide, once she stepped away from the edge, she was going to get yanked back in and thrown to the floor with a vengeance before she could change her mind again. "You've seen someone who looks like him. Don't let it confuse you."

"He knew me," Casey countered.

"So, he escapes some sappy daydream to seek you out—no small feat, you'll have to agree. And after all that, he just sits there without saying a word? I can't believe I'm saying this but does that sound like something a nightangel, or whatever the hell he's supposed to be, would do if he were the real deal?"

"I told you. You do think I'm crazy."

"Of course I don't."

Casey, observing her friend, did not believe she was confident in what she was saying.

"You know what this is all about? You've been working too hard and putting in too many hours. You're overworked and stressed out. You're not taking care of yourself, either. You never get enough sleep—ever. Stress, overwork, exhaustion; they can affect our perceptions sometimes." Ricki peered over at her. "Are you willing to admit that much is true?" For the first time since they had begun this discussion, Casey was wavering on her stance. Ricki was right on this one point. She never stopped working and she never gave herself a break from the pace she maintained. She was drowning in stress. She was exhausted. This was not going to change. She supposed all of that could make it easier to become overwrought about something that wasn't what it looked to be. "I guess so," she conceded.

Ricki nodded her head in agreement. "When we get stressed and drive ourselves into the ground, we have to expect it's going to take a toll on us. Isn't it possible, when you take these factors into consideration and then throw your vivid imagination into the mix, you could have been mistaken about what you thought you saw tonight? Just maybe?"

"Okay. I guess it could be true." A trickle of blind relief began welling up inside Casey. It would be so good to have not seen him. And even if she had, Ricki's solution for removing Gabriel from her life was still straightforward enough to be dead on. If thinking about the nightangel was what caused these visitations, then not thinking about the nightangel would shut them down.

"You know what you need?" Ricki did not wait for a response. Casey was sure she did not expect her to know the answer anyhow. "You need a real man—one you can meet in this world."

Casey wanted to argue but she controlled herself. She had to because Ricki had settled on the principle thrust of her argument and her words were coming rapid fire.

"Not some vampire with wings who sucks up your life and replaces it with a daydream. And it doesn't help that you put up walls and second guess yourself when it comes to romance because your brother screwed his life up in the name of love. He made terrible choices. That doesn't mean you will."

"I don't want to talk about my brother."

"Have you heard from him?"

"Drop it, Ricki."

"There was nothing you could do to stop him or fix it, Case."

"Subject closed."

"Fine. Let's focus on your immediate problem." Ricki wasn't about to let this opportunity to reform a friend pass her by. "You're lonely, Case. That's not good. Look where it leads."

"I haven't met anyone I like. What am I supposed to do?"

"Try harder. You're too picky. And no wonder. Who can stack up to some hybrid angel-vampire with a castle, a set of wings, and a big crush on you? It's not about him. It's about you. Find someone real. That's the key."

"I go out."

"Not that often. Hardly ever."

"I went out with that guy from DOJ last summer."

"Once, for drinks, no dinner."

"It was twice with an action film and lunch."

"Are you trying to make your point or mine?"

Casey was happy they weren't sitting across from each other in a courtroom.

"And no one since then. What are you waiting for? And don't say someone like Gabriel because there is nobody like Gabriel."

Ricki was so right. *There was nobody like Gabriel.* If there was a glimmer of a chance someone was out there who could stir her heart in the way Gabriel did in the dreams, she would do what Ricki said without feeling so miserable about it. Ricki could not fathom how much walking away from the nightangel to settle for what reality had to offer instead was going to kill Casey.

"Admit it. You have a full-blown obsession with a daydream."

"I don't." *Oh damn, I do.* The realization hit her like a solid punch to the stomach.

"Not true. And it's not cool. You've endowed him with qualities no real man could ever hope to have and then despise every guy who shows any interest in you because he's not this Gabriel. You're deluding

49

yourself. There is no Gabriel. Nobody can ever be like him, either, because he's not real. It's easy to fall in love with some figment of your imagination because you never have to deal with it when it's being an ass, or making you cry, or otherwise acting up. A fantasy is always perfect. Real men are not. Deal with it. This is one time when, despite the current cultural wisdom, it would be best for you to ditch the dream and get on with life."

Casey grabbed her wine and brushed past her friend. "So you think it's all in my head."

"Change your perspective and everything will change with it. See, Case, you're not crazy, but dreaming the way you do is a little nuts. No offense."

"None taken." Casey curled up like a weary kitten in one corner of the living room sofa.

Ricki flounced down on the other side, bringing her legs up and curling her arms around them. "Stop thinking about things that aren't there. You'll see. These 'sightings' will stop." She gave Casey an encouraging look.

Casey set her almost empty glass down on the table. She was the dreamer. He was just the dream. How had she forgotten this elemental fact? The dreams were a habit. Habits are hard to break. Ricki had that pegged. She was going to do it anyway. Ricki said she was determined but that was just a polite way of saying she was stubborn. She could do this. She could do anything that gave her a way out. "It is my dream to stop or start, isn't it?"

"That's right. Toss it aside. Walk away from it."

It would be a loss. The dream would call after her. Resisting was going to hurt like hell.

"I can do that." She had made up her mind. She was trying not to feel guilty about it. "I won't think about Gabriel again. I won't daydream anymore." She began to fiddle with the ring that circled her finger like a secret patch of the garden she had carried out somehow without even knowing it. It was the closest she was ever going to come to walking those charmed garden paths in the daydream with the nightangel again. "How hard can it be?" The golden flowers winked up at her. *Hard.*

"It'll take practice. That's all. Remember. No dreams. No Gabriel. Problem solved. Pretty simple, huh?"

No dreams. No Gabriel. What a dreary thought. "Yeah, so simple it might work. Where's the wine?"

Ricki poured some from her glass into Casey's.

"Your hostess skills leave a lot to be desired."

"You wore me out with all that crazy crap. I'm too tired to get up. Just drink it."

Casey did. Their eyes met above the heavy crystal glasses.

Ricki bumped her knee against Casey's leg and chugged down the last of her wine in one gulp. "Damn, Case. I'm glad you're not crazy."

Casey pressed against the door of thoughts she had slammed shut within herself. It felt good and solid. She made sure to lock it behind her. "Me too, Ricki Lee. Me too."

≪ CHAPTER SEVEN ≫

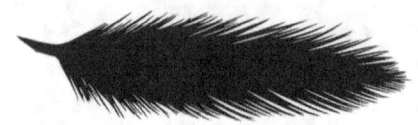

CASEY STEPPED ASIDE AS her favorite law librarian, Mira Shepard, stood up behind the reference desk and began shooing away the two fresh-faced male associates who buzzed around her as though she were some kind of rare flower. "It's not enough to have your IDs, you know. You have to do the training. The rep will be in tomorrow morning at 10:30 to give a class. You need to be there."

"I don't have the time to do some training class," Jack, one of the second-years, began to protest.

"Yeah, you do. Look at all the time you're wasting online trying to figure this stuff out on your own. I see the bills and you're just wandering around the high-priced databases hoping to hit it lucky. That's not where you want to create a high profile. The managing partners hate explaining unnecessary charges to clients." Mira favored him with a melting smile that caused him to mumble something indicating his willingness to appear at the appointed time. Casey thought he blushed but she could not verify this before he rushed off. "She brings breakfast rolls. You'll love it," Mira called after him.

She turned to the other associate hanging on to the edge of the reference desk like it was a life raft and Mira was the one who could either pull him in or kick him back into the water. "I'll gather these industry stats together for you first and then I'll start working on that legislative history. When do you need it by?"

He grinned. "I need it right away."

Mira's cocoa-brown eyes rested on him with the patience reserved for naughty puppies and small children on the verge of tumbling into a heap of trouble. "The legislative history, Richard. When do you need the legislative history?"

"Tomorrow?" The lopsided grin was gone.

"That's do-able. Give me what you've got there and I'll get started on it this afternoon."

"What about my other question? The one I asked you earlier?"

"That's not do-able. I told you why already." She stood up and tapped the papers he handed her against the high edge of the reference desk. "A little refresher wouldn't hurt you either. See you tomorrow morning."

"Tomorrow morning. Sure," Richard agreed, looking like he'd been spun around by a cyclone. Maybe he had been. He hurried away, making up for any perceived malingering with a burst of speed.

"And remember," Mira shouted after him. "She brings breakfast rolls. You'll love it."

"I've got a question for you, Mira." Casey said, shaking her head. Mira joked about being an information warrior and Casey thought there was some truth to that. A petite powerhouse, Mira dressed like a 1950s librarian who had fallen through a time warp and on the way to the 21st century had spent her time playing post-apocalyptic video games. She liked pearls, pencil-slim skirts, stiletto heels, petal pink nails, and the color black. "I'm going to ask you if you don't make me come to a class tomorrow."

"Nah, Tweedle Dee and Tweedle Dum there need a refresher class—basic 101. Sad, really. No online legal research skills and all those law school debts hanging over their heads. It's my duty as an information professional to help the lost and befuddled. There'll be an advanced class coming up on searching the Invisible Web. I'm teaching that one myself. That's your ticket."

"Got it. Actually, that's kind of why I came by. I need your assistance. Can you borrow some books for me on interlibrary loan even if it's not work related? I wouldn't ask but they're not available for purchase anywhere."

"For you, Casey, sure."

"The books aren't for me, actually." Casey avoided looking directly at

Mira and started rummaging through her purse for the list. "I have this friend who's doing some research—it's a little off the wall. She doesn't exactly know what she's doing." *Boy was that true.* Casey hesitated; she was thinking maybe it was a good thing she could not find the list in her bag when her hand landed on the sheet of paper. "But she's trying to find some answers to a few questions and doesn't want to leave any stones unturned. I told her I might be able to get them for her faster than if she went through the public library. She's a little embarrassed to ask for these. They're not the most standard fare." She handed the folded list to Mira.

The librarian read it over without blinking an eye. "Hmmm. Interesting titles. I'm always happy to help those on a quest for answers. I'll track these down and deliver them to you personally. And don't worry, I'll put them in some inter-office envelopes when I carry them down the hall so they'll look boring and legal. It doesn't hurt to be discreet at Phillips and Row."

∞ ∞ ∞

Casey took a swig of her vanilla latte. Cold. Again. She was feeling pretty good about life at the moment, except for the latte, and she could fix that. She got up, took the carryout cup down the hall, and leaned against the counter to consider the contents of the vending machine tucked into the corner while her espresso drink nuked up almost good as new in the microwave.

Her conversation with Ricki had helped her accomplish a few things. First, she was no longer as worried about being crazy. Second, she had survived a whole week without repressing the thought of Gabriel more than about a hundred times a day. And third, she had settled back into a routine that had work as her major focus, causing Ed Johnson to look at her without frowning that very morning.

He had scheduled a meeting with her later in the afternoon. His executive legal secretary and no-excuses-about-it gatekeeper, Jo, could not give her much of a lowdown on the meeting when Casey had stopped by her desk earlier in the day—just that it was not a continuation of the lecture she had received over the missed filing but something about being teamed with a more senior associate on another case. As long as it was not Derek Rider, Casey was good to go. She was eager for the extra work; anything to keep her thoughts from drifting back to the angel.

Casey was curious about it but if Jo knew who it was, she wasn't telling. Casey had been tempted to inquire but she didn't press it. She would have told Casey straight off if she wanted to provide her that detail. Asking Jo questions she didn't think needed answering was a sure path to getting on her bad side and getting on Jo's bad side was a dire error at Phillips & Row. She had Ed Johnson's ear and some said, at least at one point—his heart; he trusted Jo implicitly. Considering she efficiently managed every aspect of his life for the last ten years, Casey thought that was a smart move.

∞ ∞ ∞

Casey took a sip of the latte that had been sitting untouched on her desk for the last hour; cold again. She had just enough time to grab a legal pad and pen and race to Ed's swank corner office. Already sitting in one of the two chairs straight across the desk from Ed was her worst nightmare, Derek Rider.

"Good. Sit down. Let's get started." Ed barked commands instead of speaking to people.

Casey took the other chair without looking in Derek's direction.

"Casey. Derek. You know our firm prides itself on our pro bono work. I've looked at the numbers for the last few months and you two are at the bottom of the list for pro bono hours worked."

"I'll put in some extra in to catch up. My caseload has been heavier than normal."

Derek snorted. "And you've had to clean up some messes lately, as well."

"What's your excuse, Derek?" Ed asked him without blinking an eye. "Your pro bono hours are the lowest of any associate working at Phillips and Row."

Casey felt a smile swimming up to the surface and she pushed it back under. Derek was already a thorn in her side. Why provoke him?

"I had the flu," Derek replied.

"And why does that matter? Half the office had it." Ed Johnson was not one for excuses, as Casey had learned firsthand.

"Our pro bono program is one of the best in the country and maintaining the level of our pro bono hours is something we take seriously. You two are not exempt. I've talked to our Director of Pro Bono Activities and he is delighted the two of you are now available."

Casey believed in the importance of pro bono work. She could do this as long as she did not have to deal with Derek in order to get it done. Maybe it would help take her mind off Gabriel. She glanced over at Derek. He saw pro bono work as a waste of his talent and energy. His approach was to do enough pro bono work to fly under Ed's radar—and that was all; picking what would make him shine and nothing else. He'd miscalculated this time.

"You two contact Russell. He has several potential pro bono matters but they all require a team of two. Guess what two people got pushed to the top of the list for one of those pro bono assignments."

Casey shifted in her seat when she caught Derek's smirk. *Pro bono work with Derek. Big NO.* "Can't we pick something we can go solo on?"

"Be a team player, Sloane." Derek was eating up her obvious discomfort at the idea of working with him.

She had reason to be uncomfortable about it. She had done the unthinkable. She had once turned down Derek for a date. She did not want to go out with someone she worked with; there was something about Derek that felt off. Derek had been offended by this slight. He had never asked again but when given the opportunity, he punished her for it in whatever way was at hand. When she had missed the filing, he had spread the story to everyone at the firm who would listen. A surprising number of people must have wanted to listen because everyone from the mailroom staff to the top partners gave signs of having heard Derek's spiteful retelling of the missing filing and the shocking consequences.

"He'll explain what you'll be doing. Just do it. I told you both before—get along. It's teamwork all the way here at Phillips and Row."

Casey wanted to laugh. *Teamwork? All the way to where—hell?* Half the associates at the firm would deep six each other to become partner. With the competitive stakes what they were in such a workplace, there was no room for true teamwork. Casey thought it was funny that Ed felt compelled to put such a positive face on such a dire environment. Did he believe what he was saying?

"I'm happy to work with Derek but I'd prefer to choose the pro bono work I take on."

"Then you should have picked something else when you finished your last project instead of waiting to get on my radar. Derek, don't look so smug. You may be more senior than Casey but you're not a partner yet."

Ed Johnson gave them a dismissive nod and began to study

something on his computer monitor as if they had ceased to exist. The meeting was over. They both got up and left before he could think of anything else to say to them.

"Looking forward to working with you, Sloane," Derek said when they were walking down the empty hall that would pass by his office.

Once he marched inside, Casey would be able to go on to the elevator lobby and the coffee shop next door by herself. She was going to get another vanilla latte. She could not wait for no Derek and a cup of coffee. Casey sped up. "I bet."

"Pro bono work is so nice and snug. We'll get to spend some quality time together. And since you're more junior than I am, I'll be the lead. Bossing you around in the name of doing good is going to be fun."

Not hating Derek Rider was difficult.

"I'm not that easy to boss and pro bono work isn't like a regular case we take on. I'm sure we'll be working more as colleagues. You're not that much more senior than I am, anyway."

"I'll make sure it doesn't work that way. And I'm senior enough. Besides, face it, Sloane, one way or another, someday you're going to be working under me on all your cases. And loving it," he added, with the kind of emphasis that made Casey want to pop him one right in the nose.

She thought about it for a second before letting the idea go. *Not worth it.* She'd get fired for assault, lose her ability to get another job, and be cast into the gutter of the legal world while he kept climbing the partnership ladder and harassing women with impunity.

Life without Gabriel wasn't just boring; it was fraught with living, breathing reasons why she found the nightangel so irresistible and unforgettable in the first place. Derek Rider was a perfect example of that. He was one of those people the phrase "total jerk" was meant to describe. She said it under her breath as she headed back to her office to grab her purse. She thought saying it helped. And so she said it again under her breath as she trudged back to her office, more disgusted with the real world than ever. "Total jerk." *Yup, it helps.*

Unfortunately, there was no help to be found with regard to forgetting Gabriel. And no matter what she had said to Ricki, Casey wasn't sure she wanted to forget him anyway.

≪ CHAPTER EIGHT ≫

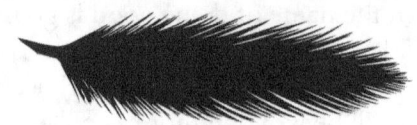

FORGET GABRIEL. **THAT WAS** what Ricki had said. Like that would be such an easy thing to do. Like dropping out of the dreams would be as easy as pie. *What was so easy about pie anyway—except eating it?*

She shook her head to stop the flow of ideas slipping past the depressing vigilance of her inner censor. She was thinking of Gabriel again. In a roundabout way. Still. She had promised herself. She had promised Ricki. She was not going to do it anymore. And yet, no matter how much she tried not to, she did it every day.

Thinking about Gabriel was a waste of time anyway. There would have to be such a thing as a nightangel to begin with, for anybody to see it. Anybody sane, that is.

Oh yes, Ricki had managed to pound that one fact into her thick, resistant skull. There was no such thing as a nightangel. There was no such thing as Gabriel. Ricki had said so. That meant it must be true. It had to be true. Miserable things like Ed Johnson and Derek Rider could exist in the world but resplendent angels who longed after you for no good reason you could think of—no, those could not be. How crappy was that?

Sanity had its price. Her nightangel was her payment. It seemed a heavy price to pay but she was paying it anyway. She did not feel as though she had much of a choice about it.

And what did Ricki know anyway? Ricki knew nothing about

nightangels. Real or not, the memory of such a being did not just fade away. She missed him. Not thinking about the angel was trickier than it sounded and involved serious heartache. If Ricki had to give up a nightangel, she'd be moping around some too. As it was, Ricki was unsympathetic about any overt nightangel mourning and so Casey kept it to herself as best she could. Failure to do so led to a scolding lecture that always ended in Ricki saying, "I'm telling you this for your own good." Casey hated that part the most. Ricki did what she did because she believed she was right. Because being right and being for Casey's own good coincided this time, it was impossible for Casey to argue with Ricki about it with any hope of prevailing.

Casey was grateful to Ricki for convincing her of the nonexistence of Gabriel—in a dull, grim way. She needed to be convinced. She could not go on as she had been doing. Something had to give. She had not expected it to be the otherworld; it had been so potent, so compelling, so powerful. And now, it was lost to her. The otherworld was more fragile than she thought. Rather than fight her, it had yielded to her wishes. She had turned her back and walked. Nothing happened. It was over. Life went on. She was surprised.

Enjoying this no-Gabriel zone was turning out to be a lot more difficult than she had imagined. She had never realized until she stopped, how much she had thought about him before. The void it had created in her life was significant and the difficulty she had filling it up tempted her to fall back into the dreams during every waking moment.

In spite of this, she had been careful to at least try not to think of Gabriel. She did not believe she dreamed of him at night. She worked. She ate. She drank lots of coffee. She collaborated with Derek on their pro bono case, and laser-focused in on every aspect of her career. She went to the gym. She watched TV. She checked in on Facebook and surfed the web. She read. She tried to remember to go out with friends. She slept. She did all the ordinary things. She did them over and over. And it was not getting any easier. Maybe it was getting worse. She had never recalled it all seeming so mundane before.

The day stretched out before her like a long desert trek with no end in sight. Not thinking about Gabriel was a lot of work. She was exhausted but she knew sleep would not come to her. She would opt for wolfing down a hearty dinner and moping in front of the TV. Her appetite was withstanding the stress just fine. In fact, the stress might be enhancing it. A soda machine and a coffee maker stood at the ready in the kitchenette down the hall from her office but no snacks were available. Casey had survived the day on lattes from the coffee shop.

She walked into her own kitchen thinking about the lack of chocolate and salty treats at work with mixed feelings. She could have used a dose of chocolate about three in the afternoon and by four o'clock she would have even settled for pretzels or a bag of chips. She opened the refrigerator and stared into its depths as though she did not already know she was in bare cupboard status at the moment. The only things left that didn't look like biohazards were a half-empty bottle of white wine and a loaf of white bread she should have tossed out the week before. She grabbed them both and slammed the fridge shut. So much for the hearty comfort food approach to squashing her pain.

She stretched up and snatched a stemmed glass from an upper shelf, flipped the cupboard shut, and poured herself a glass of wine. She dropped two pieces of bread into the toaster and threw the rest in the trash. She was thinking about not thinking of Gabriel, which meant she was thinking about Gabriel after all. She began to pace back and forth across the kitchen floor. She was relying on the movement to drive away the thoughts.

Pacing did not help.

Her angel always did like to walk along with her wherever she would go. Even called up in memory, he was a diligent companion.

Gabriel. The sound of his name ricocheted around in her head and the lack of response emboldened her to continue. *Dreamangel. Nightangel.* The names flew fast and anxious into the shallow silence she had created for herself over the last few weeks.

You ought to stop, Casey thought. Having begun though, she would be a coward not to go on. She was hungry for a quick word with the one who resided in silence now in the otherworld. It was necessary to her peace of mind.

Ricki would kill her if she knew. But then, how would she know if Casey did not tell her? And Casey had no intention of telling her—ever.

Outside, the dark night pressed against the windows. Inside, the round sun of the kitchen light filled the glass panes with a false noon. Did dreamangels ever stand in the plain white glare of home? What did home look like to something like that? She yanked the curtains across the window and turned away.

60

Casey felt guilty about Gabriel and the way she had left him languishing in the ruins of her daydreams. "I'm sorry." The sentence slipped from between the tight line of her lips and the sound of it startled her. She did not want to be sorry. Sorry made people feel better. And worse yet, sorry meant maybe there was a Gabriel out there waiting to forgive her. "I'm so damned sorry." She said it again anyway. "For you. For me. For everything." She should shut up. She knew she should shut up. She snatched her glass from the counter and took a drink of wine. She spilled the rest into the sink.

She wanted to talk to the emptiness inside her and pretend it was something else. With no one there to stop her from doing it, the words bubbled up within her. She poured them into her imaginary nightangel's ear without speaking a word out loud. *It wasn't my idea to abandon you this way. You started it. You're the one who broke the rules, not me.*

She drifted into the living room and draped herself across the sofa. The soft green design of stylized flowers and foliage that covered it was a washed out version of the lush greenery in her dreams. She fingered the fabric in disgust. Here she was reclining on a flat, green garden in the middle of suburbia when her heart wanted nothing more than to seek out the nightangel prince lost in the dream. She knew a place where dreamangels trod along lush garden paths thick with color and scent. She needed to be in that place. Maybe it wouldn't hurt to pay it a quick visit. Something about the rose beds edged in amber stone and the garden flowers tucked along the crisscrossing paths made it a refuge from the world and the stresses it threw her way. The angel's presence filling every corner may have had a little something to do with the high quality of the peace and quiet there too.

It would be nice to walk in such a garden again. Very nice.

She was feeling pretty stressed. Maybe strolling the garden looking for nightangels would help. Ricki did not understand how hard it was to stop dreaming. How could she? She had never been there. She had never seen. If Ricki was right, and she must be right, what harm was there in a brief return to the otherworld? If the dreams were nothing more than what they should be, then where was the danger?

Besides, it seemed fair. Gabriel had crossed the void to pay her a visit of sorts. Whether it was real or imagined did not matter. She owed him this call. She owed it to both of them. She had something to give to the archangel—a goodbye, a thank you, a closing dialogue, a reasonable parting. Paying him this final visit was the right thing to do. He was a friend. He was more than that. She knew he loved her. The problem was he did it in the way she had found nightangels tended to do things—with a vengeance and displaying no real interest in any other result than what they wished as an outcome. She didn't care. She could work around that.

She wanted to say her goodbyes and see him one last time. She was certain now. Because then, she planned never to draw up the memory of his face again. It would be too painful. It hurt already. She would have to learn to tough it out. This one last visit was going to have to last them forever. After this, she was going to find a way to forget and then settle on another method for reducing the weight of the world pressing in on her without resorting to nightangels in secret gardens. She could not imagine what would do the trick beyond a case of permanent amnesia or some kind of heavy-duty anti-daydreaming patch similar to those smokers wore when they were trying to kick the habit. She would figure something out. And once she had, she'd help the forgetting process along by taking up knitting, or running, or flower arranging to lower her daily stress level instead—well, maybe it would be better not to focus on anything involving flowers, but she could worry about the details later. The point was she would find something dull and ordinary to replace Gabriel and pretend she liked it. Ricki would be so proud.

She stretched out on the sofa. She folded one hand over the other—as if in quiet supplication, or calm sleep, or cold death. Snow White resting in a coffin of gold and glass in the forest; Sleeping Beauty dropping into an enchanted sleep in a castle chamber—waiting for the arrival of the one who would release her.

She was about to go over the top. She had no wishes to make. She had no prayers to say. At least, none she cared for the nightangel to overhear. *Fairytale princesses of storybook and film; pay attention to how it should be done. Casey Sloane is going in. Maybe you should be taking some notes.* Casey shook her head in disgust. She was pretty sure Casey Sloane did not know anything about how it should be done. Gabriel was probably counting on it. But why dwell on the negative? Better to think of the angel.

Casey smiled. How dangerous he was. How irresistible he remained.

He would be there in the dream. Somewhere. He would know she was coming. He must. He would be waiting on her. The way all good dreams wait on their dreamer. Never far away. Impatient to begin. Whispering in the dreamer's ear the soft words of seduction that will call them back. And back. And back again.

Here she was once more, thinking of him as if he was real, as if he had a will of his own. Why could she not stop doing that?

Her eyes closed in a slow, purposeful flutter. Her lashes slid down against her cheeks like locks falling into place against the world. She was on her way. The smile lingered on her lips. The air around her was warmer, lighter. Yet, a chill passed through her. She took a deep breath. She steeled her heart as best she could against him. She pushed her qualms aside. She knew where she was going. She would not rest until she had made the journey one more time.

Gabriel. Hear me. I am coming. I am falling. I am almost there.

The smell of roses spilled into the room; the heady scent saturated the air. She kept her eyes closed tight. She took a deep breath. Her eyes opened wide with expectation. The garden spread out before her with a welcoming sigh.

She had arrived.

The sky hung lavender-blue and darkening above the garden. Her eyes jumped to the expanse of chamber window cut into the façade of the highest turret. No nightangel stood in that rough gray arch, watching the garden for her arrival. No dreamangel called out his pleasure at her coming. No fairytale prince appeared swift and smiling beside her as she began to move within the dream.

Fairytale princesses, hold off with the note taking.

Damn. Already this was not turning out the way she planned. She had to stop watching her favorite happily-ever-after animated films or at least cut back. They were giving her unrealistic expectations with regard to men—inside and outside the dreams.

Casey kept her eyes on the window anyway. She had a penchant for being ever hopeful. She breathed in the garden smells and tried to think positive.

The scent of roses sweetened the air. Musk roses, damasks, and chinas. Floribundas and teas. Old-fashioned apothecary roses and tall Victorian hybrids. There were button-eyed cabbage roses that never opened to reveal their center and wild sweetbrier with leaves that, after the rain fell, smelled of ripe apples. Roses bloomed like scented fireworks along every walkway the garden held.

There were other flowers too. Heavy-headed peonies bowing beneath the weight of their own frills like flushed Southern belles. Gray-leafed maiden's ruin and dusty-pink valerian pressing against the catmint and mignonette. Jutting swords of ice-blue delphinium reaching toward the cooler, bluer sky. Lilies of gold and orange. Bright yellow sundrops. Wands of lacy fairy primrose. Purple orris root Casey called by the newer name of iris, and star-shaped clematis with centers that hung like eiderdown when the blooms had dropped from the vine. But Gabriel, like Casey, preferred the roses to everything else. No visit between them was complete without at least a few moments lost in the rose garden.

She set off toward a long wall of lilacs that screened the farther end of the garden in a froth of heavy blooms. Her attention was distracted by the window spread in a curve of harsh stone above everything within the rose-wreathed walls. It still stood empty.

She forced her eyes from the lure of the window. She looked about her as if she must be missing something. The garden was empty. No angel loitering by the wall. No angel lingering by the gate. No angel pausing, still as a statue at the turn of the path. *Where was he?*

Nightangels were so unpredictable. Not too long ago he could not leave her alone and now he was nowhere to be found. If he was trying to confuse her, he was doing a good job.

She considered calling out to him. "Gabriel. It's Casey. I'm back. Where are you?" But that sounded a little pathetic. She could step it up to a demand by tacking on, "You'd better get here fast or I'm taking off again." But angels dislike demands and are good at recognizing lies when they hear them. So she kept her mouth shut. She had no intention of leaving. She would have to go find him.

She walked through the gate of the empty garden and beyond the crowd of wood lilies that watched her with marmalade faces and purred in the breeze as she went by. Darkness crept over the dusk. A full moon climbed through the treetops like a plump-faced Cheshire cat. A dense purple melted over the bottle blue sky, turning it a darker shade than the lilac and lavender that Casey favored in her dreamscapes.

The air stirred her skirt and it fluttered around her legs. Casey paused and looked down at her dress. She had been so busy searching for Gabriel that her outfit had been the last thing on her mind. Now she gave it her full attention. The dress was of a delicate blue material cut low across her breasts and falling all the way to the ground to end in a filmy demi-train at the back. The blue of the dress was a paler version of the blue of her eyes. It clung to her body as the evening breeze traveled past her. She had a feeling she looked hotter in this gown than was appropriate to the occasion. For something that covered so much, it revealed an awful lot. She wished she could switch it out for jeans and an oversized sweatshirt but it did not look like that was going to happen. It seemed the dream instead of the dreamer was in charge of wardrobe tonight. At least she wasn't wearing something that made her feel as though she had stepped into a dark-edged video game—something tight, black, and promising more attitude than she could deliver. She said a silent thank you to whatever it was in the dream that had taken control of her attire tonight for showing a little restraint.

She started off again. She had to find him. Her goodbye to Gabriel was what was needed to set everything in her life right again. He was not going to avoid her tonight.

Her path wound past a few essential spots in her otherworld. The patch of giddy daylilies. The grove of chalk-limbed birches reaching up to the sky. The thicket of berry bushes heavy with bright fruit. The butterfly garden vibrating with the movement of colorful wings. The rock-strewn edge of the pond where the black swans gathered. The sea of promiscuous wildflowers whose names were cleverer and more eloquent than those of their more sophisticated cousins behind the garden wall. All of it waiting on her as she waited on Gabriel.

She began to amble instead of march. She had plenty of time to take it all in. It was a long, lovely walk to the meadow and the picture-perfect view it provided of the great forest at its far edge, where the nightangel roamed—free of sunlight, free of dreamers, free of all constraint.

She listened to the evening noises in the cooling air. The calm whisper of the wind punctuated by birdsong drifted past her. Casey thought it was the mockingbirds, a bird of her own Virginian backyard. They winged through her dreams along with a modest population of cardinals, jays, wrens, and sparrows. Tonight a flock of daffodil-yellow goldfinches flashed across the landscape like a shower of shooting stars but she hardly noticed. She had other things on her mind besides small songbirds.

She walked on toward the field that separated her from the thick forest spilling out from the tumble of impenetrable hills rimming this side of the dream. A scattering of butterflies drifted past her on heart-shaped wings the color of Valentine's Day candy boxes wrapped in red cellophane. At any other time she would have followed them to the

65

isolated spread of neon-bright lantana plants to better admire their oversized wings. Not tonight. She was only interested in angels tonight. She hurried her steps. If he came, he would come through those woods.

The field was one of her waiting places, a point of departure to destinations deeper in the dream. Casey had made a beeline to this spot so she would be there to greet him. Even if she was going to turn her back on him forever after this dream, it didn't hurt to start things off on the right foot. She could be a gracious hostess this one last time.

The field and the crest far past it stood empty. She kicked at a small, round pebble and sent it flying into the weeds. She would have liked to kick a volley of smooth stones in the direction of Gabriel's comings and goings, like a small child throwing rocks at the dark. She looked for another.

She did not see a stone. She did not see anything. She started across the meadow. The grass grew high here. It rubbed with a provocative little hiss against her legs as she walked. She quickened her stride.

It was a pretty night in dreamland. That was as it should be.

Except, it was jumbled like her thoughts. Warm and cool. Breezy and stiff. Empty and full of life. Something was off. She just did not know what it was yet.

She yanked at the train of her dress and pulled it away from where it was tangled in the weeds. She shivered even though she was not cold. She knew she should not be there, standing around at the place where so many encounters with Gabriel had begun before. That made her more set on doing it.

So what? She would stand where she wanted. She was not going to swoon with desire for a made-up angel in a damn daydream. Even if he was unbelievably gorgeous and made her insides turn to mush every time she looked at him. That was then. This was now. Now she was more irritated than beguiled. She just wanted to say goodbye.

The field went silent. She lifted her head and scanned the horizon. She was not sure whether to be satisfied or horrified. Where nothing was a moment before, there was her angel. Gabriel had arrived at the edge of where the dream became dangerous as if breathed to life by the very breaths she took. The nightangel broke through the jagged edge of the forest astride a dark, powerful horse. Just as always, he was an attractive danger. She tried to breathe but the air lay leaden in her lungs. That was not all she saw.

66

He was not alone. Not at all.

Three riders descended upon her in great haste. She was not prepared for three. One was bad enough. Three was a guarantee of trouble. She should have known Aric and Rane would not be left out of this dream. He was never long without his brothers and they were never long without him. Why didn't she see this coming? Already the dream was taking its own course. If Casey was not so shaken, she would have been annoyed.

Now, she would have to say goodbye to three nightangels instead of one. Who could know how eager they would be to part with her when, unlike Gabriel, they were still dream-bound. She had not realized how fortunate she was to only have one such being harassing her. If she had a gratitude journal back when Gabriel was chasing her around the city until she was shaking in her boots, this would have gone into it: "I'm grateful today for one stalking nightangel making my life a total living hell instead of three." Sometimes one of something was more than enough.

Tonight it seemed there were three. Casey was sure that was going to be inconvenient.

They were all in black; all in wings. The stark moonlight radiated off the surface of those wings with such brilliance she wondered why her outfit didn't include a pair of sunglasses.

She thought about ending the dream right then. She imagined the nightangels dropping into nothing and opening her eyes to what she called home. A pale flowered sofa. Stale toast and white wine. The hard artificial light from the kitchen shooting in a dull spike across the living room. A pile of work and a half-read newspaper on the floor under the coffee table. The day and evening; spent, lost. Her waiting bed; wide, empty.

She shaded her eyes with her hands and remained where she was. She watched their progress with uncontained expectation. She could not help herself. She could not control her need for the daydream and the nightangels within it. *Talk about looking for trouble.*

Gabriel broke away from the others; riding as though he was racing straight into battle. The jingle of the bridle and fall of the horse's hooves beating the dirt filled her ears. Rane and Aric rode his flank a distance behind him. The cadence of their horses' strides rang in time to the first.

She had the urge to dart away as fast and as far as she could from the descending nightangel astride his wild steed. But she did not. She stood and waited, as she had stood and waited each time before. She watched her fate approach. Her eyes opened wider and wider. Her heart beat as though it would burst. She waited, poised to run but not running at all. Enthralled.

Their horses were black with blacker manes and tails. Gabriel's horse was fine-boned and bred for speed. The others rode on huge stallions with thick manes and lush, trailing tails that flew in silky banners of gleaming ebony behind them as they galloped. These horses were heavy with the glitter of plate that evoked a world of bygone battles and tournaments. The polished metal shone with the light of the oversized moon and the glow of the nightangels' wings.

Those wings, raised wide and high, cut apart the sky and knit it back together again. Their eyes and mouths, vivid as bright-colored gems, stood out against their pale faces. For some reason, they did not think she should be able to see the rush of wings, the flash of white teeth behind red smiles, or the glint of the supernatural in their glances. Casey didn't get that. "What's the big deal about it? I bet anyone could see that," Casey told them when the subject came up for discussion. The nightangels disagreed. It seemed she had the gift of seeing nightangels for what they were down to the wings and this was a unique ability among mortals, even in daydreams. "Lucky me," Casey was always quick to respond. Although she wasn't so sure how lucky it was.

Gabriel reined in his horse just in front of her. She staggered back and gasped as much for pleasure as fear. Like a dragonfly alighting sharp as a shadow on the fragile surface of a sky blue pond, the rush of his wings slowed and then stilled as he settled into the daydream.

Gabriel understood the value of a proper arrival. Casey appreciated that.

She let out her breath and caught it again but the air did not seem to fill her lungs. She took another deeper breath. She held it and let her eyes fill with his presence. His face was so hard, so sweet; she was torn between craving and cringing. The air trembled around her and she drank it down like a triple-shot latte.

The goodbye was gone from her lips. Yet, she could not bring herself back to her place on her sofa of flowers. She was too busy gaping at the nightangels to retreat. They were looking back at her with a predatory presumption she had come to find was standard operating procedure for this particular breed of vampire. She was not sure about the more ordinary kind. She had never met any of those. But given her experience with the nightangels, she imagined vampires not graced with wings would

68

be of a similar mindset. She had no intention of testing this theory. She had enough problems already.

Aric's wings turned the air to storm as he rode past her, catching up her hair so it flew around her face in a whirl of long dark waves. She shoved the thick rush of tangled strands away in time to meet his somber slate-gray eyes. Aric rested his glance on her in the unsettling way he had of taking a person's sum and sifting it out so he knew every fragment of who they were in the blink of an eye. Aric and Gabriel traded glances. *Message transmitted.* Her soul had been bared and shared just like that. Holding an advantage with the nightangels was tough. Privacy was not a given.

She stopped fiddling with her hair and turned her attention to Rane. He kept the closest to the woods. He had Gabriel's back. His horse was skittish and wild-eyed. It tugged at the bit as if, given half a chance, it would bolt. Rane held his wings quiet and lifted, as a glossy-feathered bird in high summer keeps the power of flight held apart from its body until it's needed. One of Rane's hands tightened on the reins while the fingers of his other hand caressed the taut neck of the animal that strained for its own way. His lips formed some soothing words. She could not hear them. He patted the animal with a firm, open hand. It settled beneath his control and the calmness of his touch. Casey's heartbeat slowed, as if he stroked it calm with that same compelling hand, as if her heart had heard his secret words and took comfort from them. How odd that Rane, the one she often saw as the most formidable of the three, would be the one to cause her heart to stop racing now.

As it was, she was hemmed in with the nightangel; the one she had come to see, and a couple others she had not meant to run into at all. She was not frightened. She could not be frightened when she looked up into Gabriel's face. She saw no threat, no danger. She only saw her dreamangel, arriving at hearing the call of his name and choosing to answer.

She wanted to hear what this dreamangel would say. She wanted it more than was good for a woman who did not believe in daydreams and angels anymore.

Damn, I'm stupid sometimes.

≪ CHAPTER NINE ≫

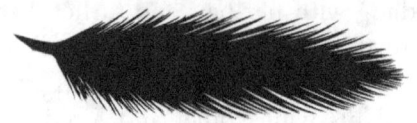

GABRIEL'S MAGNIFICENT WINGS BRUSHED shut. Casey admired the graceful action of that closing. She did not look but she heard the scratch of feather upon feather pressing one upon the other and she knew Aric and Rane had followed suit.

Wings upon vampires were a wonder to Casey; so unexpected, yet so reasonable. She was fascinated by the wings. Their movement could hypnotize her, render her weak, and reduce her to something ridiculously close to willing. The sight of the nightangels' elegant pinions could cause her head to spin into flights-of-fancy mode without warning. She saw the mythic in their sweeping form, and forgot in the seeing, to beware their magic. Not a very good idea with the non-mortal crowd, in general, but hard to avoid. The nightangels dazzled the mortal mind with every ounce of who they were without meaning to do anything more than exist in plain sight down to the last feather. Casey accepted regular bedazzlement as part of the price she must pay to know those who walked in wings, the same way she accepted paying a toll to drive across the Chesapeake Bay Bridge so she could get to enjoy a perfect day at the beach. Both tolls came with a major view, so it was hard to complain.

She focused on the wings even when she tried her best to pretend she did not. And that was annoying because it was difficult to pretend you did not care about the wings when you could not take your eyes off them half the time. The wings were mesmerizing. Each set different—in cast and color, in texture and size—angel to angel, time to time. She would study them. She would wait until she thought the nightangels did not see, and she would gaze at them for long, secret snatches of time. On occasion, she would reach out to feel the motionless edge of one like a child reaching for what might be forbidden but could not be resisted. Their wings were hard and soft at once to the touch; a rigid curve of feather and bone.

It did not matter how light the touch of finger against pinion. The nightangel would know. It would sense the electric connection of flesh to feather. It would turn. It would look into her eyes. Sometimes, it would touch her back with a new intimacy and she would stand, too bewitched to move. Sometimes, it would spread its wings and hold them out full and high so she might better satisfy her curiosity. Once, Rane had caught her hand and run it along the great curve of a settled wing until she had begun to shake. And not so many weeks ago, Gabriel had pulled her tight against him within the cool, dark shelter of his wings as though he was not sure he was going to let her go again—and she had clung to him as though she was not sure she'd step away if given the choice. But he did and she did.

That was how it was. They touched what touched them and in touching, held forth their beauty and strength as they held the moment and the dreamer—frozen and revealed. When your fingers were stuck like glue to a nightangel's splendid wing, it was difficult to insist you were the one who ran the show. Claiming you had the upper hand was fruitless when your secrets danced in their eyes like they had read all the best parts of the diary you knew better than to keep.

The dreamangel would say her name then, or smile, or turn its eyes away, or thrust her aside with a gentle movement; it would free her. And she would drop her hand. She would draw back in new awe, more fascinated by the wings and by the angels who bore them than she was before.

Gabriel's wings were deep azure edged in crimson now. They were stiff and luminous like the edge of day falling into night would be painted by a Renaissance master. Rane's wings were most often glossy black and spiky, although Casey had seen them red on occasion and icy crystal more than once. They were anthracite this evening—dense and polished. Of the three nightangels, Aric's wings were the finest. They were the wings of a seraph. Three sets lay upon each other. They opened and closed with a pulsing, changeable fire when he moved them. They emanated a soft, pervasive light no matter what their color. Now, they were black-tinged violet banded in gold. When he settled them down around himself, they rested about his lean hips and long, powerful thighs in a provocative gleam of furled strength.

"You are here." Gabriel did not smile but his wings crackled with the force of his pleasure in seeing her standing there, staring up at him. "You have kept us waiting a long time, dreamer. We have been impatient for your arrival."

"How is it she has no time of late for dreams?" Rane demanded.

"Ask her," Aric said in a low, curious tone.

Gabriel did not speak. He was assessing Casey. He rested an arm against the silken neck of his stallion. His stare deepened.

"No?" Rane said, his wings rattling like rain against metal. The horse beneath him snorted and pawed at the ground. "I shall tell you then. She is unkind."

"She is busy."

"Too busy, Aric, to consider us?"

"Too busy to consider herself."

"Is that why?" Gabriel's voice, upon beginning again, sang in her ears until she could not think for listening to it. "Were you so busy, my heart?"

"Yes." She whispered without conviction. She had made sure she was too busy to consider anything for weeks now so it was an honest enough answer. Still, it did not sound like the right one when she spoke it out loud. Gabriel's question, and the way it had been formed, unraveled her thoughts. "No."

"Yes. No. Which is it, Casey?" Gabriel inquired in a voice so soft and firm she felt as though she were falling backward into a cloud of hard-packed feather down.

She dropped her eyes and tried to keep the sound of it from smothering what little good sense she had left to call her own. She could not look at him and speak. "I don't know." *Where was a peel-and-stick nametag that said, "Hello, I'm Stupid" when you needed it?*

"She must know."

"She does not know. She has said she does not."

You tell him, Aric. Casey cast a grateful look his way. Someone was taking up for her.

"How can she not know? What kind of answer is that?"

72

And shut up, Rane. As usual, he was the one to point out her every flaw. Maybe it was good there was no peel-and-stick nametag action going on tonight. Why highlight the obvious when Rane did it so well without any help from her at all?

"She does not know, Rane," Aric said. "That is all. There is no secret reason. Perhaps she is just confused."

"What then? Where have you been, my own? Why so confused when before you were so sure?"

"I've been thinking." *Oh, that's genius.* She waited for Rane to chime in and he did not disappoint her.

"Thinking? Is that what she's been doing?"

Casey flashed an angry look at Rane. Did he mean to repeat every word she said, question every statement, in that cool, mocking voice?

"About what?" Gabriel asked, as if he heard no one but her.

"You."

"What are your thoughts—on me?"

"Nothing." She stumbled over the word. "It's hard to say."

"Try." Rane's voice was sugar.

"I don't know."

Gabriel waited.

"I don't. I'm not kidding, Gabriel. And I'm tired of thinking. It doesn't help."

"I don't know, Gabriel. All this thinking is hard." Rane mimicked her. "Why so ignorant tonight when she is usually too clever for her own good? I believe she does not want to say."

"No one asked you what you thought. I wasn't talking to you. I was talking to Gabriel. You can be quiet."

"Speak without lies and clever avoidances. That would render me speechless, I assure you."

"I'm not lying."

"You are not speaking the truth."

It was unfortunate the nightangels were so intuitive. It always gave them an advantage and that was unfair. After all, she was the one doing the daydreaming, Casey thought, trying not to look as irritated as she felt. Aric gave her an all-knowing smile.

"Her answers are mine, Rane. I understand their meaning. Casey does not have to lie to me."

"Give them their peace, Rane."

Rane continued to scrutinize Casey but urged his horse backward a few steps. He acted as if he was willing to relegate himself to the role of a sentry—detached and indifferent—but he was taking it all in and was primed to interfere as he saw fit. Rane was like the big brother she never had and had done very well without up until he arrived in the dreams— all bossy and annoying and controlling. The problem was there did not seem to be a delete character procedure in the daydreams that was of any use in expelling nightangels. Casey wondered about why that was a lot at moments such as these but as the angels were all staring down at her in an unnerving fashion, she proceeded with the conversation before they took matters into their own hands. "I'm not lying, Gabriel. I just don't know what the truth is."

"No matter. You are here."

"Yup, I'm here."

"Why have you come, Casey?" He was noting the way her concerned eyes darted between Aric and Rane and back to him again. "Look at me, just me. Tell me the reason for your arrival. Or is it a secret you mean to keep even from yourself?" He gave her a challenging stare.

"It's not a secret. I don't care whether you know or not. Anyway, I don't think you're stupid." *Like me, tonight, standing in an empty field with a bunch of dangerous angels with really pretty wings.* She took a deep breath. "You're already aware of why I'm here, so why shouldn't I tell you? I came to see you, Gabriel."

"There, you see. She can speak the truth well enough." His glance wandered toward Rane, then flew back to her face. "I knew you would come. You could never walk away without a word of explanation—not for good. You would not be able to stay away forever. You would not want to. I imagined you would miss me after a while no matter how 'busy' you grew. I am glad you are here and you aren't afraid to tell us why and for whom. Tonight, it is important to tell us what you think."

"Why not?" Casey kicked at the grass with studied carelessness. "Why shouldn't I let you know what I think about things?"

"Why not, indeed, Casey?" He held her glance as he spoke. His eyes asked the question he voiced in an altogether different manner. "After all, this is not the time to hide from the truth."

She looked away and then back again. She was shaken. She was almost annoyed. As much at herself as the nightangel. "I need to talk to you."

"Talk of what?"

74

"Everything."

"Everything? What can that be? What is everything?"

"Everything. Everything. That's all. That's what I came about. Don't repeat what I tell you like it's beyond believing." Sometimes the dreamer had to set the dream straight. And he was making her do it with all his questions and that smile hidden in the words he spoke. Now she needed a peel-and-stick badge that read, "Hello, I'm a big bitch tonight."

"Forgive me, Beauty." His lips closed against each other. "Everything is a great deal to consider between us in one small dream. That you should want to speak of everything—it surprises me. But I shall do my best to oblige you. It shall be as you wish." He smiled too quickly then. His eyes were cool, fern-green lakes—no emotion rippling across their surface. "Where shall we go then? Where shall we ride?"

"Nowhere." Casey was shocked by his assumption.

"You wish to stand about in a dark field the night and chat of everythings?"

"No," she hissed, frustrated by his calm disregard of her wishes and mood. "Of course, I—" She stopped herself. "Why are they here? I don't want them here."

"They have come a long way."

"I want to talk to you. Only you." She tried not to look toward Aric and Rane. They were not above inducing guilt or taking offense—neither was an alternative that promised a good outcome.

"So you shall. Rane and Aric will leave us. Later. Then, Casey, we shall find a place to be private."

The idea of being private with the breathtaking nightangel Gabriel, looking at her like being private might entail quite a bit more than a little chat, sent a swarm of wild butterflies to fluttering in her belly.

"Then you shall speak to me of your concerns and I will understand what you would have me know. But come. First, we ride. The dream awaits."

Damn dream—it had a lot of nerve waiting when she had just opened it up for a quick goodbye before heading off again for a plain vanilla life with no cool-factor, please. Gabriel was taking the high road but Casey did not want to take any road at all with him tonight. That way led to trouble. "I have nowhere to take you."

"No matter. We shall take you."

Casey had not seen that coming. Shouldn't she have seen that coming? "In what direction, I wonder?" She asked the question to herself more than to him, stunned.

"Come see." He flicked the reins and the horse took a few fast steps forward.

Casey was startled. He was very close now. But she stayed put. She had to tilt her face up to look into his. That was what she did. To her mind, stepping back was a show of weakness, poor-spirited; unnecessary at this point. Why, this was nothing. A little conversation and moonlight. She could handle this. She did not intend to be pushed around by a dream. "Tell me," Casey said.

"Past the usual places. Somewhere you have never been. Would you like that, my own?"

His voice was all seduction and Casey was not immune to that tone.

"I like it here. Make them go." Gabriel had not expected her to come back to their dismissal. She watched as he weighed the idea of abduction in his mind and cast it aside in favor of a more moderate path of action. He was very good at the occasional abduction laced with the special fire only a nightangel could bring to the experience. If she hadn't switched from being stupid to being bitchy already, she'd have almost regretted the loss of such an adventure. "Well?"

"How could I do such a thing? Have you forgotten?" His smile grew thinner, harder. "The dream is yours, dreamer. You would remind yourself of that fact but I am confusing you with my offer and my questions. You should have come to it on your own in another moment or two. Remember yourself, Cassandra. Remember who you are and what you are about this night. You think all of this is yours. The field. The forest. The sky. The nightangels beneath the false violet heaven. You think it all yours. Do you not?"

Hell, yes. "It is."

"Is it?"

It had better be or she was in trouble the likes of which she could have never imagined. Casey tossed her head in a dismissive gesture that belied her true state of mind. To underestimate the power of a vampiric angel not seeing eye to eye with you was never smart and it was no good letting them see the chinks in your armor at such moments. "Yes, it is. You know it is."

"Then send them away yourself."

"I will." She dragged her eyes away from his calm smile and the

76

searing green eyes that sifted through her thoughts; knowing them before she did, laying them out for her to act on. *Okay, I'll show you who is the boss here, Prince Charming, and, by the way, it's not you. It's me. Little Miss Dreamer.*

But she could not dismiss them. The field was empty of all the dark riders atop their dark horses except one. She was alone with Gabriel.

She sighed. This dream was hers. Her mind moved it, gave it voice, filled it with dread and desire. The fact that he had anticipated her thoughts and spoken them aloud for her was proof he was a facet of those thoughts. Nothing more.

He was the loveliest thought she had ever had.

His eyes shone like the sun through the treetops on a summer day. Casey thought that was kind of crazy considering he was a nightangel and preferred the darkness. All that light raining down on her was banging against her heart like it was a tin roof in a summer thunderstorm. The curve of his lips told her she would be swimming in the fiery glow of his attention if he had his way.

She couldn't help but admire him. She gazed up at the nightangel, the way an artist studies her own handiwork with proprietary pleasure. He was handsome, more than handsome; he was the definition of masculine in her personal dictionary. His nature was undiluted by modern convention. Everything about him was unequivocally male—strong, purposeful, and confident. He had a little bit of the knight in shining armor thing going but he played by his own rules. And he was smart as hell. Gabriel was perfect. He was everything she had ever wanted in a man and was afraid to get.

A fan of soothing light stretched behind him and Casey realized it was the radiance of the nightangel's wings spread out at his back. Yes, he was perfect and it didn't hurt that he had a Class A set of wings sprouting out of his back either. He was some dream. He beamed down at her. The world tipped on its axis.

The dreamangel was looking more irresistible than she had ever remembered him being—and that was saying something because vampires with the wings of fierce angels had a certain natural tendency to hold a mortal in thrall by virtue of their very presence. She tried to shake herself free of the spell he was casting over her. Doing this was difficult. She could not get enough of her angel. Maybe she was a kind of angelholic. She shouldn't like nightangels so much. They tended to take advantage of it.

"Come up beside me, maiden. They are gone."

"No." The word sounded false, uncertain. Casey looked down at her gown; feeling the fabric changing from a flutter to a swirl. The blue gown that had taken her down to the field was gone. She was dressed in a velvet riding habit of some indiscriminate period nipped tight at the waist and falling in elegant folds to the ground—forest green with kid boots the shade of the field grasses, minus gloves and other riding paraphernalia. The veiled edge of a hat tickled her forehead. She was glad for the change in outfit but not the conflict of wills it indicated. She was sure this new look was incredible but she was not going. "No."

"But we are alone now." He was admiring her with eyes the dark green of the deep forest; all that blinding light hidden behind its cool leaves again. "Besides, my love, you have changed your gown for a ride. And that hat is quite charming. You must wish to go."

She wasn't too sure who was in charge of her wardrobe changes tonight because she had not been thinking go-for-a-ride green velvet gown but rather get-the-hell-out-of-here gray sweats, when she had found herself in a whole new outfit courtesy of the dream.

"I can't." *Cowardly, So Cowardly. Or maybe not. Could cowardice be a virtue in a situation such as this?*

"I will pull you up," he said, as if he mistook her words for helplessness. "Take my hand."

Casey thought about that with the same quick intensity with which Gabriel had considered the efficiency of a simple abduction. If she agreed, she would get the pleasure of being held in the strong grasp of the nightangel as they rode off together like there was nothing wrong between them. To go riding off with angels was always a treat. And tonight she imagined that treat would get amplified about a hundred times over if she took the nightangel up on his suggestion. "Where would we go, Gabriel? Where would you take me if I gave you the chance?

"There." He looked across the field.

"There. Just there. And will we come back—from there?"

"If that is what you wish." He paused to assess her desire in the matter and when she said nothing, continued on with pointed civility. He still held his hand outstretched. "It is your dream, Casey."

It should be but was it? Casey was not sure she should believe him.

"It's what I would wish if I were to go. I don't wish to go, however. I'd rather stay here with my feet on the ground. After all, what is it—

there? Even if you say it's heaven, how can I know I wouldn't call your heaven a hell? Heaven and hell are very personal things, don't you think?" Who needed a treat amplified a hundred times over when instead you could stand around being difficult and pissing off beautiful nightangels who wanted to whisk you off into the deep, dark dream for some quality time together?

He was silent. The wind kicked up and settled again.

"Your wings are tipped black now, nightangel. Do you know it?"

He tightened them against his body. He gave a sharp, quick laugh. "You vex me, dreamer. You refuse my hand." The ruby fringe on his wings blackened further as he spoke. The darkness moved through the deep red and into the melting blue it edged like streams of spilled ink running the wrong way across bright fresh paper. "You have never done so before. Suddenly, you do not trust me when before you were happy to go where I would take you without question."

"Before was before. This is now."

"I see." His wings were solid jet now. "Yes, I see, Cassandra. You give a very simple explanation to what you think a very simple creature within your clever dreams."

He didn't believe that. He was trying to rattle her enough that she would tell him what barriers she had put up against him so he could tear them down.

"No, you don't see. If you did, you wouldn't say that. You would understand. You know you are anything but simple. That's the point. I am. I'm a mere mortal. I don't know how to fly with the wind, come and go from the far reaches, or find the hidden pathways without your assistance." She wasn't sure how it had happened, but Gabriel had become the key to accessing some of what was most secret and surprising in the dream.

"You have always had my assistance."

"Which you could withdraw at any time if it suited your purpose."

"What purpose would that be?"

"How should I know?"

"I have not done so yet." His eyes were sincere. His smile was soft, pleasant. He was trying to enchant her with his words and that look he was giving her. He was doing a solid job of it because she was aching to go with him.

"Call me paranoid but it's enough that you could."

"And how is that? You believe I am but your dream. You have told me so. How could I do anything you did not wish? Don't you trust your own daydream?" His smile tightened.

She trusted him a lot more than she trusted herself right now—as if that made any sense.

"You are not a dream, are you?"

"You tell me, dreamer."

Hey, this isn't Mystery Date. I need some answers. Casey sighed with frustration. "I can't. I'm not sure what you are. I know what I'd like to think about you. That's not enough. Now I'm uneasy with you. Before, I was not."

"You do not think you should trust me though you have always done so before."

This was as good a time as any to put that old saying "honesty is the best policy", to the test. At least, kind of. "My knowledge of you has changed. I have seen you outside my daydreams and I would like to know why."

"Why would a dream walk outside of itself?"

"Because—" she faltered. *This honesty thing isn't all it's cracked up to be,* Casey thought. Gabriel was staring at her like he wasn't so impressed with her attempt at honesty so far either.

"Because? Is that your answer?"

Was he taunting her with those angel eyes? Was he teasing her in that seraphic voice?

"Because—no reason."

His eyes narrowed, as if unconvinced and now hungry for hidden war. "No reason, dreamer? Should I believe you? Do you believe yourself? How good you have become at the art of deception in the span of one dream."

"Because—because of me, then," she stammered. Hot-faced. Stung. Her words were brittle with shame. "Because of my overactive imagination. Because I've been working too hard. Because I've been hanging around in dreams with nightangels when I need a break instead of living a real life, finding a real guy. It's me, isn't it? It's not you."

He did not respond. She was annoyed he did not answer. *Now, wasn't that just like a man? Any kind of man—even one who came complete with wings and special dietary requirements.* "Isn't it?" She repeated the question.

"Knowledge changes things."

"Yes, it does." She knew some stuff alright. Like that she did not have a chance of figuring this whole thing out in a satisfactory way now that she had opened herself to the dream again. She also knew enough to realize if trouble had a definition this would be it and the core of all her problems was smiling at her like that would make everything good again. She did not smile back.

"Fear changes things too."

She glowered at him. "I'm not afraid of you. You have no substance outside these dreams."

"Your worries seem groundless then. Give me your hand, Casey. We can go."

And now he was rubbing it in or just making a valid point at her expense. Casey was not sure which it was. She didn't like it either way.

"I told you, no." It was never a good idea to cooperate with trouble, even if it looked at you like butter wouldn't melt in its mouth.

"So you did. But I did not think you could mean it, my love."

She pulled the veiled hat from her head and let it drop to the ground. That was too bad because really, where else did you get to wear a vintage hat and veil these days? "I do."

That smile again—cooler, longer. "What do you wish from me then, fearless girl?"

Nightangels were such a pain sometimes. Never more than when they thought they were winning the day—or night. She blushed with anger. She did not like to be considered a coward. Especially not by Gabriel.

"To say goodbye."

"Goodbye?" He sounded amused. He should not have been. She had not meant for him to sound amused.

"I have some questions first." Maybe the angel could clarify a few things. She might as well at least try to get some answers because saying goodbye wasn't going anywhere.

"For me? Why me?"

"There is no one else to ask."

"Ask them, then." His intonation was as much rock salt as cream.

"Will you answer?"

"I am yours to bid."

Casey waited for another sugar-white smile, for his darkened wings to grow bright again.

Gabriel did not smile. His wings remained black and still. After a long instant, his lips parted like a piece of sharp, red glass fractured in two. "Begin," he said.

Casey, staring at the way his mouth curved around that one word, began to think perhaps it would have been a safer bet to let him lift her up with him on that impatient black horse and be off.

Too bad she couldn't figure out how to take out a little traveler's insurance for such a journey or she just might have done it.

≪ CHAPTER TEN ≫

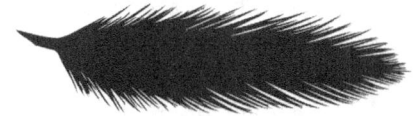

BEGIN. JUST BEGIN. AS if that was such an easy thing to do.

"No wings. No horse. No more company. Just you. Just your answers."

His feathers fell into air. He sprung from his horse to stand beside her. "Shall we walk?"

She hesitated. She looked at the dirt beneath the soft suede of his boots. She looked at the red-rose line of his lips. She looked at the dark, hovering curve of sky beyond field and forest. "Why not?" She shrugged, finding his face again.

She allowed him to take her hand. His fingers curling around hers said he was her personal angel and now he was in charge. His touch was protective and compelling; as controlled as it was controlling. He was being presumptuous but Casey was okay with that. She'd expect nothing less from the angel. Besides, there would be a dearth of nightangels to hold hands with after tonight. She might as well enjoy it while she could.

"The garden is beyond. It will be private enough for your questions and my answers. That is the place I would choose. But what do you think, dreamer? Name your direction."

"The garden," she repeated; pictures of the two of them standing close, heads bent together in conversation as they had done so many times before along its flowered paths flashed in her mind. "Yes." She was lost to his magic already. "The garden is good. I mean," she said, catching herself up again, "the garden will be fine, I suppose."

He turned without another look or word and began to lead her along the path up to the garden gate. He drew her along the narrow way in such a rush she found herself walking behind instead of beside him. He did not look back at her. She frowned at the strong line of his shoulders, bare now of heavy wings but she let him lead.

She was thinking—about her questions, about his answers. What would she say? What would he do? What would happen then?

They rounded the gate and Gabriel swung it shut behind them. He leaned against it and then he did not stir. For a moment he did not seem to breathe. Everything stood still, even the beat of her heart. Casey stared at him; waiting for him to start the world up again as he had stopped it. He shifted his gaze from her hand held in his to her face and everything came to life in a rush. "We are alone now."

Casey found it difficult to breathe when she heard his voice. The sweet heaviness of it. The subdued power behind it. She listened for his next words; her lips parted as though she thought he might feed them to her instead of speak them into the air.

"It is as you wish. Here we are. Speak to me. Give me your questions."

He was full of commands. Yet, so far, so good. They sounded like words she would choose for him to say; right in character for the nightangel Gabriel. Bossy with sugar on top. Just as always. He was either obliging her or, as she preferred to think, it *was* her story. And it would end in a goodbye. She was reluctant. So was he. Why shouldn't he be? Her goodbye was his demise. A beginning for her. An end for him. They both knew it. Even if they did not speak it. Casey was beginning to feel she was indeed quite cruel.

They stood together at the sealed entrance at a momentary impasse. Casey did not know what to say now that he was right in front of her, ready to listen. The nightangel still held her hand. She did not think he meant to let it go. The hand that gripped hers was as purposeful as the rigid curl of his mouth was stubborn.

She did not try to pull away. That would be like admitting he had some power over her at the moment he did not. The best thing to do was come out fighting. "I saw you, didn't I? I saw you on the other side. You've been following me around. I think you should know. I don't appreciate it."

He was silent as if knowing there would be more and wanting to hear everything before answering her.

"Did you think I'd stop and have a big chat with you in some library reading room because you put yourself in my path?" She thought about how she flipped him the bird that night and whether that counted as conversation and decided it did not count in the formal sense. That was probably fortunate. "I didn't, did I? I didn't say anything to you. You know why?"

The corners of his mouth began to curve into the hint of another consoling smile.

"Don't you do that. I hate when you do that."

The edge of the smile remained. Casey chose to ignore it and forge on. "Guess what, I don't have to talk to you just because you think it would be nice. And you know something else? I didn't want to talk to you anyway. I'm never going to want to talk to you. Get it?"

"Yet, you are talking to me now, my own. How do you explain that?"

"I mean there. Not here." She rolled her eyes up to the darkened sky as if it was all she could do to find the patience to explain such a simple thing to him. "And stop calling me that. I am not your anything. My name is Casey."

"I know your name, Casey. Still, you are my own, whether you like to admit it or not."

"Are you trying to scare me?"

The angel was beginning to look perplexed. "Why would I want to do that?"

"How should I know? The point is, whatever reason you might have for it, you don't scare me."

"I'm happy to hear it."

"Good because I'm totally not afraid of you." She glowered at him in a way she hoped communicated a don't-screw-with-me attitude.

"Point taken."

I am totally so full of shit and he knows it.

His eyes, looking back into hers, confirmed the point he had taken was the unspoken one that required a pair of wading boots to navigate.

Casey frowned. She hated that he was being so understanding, when she was being so difficult. This saying goodbye thing wasn't turning out the way she thought it would at all. "Maybe you are the one who should be scared."

The smile was surfacing again.

"Maybe you should be scared of me." *Okay, now she was sounding crazy and her goal in life right now was to be non-crazy.*

"Afraid, of you?" The smile turned into a laugh. "Oh, Casey." He brought her hand to his lips and brushed a light kiss against it. His breath was cool on her skin and a wave of calm flowed through her. How dare the nightangel snatch her fear from her with such a small act. Her anxiety was imperative to her carefully engineered justification for leaving him behind. She needed that anxiety to drive her to turn and go. And now, at least for the moment, it was no longer available to her.

"You are so arrogant. You're just a dream, you know." Casey stopped short. She knew it was ridiculous to be angry with him for releasing her from the grasp of her rising anxiety. She detested herself for talking to the nightangel this way. He did not deserve this, yet she could not stop herself from lashing out at him.

A rogue wind moved a scattering of dark curls across the smooth whiteness of Gabriel's brow. Casey stared past him to the wooden gate that his shoulders, wingless still, rested against. His understanding frightened her more than his anger could have. It brought her to a sudden realization. Her voice grew sickly calm. "You knew I wouldn't sit down across that table from you. You never expected it. You didn't come about that. You didn't come to talk, did you?"

Gabriel did not respond. He did not move. He was listening to her. He was watching her. Her eyes. Her face. The movement of her body when she spoke. The way her breath rose and fell in her chest. He was listening and watching with an attention as meticulous as it was comforting. She pretended she did not notice. Casey found it irritating. She did not want to be comforted. She did not want her state of mind assessed with such care. She wanted answers from the nightangel loitering with her in a nonexistent garden under a nonexistent sky within a nonexistent season—a sunless merging of spring and summer. She wanted to understand what had been happening to her because of him.

"Fine. Don't answer. I don't need you to answer. I'm not stupid. I know what you were doing. You were letting me see you could be there whether I was ready or not to believe you could be sitting right in front of me instead of hanging around in this damn dream. You were letting me get a closer look. You were giving me a chance to get used to the idea. Like that would help. Like anything would help."

The sky turned an inky indigo. The moon grew more silvery. A few stars appeared. Casey paused to take note of these things before continuing. The night was getting much darker than she envisioned wanting it to be. She didn't care to think what that might mean.

"Like you're something normal I could get used to seeing walk around my life the way I've let you walk around my dreams, if I had enough time to really think about it." She was waving her free hand around in quick, nervous circles. She yanked it down against her side. The angel smiled at her some more. "Well, it didn't work. And it won't work. I can think about it forever. I won't get used to it—not you out there in my world. That's not where you belong. You can't be there anyway. And even if you could be there—I don't want you there. I would never want you there. Not three weeks ago. Not tonight. Not ever. Not for a second. That's something you ought to face."

She was getting confused, talking to him one minute as if he had been there and the next as though he had not. Now that she was with him again, she was not sure what had happened and what hadn't. It seemed very real at the time. She met his eyes again. No reaction there— just cool, green eyes looking back at her in curious silence. He was not confused at all.

She had worked so hard to believe she hadn't seen him. Ricki had told her it was the sensible thing to think and most of the time she was sure Ricki was right about this. Thinking of Gabriel as being anywhere but here in the dream was bound to be a big mistake. Now she was questioning herself again; questioning everything. *What was wrong with her?*

"It was you," she stammered. Her statement verged on a desperate question. Her body vibrated with the tension of knowing and not knowing at the same time. "You were there, weren't you?" As frightening as the idea of his being there was, the idea of his not being there now seemed worse.

"Did you see me there?" He was calm.

She reminded herself of all the things Ricki had said about why she couldn't and hadn't, then sighed. "I thought so."

"You should trust yourself. You know what you saw." He was so very calm.

Hello—just an FYI—hallucinations are never good. "I don't think I want to trust myself on that point."

"Because it might mean you are going mad?"

87

Casey responded with a giddy laugh that pushed the crazy-meter indicator up a notch. She tried to yank her hand away as if by removing his touch she could remove her fear of him and everything that seemed to be happening to her because of him. He was just a nightangel in a dream. An imagining. Removing her hand from his ought to be easy.

But it was not. The problem was he still would not let go and there was something about the pressure of his hand over hers that made her struggle turn halfhearted, made her dizzy with desire. No need to share this information with the nightangel in question though.

"Cassandra. Look at me." Gabriel used her given name when there was something serious about to go down. Casey glanced around like maybe she could find somewhere to hide before she had to look back at him. "Casey."

"What," she snapped back. She forced herself to look him in the face. Cassandra and Casey were very different forms of address when they came from Gabriel. Tonight the difference was enough to damper down her sudden spike of anxiety the exact degree necessary to brave the angel's gaze again.

"See me. I am your sanity. I am your truth. You saw me on the other side three weeks ago tonight. You told me so."

Casey straightened a little. A petulant curve came to her lips. "I was wrong." Now she was choosing crazy over a Gabriel who was more than a dream. Maybe she could find a place to land somewhere between the two.

Gabriel's eyes held one of those merciful angel glimmers that made Casey feel like she was the one causing all the trouble when she knew that wasn't true. "There is nothing wrong with your eyesight or your perceptions. You are not insane, my own. You are not overworked to the point of a breakdown. You are not in need of a human lover to ground you in the ordinary world. You do not want one anyway. I think you want me."

Casey wished she could interrupt him to say he was wrong but given she was still standing there with her hand in his like that's where it belonged, it seemed stupid to pipe in with a denial.

Casey stopped focusing on the hand-holding thing and concentrated on what the nightangel had said to her. These were not the words of the dreamer spoken by the dream. Something was wrong. "I want to walk."

"Then," he said, drawing himself up and pulling her arm through his as if they were a pair of lovers in an old painting off for a secret stroll,

"Let's walk together. The proverbial garden path lies straight before us. We have only to take it."

He smiled but Casey did not respond. Dread roared through her body like a double shot of chemical adrenaline; a bolt of jarring energy with no place to go that shivered within her. They started the long walk toward the wilder, older end of the garden.

"Who are you?" She walked numb at his side, letting the force of his movement pull her along beside him.

"How is it you no longer think you know such a simple thing as that?"

"I don't know anything anymore." The fabric of the dream was reweaving itself about her, so its essence was not all of her making. "Things are different."

"Yes. Things are different. You have begun to notice. Good."

"You're different."

"Yes. In a way. And yet, I am the same as ever, Casey."

"Who are you? Tell me."

"I am Gabriel."

Casey believed it was imperative she be honest to this piece of the dream walking so close to her before the changes working within the daydream continued any further. "There are no Gabriels. Not really."

"Are you so sure? I walk beside you. Do you not see me? Are we not speaking together? How strange you are tonight."

"There are no Gabriels. No Arics. No Ranes. No nightangels. No vampires. No blood-drinking seraphs or archangels or angels of any sort."

"Why do you tell me? It is your mind that needs assurances. Convince yourself."

It was difficult to be confident in her opinion when the angel was having none of it. Fine then, but he would not avoid her question. She would ask until he answered. "Who are you? What are you? I want to know." There was something more to Gabriel than she had assumed before.

He reflected on her demand for an unsettling moment. "I am your prince, fair maiden," he said, as if that was that and there was nothing more to say beyond it; that somehow she ought to understand what he meant without further discourse on the matter.

His unexpected response flustered her. What if she didn't want a damn prince? Had he ever thought of that? "I don't think so. Try again."

"I am Romeo, Juliet. But we will not be star-cross'd lovers. We will form our own happier destiny."

Well, she would hope so. Those lovers didn't fare so well. "We have no destiny together. You're a nightangel living in a daydream. I'm a mortal living in the real world. End of story."

"Our differences won't stand in our way. There's more to the story than you think."

He's rewriting stories now. Super.

Looking into the angel's radiant face gave her pause to consider his statement. She feared he might be right. And she couldn't let him be right about this. She flirted with the idea of falling into a small fit of hysterics when she thought about what more there could be to the story, what the fallout would be if the angel could rewrite it, and what could happen if their differences didn't stand in their way. But she couldn't indulge herself. All that peace on earth stuff the angel was sending her way wouldn't allow for a therapeutic meltdown. That didn't make her any more willing to hear him expound on the hidden aspects of the story and how he thought it should go. "I don't want to have this discussion. Just answer my question."

Her reaction seemed to confound him. "Are you refusing to understand me on purpose? It almost seems you are not listening for you should take my meaning by now."

Oh, now I'm the problem. Romeo, my ass. Casey glared at him.

"You look perplexed with my answers and frustrated with your angel. You should not be. Cassandra, it is not really fair of you."

It's so totally fair. "I'm listening the best I can. I'm trying to get it. Go on, then. Try again."

He bowed his acknowledgment of her sudden flash of cooperativeness as if he appreciated it despite how grudgingly it was given. She hoped he didn't expect it to last long.

"It is as I told you from the beginning. I am the rescuing prince, lost and sleeping damsel." He spoke with a disturbing air of confidence.

Screw this prince and damsel talk. She tried to wrest her hand from his.

"That's not an answer." Her voice shook. She stood somewhere between rage and panic and the power of these two emotions pulling against each other was all that kept her from falling victim to the ravages of her spiraling alarm.

"It's not the answer for which you look." His tone grew gentler in the face of her distress; his molten voice incinerating one after another of her apprehensions. "There is a difference, dreamer."

She wanted nothing more than to go, yet she stayed, listening. To be near this angel was dangerous but it was impossible to leave his side when he spoke to her in this way.

"Casey, I am your heart's desire. The one true love you have dreamed about. Your very own knight in shining armor. Don't you recognize me?"

"You're no fairytale prince. No knight in shining armor. You are certainly not my true love." She had to break this spell he was holding her under. "And we are especially *not* like Romeo and Juliet."

"Wasn't that my point?" He looked perturbed by her lack of understanding.

Casey flushed. "I—I don't know. I guess I don't get your damn point."

"They were star-cross'd, Casey. But we are not. We are not ill-fated," he explained in a voice full of serene conviction. "We could never be that."

"Oh," she exclaimed without meaning to make any sound at all.

"Far from it," he added, as if he wanted to make sure she saw his point.

"Forget them then," she said, avoiding his amused glance as she struggled to regroup in the face of his correction. She bristled at the thought of this archangel in a dream laughing at her when she had made him up—well, most likely made him up, anyway. He was not in a position to laugh about anything. Yet, there he was looking as though he'd like to press that smiling mouth against her frown until she didn't care what was what anymore.

Casey was starting to yearn for home. She did not like this dream such a great deal anymore, yet she could not seem to remember there was a way out. "You're not going to help me sort this out, are you?"

"I cannot do it for you. You need to help yourself, Cassandra. Set aside your anger; push aside your fear. There is nothing to be angry about, nothing to fear. These emotions cloud your reason."

Why did she think maybe he was right? Casey shoved her hair away from her face in frustration. As much as she thought her anger and even her fear might serve her in this instance, she hated them.

He pushed aside a stray strand that had fallen back against her cheek with a cool, light touch of his fingertips. "I have told you the answer but you choose not to listen. You do not want to know."

Maybe it wasn't as simple as the nightangel thought. "You're wrong. I do. Tell me right now. In a way I can understand. I command you."

He gave the barest nod of acquiescence. "Everything in the dream is

91

as you command. Is that not so?"

She gave him a haughty nod in return. She had to yank things back to what they should be again. She had to seize control of the dream slipping away from her. He had to understand the dream obeyed the dreamer and not the other way around. "Yes, of course, dreamangel. How else should it be?"

His voice dropped to a near-whisper. "How else indeed, dreamer?"

"What do you mean by that?" She had the distinct feeling that when he responded to her question; she wasn't going to be wild about his answer. Casey stared straight into his eyes. She was scared to death by the determination she saw there. She did not want to hear the next words that would come out of his mouth even though she had insisted upon them being spoken in the first place. She almost wished she could command nothing from him.

"I am the dream, dreamer—and yet, I am not a dream at all. I am Gabriel. The nightangel. The bloodangel. The vampire prince all in wings. I am, as you have always insisted on calling me, the dreamangel."

The air shimmered around him. Casey waited for the wings but they did not come.

"I am everything you ever dreamed of and more. I am yours, as you are mine. For whether you acknowledge it or not, we are each meant for the other. What more do you need to know? What more could there be? Everything follows from there. Just not quite the way you might have anticipated, my dearest dreamer."

Casey retreated step by step with every sentence he uttered as if she could erase the implication of each of his statements by her movement away from the one who spoke the words.

"Why do you look at me so, as though you have never seen me before?"

"I haven't." She stumbled over her words. "Not until now." She shrank further from him.

He matched her steps. His hand tightened over hers. It felt solid; more real than it had a moment earlier. "I am as I have been each time you have come before. How have I changed?"

"I don't know. You have, that's all."

"Ah." He took a sudden step toward her. "She wakes. She sees."

The wind rustled like stiff, black wings in the mock orange tree boughs hanging low behind the wall. Casey stumbled back a pace and then stood frozen, doe-eyed.

Gabriel advanced, closing the space between them. "But what is this? How can it be? She is freed from the prison of her sleep by her prince but she does not smile upon him." He touched a finger to her paling cheek. "She only looks at him with storm-cloud blue eyes." He dropped his hand from her face. "Does she not at least owe him one kiss for all his trouble?" He stepped closer, taking hold of her shoulder. "What can she be thinking? How can she be so unkind?"

The small span between them was charged with an unpredictable energy, like the air before a storm. Casey did not move. She was surprised by this sudden change in tone and demeanor. She was not sure what it meant. And the kiss. The prize this prince had set his heart on. Why did he want it now? When she did not even recognize him on looking into his face, for what he said he was.

He is not going to get any damn kiss.

"How sad for me," Gabriel continued in a new voice, seeing her denial in her face and reacting to it as a battle call. "How unfair of you to refuse me such a small thing. I shall have it though. Later." His smile stopped at his eyes. "Won't I, my beauty? You shall give it to me. I know you shall." He let go of her shoulder but kept her hand within his.

No. Casey mouthed the word. If she could pry herself loose, she would shoot up the path in a very un-fairytale princess-like way. It would not be pretty. Maybe he would rethink this whole prince thing then. She put as much distance as she could between them given he was still in possession of her hand.

He followed the glance she threw over her shoulder. "Don't run away. Come here. Come closer." He moved forward until he had closed the space between them again. He brushed the small betraying tremble of her bottom lip with his free hand. She stood there instead of fleeing.

Since she couldn't bring herself to run off, she twisted away from him so she could walk on. Head high, jaw tight, the fingers of her free hand crushed within her damp palm. "Please don't say anything about that rescuing prince stuff again. I don't like it."

He shot a look across at her that said he had no idea why she wouldn't be enchanted by the prince-awakening-the-sleeping-maiden scenario he had presented to her. He really seemed to want to be her prince; like one stupid kiss was some big prize. She worried what that could mean. Nightangels did not waste their time wanting things not worth having.

"Then what do you want me to say?"

He brushed against her shoulder. A chill seeped down her arm but she felt warm. She stretched out her hand. Rosemary, lavender, and rue reached to meet her fingers. She did not look down at them the way she did not look at Gabriel. She looked straight ahead. "Nothing, I guess. I just came to say goodbye."

"But now that you are here, you would like to know a few things before you depart."

Casey shrugged, as though she couldn't care less. "Well, I did, but you've freaked me out with your answers so far. I think I'm going to stick with saying goodbye, thank you."

"Let's walk a little farther. You might find you have a few more questions after all."

Yes, Casey thought. *Some fresh air and a nightangel pulling you along beside him like all was well in the world and you were just out for a stroll together will do the trick. Sure it will.*

"You think you know all the answers, don't you?" Casey halfway hoped he did, though she would resent him for it. "What if you don't?"

"What if I do?" He smiled his most beguiling smile and she caught her breath.

"What does that matter if I can't make sense of them?"

"I can help you make sense of everything you want to know and more if you will let me."

Accepting help from nightangels was a tricky business. They had a strange idea of what was helpful and once they started with the helping they didn't like to stop until they were satisfied with the result of their efforts on your behalf.

She appreciated the gesture though. Casey fought the urge to draw closer to the angel.

"I do want to know more," she admitted in a begrudging whisper. "Even though I haven't cared much for your answers so far."

"I will try to do better." His desire to please her vibrated between them.

Casey thought how fortunate it was he was not all in wings or she would be melting into a compliant little puddle in the palm of his hand right about then. His casual acceptance of her criticism and the way he did not take offense at it caused her to smile down into the faces of the garden flowers with relief. The scent of roses drifted across the path. *At least they were happy.*

94

"It is reasonable, Casey, to want to know more." They were sauntering along as if they didn't have a care in the world. Just as always. Everything so serene and her companion so understanding. The garden was growing wilder and more overgrown. Gabriel was drawing her farther and farther away from the path home.

She stopped dead and pulling her hand from his, looked up at him. "I don't think so. Nothing here is reasonable. Especially, not you."

"I am everything reasonable, my own. You just do not understand that yet." He took her hand back in his as if, this time, he would never let it go.

Fine. Go ahead and touch me. Her hand in his felt right even if the angel was all wrong for her.

Calm poured from his fingers and saturated her being. They continued on, side by side. She almost forgot about the kiss and what it could mean. All the worries about what would happen if he was the kind of thing that could turn up any place he wanted to be—like in the real world—disappeared as the rivulets of peace moved through her from where his fingers touched her skin. His hand tightened on hers and she shivered. What was she doing? He was not her companion, not her trusted friend. He was something else altogether. The peaceful feeling disappeared.

He quickened his step. "Come along. Ask your questions." The garden had gone silent.

Peace and quiet and taking long, thoughtful walks through twilight gardens wasn't all there was to nightangels. There was also the part that was all about having their own way in things—like a kiss that would serve as some key to a door that, if Casey could find, she would throw herself against without delay. She meant to keep him out of whatever it was he wanted entrance to in her life. He was not even going to get a day pass out of Dreamland again if she had any say about it. She hoped like hell she did.

"No, thanks. I figure it's best I don't know any more about you than I do already—which boils down to pretty much nothing. I guess that's okay seeing as we're saying goodbye anyway." She meant to stop but she was still walking with him, her hand still in his. His touch was more controlling than peace-inducing now.

"So soon? I thought you wished to speak of everything."

Casey bowed her head and said nothing.

"Not one more question? There is nothing else you wish to understand?"

She was ashamed of her silence but what question did she dare to ask him now that she was so sure he was not the biddable dream she had always assumed him to be? Dreams tell you what you wished to hear. Nightangels running wild might tell you everything you ought not to know in the speaking of one soft word. Some people say ignorance is bliss. Casey didn't know about that but she considered it a good enough excuse to get her out of a sticky situation while she might still have a chance of scurrying back home to more ordinary things than nightangels dwelling beneath darkening skies making ridiculous demands. "Why should I ask you any more questions? Your answers confuse me. Nothing you say makes sense."

"I am sorry you are confused. It is not what I want for you."

"I don't think you're sorry. It's what you meant to happen. You're trying to confuse me." She could have sworn he sighed but by the time she looked toward the wingless being at her side, there was no way to tell whether she had imagined it or not.

"It does not please me to see you bewildered. I find it hard to fathom. The truth stares you right in the face and you look past it, as if for something else; anything else but what you see before you. And all the time you call its name, as if the truth escapes your vision. This is not my doing. It is your own. You confuse yourself, Casey. You do it for your reasons, not mine."

"There are no more questions," she said, dismissing his observations as she dismissed him. She clung to the hope he was less than he suggested to her, less than she was now beginning to think him. She needed to escape without further hesitation before escape of any sort was impossible. "I don't like this dream. I'm going. I wanted to see you one more time. I have. That's enough." Casey was getting the creeps standing there thinking about how she was sinking deeper and deeper into the power of this fantasy gone wrong as she looked into his resolute eyes.

"For you perhaps. I would have more."

'More' could mean so many things, Casey thought. *And none of them particularly good in this context.*

≪ CHAPTER ELEVEN ≫

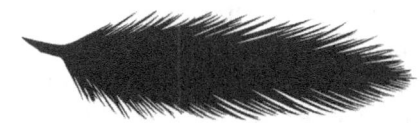

SOMETIMES, YOU CAN'T HAVE more, *no matter how much you think you should have it. Even a nightangel should get that.* As far as she was concerned, there was not going to be any more anything. She was heading out. He was staying behind. End of story. She was not going to feel bad for leaving either. She had tried to close things down with compassion. He wouldn't let her. Maybe it was just that he wanted her to stay and stay but if there was a way to sort it out so the story could go on, she would have done it already.

"There is nothing else but goodbye, whoever you are, whatever you are." Casey was watching Gabriel's face; waiting for his reaction, trying to hide hers.

"There is your kiss. I will have it."

Not the kiss thing again. Casey's face burned just thinking about what this kiss would be like. If there was one thing Gabriel knew how to do, it was kiss the living daylights out of her. But this sounded different from anything that had come before. "You've already had plenty of kisses from me. I don't see why you need one more."

"This one shall be different. It shall be given in knowledge, not ignorance."

The fact that he argued with her made Casey more certain she was right to deny him. *Time to go home.* "Don't hold your breath waiting on it."

"You owe it to me, dreamer."

Casey would have been flattered he wanted that kiss from her so much if she didn't feel the danger oozing up around her. She yanked away from him. "You are seriously mistaken. I don't owe you a thing."

"It is you who mistakes things. Why should I let you leave before you give me what is mine? I am the Awakening Prince and you are my own Sleeping Beauty. And Sleeping Beauty," his voice turned the kind of soft that held danger. "Anyone ought to know what comes next."

Although it was never spelled out in all those fairytales, Casey had always imagined what came next was happy-ever-after punctuated by lots of amazing sex. Considering the tone of his voice, she was pretty sure that was what the nightangel thought too.

"Every fairytale such as we have been living out has a kiss before the rest of the story unfolds. It just has to come to this moment. We are here. You shall give me that kiss now."

"Because you've awakened me."

"Yes, because I have awakened you."

It seemed that rescuing princes were very single-minded. Maybe that's the way they had to be. And if awakened meant she now understood Gabriel was quite a bit more than she had always thought him, then okay, she would give him that. She was awakened alright. She wasn't finding it a lot of fun so far.

"To what, if you don't mind me asking?" Casey was getting more and more ruffled by the air of assurance he exuded regarding the outcome of this encounter.

"Why, to everything, of course. You'll see. You'll see more and more as we go. I don't expect you to understand it all at once. It takes a while to unravel, dreamer—even for a nightangel with a talent for solving puzzles as delicate and complex as you. But first, we must begin. We must begin now."

"Maybe I'm not all that awakened. I'm not seeing what you want me to see."

"How can you say that, when you provided such an eloquent, if unladylike, gesture of outrage at my presence the other night? Obviously, you see what I want you to see because you see me not just here but in the world beyond. The problem is you want to pretend you do not." His gaze sharpened. "You have been asleep for so long, dreamer. But your eyes are open now. I have been patient. You have made me want you so much that waiting has been a great trial to me. Be kind, my love. End this waiting. Give me what is mine. It is only fair."

"Your notion of what's fair is a little off-kilter if you ask me."

"Fair is fair, Casey. There is no use trying to argue it away."

"You're wrong, you know. You're wrong about everything tonight." She had to set him straight before the situation spun even more out of control. Casey hoped he was the one confusing things and not her. "This isn't a fairytale. It's just a daydream. This isn't the beginning of anything. I only meant to come for a minute. I've already been here too long. I can't stay. I can't come back. This is the end." She was sorry for having to tell him the truth when he thought he had it all figured out. It felt like a betrayal.

The angel appeared unmoved.

His stoic response increased her guilt level. "Oh, please don't look at me like that. I'm sorry." The tears began to rise in her eyes but she drove them back. She needed to calm down or she would be trapped in this guilty spiral of longing and fear he incited in her tonight. "I'm sorrier than you will ever know but this can't happen anymore."

"I wish to begin, Beauty."

Oh, hell. Begin? Why didn't he get it? The dream was finished. "Begin? What is there to begin? We're done. I'm going. It was stupid of me to come here tonight."

"Yet, you did it anyway."

"I'm an idiot."

"You are a dreamer. You are my dreamer." His eyes softened for an instant and then turned dark and cool. "You will never be happy without me in your life, Casey. Not here, not there, not anywhere." She would have tossed out an indignant denial but he interrupted. "Even though you do not understand all the reasons why yet, you need me at your side. And that is where I will be, must be—in the dreams and in the world."

What he must be is pressed down into the dream so far that he never swam up to the surface of it again. She didn't have the heart for that though. Gabriel's alpha-angel demeanor made her want to resist and comply at the same time. "No," she managed to sputter.

"Count on it, Casey."

"I'm done with this. I'm leaving now." She turned and began walking back the way they came.

"Done? We are not done." He was following her.

"Goodbye, Gabriel. There, I came to say goodbye and now I have. We're finished here."

"Not yet."

She felt the soft pressure of his restraining fingers upon her arm. "I'm going. You can't stop me. You're just an angel in a dream I made up." *Keep telling yourself that, Casey.* She could almost believe what she was saying. She was on the way home and she did not think the dream could hold her back if she was this intent on going. At least, this was what she hoped. Casey looked down at her clothes. The riding garb had been exchanged for the blue dress she had gone to greet the nightangel in when she had entered the dream so expectant of an easy goodbye. She was starting to feel like a Barbie doll having a serious wardrobe crisis.

Still, the blue dress was a good sign. It meant she was on the path back to where she started this dream. The problem was, the nightangel did not let her go. She started toward home anyway as though his hold on her did not matter.

The pressure on her arm tightened. *What was this?* Gabriel swung her around to face him. He thrust her back before him in one abrupt movement and she lost sight of the way out. She stumbled and he caught her up before she could fall. She blinked. She tried again to open her eyes to the other side. It should be there. But it was not. The angel still held her fast in his grip. In her surprise, she could not find the strength to struggle against him.

He was touching her—as he had never before touched her—with a raw possessiveness. He forced her against a tumbling wall of rough-cut stone covered in a tangle of ivy, climbing rose, and honeysuckle.

Maybe I'm not the crazy one, Casey thought, her heart banging away as his sudden closeness pressed against her senses.

"What do you think you're doing?" She scanned the garden behind him for the way out but the light from the angel's eyes obscured everything else.

"Providing you some clarity."

"I've got all the clarity I need, thank you." She tried to sound enraged but her words came out small and shaky.

"Closure then. Isn't that what you came back for tonight?" He gave her another tiny shove so her back was flush to the stone. He laced his fingers through hers. His hands were as hard as the wall to her back. "I believe we are both in need of closure."

100

"You need to stop now. That hurts."

"Impossible. It is only a dream, my love."

Oh, damn. What was she supposed to say to that? He was using the dream and everything she thought about it against her. "This is ridiculous. Move aside, dreamangel."

He smiled a sharp, ice-edge smile but he did not obey. He should have obeyed. He was the dreamangel. And the dreamangel did what the dreamer wished within the dream. That was how it had always worked. Hadn't it? Why wasn't it working that way now?

"I want to leave."

"Leave then. How can I hold you back?"

Casey knew the answer should be that he could not—not for a minute. Too bad that answer wasn't right anymore. She just couldn't quite figure out why or how to fix it before Gabriel could stop her doing it.

"I am only a nonexistent nightangel in a daydream. What happens here is at your command. I have no power over the dream, no power over you. You told me so."

She didn't have time to try to figure out why things weren't working the way they should tonight. She was getting the feeling she couldn't do a damn thing about it anyway. Something had shifted. And not in her favor.

She was going to untangle herself from the web the dream was weaving in a new pattern around her and walk away from everything in it forever, including the adamant angel daring to hold her captive within it. "Let me go."

"Why should I do that, my darling dreamer? It would not be what is best for either of us."

"You aren't thinking about what's best for me. You want your way."

"I think of you. You are always in my thoughts. I consider your welfare before mine."

"It's not true."

He brought his face closer to hers. He held her hands high and close together above her head. The scent of crushed flowers filled the air. Wounded honeysuckle. Bruised rose. Green ivy leaf mixed with pale rose petal. The rose thorns pricked at her fingers and scratched her bare arms. The gray stone scraped her skin. "I always speak the truth, although I know you do not always like to hear it. And I do look to your welfare first, whether you wish to believe it or not. Who do you think has been seeing to your safety in these dangerous dreams?"

"There's nothing dangerous about them," Casey lied.

Except for you. She couldn't lie to herself. *And Rane. And Aric. Aric probably most of all. Although Gabriel might be edging him out for that prize given his current behavior.*

The nightangel had the audacity to let a smile flash across his face but the concern never left his eyes. "How can you be so oblivious to the danger all around you? Can't you feel it?" The stir of his hidden wings snapped like downed wires on a rainy highway as he spoke.

She could feel it alright. Danger was holding her against a garden wall like it was just getting going. It was stronger than she expected it to be.

The roses were dead silent. *Damn roses.*

"I do, dreamer. I am good at seeing dangerous things and knowing what to do about them. I ward off the dangers that would beset you. Haven't you noticed?"

She was incensed. "I don't believe that. Anyway, don't bother. I can take care of myself. I don't need any help from you to know what's best for me. I know my own mind. It brought me here and it will take me away again. That's what gets you—that I will go and you can't stop me."

His lips brushed against hers. "Is that what you believe, Casey? Why don't you prove it to us both then? Go ahead. Leave." He challenged her. "Why do you wait?" His mouth wandered across her face. His cold breath burned her cheek. She flinched. "Why do you stay here; my prisoner, my prey?"

Casey didn't have a clue. She felt pinned to a board like a hapless butterfly caught mid-flight, still meaning to flutter away, if only the opportunity of freedom presented itself, though nothing could seem less likely.

Her lips moved to form the words that would explain everything to this creature she did not quite recognize as hers anymore but nothing came out.

"What? No answer? Shall I tell you what I think, then?" he asked.

He was really starting to piss her off. "Go ahead." She meant it to sound snide but it came out in a breathless whisper that caused Gabriel to flash a tender glance down toward her before tightening his grasp on her.

"You cannot say because you no longer know where the power lies, what it truly is, where it stops and starts. You are afraid something you have said or done tonight has released me from what little hold you believe you still retain over your disobedient angel." He swept a kiss against the corner of her mouth and then began speaking into her ear, his words rolling from his tongue like drops of molten honey. "And if that has happened, oh my Casey," he breathed with a hungry sigh. "You are afraid you will not mind so much because you are ready for more even if you will not admit it. You begin to see now. You begin to understand."

Casey wanted to scream "no." No, to being ready. No, to seeing. No, to understanding. No, to anything else he could come up with too.

"You begin to perceive there could be much more for us but you do not know how it is to be achieved without hazarding everything you believe in, without having to endure the struggle to overcome your greatest fears. The dream does not do anymore. And it is not quite what it seems, besides. Is it?"

Casey's heart sank as something in his gaze pulled a small answer from within her. She could taste the mingled scent of honeysuckle and rose in her mouth as she breathed in to respond. "No," she said, dazed by the implication of this tiny word. *Oh, damn. That was not the "no" she meant to give him.*

"No." He breathed back her word to her and his breath was a sweeter echo of the flowers that surrounded them. "That is right. You have thought about what more means but you chase away the ideas that form in your head and ignore my presence on the other side as though you could erase my very being in that way. How foolish this seems, my own, when you think on it even a bit. I cannot be wished away—not even here in this small daydream of yours. Still, though you wished to deny my very existence, you had to come again to seek me out because you must have something. You cannot quite do without your nightangel."

Casey flashed an angry look at him and he returned a knowing smile. He leaned in a fraction closer. "But why settle for this? Why settle for the dream when the whole world stands waiting outside it. Admit it. You were glad to see me on the other side, weren't you? You just don't know how to justify it to yourself. You are just afraid of what it will mean. I will help you with all of that. We shall sort it out to your satisfaction and mine."

Oh, no we won't. We're never going to do that.

She imagined the moment she had seen him in the reading room, present and waiting. She pictured herself sitting down in front of him instead of fleeing him. She saw her future tumble into his hands in that moment. She caught her breath. *But I did not do that. I would not do that. He wasn't real. Not there. Not now.*

"Casey." His voice held an intensity that caused her to dare a glance at him. She wished she had not for even the briefest look between them said too much; all her secret thoughts spilling out of her eyes despite her reserve toward him. "Yes, you are ready," he said, as if speaking out loud his own conviction to himself. "And you are right. It is time to leave this place behind. It has been a fine testing ground. I have seen enough here in the dreams to know how to proceed. Better now to have you in one place than two. How much trouble can you get into in the world with me to keep an eye on you and everyday concerns to keep you busy?"

She didn't think that was a real question. She was pretty sure he had an idea how troublesome she was capable of being when she put her mind to it, no matter where she was and what she was doing. Maybe he thought he had it in him to discourage any bad behavior.

Casey was confused. What did he mean by ready? What was he testing under her cloudless lavender skies? Would it be better to pass or fail?

Why should she care? The disturbing utterances of an angel about to fall into oblivion weren't worth her worry. The only thing she was ready to do was leave—without him. She was going to do it as soon as she could extricate herself from the grip of this surprising daydream. "The dream is done. I mean right now."

The air grew colder. The angel's chilly breath mingled with hers and she was weak with desire to breathe him in again.

"Is it?" He leaned closer as if to kiss her.

"Check out the sunrise, nightangel." A bloody pink tint rose along the skyline as she spoke. There was nothing like a smidge of sunlight for shutting down a vampire with or without wings.

"So it does, dreamer." He seemed unconcerned. His lips grazed her neck.

The threat of daylight did not appear to be cramping his style. *Not good.* "Don't you see it? Don't you know what it means?" Casey knew she sounded frantic. "It's my dream. I'm in control."

She felt the upturned brush of a smile laid upon her flesh. She could imagine what it looked like—a rebel's bow with arrow ready to fly, a hard perfect weapon of deep, wounding red. He lowered his head and kissed the moving swell of her breast where her heart beat. He trailed that kiss back along her neck. The sharp tips of his teeth rested there for the barest instant. And then he lifted his face to look into hers.

"So shall it be a while longer—if that is what you need, my own. I do not wish to be unkind. I only wish to be alive in your reason as well as your imagination."

Damn. She loved it when he talked like that. Like a real prince in a real fairytale. No wonder he thought he had a kiss coming.

"Congratulations, mission accomplished. Now, leave me alone and go back to wherever it is you came from before you turned up tonight," she said, set on ignoring his wishes and focusing on hers. "We're finished here."

He tensed. His fingers laced more firmly through hers. "Not yet." A determined light filled his eyes. He brought his face over hers. "First, dreamer, I will have my kiss."

Uh oh. Casey knew with a certainty the nightangel was now officially done with talking and tempting.

He sucked the breath from her lips. He swallowed her small "no." He pressed his mouth down hard on hers. Casey kept still. She was going to have this kiss. After all, no matter what he said, it was just a fantasy, all made up. This would not be the kiss of an awakening princess to her rescuing prince. It would not cause anything to begin. As a last kiss between dreamer and dream, in a way it did not exist, and so maybe they could be allowed it. She would wonder after it forever otherwise. Besides, he was more taking it than she was giving it. She was not acceding to his demand if you looked at it that way.

Even considering this, it was quite a kiss; she quivered with the power of it. The cold pressure of it moving against the warmth of her crumbling resistance exploded her fear. How she lied to herself. She thought of nothing but her beautiful dreamangel and all the ways he would love her now if she would let him.

She returned his kiss, her mouth moved with a soft violence against his. His lips parted. She sighed. Her tongue curled around his like the ivy behind her clung to the hard stone wall. She longed to sink with him onto the bed of moss where they stood. To slip to the ground and fall into his embrace was what she wanted—everything she wanted. Allowing herself to accept his love was going to be like lighting off a whole bunch of firecrackers at the same time, when you knew damn well they were illegal and you really shouldn't; it would be dangerous and spectacular and memorable. But mostly it would be daring. And probably there would be trouble afterward. There would definitely be trouble afterward.

Still, she was all for rushing past the kissing if her dreamangel would go for it. The problem was he was not going for it. Here she was willing to potentially blow her nice, neat life to smithereens for him and he wouldn't take the flame he had lit between them and do something useful with it. Gabriel held her fast against the wall. The strength of his arms shored her up when she could have dropped to the soft, green ground. If he wished to consummate the passion that burned between dream and dreamer, it was certain he did not mean it to be then or there.

Casey did not understand. *What was he waiting for?*

She was not having any of this. She was the dreamer. The dreamer got her way. That was the rule. She was going to remind this dreamangel about that right now. She kissed him again, tossing every drop of caution to the wind. He allowed her to close the space between them; she began to move her body with torturous lightness against his. She sighed with frustration and pleasure. Gabriel did nothing beyond return her kiss.

Casey was stuck. That was pretty much her best effort. She wasn't sure where to go from there. His lack of response mystified her. She was not expecting it. He should have exploded into a flurry of vehement action in response to the intensity of her resistance and her sudden turnabout. He should have taken it into his head to possess her without delay. He should have told her he loved her as only a nightangel could express it. He should have shown her how much that love burned within him.

Could it be true the love he had shown her in the past had been of her own manufacturing; created for her, by her? Was it possible it was not his?

Their lips parted. The rhythm of his breath was uneven.

"Give me the words."

Oh, that was it. That was what the holding back was about. He was stubborn about the words. He wanted her to tell him what was in her heart; nothing else would do for the nightangel. Everything had to wait on this.

Casey thought, looking into the face of this illusion of her mind that could not exist but seemed to anyway, that he did indeed love her. He was solemn. He was paler than she had ever seen him. Casey felt the thoughts behind his words as he spoke them to her through red, unsmiling lips. Sweet thoughts. Good thoughts. Forever thoughts. She saw it in his eyes. All of that and something else too—a sadness. And past the sorrow, his resolve burned like a brand.

"Do it. You know them. Do not be afraid, Casey. Now is the time to speak." His voice was hoarse with desire. He wanted her. Love was behind the want. How could she have ever doubted? But it was to be his way. All his way. No other way would do.

Stubborn angel. Okay. Fine. Be like that. See what it gets you.

"I don't think so." She could be stubborn too.

"I'm only asking for you to tell the truth tonight. Is that so hard, Cassandra?"

Casey thought it was. The truth opened doors and set things free. She couldn't risk it.

"I will make it my business to hasten you on your path toward the truth between us, dreamer. For both our sakes. After all, my own, we cannot be about this forever. There is more for us than this."

If nothing else, this nightangel was efficient in his pursuit of her love. He knew what needed doing and he intended to get the job done. He had presented her with some specific milestones. He had set a deadline of sorts. Casey, however, did not think she would be an easy resource to manage. Although she was good with deadlines, she did not like them. And orders—she was especially not good with orders.

Still, it would have been an easy enough thing to make her say what he waited on right then and there; a look, a touch, a few more well-chosen words, and the cover of his wings to mask the future. These would be all it would have taken to pluck the words from where she had buried them beneath her fear and tear them from her throat. 'I love you' might have spilled like heavy wine from the secret goblet of her being. He might have drunk the phrase from her lips like a hot geyser of heart's-blood gushing from a mortal wound. And what vampire prince worth his salt wouldn't like that?

He could have her then. Once those words had poured out of her and he had drunk them in every manner possible, it would all be his way. How could she have stopped him? How could she have stopped herself? The act would be a final souvenir of the daydreams and the nightangel prince at their core who loved her alone; a last gift for the angel before he vanished forever.

Gabriel held himself back from such a resolution. He meant to have what she would not give him. Words—spoken and meant. Words—given and then lived out.

Were the words a sort of inescapable contract or a key that started something up that the nightangel hadn't gotten around to explaining yet? Casey wasn't about to whisper all her secrets to the angel so she could find out. "You're never going to hear it from me. I'm not as stupid as that." Well, maybe she was but she didn't have to tell him so.

This imaginary nightangel, very substantial now, was nettled by her answer.

Disappointment smoldered in his eyes. Anger shuddered in the wings that had sprouted again, purest day-flame. They were painted in the particular color of a nightangel's rage; a shade darker than the color of his mortal dreamer's eyes; her answer still reflected within their center. Blue—savage and bright, burning against the empty air, edged in pain. They rattled like armor, feather against feather. They opened, wider and wider. They snapped shut again with a harsh metal whisper behind him, falling in two thick shining daggers that scratched the fat carpet of moss at their feet.

Gabriel had become the embodiment of her fear and her desire and she did not know which way to turn. She stared into his face in wonderment. That was how she saw it. Not the light of victory in his eyes. Or the low fire of revenge. She saw his intent. She saw the pause. He was waiting. He was still waiting. He was waiting on a final change of heart from her.

He was waiting on those damn words. As he had always waited.

And the worst part was, all she wanted to do was give them to him— every last word and more.

Maybe I really do need one of those Hello My Name Is Stupid nametags after all, Casey thought.

❮ CHAPTER TWELVE ❯

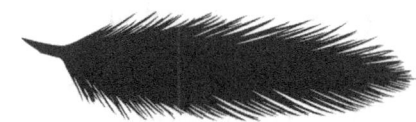

A SORROW WELLED UP inside her for Gabriel. She ought to say the words. Her heart, as Ricki was always quick to remind her, was not the Holy Grail. It was just a heart. They were just words. Her heart, her words were not so much. She ought to give them to him like a polite farewell gift before she heartlessly tossed him into the black oblivion of nothingness forever and ran away home. It seemed like a questionable gift to give, considering the circumstances.

Nothing was working out like it ought to tonight. The no kiss thing had turned into a regular kiss-fest and now he was pressing her against a rough garden wall as if he might never let her go when she had told him in no uncertain terms to cut it out right away. Besides, even if the words would be a nice bright gift before the blackness, that didn't mean they wouldn't get her into more trouble than she could ever imagine now that her Prince Charming was turning into a bit of a Big Bad Wolf right before her eyes.

The nightangel took a ragged breath and looked at her mouth as if he could pull every word from it by sheer desire to hear them spoken.

Casey pressed her lips together. *The dreamangel does not need your pity. And he certainly should not have your words.*

It was true. She knew it was true.

It was hard not to feel sorry for him but she had to leave him behind.

To do that, she would need to change the story of what had gone before so it would be as if it had never happened and what she felt for him did not exist. She would have to tell him this new story like it was the way it had always been and he was the one who was confused. Maybe then, he would turn and go before she gave in to all his demands or began to think he was quite real after all, just as he insisted he was, for who knew what would happen then. Look at what had happened already. In the course of one small dream, she was totally at his mercy.

He was still watching her mouth and it made her want to begin kissing him all over again. Too bad her next words were going to spoil the moment for both of them. His eyes brightened as her lips parted and then, as she began to speak, they melted into two darkening pools of phosphorescent light.

"I don't even care who or what you are anymore. Go. Just go. I don't love you. I've never loved you. I'll never come to love you. So how can I ever tell you the words you are waiting to hear from me?"

She couldn't tell if he believed her. She had to make him believe her.

"Who knows what the hell I'm seeing when I look at you; what I really hear when I listen to your voice. How could I ever love something like you? You may be everything that isn't right and should be avoided at all costs. How can I tell? I just want you gone."

Liar. Liar. The words screamed inside Casey's ears.

"You are timid and stubborn, Casey. And yet, I know for a fact you can be brave. You ought to have been brave tonight instead of hiding behind such an ill-contrived set of falsehoods, as though somehow they could save you from the truth. I am disappointed in you."

"I'm telling you the truth," Casey said, averting her eyes. She wished she could find a way to be a much better liar for just a little while tonight.

"Casey." Gabriel's voice was even. "Look at me."

She turned her head as far aside from him as she could. She squeezed her eyes shut. She didn't want to look. He couldn't make her do it.

He slid her arms up the wall in one quick, sharp movement. The rose thorns that had pricked her before now bit into her flesh. *Ouch. Ouch. Ouch. That really hurt.* The shock of it forced her eyes—teary with surprise and pain—back to the nightangel.

"It seems I have your attention after all."

Casey gave a little cry of shocked outrage but the nightangel's words cut it short.

"Listen well, my beautiful little flower, and understand." He pressed her hands harder into the petals and their prickles.

"Stop it," Casey demanded. "I told you before to stop. Now you've done it again. Please." Her voice shook. "You're hurting me."

Casey thought he looked a little sorry for it but when he spoke his voice was nothing but decisive. "Hurting you? It cannot be. I've told you already, it's impossible. Why do you look as though you don't believe me? I'm repeating what you have presented to me as fact this evening. Have you forgotten? Pretty or ugly, it is but a dream. I am but a dream. You have stated it with utmost confidence. You left no room for doubt about your view. How can I argue with it?" He released the pressure with which he held her hands into the thorns and pressed them back again as if for renewed emphasis. "Unless, perhaps, you have changed your mind. Have you, Casey?"

"No. Never." They each stared into the other's face for a moment. She went on in a more patient voice; this must be hard for Gabriel and she was making it worse by being a miserable failure at helping him grasp the truth of the situation. "You can't love me and I can't love you. Don't you understand? You're not real and that means we can't be anything to each other. Gabriel, you don't exist. This isn't happening. It's just a dream and we can't continue any further with it. Not ever. We're finished here. I have to go and you have to step aside and let me leave."

He twisted her hands within the sharp clusters of white roses and Casey let out a small sob. "It is you who does not understand. You are here with me now and you will stay until I give you leave to go. I will not step aside until I have finished."

Why wasn't she on the path home already? He should have released her. He should have stepped aside. In truth, all she should have to do is open her eyes from where she lay on her sofa dreaming this daydream to be done with it but she could not seem to do this simple thing.

He brought his face near hers so all she could see were those green eyes, burning like a forest set on fire by a careless camper. The angel began to speak; each word striking the air and then pressing against her in a soft bruising caress.

"You want me. You look for me. You catch your breath when you come upon me in dream and life alike. Do you think I do not know? Never mind. I shall go, Casey. It is time. I know what I must do and I am impatient to do it. I am satisfied as to my path."

Casey was bewildered by his words, as they were angry and gratified in the same breath. Gabriel pressed a light, certain kiss upon her mouth that sent an alarming thrill through her.

"Before we depart, I will give you my promise, cautious maiden, careful girl."

Casey would rather he hand her a rattlesnake than give her a promise sure to be the precursor to many a restless night back home.

"I do not go but to arrive. I do not seek but to find. I will have your vow. As you have mine. I will have you. As you have me."

Only a vampire prince in a huff could say something like this and make you think—for a second—that maybe you should be happy about the whole thing.

"I will chase you down until you cease to run." The angel continued in a sharp whisper. "I will haunt you until you acknowledge me."

Until he finished his thought and that happy second was washed away by a tidal wave of panic.

Was being haunted better or worse than being hunted? Somehow she thought the two were going to wind up being close to the same. He seemed flexible in his approach to hounding her into accepting his reality; into accepting him. She, however, did not feel like being flexible about getting cozy with him on the other side just because he thought she was his one and only. "I hope you bring a good pair of walking shoes because it isn't going to happen no matter how much you follow me around. You're bound to get tired of the chase after a while."

"I never get tired, Casey. And angels of any sort are steadfast creatures by nature."

Steadfast? Try flat-out stubborn. This is what she got for not taking Ricki's ode to the common man speech to heart. If she had gone that route, she would always be disappointed but she would never have had to worry about being the object of a nightangel's steadfast love. "Doesn't matter. I'll ignore you."

His wings began to rise behind him—higher and higher—and the roses sighed. Casey wanted to sigh too.

"Ignore away, if you can. I will always be there. Even when you pretend I am not. There will be nowhere to go that does not lead to me. Every space you step into will be a potential avenue for my entrance. Every corner you flee around might only bring you closer to me. Everywhere you would run to escape me will be so full of your angel's impatient presence you will have to fall before it. And when you do, you will fall straight into my waiting arms, Casey."

Casey thought about those arms, thought about how satisfying it would be to fall into them in the midst of the ordinary world. And then reminded herself about why it was such a bad idea.

"You will turn to face me in the end, then we will begin on the other side. I will drive you to it, my love, and your own heart will assist me in the effort. I will woo you. I will court you until you cleave yourself to me—most happily. You will come to see the wisdom of my arrival. You need me, dreamer, in more ways than you know."

Cleave herself to him? What the hell did that even mean? Sometimes he spoke to her in the strangest way and there was something very appealing about it. His next words brought her to her senses again.

"You will be mine. You will love me without cease or reason and you will tell me so. 'I love you, Gabriel' and 'Yes, Gabriel' will fall from your lips and you will mean these words with your whole heart."

"You'd better get used to hearing 'no' instead because you're mistaken about that."

"Mistaken? Hardly. You want to tell me right now."

He was looking at her mouth again. Casey found she was speechless.

"No? Not yet? Soon enough it will be your pleasure to say 'yes' and so much more to me. There will be no more partings. We will be bound together. Even now, we only say goodbye to say hello again, Cassandra. Even now, I await you."

How could he delude himself so? Her poor broken dream, her dearest angel; he was clinging to her when she must let him fall back into an abandoned dream forever. Feeling sorry for him was no good. He was growing harder to handle by the minute; more dangerous with every moment she let herself feel anything for him that reeked of pity. She hardened her heart against him and turned her voice to ice. "The sun is rising. Have you forgotten? You should go."

He dropped his hands from where they held hers against the wall. He stepped back and she staggered forward without his support. Gabriel made no attempt to catch her. She landed on her hands and knees before him. She stayed crouched a moment—stunned as much by his sudden indifference as by the sight of her own blood, bright red on her arms and hands. *This was definitely not a Romeo and Juliet moment.* He had wounded her—even if it was just in the dream. It felt real. Actually, it hurt like hell.

He had done it on purpose to prove a point she wouldn't have believed any other way.

What a rebellious, insolent dream.

She glared up at him. Her eyes said everything she did not voice. Some emotion she could not read flashed across his face. She shoved the stray strands of whisper-dark hair that clung to her damp cheeks and fell into her eyes back away from her face. She stared at his booted feet and the jagged tips of his wings, ablaze with reflected moonlight. His legs were lean and hard beneath the heavy black material of his trousers. His face, when she looked up at it again, was sedate and confident. Casey sighed. He was beautiful, and dangerous, and way too smart to keep playing games. She needed to walk away while she still could. He looked hungry—on a lot of different levels. She couldn't help him out with that. And besides, he was being kind of a bastard right now—not like the angel she thought she knew, was sure she knew. Why stick around any longer?

She pushed up off the ground and brushed the mossy soil from her hands. She did not have time to shove by Gabriel or toss icy words at him over her shoulder upon departing. He turned first, without a word. Casey could think of nothing to do but follow, when an instant before she wished nothing else than to run the other way. She did not know what Gabriel thought about this. He strode off and she scurried to keep him in sight.

They were at the pond set to the side of one of the well-worn paths that led from the far side of the garden down to the field now. The dark water was edged in sand and large rust-colored stones. He swung around to face her. She stopped dead in her tracks so the still water stood between them as a barrier while she waited to see what would happen next.

Gabriel's voice caused ripples to stir on its surface as he began to speak. "I can depart this dream or not. I can do as I please. But I shall leave you. It is of little importance now. Nothing you do will make me disappear. Not here. Not on the other side. There is not a dream you stop that will not begin again with me. There is not a step you can take on the other side I shall not follow. I will not go away." The water broke into a thousand sharp, choppy waves. "I have chosen you. You are mine. To have and to hold. To love and honor. To cherish and keep. Forsaking all others. You are mine, Cassandra. As I am yours. For you have chosen me, too. To think otherwise is to embrace a lie."

Her heart was skipping like a stone tossed across the pond toward the nightangel—exquisite in his anger; she was moving toward him even as she held herself apart. "So you say." Casey studied the center of the empty pond instead of the angel. Staring at the water was the only way she could take in what he was saying without fleeing back up the path like a frightened child. She would not do that. She would not give that to him.

I have chosen you. You are mine. Such a possessive dream. Why wasn't she terrified? Why did she wish it could be as he said somehow? Why did she keep this dream so close to her heart when she ought to wipe it away? She cast her eyes up to take a secret glance at him. She could not resist a last chance to see the nightangel speaking to her with such solemn intent.

Gabriel caught and held her glimpse for a small eternity before responding. The force of that look yanked her to him and shoved her back again in the span of a few heartbeats, even as she stood rooted to the shore opposite him. Somehow, she knew she had whispered every secret she had in the world and dream alike to him in those few seconds without saying a word.

"Remember my promise. I will keep it. Maybe you will be happy to see me when I find you on the other side and we will laugh over this. Don't look so doubtful. It is not so farfetched."

"My, my. Look how light it's getting." Casey glanced at the horizon, then back at the iridescent surface of the pond, smooth as a mirror again and reflecting the pale dawn light. "You'd better hurry." He gave no response. Casey looked up from the water. Gabriel was gone.

It could not be that easy. She had left something undone. She began to chase after him, guessing his direction. She was going to make sure this was finished the right way so it wouldn't start up all over again. He would stay put in the dream. She didn't care about his promises.

Casey began to run, faster and faster. She passed through the gate, flung open now. She ignored the querulous mewing of a patch of wood lilies. She found herself at the intersection of the path she and Gabriel had taken to the garden at the beginning of the dream and she sprinted down it until she reached the curve that once turned would reveal the field where they had started. There, she slowed to a trot and came around the bend wary-eyed and out of breath.

115

Gabriel was already astride his horse. "Checking up on my whereabouts so soon? Are you afraid I already follow, dreamer? Or that I will be on the other side before you, waiting?"

"I am not afraid of shadows."

"You shall be, my love, if that is all you still think me."

Like haunting her wouldn't be scary enough.

"Be a shadow then. It doesn't matter. What are shadows?"

"You shall see what they are. A shadow never leaves you. A shadow always stays close."

"Do whatever you think you can. I will never acknowledge you."

"I will be your shadow then and you will come to dread what walks behind you, beside you, before you. At least, given your stubborn nature I imagine you will choose to do so at first. What a waste of time. No matter. You shall soon come to look for it with desire."

"That will never happen. I'll lock you in this dream. You won't be able to follow."

"For it to be my prison, it must be yours to warden."

"It is. The proof's in the sky."

"Very true, dreamer. So it is." His horse reared up and danced backward. Its hooves stabbed the ground as it came down to all fours again and pounded the gentle grass into flat half-moons of raw green. She saw the white rims of its eyes, the flare of its nostrils, and the tension of its muscles straining hot against the cold hand that held its power firm in its grasp. Gabriel did not rein the stallion in as he might have done. His wings fanned out like a midafternoon heaven behind him—brilliant blue with tips of blazing white. Casey was dazzled and then dismayed as they changed to a blunt, colorless black, a great whirl of dark, sharp energy. She felt their power. The stir of the wind they created as they moved against the backdrop of the coming dawn—Casey's dawn—tugged at her hair and tore at her gown. If a wardrobe change kicked in again, she was going to go ballistic.

Gabriel raised an arm and pointed at the sky. The brightening horizon blinked and the scarlet edge of the rising sun, falling like a red ball cut from a string, dropped behind it. For an instant, Casey thought he had blotted out the light of her sky with the vastness of those wings, outstretched and moving as they were. But no, that was not it. The sky was a sheet of midnight glass; the color of the nightangel's wings but not part of them; its light—Casey's light—was lost. A colder, denser

116

firmament, sharp with an icy dusting of steel-edged stars set like sparkling seals upon the promise he had made to her, replaced it.

The nightangel did not smile at his trick. He turned to her with a look of quiet satisfaction and stared into her face one more time. He seemed content with what he saw there. He brought the stallion under control. His heels pressed into its sides and the animal began to race with him, back the way they had come—straight across the field of outlaw green.

Casey staggered forward. She was startled by the sky of black velvet studded with the eyes of so many far-off fiery stars fastened on her; by the rigid back of the nightangel as he rode away, confident and sure of his victory; by the sudden, certain silence that surrounded her. Most of all, she was startled by how much she already missed the presence of the nightangel, departing in such a quiet rage into the secret heart of this black-skied daydream.

She waited for him to turn. He did not. Still, she waited on it. She had to wait. She did not want to miss a fraction of his going. She did not want to lose a final look, a last farewell. Not for anything in heaven or earth.

Gabriel did not turn. He did not call back over his shoulder to her— not to taunt her with her precious fears, not in the defense of her dreams. She supposed he did not care to defend the dream anymore. Why should he, when it might be his more than hers? Why should he, when he did not think he required it anyway?

He raced off across Casey's meadow of stirring celadon toward the black-branched forest. A goodbye formed in her mouth but she was smart enough not to give it breath.

He rode on. Casey let him go. She did not think he would return. She did not mean to follow.

Gabriel was no backward-looking angel. Casey was no fool.

≪ CHAPTER THIRTEEN ≫

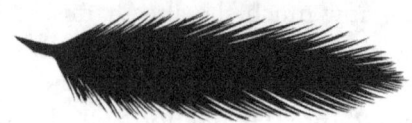

THE FIELD STRETCHED IN a slab of polished malachite straight
before Casey. A breeze feathered its top; racing, spinning, whirling
around itself, building in strength until the calm surface was shattered
into a legion of sharp, living arrows that made an ominous noise as they
rattled one against the other. A voice arose from its center. A sound that
formed itself from the rush of the wind and the movement of reed and
stem into a meadow-grass voice tipped in stone. "Sad," the grass sighed.
Dew clung to the reeds like tears.

Casey did not cry. She had done what she had come to do. She
moved deeper into the midst of the moaning meadow grass.

"Sad. Sad."

The grass usually tended toward whispering positive affirmations or
quoting the angels when Casey would have preferred it would shut up
and let her think. Its current maudlin outpouring, complete with subdued
wails, was even more annoying than a barrage of nightangel quotes and
peppy thoughts of the day. She let it clutch at her ankles as if that might
provide some silent consolation.

"So sad. So sad."

Obviously not. And it was wrecking the delicate material of her dress by
tangling in the hem of her skirt as she moved through it. "Stop fussing
about what can't be helped. Why don't you say something cheerful like

usual?" She stood watching the emptiness.

"The dreamangel loves you," the stirring grass moaned.

That was so not helpful. She ignored it. The dreamangel's love was not what it seemed. Nothing in this place was what it looked to be. Not even the whining reeds of grass clamoring for her attention and catching hold of the secret thoughts she despaired to think within herself.

"He loves you. He loves you," the grass repeated in a shivery voice. "Call him back," it implored, poking through the material of her skirt and scratching at her legs.

Stupid green-grass thing. What did it understand? Would it never shut up? Where was a lawnmower when you needed one? Not that she had ever mowed a lawn in her life.

"Why?" The grass called out in an emerald whisper that cut across the night air.

One look at the angel could provide the answer—to save herself. From what, she still was not quite sure.

"Call the angel back. Call him back," the grass demanded in a sulky green voice.

"Stop it. Stop it." She put her hands to her ears. "Be quiet. There is no wind and the wild grass has no voice." Casey crushed a whimpering patch of it beneath one foot. The grass gave a soft whine of protest but no words rose from it again.

Okay, that was mean, but it worked. Besides, she stepped on the grass all the time at home and it never seemed to do it any lasting harm.

Casey took a deep breath and sighed. *Silence.* The dream was quiet. The grass stood stiff and wordless. The wind had died to nothing. Nothing stirred. Nothing at all. The dream was still. *Good.* At least something in this dream was listening to her.

Casey's eyes were glued to the sky above her. She had recognized it for what it was at once. That smooth obsidian sky exploding with hard, cool stars was a parting sign of Gabriel's power over her, over her worlds. Everything she thought she understood had been swept away to reveal a mystery in its place. Even standing under Gabriel's brooding sky, it was difficult for her to believe the dream had not been hers alone.

For crying out loud, most of it had to be mine. It had to be. After all, whose idea was it to get the tiger lilies to purr if not her? And there were other things too, except she was having some trouble remembering what they were. But there were some things. Lots of little things. At least she had that slight comfort. As comforts went, though, it was not much; almost nothing. She was full of questions; more questions now than when she walked the path with the nightangel earlier. She felt she had as many questions as there were stars cut into the sky. And at the moment, there was no nightangel standing by to give her any answers.

She supposed that until now, Gabriel, Aric, and Rane had played her game, more or less. It suited their purposes just fine. They roamed her dreams with casual abandon—as if the landscape were theirs to range without restraint and she, theirs to draw near without permission or invitation. And she had let them do it because having a bunch of nightangels moving through your dreams like they own the place amped everything up. *Guess they had it right.*

They waited for her comings with the casual assumption she would arrive. And she always did. Once there, they stalked her with a sort of gentle concentration that somehow made her feel treasured instead of frightened. They listened to her like no one had ever listened to her. They spoke to her as no one had ever spoken to her. With a pure, deep understanding and acceptance of everything she was, had been, and someday wished to be. And why wouldn't they understand her? When you hang around in someone's daydreams, you tend to know a whole lot about them, more than was fair for anyone else to ever know about another person. Nobody knew her as they knew her. What a powerful thing that was. Knowing. Knowing everything. A rising fear burned in her chest at the thought of all that had passed between them and could not be taken back. What had she done?

"Nightangels are make-believe," she reminded herself sternly. "You can do without a vampire prince at your beck and call. You don't need nightangels littering up your life with all that wisdom and beauty. You have a job, a best friend, a mortgage, cable, and maybe you can get a betta in a bowl and put it by your bed. That will have to do. You sent him away and he's gone. He's not coming back no matter what he thinks. It's what you wanted. Deal with it."

If she had paid more attention to what was going on around her, instead of berating herself and glaring at the stars disappearing like lightbulbs being shot out by a sniper, she would have noticed the fabric of the dream was changing again. The grass quivered against her legs in expectation. The rush of the wind caught in the high tops of the trees beyond the field. She yanked her eyes from the sky.

She had company. And not the kind that came for tea and cookies or a nice glass of chardonnay either.

Rane and Aric rode across the wide green meadow between them at a sharp gallop. The clouds fell away from the moon like a cover lifted from a lamp. She shaded her eyes with her hand. The nightangels shot toward her, quick as arrows of blackened gold.

If there was ever a time to leave, it was now.

Still, she stood, greedy for a final look. They were glorious, sumptuous, unreal; a splendid fire against the darkness that had settled over her heart. The brilliance of moonlight on gilded feather stung her eyes. There was nothing like a vampire in wings to cheer up a daydreamer; and then make her quake with terror.

She had to get back to the garden. Why had she ever left it to follow the nightangel down to the field? The garden was no longer in view; it was far behind her. She had seen the glimmer of warm incandescent light that marked the way back out pushing against a corner of the garden when she turned to pursue her dreamangel down the path. She had closed her mind to it and kept her attention on the angel. Maybe that hadn't been such a good idea. She hoped that light was still shining and she would find it with as much ease as usual when it was time to leave the dream. She was a little worried about that. All she saw was the palest edge of light at the top of the path and nothing was going as it ought to tonight.

If I ever manage to get out of this daydream, I'm going to be a better friend, upgrade my cable, and get a whole aquarium of fish. Except for angelfish. She was not getting any of those.

She focused back on Aric and Rane. She had the feeling she had overstayed her welcome.

She spun on her heels and the dewy green field turned slick as ice under her feet. She hit the ground with a painful thud. The grass gasped and then grew quiet. She was too surprised to cry out. She could see their faces now. Faces plucked from windows of sunlit stained glass. Yup, they were glorious alright in a winged-warrior-glaring-down-at-you kind of way.

Now that the nightangels had arrived, leaving would be more difficult. They had driven themselves between her and the path to the other side. She could not see the tiniest ray of the milky light of reality glowing in the distance. She had nothing to head toward; no marker rising up out of the ordinary to show the way. Their light blinded her to such dull things.

She would regain her bearings in a moment. She just had to get up and she would find the way again. They could not keep her there forever. *Could they?* She wasn't so sure what the dream was capable of anymore. The words "whatever it wanted" came to mind as the possible answer.

Aric and Rane raced around her on horses that pounded the earth with metal-shod hooves. She had no time to get up. She clung to the ground instead. She closed her eyes. She dropped her head tight against her knees.

The banging of hoof to ground slowed and then stopped. The jagged breath of the horses and the eerie, elegant music of the angels' wings slowing to a close were all that broke the silence.

"Get up, Cassandra. We wish to speak to you."

She dropped her hands from where they had been covering her head in an instinctual gesture of self-protection and peered up at Rane. She straightened to sit on her heels. She pressed her fingers against the fragrant earth, gave a quelling look to the grass whispering encouragements at her, and stayed put.

"Stand, girl." Rane flung the words down at her. "What are you waiting for? Did you not hear me? I told you to get up. What do you think we will do to you?"

"Casey, get up off the ground. We mean you no harm."

She believed that voice. She did as she was told. The ground under her feet was now quite dry.

The two nightangels remained on horseback; their wings furled tight about them, their mouths set and scarlet. Casey, standing between them, was forced to look up at them as they wove a small confining circle around her. They did not mean to let her pass. She did not try. She found herself twirling around so her back was never to Rane. That was important.

He drew in his horse. "Look how she flushes."

"She is frightened, Rane."

"At first. Not now. Now, she is becoming angry with us." Rane laughed. He was pleased.

"She is a pretty thing." Aric's voice behind her. They had begun to move again in that relentless circle of angel astride horse, angel astride horse; around and around. Aric smiled as he came in front of her.

"Prettier still when angry or put off her guard."

Like any proper angel, Aric had a smile as addictive as crack. Casey glanced away from Rane to bask in it a moment.

"She has charmed you."

"And you?"

"Certainly. She is perfectly charming." Rane's tone lacked conviction.

"Gabriel thinks she has intellect and beauty. He thinks she has a special spark."

"Gabriel thinks. Gabriel thinks." Rane pronounced the name with indulgent annoyance. "What else should he think? He is smitten with her."

"What else should he be? He has found his bespoken."

"Finding his bespoken was not on the agenda."

"It's never on the agenda but there it is."

"Bringing us to something else Casey possesses that is on the agenda."

So angels had agendas. Casey had no idea what she had that could possibly be of enough interest to the three nightangels to land her on theirs.

Aric flashed a silencing look Rane's way. "And why shouldn't he be smitten? She is more than beautiful. She has substance. She is a clever girl. She can be amusing, too." He shot another of those brilliant smiles at her. "She's smart, but she's thoughtful."

"That's fortunate for her. I like smart. Stupidity never sits well with me." Rane eyed her as though he were waiting for her to do something stupid just to annoy him. "And she has a kind heart. Don't forget that. That's bound to mean nothing but trouble."

"What's a little more trouble? You know what mortals are. Still, she is all the things she should be and an elusive something else that enchants."

"Enchants? My, my, what a paragon our Casey has become. Clever. Thoughtful. Intelligent. Amusing. And imaginative. Let us not forget that." He gave a meaningful pause. "She does have quite the imagination."

"Ah, her imagination. Who could forget that? She does have an abundance of imagination. We must all appreciate that. It has given us so many intriguing moments. Maybe that is the something that takes her from interesting to enchanting. There is some magic to that imagination of hers."

"I'm not magical," Casey interrupted. "I'm ordinary. Just ordinary."

The nightangels stared down at her, then looked about the part of the dream they now occupied. Deep-skied, evergreen-tipped, evening-scented.

With a scoffing laugh that could have held an edge of outrage to it, Aric contradicted her statement. "Ordinary. Not at all. Not you. Never."

"I don't agree." She glanced at Rane. "And actually, I don't think Rane does either."

"But Gabriel does."

Perfect. She was beginning to feel very dizzy, following Rane's slow orbit around her and looking from one to the other as each spoke. She wished they would dismount and say what they had to say on the solid patch of green grass under her feet. She was growing rather sick.

"Casey, you remind me of an old illustration I once saw in a book; a picture of a princess."

"A princess? What nonsense is this, Aric? Casey is not a princess."

"In a fairytale. The one about Snow White. She looks remarkably like her but with a beauty no faded plate closed up in a children's book could ever capture."

"Snow White?" Rane snorted. "Hardly. Goldilocks running through the forest as though the bears could not catch her if they wanted, or that foolish Alice going around in circles only to wind up in the same place she started. Those would be better choices. It's like you to compare a simple human girl to a fairytale princess. Your heart is softer than it should be, Aric."

Aric laughed.

"Snow White," Rane cooed. "Snow White. Why do you not answer, Princess?"

A girl. A girl. She hated when he called her that. She was a grown woman. Not a child. Not a girl. And now this. A princess. Again. *What was with all these angels tonight?*

Casey ignored him.

"I am calling for you, Snow White," he continued in a wheedling tone. "Honor me. Give me audience. I would speak to you."

She bit her lip. Sleeping Beauty would have napped through this whole thing and Cinderella would have sprinted away minus a shoe. She, however, stood frowning up at Rane, thinking without much success of some brilliant comeback to his teasing. Punching a nightangel in the arm or calling him an asshole would not be smart but she'd like to have done it anyway.

"She does not answer, Aric."

"Nor should she," Aric said with more irritation in his voice than Casey thought he felt. "I see the resemblance." He continued to make his point. "Not to the story but to the princess. The same dark hair. The fair skin. The blue eyes. Even though the plate was faded, I am certain the artist meant her eyes to be bright blue." Casey's cheeks flamed under his scrutiny. "And red lips. Snow White had lips as red as the red, red rose." He quoted the phrase as if he were reading from the story itself. She half expected the book to materialize in Aric's hands and for him to hold it up to the drawing in question for them to view as proof of his statements.

"Casey's mouth is not such a red as that. Barely passing. I'd call her lips pink."

"They're not as red as yours. That's all," Casey blurted out.

"They could be, should you care for it." Rane's voice held an invitation.

"I would not care for that, nightangel. Not ever."

"Is that so? Time will tell." He smirked down at her.

"You think you're so smart. Do you even know how to tell time? Maybe you could learn. Then, you'd know when it was time to go."

Rane spread his great wings for an instant to remind her to whom she was speaking. They were dull black and jagged at the edges. "She does not quite have the niceness of temper a maiden such as you insist on comparing her to ought to possess."

"She can be pleasant. Sweet-natured even."

"On occasion, but not enough to suit my wishes. If she were mine, her tongue would soon be tamer. I will agree she can be pleasant enough when she has a mind to be. She does have that insufferable air of innocence about her."

"Exactly. All the time. I do not believe she will ever outgrow it."

"Not in a human life."

"Not in any life."

"I am not so innocent."

"You are a child."

"You are—"

Rane leaned forward as if to make sure to hear what came next. He raised a challenging eyebrow.

She knew he was goading her on but she did not care. "You are a—"

"What, Casey? Go on. Make it worth the listening. You will amuse Aric."

"You're a—"

"But you might anger me. Do you want to anger me, Princess of Aric's fairytales? Do you? Think on it a moment."

His horse danced a step closer to her. She backed up until she felt Aric's hard thigh against her shoulder. She would have drawn away but Aric caught hold of her. The horse had become still beneath him. The shiny prickles of its coat and the studded leather of the saddle chafed her back as she attempted to squirm out of his grasp. "You're the child." She threw the words at Rane, giving up the struggle with Aric at the same moment.

"I am?" He seemed surprised.

Casey was pleased. To manage such a feat with any of them was rare. "You have to be. When did I dream you up? I'm sure it hasn't been that long. You can't be more than a kid. I'm the adult here. Not you. You're just a bad little boy. Why, you're not even grown enough to be a juvenile delinquent."

Aric roared with laughter.

"You, too. You're just as bad. Maybe worse. I believe you're the oldest. Although I don't know how that can be because Gabriel came first. Anyway, you should know better." She tried to shrug out of his grasp again.

The angels were quiet. She could not see Aric's face but his strong fingers wrapped around her bare arm. Casey looked at Rane. She was watching for a reaction—his—or Aric's, reflected in the eyes of his companion. She could not gauge either.

Rane was smiling a boyish smile with a glimmer of something else behind it. He teased her with it. She stared at its pointed edges. Aric and Rane were not boys. They all knew how foolish she was being. She pressed into Aric's strong grasp.

"You are," she said, digging herself in deeper instead of reneging. She was never very good at backing down and Rane brought out the worst of that trait in her. "You both are."

"Then, why shy away so? Do you mean to melt into Aric's horse or the ground upon which you stand? I don't believe you will be able to do so. Come here. Come along. We are but children. Yours, it seems. You must love us then. Do you not love us, Casey? Tell us."

Tell us. The familiar demand rang in her ears.

Gabriel might think she wasn't crazy but maybe Aric and Rane hadn't heard the news. And now, they were directing expectant smiles at her— like she was going to divulge one of the last secrets she had left to keep from them because they told her to do it. Love the nightangels and tell them about it? Even if she was crazy, she would never be crazy enough to do that.

"You do love us." Aric pressed possessive fingers down against her shoulders.

"Your heart has told us so already." Rane was no longer smiling.

His statement shook Casey out of her silence. "You don't know that at all. My heart didn't tell you anything. Maybe I don't even like you." She hated to lie to them but there were some things better left unsaid between dreamer and what haunted the dream.

"It does not matter what you say. We know the truth. Come along then. You are the adult. We are small boys. Easy to manage. Quite within your league. Playmates. Why are we waiting?" He crooked a finger at her like a summons. "Time is wasting, Princess. Don't look so clueless. Come here. There's no reason to hesitate."

"You are such a bastard."

"And you are such a stubborn slip of a girl. I do not know how it is you manage to be so very much trouble."

"All I'm trying to do right now is stay out of trouble. And that means I don't have time to play these games with you tonight."

Rane leaned in so there was no space left between them—just angels and dreamer and horses standing like statues, all drenched in moonlight and the night closing them in. "So serious tonight. Have we ceased to amuse you? Have you no games at all to play with us this evening? Why, usually you have so very many. And we like your games such a great deal too."

A terrible shudder ran through Casey. *What next?*

Aric pressed his chilly lips against her ear and breathed something more like a feeling than any words she could discern. It melted along her body in a tranquil wave. When he had sensed her calming, he lifted his head to speak to Rane. "Enough. Ask her."

Rane drew back so he could state his questions and assess her responses with special care. "You did not wish to go with Gabriel?"

The inquisition had begun.

"No."

"Why not?"

"Ask him."

"He is not here to ask, is he?"

"Maybe you ought to go find him then."

"We have found you."

More like headed me off at the pass. "You know so much. Why ask me anything?"

"Curiosity. We are interested in your answer."

"Curiosity killed the cat."

"Ah, but we are not cats, are we, Princess?"

This princess thing was getting annoying. First it was Sleeping Beauty, then Snow White, and now the all-encompassing Princess. She did not know which was worse. "Stop calling me that. I'm not a princess."

Fairytale princesses might have a thing or two to teach her about how it was done though. She had a feeling selecting an appropriate prince for your fairytale ending would be the key tip—one who could sing songs, pick up crystal slippers, dance the waltz with you at balls, and be willing to slay a garden-variety dragon or outwit a vindictive stepmother along the way. She was sure they would say, "No wings, no blood, no vampire princes, not ever." And then they would have rushed off to lose a shoe, or eat a poison apple, or prick their finger on a damn spindle. Casey would not have listened. She liked the wings and she ignored the vampiric aspect of their nature as best she could.

"You see, Aric. Casey does not agree with you either. She is just a girl standing in a dream. That is all."

"At least we know what I am."

"I see. You would rather not believe in nightangels tonight. Perhaps we are nothing but a bit of undigested beef or a blot of mustard then."

"You could be anything, I suppose, but not a line from Dickens, I'm sure you're much more than that."

Rane sketched a mock bow and then inquired, "Such as?"

"How should I know? You could be a spectral beast straight from the bowels of hell."

"That imagination again, working overtime." Aric shook his head. "A spectral beast? From the bowels of hell? Oh, Casey, that's very dramatic. Even terrifying. But in the best possible way. Is Gabriel a spectral beast too?"

Rane gave a low snicker.

Exactly what was so freaking funny about spectral beasts from hell?

"Okay. I'll take it down a few notches. Maybe you're just some seriously annoying stray cats who wandered into my dreams by accident. Maybe once you got inside you shifted into what you are now." Casey was starting to wish she had dreamed up a big barky sort of watchdog, maybe with multiple heads, to discourage stray anythings from stopping by tonight.

"Now we're shifters. Better and better. I'm not sure which I like more." Aric beamed an approving smile her way. "Dearest, you are outdoing yourself tonight."

Rave reviews from a nightangel with wings rising behind him like heavy wrought iron gates about to clang shut were not always a good thing. Casey didn't smile back. She locked eyes with Rane.

"I have already told you, dreamer, we are not cats. Why do you keep coming back to that? Is it a reference to yet another fairytale? I believe she might be Alice after all, Aric. I thought you said you were not a princess but a woman. Alice was just a girl who spent her time talking to Cheshire cats and such. Girl or not, I think you are more than that, Casey."

Great. Rane's words, and the way he shot them like small, sharp darts against her desire to say nothing more to him, tore holes in her resolve to be silent and made her speak when she would have stopped. "I have no idea anymore what you are and I wish I did. It would help."

"I can tell you. Come here. You shall know everything you wish to know and more."

I have to learn when to shut up, Casey thought.

"Leave her be, Rane."

"I don't care what you are."

"But you just said you did."

"Well, guess what? I changed my mind."

"I am only trying to oblige. I always seek to serve you."

"No, you're not. No, you don't. You're trying to upset me. Like always."

"I would never strive to upset you, Princess."

"Yes, you would. You do it all the time. You're doing it right now."

"How can you make such an unjust charge against one of your own nightangels? You are quite uncharitable tonight, Casey."

"I'm not trying to be. It's just the truth."

"Be that as it may, you do want to know the answer to that question of yours, don't you? You said it would help."

"No. Nothing will help. I don't need to know. I don't even know why I said that."

"Yes, you do. You know exactly why you said it. You are the curious one, aren't you, kitten."

Now he was the one talking about cats. "No, I don't care what you are anymore. And I am not a damn kitten."

"Rane." Aric interjected.

"My mistake, Princess. I see you are more wildcat than kitten tonight. I must disagree with you on your other point. I think you do care. I think you care very much."

"I don't. I don't want to know. Not at all. And I am not a wildcat either, by the way."

"Aren't you, now? And you do want to know. It's all you want in this moment, gi—"

"Rane, be done." Aric cut him off.

He glanced across at Aric, gave the slightest nod and leaning a fraction closer to Casey, finished his sentence. "Isn't it, girl?" He drew the last word out.

Casey bristled. *Maybe I am some kind of cat. The kind that needs to stop being so damn curious.* "Dammit. I told you, I'm not—"

"Why so angry with your angels tonight?" Aric asked. He leaned around her, lifted a handful of her hair away from her face so he could peer into it, and let the dark strands slip through his fingers while she considered his question.

Casey yanked the hair away instead of answering and pushed it behind her ears.

"You know Rane is teasing you," Aric said, unperturbed by her reaction.

"She does not like it, Aric. What she does and does not like, what she does and does not want—that is all that matters to her. She is not interested in our perspective."

"I can speak for myself, Rane."

"Speak then. I grow impatient to hear what you shall say. Go ahead. We are waiting."

"Don't tell me what to do and when to do it."

Aric cut them short. "Quit this quarreling, both of you. It is I who becomes impatient. For some peace, Rane. For some answers, Cassandra. I expect both now."

"I was telling him something he ought to know already. What's wrong with that?" She said it like a kid trying to explain away an ongoing argument with a sibling. "I'm not quarreling."

"Nor I. Cassandra and I never quarrel. Not really. Do we, Princess?"

"No, never," Casey responded, trying not to heap on the sarcasm. Rane grinned at her as if they had entered into a secret conspiracy and she found herself flashing him a small half-smile back. She could never remain at war with him for long. Besides, why deny it? They liked their arguments.

The air pulsed, although the angels' wings had gone perfectly still. Casey held her breath as if even that could put something unexpected into motion if she wasn't careful.

Rane extended his hand to her as he had done so many times before. "Come. We ride."

Aric released her as if he assumed she would let Rane lift her up with him and they would gallop off without further discussion but Casey stayed put.

"Come with us, dearest." Aric pressed the request against the top of her head in a small kiss that scented the air so heavily of winter the frozen sweetness of it caught in her lungs.

"There," Rane stated to clarify the matter. Something in the way Rane breathed this one word into the air over her head caused her to lust for that place. She followed Rane's glance with obstinate but interested eyes. The forest loomed high and mysterious against the shrouded sky. Something shimmered behind it.

"There and back." Aric refined the lure; made is sound safer.

Her eyes lingered on the bank of trees; picturing the far edge, the rider who might be waiting. *Not safe.*

"Stay awhile."

"You can run home anytime you like."

"Look, you can see the light of your living room window from here."

The watered-down beam of light trembling past the curve in the path behind her was difficult to make out. She could swear it was fading. The angels were looking at it like that dimming light was a brilliant beacon that would lead her home in a snap. *Now who's full of it?* Casey thought.

"Do we ask so much, weaver of dreams, that you cannot oblige us?"

131

Rane held out his hand again with more purpose than before. "Come. Gabriel awaits us."

She caught her breath. Again. That was happening a lot tonight. She was pretty sure she turned as pale as the angels. She was glad Gabriel was still there somewhere but she was concerned everything in the dream led back to him. It was just like Rane to tell her something such as this; confirm all her fears with a smile.

She could not help but look at his hand—a strong, dangerous hand. He was holding it out to her with an air of certainty. She stood between the two nightangels, between the two great ebony horses, like a shaft of moonlight that had fallen between two sharp sides of the black night sky and was not sure which way would bring it back out again. She had thought it was finished but they did not. She stood there considering the hand and all the possibilities it represented if she took it.

Was it bad, Casey wondered, that, for a moment, the inherent dangers looming in the invitation didn't concern her as much as the potential for another unsolicited wardrobe change?

⪻ CHAPTER FOURTEEN ⪼

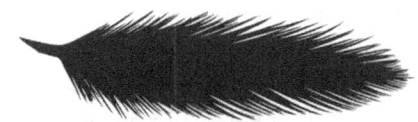

RANE'S HAND GRAZED HERS and paused above it like a heavy-winged butterfly about to settle on a delicate flower. His fingers moved to close on her wrist. Casey watched in fascination. She imagined them tightening like an iron cuff around her arm. He had set aside her tentativeness. He had taken her answer from her touch. He slowed his hand, his smile steady. Having brought her so close, he did not mean to scare her off.

Rane was of the same mind as Gabriel where Casey was concerned. *Sometime—sometime soon—this girl would tell Gabriel what he waited to hear. She would tell him "yes." And failing that at the moment, she would tell them "yes" instead and come along, as she was asked to do, without further argument.*

Maybe they wanted to give her a final opportunity to pour her heart out to their brother; to tell him she loved him without cease or reason just as Gabriel had told her she would—so they could all get on with things.

Casey pictured the moment they would deliver her back to Gabriel. The way he would smile at her so all her fears fell away. She would slip from Rane's saddle then, down between the two horses. Gabriel would catch her as she dropped and lift her up so she was held tight against him. And she would be glad—so glad. She would never want him to let her go again. Then they would race away. The three riders riding fast.

The archangel out in front. The maiden in hand. Everything as it should be. Everything as it had always been. Her fear would be a lost echo falling into a jumble of sharp nothings, already forgotten. They would trample it into a silent dust beneath their beasts. And Casey would not notice; she would not care. She would not be able to recall why she ever wanted to go.

Until he turned up on the other side. Full of renewed expectations. And maybe a few extra angels to keep him company.

No wonder they were calling her "girl" every time she turned around. She was being ridiculously naïve. One thing was bound to lead to another. She had to leave. She snatched her hand away. "No. No more. No more rides into the wilderness or anywhere else."

She was certain "no" was not a word the nightangels were used to hearing. She did not like to say it to them either. She did it because her desperation to escape the dream was winning over her desire to be polite. She wanted to be courteous to the angels tonight. Like someone was going to report her to the etiquette police if she laid the hard-ass routine on too thick. Standing up to Rane required her to embrace her inner tough girl. He looked like the Big Bad Wolf right before Little Red Riding Hood figured out maybe it wasn't such a good idea to chill out with anything that smiled a sharp, red smile every time it looked her way.

His glance slid back to her face. His eyes were unnerving—dark and deep; full of storms and long starless nights. She wished she could bring herself to look away but, of course, she could not. She wanted to look into those black eyes. The feeling, though unsettling, was pleasant, and the more she looked, the more she wanted to sink into their darkness and pull it around her like a blanket on a cold night.

He leaned closer again. She moved nearer to his companion. Hiding within the shield of Aric's arms made her feel a fraction safer.

"Don't confuse me with a guardian angel," Aric had told her once. She had never believed he meant it, even at the moment he said it. She knew bullshit when she heard it. He had a penchant for looking after her welfare. He could protest all he liked but she needed a guardian angel of some sort at least once in a while and as far as she could tell he was the closest she was going to come to one. He had the job whether he liked it or not. She didn't think he minded as much as he wanted her to believe.

He seemed willing to take on the role of guardian again tonight, whatever the reason. She melded herself to the angel and his charger.

"No more rides, no more dreams."

"So sure," Rane uttered the observation in a low voice.

"Very. It's over."

"She has decided against us."

"She does not understand. Patience, brother. There will be time for other choices. Later."

Oh, hell. Casey did not like the sound of that.

"I do not have the confidence that you do in Casey's ability to make the right choices. I leave that to you. I have little faith in mortal girls— even one who might be a princess. I am happy to be wrong in this matter for Gabriel's sake. Prove me wrong, Casey."

Casey did not think that would be such a good idea. She stood there gaping up at him instead of answering.

"You cannot force her to it. She must come to it on her own."

"Again, we must wait on the whim of this stubborn mortal girl. Well, time will tell whether the wait was worth the bother. For now, I remain unconvinced."

"Time will not tell. There's no more time," Casey said.

"No more time? No more time at all?" Rane was smirking down at her again.

"That's right. Time's up." She did not like to sound so callous but this was a nightangel she was talking to and Casey had found nightangels often had a hard time hearing answers that were not what they wished them to be.

"What happened to our goodbye?"

"This is it." She made the mistake of turning from Rane to glance over at Aric. The idea of waking tomorrow knowing she could never talk to Aric again made her sick with grief. She thought maybe he was going to miss her too even if he didn't say so and a wave of regret overrode her resolve to present a hard-hearted front.

"It's not like I'm happy about it. There's no other way. I'm sorry. I am so sorry." *Crap.* She was not supposed to be sorry. Sorry might be interpreted by them as an opportunity to open negotiations on a topic she wanted them to consider closed.

"And what good is it to us that you are sorry when you still mean to go?" Rane asked in the kind of soft voice that was all steel underneath.

He was right. She looked, one to the other. A tear coursed down her cheek. *Sorry.* What a stupid thing to say. What a stupid thing to be. *Sorry.*

Sorry was a shallow word to describe her pain at having to leave them all behind. She had not expected this to be so difficult. She had not planned on these goodbyes. She had not expected the dream to talk back to her as it saw fit, challenge her decisions, tempt her to stay.

She swiped at the tear. This was all Ricki's fault. She had convinced her that the dream was a distracting fantasy and the angels were pure illusion. And that had allowed Casey to delude herself into believing this trek into the dream would be manageable. Ricki had been so wrong. And the worst part of it was she could never tell her so. Life was just not fair sometimes.

"We are sorry too." Aric's exquisite voice was hushed. Casey wanted to do whatever he asked next. Lucky for her, he asked for nothing at all. "It is sad to know you wish to leave us. And in such haste."

"It's not that I want to do it. I have to do it. Believe me, it's best."

"For whom is it best, careful girl?"

Had they taken a good look at themselves? They were the most exquisite, most intimidating creatures she had ever seen in her life. "For me."

"Ah, I see. For you." He looked over her head to trade glances with Aric. "She cannot wait to go. When did she come to hate us?"

"For a nightangel, sometimes you really miss the obvious, Rane. I don't hate you. Mostly, I hate myself right now. I should never have come. I've caused more trouble for everyone. And the longer I hang around here, the worse mess I'm going to make of things."

"It's true you are troublesome, girl, but not enough that the problems you create are beyond repair. The conciliatory way in which he spoke to her made her think these angels were never less hers than in this moment.

Rane leaned down toward her as if he would scoop her up, toss her over his saddle, and ride away across the green field behind them if he thought Aric would go along with the idea. His wings shuddered and tightened together as though he was locking them into place before a battle.

Aric shook his head. "Leave it, Rane. If she wants to go, then let her do it. You do not have to hate yourself for it either, Casey. Do not do that. We do not. We would never do that."

Casey was worried she was going to start bawling. Rane rescued her from this embarrassing show of emotion.

"She does not love us anymore. Perhaps we should be outraged about that."

136

"That's not true," she shot back.

Rane and Aric looked very interested in what would come out of her mouth next. Casey struggled with what to say that would not give the nightangels the words she had no intention of ever speaking out loud to any of them.

"Tell us you love us then, Princess."

"You should tell us, Casey."

Tell us. Tell us. Tell us. Talk about one-track minds. "I'm just saying I'll miss you—that's all. I figured you might want to know before I go." Her voice trailed off.

At least these two nightangels remained where they belonged. She was starting to feel positively grateful she had come upon them here so she could say her goodbyes, leave them safe in the dreamscape, and make her getaway. She did not realize how painful it would be to turn away from them and head home. She had forgotten how much she loved every element of the dream, how much she loved her mysterious, abiding angels.

They were silent and it was difficult to know what that meant. Casey took it as a grudging acceptance of the watered-down version of her feelings she had expressed instead of their quiet resistance to the idea of her going. "I can't come back again either." She didn't want any misunderstandings on that point.

Rane looked away from Casey and addressed Aric. "The dream is done."

"Truly done." Aric echoed Rane in a solemn voice.

"It's served its purpose. We've seen what we need to see."

"And always in the most intriguing ways. I'm going to miss that," Aric said.

"Not to worry. Now things are bound to get really interesting."

"Indeed, brother. I believe you are right about that."

Their eyes shone as they spoke.

Why did they suddenly seem content with the state of things? Shouldn't they be a little more unhappy?

The moon leapt from behind a cloud. The sudden light hardened their faces, making their features appear grave. Their expressions reflected a sudden change of course.

The shudder of Aric's wings behind her put a period to the conversation between the nightangels. For whatever reason, they were done with it.

137

"Then, this is goodbye, maiden," Rane said.

Just like that. Not another word of argument?

She was worried about them now that she wasn't fending off invitations to rush off into the secret dark edge of the dream. "What will happen to you when—you know—when I'm gone?" It was what she had wanted to ask Gabriel but could not because all he spoke to her about was what she must give him, and that she must have an expectation of his arriving on the other side again whether she liked it or not, and how he would be her shadow until she came around to his viewpoint. She may have let him into the other side without realizing it before. Somehow, she must have invited him. She was not doing it again. He was not going to be walking around her world anytime soon, no matter what he thought about it. This was where he belonged. And now she grew anxious for all three of her nightangels. She hated to think of them trapped in a castaway dream. However, what else could she do? They had to stay. She had to go.

"Shall we answer her? She is concerned."

"No, she is just curious." Rane addressed Casey then. "What does it matter, when you will do what you will do, whatever the answer?"

"You are going to be okay—right? You can still stay here in the dream. Just like always. Just minus me."

"What does the answer matter when you will go, nevertheless? Besides, we are disposable. You say the dream is done. What does it matter what becomes of us now?"

"You are going after all, Casey, and as you have already stated, your first priority is yourself," Aric reminded her. "Why bother to enquire about our fate now?"

"I didn't say the dream was finished—just that I'm leaving it. You can stay, can't you?"

"If we tell you the answer, will it stop you from going?"

"No. I have to go."

"Dreamer, what strange questions you ask then."

"And with such impunity. You ask questions but the answers cannot matter to you."

"Tell her anyway," Aric directed.

"You know very well, Cassandra Sloane; you cannot say what will be, and what will not be, with any certainty in a dream."

Hearing her full name drop from Rane's mouth like so many smooth stones tossed against a windowpane, sent a shock through her. How did he know that? Had she ever told them her last name? She was sure she had not. The four of them had been on a first name basis from the beginning. You did not need a last name in the intimate world of a dream.

She continued as if he had not spoken it. "I want to make sure you are going to be okay."

The angels looked at each other, then answered in turn.

"We will be fine," Rane said with a dismissive air.

"There is no need to worry, Casey. No need at all. Your concern though—it pleases."

"I have loved everything about these dreams. I will always love—" She stopped herself, sucking in her breath. *You almost walked right into that one, Casey.* She began again. "For what it's worth, I do care about you even though it may not seem much like it right now. And I wish I didn't have to go but I do." Okay, so maybe she was being an idiot who didn't know when to shut her mouth. *So what?* She gave them an uncertain half smile.

The nightangels smiled back at her and their wings rattled in a soothing way. They were pleased and Casey was not sure whether that was a good thing or a bad thing.

Casey shook herself free of the calm settling over her. Calm was not a smart idea at the moment. "I shouldn't have told you that, should I?"

The nightangels' laughter peppered the air.

"You see, Rane. She loves us. She loves us all. She is just not very good at saying it."

Casey turned pale. "I did not say I loved anyone. I said—I said I cared."

"We know what you said. You cannot change the words or feelings behind them. Not even in this last corner of this little dream of yours. We will not let you."

She ought to have resented this but she did not. She flung caution to the wind and reached up toward Aric because she was going to do something crazy. She was going to give him a kiss goodbye. Not like with Gabriel. That was pure passion. This was pure love. They were, next to Ricki, the best friends she had ever had. Some people might think it was pitiful to say that about nightangels inhabiting a daydream. Ricki would be in front of the crowd on that one. But there it was anyway. "Goodbye, Aric," she whispered.

Aric bent close over her. His breath was cold and now it smelled of frozen rain and winter. He was going to kiss her back and Casey was starting to think crazy is as crazy does when his lips brushed past her mouth to press a firm proprietary kiss on her forehead. She flung her arms around his neck and clung to him as if he was the one thing keeping her afloat in the world. And how did that make sense when he was a citizen of her dreams and no place else? She wasn't interested in figuring it out. He pulled her close then; almost lifting her from the ground. Casey was well aware he could have drawn her up in front of him. Instead, he set her free and pressed her back with a light touch until she stepped away. "Goodbye, Casey."

She turned to Rane. She did not mean to trade kisses with him and he wasn't the sort for hugs. She had never mistaken him for any guardian angel. He was a bloodangel through and through. Maybe he would do what Aric would not; call her "princess" and trap her in the dream forever. Say it was for her own good if she protested. Still, in the end she gave him her hand, laying it in his. It seemed cruel not to give him at least this. "Goodbye, Rane."

He brought it to his mouth and turning it over, laid a kiss as cool and heavy as carved marble against her fingers. "Goodbye, Princess."

She closed her hand over his and held it tight. Life was going to be so damn boring without Rane to shake things up. She gave his hand a little squeeze before letting it go.

Leaning forward, he smoothed a strand of hair away from her cheek. She tried not to act startled by this sudden act of tenderness. "You ought to go now, Casey, isn't that so?"

She nodded and stepped back. "Yes. I've stayed too long already." She realized as soon as the words left her mouth that her statement was a blunder.

"Far be it from your humble nightangels, to keep you when you would be about your business," Rane said in a tone that spoke of renewed battle. The moment of peace between them had dissolved and something else arose in its place. "What shall we give her, as a parting gift?"

"Our understanding."

"Understanding? What is there to understand? She chooses to leave. She turns away."

"Our patience."

"For what purpose? I have no patience. What good is that?"

"Our memory then," Aric offered.

There. That was it. Casey saw it. She cringed.

140

"You cannot lose a memory, Cassandra. "You cannot shut it out, or run away from it."

"Not ours," Rane purred. "You will always carry a piece of it with you."

"A reminder, dreamer, of happy times and dear friends," Aric said in a quiet voice.

"A reminder, mortal girl, of whom you left and why." Rane's words were an accusation.

"It is a picture that will not grow dim with time. The very heart of the dream for the dreamer to ponder forever."

"It is a thoughtful present. Do you like it, damsel?" Rane's thin smile made it obvious he thought she would not like it at all.

Damsel? Well, I do feel distressed. "Like it? How could you think I would?" They were playing a game. They were punishing her and acting as if they were doing her a favor.

"It is what we can give, dearest," Aric replied.

"It seems like a selfish gift. You give me a burden to bear and expect me to be pleased." Casey was angry with herself more than the angels. The gift had been in her hands all along and she had not seen it. She had been holding it there—pressing it close—since the moment Gabriel had ridden back across that sad, green field without casting her a parting glance. Aric and Rane had just made sure she knew what she had hold of and the full significance of it.

"A burden. No. You mistake it."

And now they meant to argue with her about the meaning of it.

"Thoughts of us have been your secret pleasure."

She turned her face away. She could not let them see how true that statement was. "It's a burden," she responded with annoyance. They knew their memory was no gift at all. "Why in the world should I like it or want it? Memories. Of you. I don't need to remember. I need to forget. Forget you. Forget Gabriel. Forget this place. Forever. I'm going to do it too." She had been kidding herself to think there was ever any other choice than this one. She had to untie herself from the nightangels even if it hurt them all. She had to blot them out of her mind.

"Forget, cautious maiden?"

"Forever, careful girl?"

The horses were growing restless. Rane and Aric held them in.

"Try if you must."

"See whether you will succeed."

141

They were moving around her again; the circle widened. They did not believe she would do it. They did not believe she could. Casey saw it in their faces.

"Foolish girl." Rane flung the words at her.

"Timid child." Aric's melodious voice coiled around her racing heart.

"I will forget you."

"You cannot."

Rane had better not be right about that. "I can."

"Not ever."

Aric made is sound like more of a done deal but she did not care what he said. "I will."

"It is impossible. A memory has a life of its own. A memory cannot be extinguished like a candle-flame at the end of a long evening. It shines with its own light and burns without cease."

"You cannot erase a memory. Not when you cherish it in secret," Aric cautioned her.

"I don't want any memories."

"She does not wish for memories, Rane."

"What use are memories anyway if those it summons will be near at hand. Perhaps we should give her a promise instead."

The last thing she needed was more promises from angels. "I don't want anything from you."

"Well, what do you think, Aric? Is it as Gabriel has said?"

"Gabriel has not misjudged her. Neither have we," Aric responded. "She is ready to take the next step. She is done with the dream. She needs more. I believe she knows that now, even if she's afraid of what that is and what will come next."

"So confident, brother?"

"She's leaving. She's not turning back. She has said her goodbyes. She is impatient to go. She is resolved to it."

"Then let her depart immediately. The path is cleared and ready. It has only to be traveled. Off you go, Princess. You have a journey to take."

The certainty in their tones spoke of a destiny already foreseen and now confirmed. They did not sound displeased. Casey found this change in mood confusing. They were acting as if she had done well instead of failed them.

"Don't be afraid. You'll find your way," Aric assured her.

Her way to where? Casey wasn't so sure now that she was heading

142

off that she would ever find her way back to what she had before. Knowing the angels had made that impossible.

"Until we meet again, dearest." Aric's wings were turning to a whirl of violet fire.

"Until then, girl." Rane's eyes grew as black as his wings.

That sounded a lot like a promise. Casey was starting to hate promises.

"No, we will not meet again. I am not coming back. I won't be seeing you again."

"So you say. We will not stay and argue the point."

"After all, you have things to do, as you were so quick to tell us. You must be off without further delay. You said so. You are done with dreams. Why linger?"

"Go ahead, Casey." Aric nodded to the path behind her.

"Yes. Hurry back home before you forget your direction."

Their wings banged against the air as they spoke and the wind rose around her.

"I won't forget my way. I'll forget you. I'll forget you all."

"Try then, Cassandra."

"Yes, Casey, try."

She looked up. The moon was blotted out behind a bank of rushing clouds. The sky turned to pitch. The air grew icy. *Oh, hell. This can't be good.*

She opened her mouth to speak to the nightangels.

But they were gone.

Gone. The word shivered through her. *Definitely not good.*

"I will." She called after their shadows. "I will."

"Try." The darkness whispered back.

"Try." The wind rose up from the stillness that lurked behind her.

"Try, Casey. Try." The whole night seemed to taunt her.

"Wait and see, Aric. Wait and see, Rane. I'll more than try. I'll succeed. I have a life outside this fantasy world you think is the be-all and end-all. I have a real life outside this. And guess what? You don't. That means I win." *Kind of, anyway*, Casey thought.

A line of silvered lightning slashed the sky. Once. Twice. Three times. It struck the far horizon. No riders were revealed in its glow. She turned into the black wind and headed for the plain, low light of home. A chill, needling rain began to fall as she walked. It forced a curtain of sharp raindrops between her and the place where she had begun. Casey did not look back again. She did not stop. She knew the way. Knew it well. As well as her precious dreamangels did. Better, perhaps. There was no other path to take but this, no yellow brick road to start upon that would lead her to unimaginable adventures. The nightangels had gotten it wrong. There was this path—the path that always led her home. And this path was hers—still hers. A sheeting of hard rain could not keep her from it.

She came to the garden. The gate had been wedged tight against the high stone pillars that marked its entrance. Casey was surprised. It had been open earlier. She grabbed the handle and pushed. It didn't budge. She tried again, pressing her weight into it. The gate remained shut against her. Once more. Nothing. She shoved harder, putting her shoulder into it. The gate remained closed against her efforts as if held fast on the other side by something unseen and determined not to let her pass. She tossed herself at the door a few more times like maybe she could batter it down by sheer force of repetition. The iron-hinged barricade remained solid and fixed.

The ground was mud beneath her feet. The air around her was filled with cold, stinging water. To breathe, to move, to consider, was difficult. Her body ached where it had met the door without success. She walked back a few paces, trying to reclaim her strength, trying to concentrate. She took a hollow breath and stepping closer, hurled herself against the gate. She recognized it for a final effort. She was too weary for much more. The impact threw her backward. A pain throbbed through her shoulder and down her arm. But the barrier had given way.

She could see a strip of lawn beyond the chink, a few footsteps ahead, yet the gate would not open wide enough for her to pass through. A hand of furious wind held it fast from the other side. It flew over the top of the door and the garden walls and formed itself into a churning pool of raindrop and gale that spun in a violent circle around her, much as the bloodangels had formed a circle of horse and beating wing with her at the center down beside the sad meadow.

"Open up. Please. Open. Let me in." She began to push again, trying to force the heavy gate back enough to pass through.

Who am I talking to, anyway? The wind? Casey remembered the wind lying dead in the wide, green field at the foot of the crouching forest. She had talked to the wind then. She had said something about how there was no wind and the wild grass could not talk. And after she said it, everything had settled down. Maybe it wouldn't be such a crazy idea to try it again.

"There is no wind." Her words had to still hold some power in this dream even if not in the way she had thought before. "No wind. There is no wind." Her voice reflected a confidence born of desperation.

A rebellious gremlin of air tore at her dress and pinched her body with rough fingertips, blanketing her in a howling chill. Her limbs were turning to trembling ice but she ignored it. She was staring at the gate hanging free on its hinges. It swung open in an insolent parting breeze. She flung it wide, staggering with the force of her own motion as she whirled back to thrust it shut behind her with numb fingers. *Nothing must follow. Nothing.*

The night had gone quiet. Casey's ears ached with the silence. A hollow pursuing sound lay underneath it. It hummed above the garden, within the center of the flowers, along the high walls, up and down the meandering paths, and cut across the lush rose beds. It hung suspended and menacing in the gray curve of the window that belonged to Gabriel. Gray. Like the wings of a wounded archangel. Gray. Like the rest of her life was going to be.

She wasn't that wild about gray as a rule. But right now, gray was all she had if she wasn't going to head down the crazy route. Maybe there was a way to work with gray. She'd have to wait and see.

A square of hundred-watt reality lay open before her. It was beginning to dim. Casey did not stop to think. She shoved past the dark dream. She tumbled into the light.

≪ CHAPTER FIFTEEN ≫

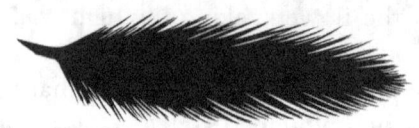

CASEY HAD LAST MINUTE tickets to the ballet at the Kennedy Center. She had meant to go alone after Ricki refused her invitation. Not that she blamed her. It was Romeo and Juliet and she was going to cry at the end if she was not careful. She could cry at the drop of a hat over that sort of thing and it irritated the hell out of Ricki. Maybe Ricki had refused because of that, or maybe it was because she wanted to enforce the real-man-in-your-life policy she had cooked up. Casey did not know for sure. Either way, Ricki had insisted Casey find someone—a male someone—and drag him along with her. And although it was under duress, Casey had.

He was another overworked associate at another high-profile law firm. Casey was not elated about the prospect of an evening out with him, but he would do. At least they had the law and the trials of living the life of an aspiring law firm partner in common.

They met at the Kennedy Center right before curtain time. She wanted to keep it simple. No dinner afterward, no rides to and from the event, no awkward moments. He had gone off to make a last minute phone call for work. Of course he had. He was worse than she was. And she was glad to be alone. This wasn't a good portent for the evening ahead.

She shifted in her seat, impatient for the performance to begin. She was dressed in black and was wearing her very best, very highest high heels. She had pretty legs. When she rated her body parts—breasts, stomach, waist, rear end, legs—her legs always won out. She twisted one foot back and forth under the seat in front of her so she could study the effect of the shoes. Very nice. Too bad they were wasted on another harried associate who gave all the signs of being chained to his caseload, his smartphone, and his ambition. This was the first date, if she wanted to call it that, and she was already losing interest.

She believed Gabriel would have appreciated the way she looked in these heels as they were a little bit wicked; an unexpected look given her usual understated, all-business-and-nothing-else-but approach to fashion. She had never worn such shoes in any of her dreams. In fact, she was confident he would have admired her tonight altogether, drunk her up with his eyes, declared her bewitching without a word falling from the hard curve of his lips. She stifled a sigh. There she was again, thinking about him when she swore she would not.

The black dress was a fitted sheath and she looked sophisticated—sexy even—in it. It made her skin seem fair instead of pale. The glossy line of her sable hair as it framed her face and spilled down across her shoulders enhanced the effect. It carried the eyes straight to the blue of her glance and the soft pink curve of her mouth.

This was the first time she had been out since she had ended the dreams. She had locked herself away as best she could to keep the daydreams, and what they held, at bay. She was not very good at it. Gabriel slipped into her thoughts on a routine basis and it was all she could do to shut her mind against him. This evening out was a decisive act for her. Now that she had come this far, she felt a little better about everything. Even the career-consumed associate she had chosen to be her companion for her evening out.

A stir emanated from the orchestra pit and a sudden hush followed. Her date returned just as everyone had settled in, causing a small commotion and lowering his chances of another evening out with her by about fifty percent. Once seated, he clutched her hand and held on to it for dear life. Make that sixty percent. Perhaps this was a typical male response to Romeo and Juliet or the ballet in general. Casey was not sure but she was beginning to regret extending an invitation to him.

The spectacular crystal starburst hanging in the recessed center of the ceiling began to darken; two thousand separate lamplights dimming together. They dropped from bright to dazzle-dark to empty black; each prism retaining a rogue fragment of rainbow glimmer before dropping into nothing. Casey tried to ignore the hand-holding. She raised her chin a fraction and straightened in her seat. She thought she might be a little bit beautiful, sitting as she was so still and upright in the vibrating darkness of the theater. She felt feminine and wished she was not wasting all this glorious femininity on the sweaty-palmed associate attorney sitting next to her.

The music began. It rolled out of the orchestra pit in a rich, sensuous wave and crashed down on the audience. She sat back in her seat and let it wash over her. The curtains opened. The dancers appeared. Casey sat spellbound. Something about this ballet—the story, the music, the choreography—sent a slight tingle to vibrating in her head until it radiated to that sweet spot somewhere deep within her that made her ache for everything that would arrive if she were to sink into a dream.

No. No more dreams. She crossed her legs instead. She crossed them up high. The soft, steady buzz of desire for something beyond the mundane, beyond the kind of ordinary someone clumsily clinging to her hand, had centered itself in the core of her like a warm, heavy bird might press into a nest of down. She was hard put to deny that urge, that call, that fire that had begun to burn within her. Denying the dream was difficult.

She had not dreamed, not once, since she had left the nightangels behind there. It had been just a matter of weeks now. Three long, dreary weeks to be exact. She had worked with grim resolve not to miss Gabriel every single day since she had shut the garden gate and run away home. She tightened her free hand into a small, desperate ball, feeling as if she was betraying him by allowing someone else to slip a hand over hers—and during Romeo and Juliet too. She should have suggested the movies instead.

It would not have mattered, anyway. Something was going to have to give because everything she did felt ordinary now, while in contrast, when she had been with Gabriel everything she did felt extremely unordinary. It made her wonder if maybe there was a way to be with Gabriel and work around the rest. *Like that would be possible.*

But a girl can dream, can't she? She could almost feel Gabriel stirring as her mind rested on him. *But a girl probably shouldn't.*

She concentrated on the ballet. She wanted to be loved like that—body and soul; heart and mind. Not for a week or a year but on and on. She needed to be loved by a man who longed for her; not in passing but with an abiding passion. Where was she supposed to find this kind of man? She was not interested in being loved with the casual hunger of the modern men who peopled her life. They talked to her as though she was a companion to banter with, argue with, compete with, or sleep with, as the circumstances dictated. How could that please?

She needed someone different; someone stronger, someone who knew what desire and passion were made of and could translate that into action. Gabriel could do that, in the blink of an eye. He could be a Romeo to his Juliet. She needed someone like Gabriel—ardent, demanding, patient, steadfast. Everything she longed for and feared rolled up in one. And who could that be? No one was like Gabriel. No one even came close. This presented a problem for Casey because he was just a dangerous sort of angel in a dream she was not allowing herself to dream anymore and yet, he was the standard by which she measured every man she met. She could not stop this regrettable tendency. She could not stop thinking of what she had lost and asking herself why she had done it. She thought she knew—because it was safe and sensible and because Ricki said she must—but she pushed aside the answer as insufficient and with her lawyer's mind she questioned herself about it without mercy.

What it shook down to was Gabriel lived on the wrong side of the tracks. When your official address is Nightangel Castle, By the Big Rose Garden, Dreamland, you're pretty much screwed in the real world. While this guy sitting next to her, thinking in turns about work and whether he was getting laid later tonight, with a mailing address somewhere in Reality-ville, Montgomery County, Maryland—he was totally A-OK. The golden boy in question squeezed her hand as if that would hurry her to his bed in payment for forcing him to sit through an entire ballet. She squelched a sigh. Yeah, she needed someone like Gabriel. And she was never going to find him.

She hated Reality-ville right now. What she needed was a little vacation from it. Just a little one. She took a deep breath. She loosened her hold on the reins with which she held back her troublesome imagination and when nothing even slightly traumatic occurred as a result, she dropped them altogether. *Let it run free for a few minutes.* She would be in control the whole time. She could do that. She was in a public place after all and perhaps her dreamangel would be chastened by her absence. What could happen? Could it hurt more than missing him

149

did? *Best not to ask too many questions.* She closed her eyes.

Released, her thoughts rushed from beneath the weight of all her carefully contrived controls as though sprung from an unbearable prison and unwilling to waste a minute of freedom. They fled, wild and quick and calling. And who they called for was Gabriel. Could she find him again when he had been lost in the shuttered dream for such a long time already? Maybe he had abandoned it as well, or slept so deep within it he would never awaken again. A real fairytale princess would not have let this happen. They'd already be happily-ever-after and she would not be holding hands with someone she had just met and already couldn't stand.

Gabriel. Gabriel. Where are you? She closed her eyes tighter. She thought of him—his face, his voice, the heavy arc of his wings and the rustle of their action, how his presence filled the space around her when they walked. She opened her eyes and brought her attention back to the stage. If she did not turn to either side, if she looked at the stage and nowhere else, she could believe him to be there next to her. She imagined the hand that still held hers was another hand and the person who sat beside her was another person. She imagined the weight of Gabriel's hand laid over hers and she felt the change—a slight shift—and her hand seemed enclosed in a cooler, more sheltering grasp. She could sense an awakening of everything she had set to rest, feel the world turning as if the archangel had been moving in it all along but had changed direction on hearing her whispered call.

Either she had a talent for finding things or he had her on some kind of preternatural GPS system. Either way, something caught her up in a flash and enfolded her in its embrace, as Gabriel had a habit of doing upon arriving within her dreams. For the first time in weeks, Casey felt a surge of excitement about something better than an extra caramel, caramel macchiato or seeing the latest episode of a favorite TV show turn up on her DVR when she snapped it on late in the evening for some big-time R&R before crawling into bed, exhausted from all her do-not-think-about-Gabriel-whatever-you-do efforts.

The theater faded. The angel was beside her now. Everything was gone except the nightangel and the rush of their movement. They were hand-in-hand; not looking at each other, not speaking. His wings beat like her heart. Beyond that beat there was nothing but the quiet night and the sound of her footsteps rushing to keep pace with his. They were walking across a dark lawn covered in frost. Casey recognized a whisper of green welcome beneath the crunch of their footfall. Gabriel was still quiet at her side, her hand held firm in his. He pulled her along, as though she might turn and run if they slowed. Urgency radiated from him. She was dizzy and chilled but she followed without a word. She looked about her as they went. She recognized nothing but she knew they had reached their destination and it was calling to her. They slipped through a heavy door hidden below a twist of vines. Once inside, he drew her with rapid steps through a maze of cold flagstone passages and up the serpentine curve of a high stone staircase. He threw open a door at the top to reveal a chamber warm with subdued light.

This was the time to open her eyes and shut down the dream or at least run like hell. Instead, she stepped inside, the angel close behind her, mesmerized by what she saw. Straight across the room was a great curve of gray, curtained in billowing white. The heavy flutter of the thick draperies blocked out the view beyond. She recognized that curve. If she drew back the drapes there would be a garden below, brimming with ridiculously red roses. This was part of the nightangel's keep. How was it that there were so many paths back and forth between her world and the dreams and he seemed to know them all? It was not fair. But it explained a lot.

The room was full of coral-tinged candlelight. It clung in radiant clusters along the oversized mantel and the long tabletops. It was held aloft, spiky and cinnamon-hued, in gilded sconces hung high on the walls. She glimpsed it above her head in a massive chandelier of rough gold; a stirring of shadowy flame that danced down the walls and played across the heavy Persian carpets that covered the floor. In the grate, the firelight crouched low like a sleepy red lion.

Gabriel turned to her in the light of the hearth. His face was smooth and cool as snowy marble; his expression serious. His lips were a stark shade of wild rose. A rose such as those American girls imagine must grow rampant against windblown stone fences in the English countryside. The kind of countryside Jane Austen's best heroines wandered about in with impunity, sometimes causing men to fall in love with them without notice.

She was still dressed just as she had been in the theater and this surprised her. In her dreams she shed the attire of the world for dress more suited to racing across the countryside or rambling through garden walkways with nightangels. Gabriel did not seem to mind. The nightangel was circling her—the fingers of one hand tracing a light restraining ring at her waist as he moved around her—as if that small touch was enough to make her stay put so he could inspect her at his leisure.

She ought to have been nervous but she stood still and concentrated instead on his orbit about her, trying hard not to turn her head to assess his progress. When he stood in front of her again, she found she was incapable of doing more than staring back at the nightangel the way he was staring at her; as though seeing each other after a long time apart and needing to take in every detail to make sure it was true. She tumbled into the evergreen depths of his eyes as she would like to tumble into his arms. She knew he saw her desire to stop with the looking and get to the part where they flung themselves into each other's embrace. Yet he held her an arm's length away, still taking her in.

"What brings you here tonight? The real world not meeting your expectations?"

Like he has to ask. The real world was always going to leave her wanting more than it could ever give her because of him.

"No surprise there," he said, taking her answer for a no. "Welcome back. I was wondering how long it would take. There is another solution. I know you don't care much for it but you really ought to reconsider." Casey must have looked like hell was going to freeze over before that happened. "Not yet? Well then, shall we push the world away and abide awhile here—for old time's sake? Will you be brave tonight? Be brave, Casey."

His words fell like cool raindrops all around her. She wish she could have caught them in a bottle so she could drink them up later, drop by drop, when she was back on her no-Gabriel program and she was thirsty for his voice. She settled for drinking them in as he spoke them while she thought about being brave and how she was going to do it even if she should not.

He was kind enough not to taunt her for turning back to the dreams. Grateful for that small mercy, she allowed him to draw her close against him and kiss her in the lingering, take-no-prisoners way she had been trying so hard not to think about for the last three weeks; letting him bring her closer still as he did so. Theirs was a single scarlet kiss melded together from two; his to her, hers back to him. A kiss that was long and urgent. But it was not an awakening princess kiss to her prince. That was never going to happen.

This kiss was more like an I'm-throwing-caution-to-the-wind-for-a-few-minutes-but-don't-get-any-crazy-ideas kind of kiss. Considering this, it was surprisingly good. Casey was confident Mr. Ordinary would never be able to whip up a fraction of the kissing action Gabriel could bring to the table. She was glad because she did not want to desire anyone except Gabriel, though she knew that was *wrong, wrong, wrong*. Lucky thing for Gabriel she was dead set on being brave tonight, very brave.

But there was no time at the moment to think about why desiring Gabriel was so wrong or being brave felt so right. The corner of the room held an oversized bed and the floor around it and the silken sheets were strewn with the petals of roses such as those gardens in dreams held. He pulled her toward it. She realized now that he was winged; those wings were clear as crystal, hidden until they began to move. The air was colder where those wings stirred it. He tightened them behind his back as they walked together; the nightangel taking measured steps back and the dreamer stepping forward at the same pace.

The voice of the fallen dusk stirred behind the moving draperies— the pretty chink of cold crystal against cold crystal—musical and hypnotic somewhere off in the garden below. A breeze pushed against the curtains and she longed to draw them back to reveal the paths they had walked along together. She let him lay her down on the bed instead.

She'd be damned if she'd play the awakening princess to his rescuing prince but maybe they could meet in the middle in a kind of don't ask, don't tell space. If they could pull that off, somebody was going to get at least a little bit lucky tonight.

She was sinking fast into the dark green pools that were the nightangel's eyes—sparkling now with the kind of golden light that shivered in the branches of the high trees on perfectly beautiful days.

Uh oh. Luck was probably not going to be such a lady tonight.

≪ CHAPTER SIXTEEN ≫

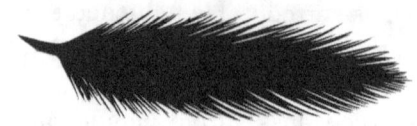

SHE WAS AWARE OF the room around them but she saw nothing but Gabriel. She did not want to look away from him. He seemed inclined to simply behold her with fathomless eyes as if she was a jewel he was drawn to examine in a multitude of different lights. He looked away from her face and his eyes swept down her body.

"All in black, my love. Are you mourning me or dressing with an eye to my pleasure?" Gabriel's caress was light and gilded with want. It moved from her ankle, where it rested for a long moment, before continuing along the length of her leg and back down again as he spoke.

"I dress for myself," she said. He did not have to know all she thought about with regard to this dress was what he would think if he could only see her in it.

"Ah," he said, recognizing her lie and letting her have it. His eyes traveled back to her face. He was poised above her now—waiting for some signal from her to begin.

She gave it to him. She pulled his head down toward hers and abandoned herself to the certain pressure of his lips against her mouth, her cheeks, her forehead, her hands as they pressed against his face before tangling in his dark curls. He buried his face in her silky hair with an audible sigh. She pressed her mouth close to his ear and mouthed the words she would not speak, "I missed you. I missed you so much."

He lifted his head. His eyes were warm with wanting her and a fleeting smile touched the corners of his mouth. "Did you, my own?" He set his mouth against her ear, pressed an electric kiss against it, and said in a whisper that was clear and dwelling. "I have missed you too."

"It's hard," she breathed, glad to be able to talk to someone about her pain; someone who would understand her, who always understood her. "It's harder than I thought it would be."

He raised his head again to meet her eyes. "It is difficult for me too." She saw in his face that it was, that she had made them both suffer.

"Won't you relent, my lovely, stubborn Casey? Won't you believe in my reality? Won't you accept my presence in your world? Would it hurt so much to try?"

He asked a lot of hard questions for a recently banished dream.

Gabriel caressed the hot pulse at the base of her throat with thoughtful fingers. "Won't you let me love you? Won't you let yourself love me back? Tell me what's in your heart."

The angel was persistent tonight.

His eyes held hers. She gazed back into his face, transfixed. For a moment, she did not know what was holding her back. And then all the reasons came to her again as his touch resonated within her and so she said nothing at all. His fingers fell away from her neck. She supposed he had taken her silence as her answer—the eternal *no* he had come to expect from her. She would give him something but not everything. *Never that.* He traced his hands down along either side of her to settle at her hips; lingering there until she let out a little gasp of pleasure. He brought himself over top of her then; pressing himself down upon her. She let him do it.

He kissed her again, with more insistence, teasing her lips apart with his tongue. *Tell me. Tell me.* The demand pulsed around her heart.

Would it be so terrible to give in to the angel in the dream? Casey wondered, although she knew the answer very well. His lips moved to the same place his fingers had burned against. *Yes. It would. He's a nightangel, a bloodangel.* Bloodangels had other kisses to give. These were the forbidden kisses. They were the reason she always said no. She never talked about it with Gabriel but she knew those kisses were what would come next. She could almost allow it too. If she did not think too hard about it. If she let his nearness drug her.

Think, Casey. Her inner voice cried out to her. She was finding it

155

difficult to hear. *Send him away. Do it now. Before you say yes to what you don't fully understand. This is dangerous.*

"Tell me you will have me, my own." He waited on her. "Be brave. You will not be sorry." His entreaty stuck to the air she breathed in like spun sugar.

She did not tell him a thing but she allowed him to settle her beneath him more securely. Wasn't this brave? It must be for the angel gave a deep groan of pleasure. He was waiting though.

If it were done then—the words spoken and the last barrier pushed aside—all acted out in the arena of a fantasy, what then? What about her reality? He began to kiss her again. They were long shivery kisses that brooked no resistance. *To hell with reality.* She'd think about it after the next kiss or the one after that. She kissed him back and back again. He took each kiss from her with hungry lips; setting it on fire, giving it back again. Forget about no and maybe. She was tempted—tempted on so many different levels—to step a little closer to yes.

There's more to him than those damn wings and the way he kisses. The small weakening voice of reason called out to her from the edge of the wilderness she was barreling deeper and deeper into without marking the path back out again. She should have paid better attention in Girl Scouts. She had no time to learn how to mark a trail now. She didn't even have a stash of breadcrumbs handy and they were lying on top of all the rose petals.

Send him back from where he came. Make the dream stop. Close the door against him again and don't look back. He's going to try to take what you tell him back over to the other side. And you're not going to like what he does with it there.

All these internal admonitions weren't doing the trick. She could not get her mind to work the way it ought to when she looked at him; when she felt him above her.

The silver rattle of moving feathers silenced the night whispering beyond the window arch. The chill of those wings closing high around them; closing out the room aflame in candlelight, blocked the world out. He grasped her hips again, pulling her into the center of that haven made of sharp-feathered ice and the solid power of his body. His hands were strong and possessive, holding her so firm in his grip there was no mistaking she was his just as he said, just as he wanted, and she found she had grown soft and yielding beneath the heavy force of that touch. *Do what you like, Gabriel. I want to be yours. I have always been yours.* She could almost tell him—almost. The almost part was a real problem any way you looked at it. One thing was for sure—she should not have come.

He began to lower his head again. Everything around her was dissolving into a golden darkness that spread from beneath his wings like streams of molten fire running through feathers the color of amethyst smoke. Only Gabriel remained. Angel or vampire? Real or dreamed. Innately good or irretrievably fallen. What was it she saw? *Why should it matter?* Her heart wanted him more than it had ever wanted anything. *Wasn't that enough?*

Gabriel's lips settled like two rose-red flames against her throat. Something sharp and sweet was about to happen. She heard her own moan. She did not want to stop.

Damn. Damn. Damn. She should not. She should not. She struggled to get out from under him; from beneath the pulsing weight of the dream itself.

"Must you, Casey? Must you?" His eyes pleaded with her not to run off just when things were going where he thought they should, but he lifted his wings and set her free.

She stood and straightened her dress. She knew better than to look over at the nightangel but it was all she wanted to do. She had already moved away from him to a place between the dream and the world. The cry of the music left behind pulled her one way and Gabriel's tantalizing presence the other. She stayed put between the two and gathered her thoughts. What was she doing? What if he should reappear outside the dreams and start chasing her around as he had promised? He was a nightangel. A bedazzling bloodangel loitering at the doorstep of each daydream she dreamed. And he seemed very real.

No, he was just a dream. Being with him was confusing her and she could not afford to be confused by Gabriel. If Ricki knew about this slip up, she would be kicking her ass right now.

And what did it say about her that she had thought someone like Gabriel up in the first place? And having done so, what did it mean that she had not banished him but invited him to stay and entangled herself in a ridiculously complex relationship with him? She craved his company. She trusted him with her secret thoughts, hopes, and dreams. Maybe that was stupid but at the time, it felt like the right thing to do. She would tell him everything because he attended to her every word like he actually gave a damn. And his advice, whether asked for or not, always turned out to be right. Gabriel was never at a loss when it came to knowing what was best for her. What he had to tell her always made perfect sense. Too bad for her that she was not very good at taking advice—even sound advice. She liked to try things her own way first, whether it was going to work or not. She appreciated that he never seemed irritated about her propensity to blow off his good counsel.

The music rose in her ears. She turned from it. She let it ebb until all she could hear was its echo. She was drifting toward Gabriel and the flame-light. Where she wanted to be was with him—right or not. She didn't care if it was perilous. *Bring it on, angel. And then let's call it a night.*

She approached the arched window of rough gray stone draped in white. She yanked back the curtain, compelled to have at least one glance into the landscape of the dream before leaving. A cry escaped her lips before she could stop it. She could not believe what was spread out before her. The sky was the color of cold mud. The garden below was barren, as if settled into the dead of winter. The roses were blooming though, on leafless stems, mostly prickle and nothing green about them. The flowers themselves were washed out and papery. The wind was a low moan and it flung itself on her now that it was unrestrained by the heavy draperies. She stood there a long time taking it in. She did not see Gabriel but she knew he was nearby. His closeness made her weak and breathless. She wished she were back under his cold wings now—safe and sound, safe with him—but it was too late for that. She laid her hands on the window ledge. She held it tight. She waited for him.

The rough-hewn stone was jagged beneath her fingers. The sky was darker now—rust-red with no light underneath. Sharp little snowflakes began to fly through the air, they cut at the flesh where they touched and began to cover the garden over. The wind smelled of nothing but the cold heart of winter. The blood began to roar in her veins, her pulse to race. She did not have to look. She knew he was there. *Draw back*, her reason said. *Stay a bit longer*, her heart responded.

She closed her eyes as he came beside her and when she opened them again it was to a sky a shade of dark lavender she had never seen before. It faded into a crisp, starless black; the wind grew lower and swept the snow away. Now that the scent of rain, green grass, and roses clung to the air, it was warmer. The roses were in full bloom and calling out to her as flowers do in dreams. She glimpsed Gabriel beside her through the veil of her lowered lashes.

"Just a while longer, Casey," he murmured through lips of hungry red. "Let us come to an understanding. It is important." He cast a coaxing smile her way; a white, sharp secret lay behind it. The harsh rustle of his transparent wings reverberated in the quiet room.

Yes, there was definitely more of the bloodangel than dreamangel about Gabriel now.

She had stayed away from the celadon fields, the scented gardens, the deep, velvet forests, and the lure of her sumptuous-winged vampires for three long weeks. She had not liked it either. In her darkest hours she had imagined they looked for her in those places, wondered at her absence beneath the jewel-dark sky, missed her and spoke her name to one another in the isolated chasm of night from time to time. Not too much—that would be unkind to desire—just a little, so as to not be forgotten by the angels. She knew it was selfish to wish they do such a thing but the alternative was to concentrate on missing them. And she was not doing that on principle. Rane and Aric were not going to win on that one.

Gabriel noted her hesitation. "There is no need to rush away when there is still so much left unspoken between us."

Like another goodbye or maybe a renewed invitation to ride deeper into the dream with the angel? She did not want to say goodbye again and the only place she was going was back to the Kennedy Center. She did not like to leave the nightangel behind in this dream that was so changed but she did not know what she would be embracing if she stayed. She had no recourse but to turn away. And she was going to do that when she was done soaking him in some more.

"Stay, Casey. It is but a dream after all. This place. The garden beyond. Our kisses."

Just a dream? A dream that spoke its own words and thought its own thoughts? What kind of dream was that? It did not matter. This holding back from Gabriel was maddening and enticing. Did she love him? Maybe. Maybe she did sometimes. More than sometimes. More like every waking second. She should not. But she did.

And it wasn't a good idea.

For all that she defended him against Ricki's negative assumptions regarding his nature and character, there was no way to ignore the fact he was a vampiric angel. Vampiric angels couldn't be all sweetness and light even though it would certainly be better for her peace of mind if she could pretend that was the case. She could not quite bring herself to believe that loving Gabriel and letting him know it without a doubt boded well for her ultimate happiness and well-being. She wasn't going to put any extra wind under his wings.

Not when the whole thing upon which the angel seemed to think everything turned was a small word or act from her to kick things off.

Casey was concerned it was the only barrier left standing between a cozy relationship with the nightangel in the daydream and a catastrophic relationship with him in the real world. Casey was relieved that she had never given herself to him fully, never said all the words. That counted for something, didn't it? It had to give her some leverage.

Okay, not that much leverage. She had thought about both plenty of times. She was only human. Normally, that would be a kind of half-baked excuse for screwing up. When dealing with a vampire laser-beaming in on the one thing he was determined to have—you; well, being human was more a detriment than anything else. And now the vampire was bent on understandings and agreements.

"Can you not let me love you?" Gabriel's words pierced her thoughts. "Can you not accept me for what I am even if I am not what you at first imagined? Can we at least agree we are not finished yet? Can you not stay with me for a few moments longer?"

"I can't, Gabriel." She stole a glance at him. "You know I can't."

"I know no such thing, Casey, and I do not believe you know it either. Your actions and decisions seemed based on nothing but fear, my own, and that is unfortunate for both of us."

What was wrong with a little fear in the face of such a force? It only proved her cautious nature had an upside. Casey had known early on with the nightangel that letting something like that know it was in the driver's seat with your heart would be a terrible idea. It seemed she was right.

Her hesitancy had come in handy. Maybe she did have some leverage with the angel. "I have to go now." Resolve cooled her tone. "I won't be coming back this time. I don't know what I was thinking tonight." If she widened her eyes she would be sitting in her plush, velour seat looking down at the ballet again. She clung to the stone casement for a moment more.

"You were thinking of us. You were listening to your heart."

"It was wrong."

"Go then. Why do you wait?"

The water rose in her eyes. "I will miss you so much, that's all."

"Why? Do you imagine you will not come upon me again? Your visit tonight has proved you cannot do without me—not really." His voice was steady and sweet but there was a challenge underlying his words. "Go, Casey Sloane. Why should I keep you any longer? After all, your leaving here is all that stands in the way of our beginning again on the other side."

What? Casey sought to protest but she could not form the word. *Not that again.*

The angel regarded her with cool, green eyes. Casey stared back at him with alarmed outrage written all over her face.

"That's what you said before," she sputtered. "I haven't seen you around though. Not even your shadow."

"Sometimes the truth is hard for mortals to see even when it's right under their noses. And really, Casey, you aren't very good at noticing shadows or what walks along with you. You like to think on things so much, you don't have time to notice half of what is going on around you. So I let you sink into your state of denial until you grew sick of it. And you see, here you are."

"I don't know why I even came here. It was just boredom. I won't get bored again," she said to the nightangel, as if she did not believe it herself but thought she had to say it anyway in case there was a chance it could be true.

"Yes, you will. Until you and I are together again, I would say boredom will be a standard aspect of your life."

He was so right. "Well, then I guess I am going to have to find a way to deal with that because there will be no togetherness happening between us. You are going to stay here and I am going to stay there. That's the way it's going to be from now on."

"Do you think it is that simple?"

She glanced over at him and she thought he was a little surprised she continued to be so uncomprehending. Something like compassion for her flashed across his face. That stung worst of all. Here was the dream, feeling all sorry for her. She blushed and turned away again.

She hoped it was going to be that simple because she did not want to add fending off nightangels to her to-do list. "Yes, I do. If you could cross over to the real world, you'd have already shown up and not as some stupid shadow. Weren't you supposed to chase me down until I ceased running because I was tired of the sound of your footsteps behind me or something like that? Wasn't I supposed to turn and fall into your arms? I think you're the one dreaming if you believe that."

The fire cracked and spit behind them. The lights flickered and reddened; the room grew darker.

"I wouldn't be so sure, my own, you know all the things you think you know or you understand as much about dreams as you assume you do."

Casey's pulse began to flutter. The chilling presence of one substantial wing had spread open behind her like a wall of impenetrable ice. She continued to look out over the garden and lifted her head a fraction higher as if she had not noticed at all. "Is that so? Well, the way I see it, things are not working out exactly the way you were planning. I wish I could help you out with that but I have to get going."

"Do you think I will not find you again and very soon?"

His question caused her heart to pound but she answered with a conviction that came near to his. "I told you. I don't think you can. You're just of piece of my dream, after all. I've been letting my imagination run wild. I won't let myself do it again." A sadness had descended over her. She didn't like to talk to him like this. She was already mourning her loss. And she felt excessively unkind.

She had to stop giving him up and then go off looking for him again; acting like somehow it was all his fault she was doing it. She wanted to reach across and lay her hand on his arm to comfort him for the fact she had turned up only to insist she must be going again but she did not touch him. She was afraid to encourage him or inadvertently give him some key that would allow him entrance back into her world. Casey doubted you could drop a glorious dark angel from a daydream into your life without some serious unexpected consequences.

"I'm sorry, Gabriel."

His wings snapped together again like a book slamming shut. "Do not be. It is what I expected. Take your leave. Things must be as they must. You cannot be something other than what you are any more than I can be so myself. Go then, Casey. As perfect as these moments together tonight have been, it is best. It must end to begin, after all, so let us not waste any more time here."

He might have been angry. How could she tell? Gabriel's self-possession did not waver. His voice remained even and calm. He spoke to her as if he did not hear her goodbye; as if there would be no farewells. Casey hazarded one last look in his direction, one last look into the yard below. His heavy, crystalline wings were beginning to cloud. In the garden, the roses had faded and wilted petals scattered like dry pastel leaves in the rising wind. The sky had turned an empty black.

She released her hold on the ledge. She began to turn away. He was no longer looking at her. He was gazing out the window as if she were already gone.

"I wish it could be different. I don't know what else to do," she said over her shoulder. It was beginning to snow again, the heavy flakes twisting and spinning in the air. The angel stood in relief against that white flurry—his wings turning as black as the night that contained the storm.

He did not acknowledge her words.

The dream began to slip away and she found herself back in the theater. She had missed something; some significant part of the dance, drifting off as she had. Someone was calling her name and the pressure over her hand had been released.

"Casey. Are you alright? I have to make a call. Do you want a bottled water?"

She could see he was just being polite. Why waste time getting water for your date when you could be making more phone calls and checking for email? Her escort for the evening was standing over her, smartphone clutched tight in his hand, an impatient look on his face.

"Sorry?" Her mind was unsettled and she would have liked to leave. She forced herself to concentrate on his question. "No. No water, thanks."

He left without another word. She was glad. Now that the house lights were up, she felt safer, more grounded in reality. She had brought herself back to the here and now out of a daydream she should never have visited. The daydreams were going to have to stay off limits forever if she was smart and sensible and all the things clever, young lawyers were supposed to be. She was beginning to have her doubts about how much of any of those things she was anymore. Smart, sensible women did not drop into dreams to make out with vampiric angels and then give them sass for their trouble. Not only was it not wise, it was not nice.

It made her sad to treat Gabriel with such disregard. To leave him sulking in black wings within the snowy emptiness of her dreams did not feel right. The problem was she had to walk away the best way she could and turn her mind to something else—anything else. The simple thought of Gabriel was a tragedy in the making. Forget Capulet and Montague. For all those problems, a vampire prince and a woman of human blood had to have it worse. Talk about lovers opposed. Not just the world would reject such a relationship, Casey's own heart and mind created barriers to such a love. How could they stand secure against so many odds? Maybe Gabriel saw a way but Casey did not. Besides, the point was he was in the dream and she was stuck at the Kennedy Center with no hope of an early escape from her super fun evening out. Like Romeo and Juliet, they were not meant to be together. They both had to face it. She was concerned that would not be the case—at least not for Gabriel.

She let the harsh lights wash away the pulsing weight of anxiety still pressing against her chest. *Pull yourself together, Casey. Don't be crazy. You're not supposed to be crazy.* She took a few deep breaths. The crowd flowed out of the theater. Now that it was quiet, she meditated on what had occurred; trying to sort it out, remembering every detail of the stolen moments with her nightangel, playing little pieces of the interaction between them over in her head. Especially the part where he was kissing her within an inch of believing the only really dangerous thing in the world was not diving in headfirst and maybe saying "I love you" to a waiting nightangel was not such a stupid thing to do after all.

She ignored the traffic moving up and down the aisle. She closed her eyes to shut it out and calm herself but all it did was make her think more about everything she needed to leave behind in the otherworld of her daydreams. How had she gotten herself into this fix? She had to forget the angel within the dreams. This, however, was easier said than done.

"Evening not turning out quite as you hoped?" Gabriel's voice was soft and distinct and even more beautiful than in the dream. It came from right beside her. *Crap.* Now she was hearing voices.

Either she was all alone or he was waiting in silence for her answer. She was afraid to open her eyes even though she was sure it could not be true; he could not be there, there was no answer to give. *Stop being crazy, Casey. Open your eyes and look. He's not there.*

"He'd better not be there or I'm going to feel like a real idiot," Casey said in a frantic whisper to the quiet space that surrounded her.

≪ CHAPTER SEVENTEEN ≫

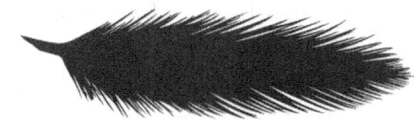

"JUST BECAUSE YOU ARE having trouble understanding something does not mean you are an idiot."

She was definitely not alone anymore. *This was bad. Very bad.* He was talking to her and she was sure they were not in the dream.

"It just means the teacher must improve upon the lesson."

And now it had moved from very bad to worse. She was in no mood for lessons taught by nightangels. They tended toward some very creative sorts of testing and she did not think she was prepared for that.

She opened her eyes. She sat up straight and turned in the direction of that familiar voice. There, in the seat vacated by her erstwhile escort, sat Gabriel. As usual on this side of things, he had shown up without his glorious wings. Casey could not pinpoint what it was but there was still something of the nightangel about him. She tore her gaze away without trying to figure it out. Her brain shouted "flee" but she clutched the seat in front of her for dear life and remained where she was. Where could she go? He sat between her and the aisle. She was trapped.

She must have looked as though she was going to find a way to bolt anyway because it was that which Gabriel addressed. "No more running. Can't you see? It only brings you closer to what you seek to escape. Besides, I am done with waiting. I think maybe you are too."

If she removed her hand from the seat she was hanging onto like it was the last lifeboat on a sinking ship, she would be able to reach over and touch him. Yeah, this was going to put a dent in Ricki's he's-not-real thesis because he sure looked real at the moment. She scanned the seats surrounding them. They were all empty; farther beyond, nobody was taking any notice of the strange drama unfolding under their noses. Casey was confident she would have noticed. *Hello—nightangel in the house.*

He was speaking to her in the same calm, reassuring tone he had used when they had stood together in the curve of the gray stone window overlooking what had once been their sanctuary. It had an edge of impatience to it now just as it had at the end of that encounter. "Be done with waiting, Casey. Leave your fear behind. It does you no service." He stood and held out his hand as if he could not wait a second longer to be going with her firmly in tow. She pulled her hands behind her back before he could take one of them in his. This only encouraged him. "We can leave right now." He nodded toward the lobby. "Come with me, Casey."

Casey shook her head.

"Follow me then and see where I lead."

Following sounded better although Casey was pretty sure it was going to lead to the same place either way they did it.

"I swear you have nothing to fear from me." His voice swirled around her; caressing her, swimming in her ears, swelling the ground beneath her shaky legs as she rose in answer. His mouth curved up a fraction.

She would follow him alright. She would follow him to wherever it was he wanted to go if it would help her figure out what was going on and how she could make it stop before she wound up paying her bills by waiting tables instead of putting her law degree to its proper use within the impersonal, beige walls of Phillips & Row. She meant to speak to him this time in her own world and get the whole thing sorted out between them once and for all. She bent to pick up her purse and coat. She tossed the program down on her chair. Technically, her date was two-timing her tonight with a sleek temptress who came complete with a wireless connection and a vibrate feature that was second to none. Maybe he would assume she had a similar thing going with her own wireless handheld device and wouldn't think twice that she was gone.

If only her life was as uncomplicated as that, she thought, regarding her visiting angel with something between consternation and fascination.

And then, she breathed an inward sigh of relief that, even if this was scary and crazy, at least it was not boring. Her fingers slid inside her bag, checking for her cell like it was programmed to reach a paranormal 911 emergency rescue service if things got out of hand. *Right.*

Gabriel backed up a step and she took an answering step toward him. She focused on his smile. He saw how it would be with her tonight. He was pleased and couldn't help showing it. Casey thought he shouldn't be quite so proud of himself. But once in a while angels had a problem with that so she didn't bother to point it out to him.

He turned and began to leave the theater. He went up the aisle, through the open doors, down the red-carpeted curve of steps, and melted into the crowd. She was right behind him. The lights flashed in the Grand Foyer. The chimes signaling the end of intermission rang out. The open terrace was straight in front of her. People were coming in through its glass doors set into a high wall of windows. The buzz of voices rose. Everyone was hurrying back to the theater. They converged on the staircase from every side.

She stopped at the head of the stairs, standing firm against those who pushed by her and concentrated on getting her bearings. Her eyes searched past the bronze bust of John F. Kennedy that dominated the enormous foyer. An ordered chaos of dangling chandelier after chandelier dropped from the lofty ceiling of the vast hall. The hard shine of mirror and glass running opposite each other down the length of the long space was separated by a span of sunset-red floor. Outside, she could see the inky line of the Potomac River, the shadowy froth of trees on Theodore Roosevelt Island, the high jutting buildings that shot up from the skyline of Rosslyn, and the line of headlights sliding over the river.

She spotted Gabriel at the edge of the tightening knot of people at the same moment she saw her date coming up the steps; still talking on his phone, not seeing her at all. This was the last chance she had to change her mind and she weighed her alternatives. Follow Gabriel to who-knows-where. Stay put and endure another hour or so with Mr. Mundane.

No contest. She turned her head away from her date and slipped into the crowd. Gabriel was already far ahead of her. She struggled to keep his departing figure in sight. She pushed her way through the wave of people, trying to be polite. She did not want to bring attention to herself. *Hello, don't mind the crazy chick chasing after the nightangel she's been trying every*

167

which way to ditch. "Excuse me, pardon me," Casey mumbled. She would like to have screamed, "Get the hell out of my way." It took all her self-control to resist the urge.

He turned right as she freed herself from the last fringes of the crowd; out of the foyer and into the Hall of States. He glanced at her and she caught the almost imperceptible summons still shining there, punctuated with a glimmer of satisfaction that she still followed. She took in those beckoning eyes holding so many answers within them, those hard, red lips showing themselves to her as in the dreams for an instant before blending in with the world again, and she knew there was nothing else she could do but follow as fast as her legs could carry her. He had the answers she needed and he was going to give them to her no matter how scary it was to be chasing a nightangel around the Kennedy Center like she knew what she was going to do when she caught up with him.

He no longer seemed to care whether she followed. He turned right again and disappeared. From where Casey walked he gave the illusion of having stepped through the stone of the soaring marble walls. He had not. He had passed through an opening cut into the far side of the passage. He was leading her to a series of escalators and stairs that provided access to the garage.

Casey rushed after him like Alice taking off after the White Rabbit. She swung around the opening, half expecting to fly straight into the shadowy trap of his arms. She was relieved when she did not. She paused at the top of the first flight, breathless, unsure of what she intended to do if she ran smack into him. Gabriel was nowhere to be seen. *Where was he?*

She caught hold of the brass railing and began to take the stone steps at a Cinderella run. She might be living out a real Cinderella moment if only there was a fairy godmother in sight and she was running away from the prince instead of toward him. That running toward him thing was the real deal breaker. And there was a big problem with her prince. He was as handsome and charming as any decent prince in a fairytale had the right to be but if he remained, as in the dreams, a nightangel prince, then all bets were off about what to expect once all this running was over. She wanted to believe he was mostly good though—she wanted to believe it with all her heart—but it was difficult to be sure when he admitted without hesitation he was something with so dark a reputation—a vampire. Tacking a set of wings on his back just complicated the matter.

She heard the sharp rap of her shoes against the stairs of speckled stone. She wondered whether he heard it too. No steps answered hers. The hum of machinery churned and knocked beside her. The slithery, black handrail hissed as it trailed around itself and back again in concert with the moving metal stairs. Fragments of a distant conversation and laughter floated overhead.

The parking levels were lettered A through C. She was at Level A. She glanced out the glass doors and at the walls straight ahead and to the right and left of her. To her right through the smudged windows was a modern mural portraying musicians in the happy frenzy of a performance. That was it. She did not see him.

She went on to Level B. She had to go through a set of black-bordered glass doors into a see-through foyer. Cars sat empty and waiting to every side. No one was in sight. No stir of movement met her ears. This was impossible. He could be anywhere. She shot a look over one shoulder. She listened to the humming silence.

There was one more level. Level C. Remember, the sign said when she had passed it coming in. Remember: Your Car Is Parked on Level C. *I remember alright.*

She looked up. The shadows of the open brass rails were lined up like ramrod-backed soldiers against the white painted stairwell. She glanced down at the brown and beige flecked steps. From here, she could see and be seen at two levels. Both lower lots were visible on three sides. A neon red exit sign hung in the dull glare between them. She was a sitting duck.

She descended the last flight as if she was simultaneously channeling Buffy the Vampire Slayer and Bambi. Not a good combination. The adrenaline rush was making her shaky. A plaque—gray edged in burgundy—identified Parking Level C. Another exit sign glowed, warning and inviting, above the somber-edged doors.

If her fate waited within, then it was best to meet it. All that was left to do was to walk through to the lot. She pushed against the brass handlebar of the door and headed into a cavern of grayish beige lit up dirty bright with line upon line of grimy white overhead tubes. The door whispered shut behind her. The lot was packed. Pipes the color of dried blood hung exposed from the Level C ceiling to form an ugly tracery of metal lace. It was cold as hell. It seemed appropriate enough. On the other side of the doors was warmth and safety. She was no longer there. She did not want to be there.

She stood in the florescent chill. She looked for him. She looked again. She gave a little curse under her breath. She was certain he must have come down to the basement level. *Note to self: Don't play hide-and-seek with angels of any sort. You're gonna lose.*

A ventilation system grumbled down the lot to the left. The traffic outside was muffled and steady. Past the exit gate, the dark curve of the outdoors lay like an open mystery waiting for her to turn the page. Her nerves were raw and frazzled. She had come so far and acted with such bravery and it was all for nothing. What was she doing anyway? The prey chasing the hunter. A woman all alone chasing a ghost into the dark. *How smart was that?* The answer was obvious. *Not very smart at all.*

She flipped open her bag, fumbling for her keys. She caught the ridged edge of one in her fingers and yanked out the whole chain. Casey clutched it tight and stepped off the yellow-bordered edge of the curb. She suppressed her desire to make a mad dash for her car, striding forward with as much confidence as she could muster. Her footsteps were loud against the soiled pavement. An occasional line of paint—the color of garden flowers soaked into the stone—would squiggle in a thin, aimless snake of color along the ground; following the cracked surface, going in its own direction in places. She stepped across a red one and quickened her pace.

A moment later she felt the car door handle silver-cool beneath her hand. She was still alone. She was almost home. She shoved the key into the lock. The latch gave a dull click as it popped up. *Hurry.* The word vibrated in her head. *Hurry.* Casey pulled the door open. She peered inside the car. No unexpected passenger there. She threw her handbag on the passenger seat. She slid in and shut the door, locking it tight and trying to thrust her key into the ignition with trembling fingers. The key struck the curved circle of the ignition but did not slide into the keyhole. She bent her head and looked down. The key found its place. She twisted it. The motor turned over with a reassuring murmur. She lifted her head, prepared to be greeted by a face at her window or Gabriel pulling at her door until it peeled back like a candy wrapper to reveal her—the tasty treat of the hour. She was glad there was nothing there because the thought of what could happen then made her sick with fear.

Now that she was in her car, she decided maybe it had not been such a good idea to dump her date and go running after something that was actually pretty damn terrifying even without its wings moving in a whirl of sharp light behind it. For the moment, it seemed she was safe and

170

sound; there was no Gabriel in sight. She was relieved, yet she could not shake the nervous feeling that scurried up and down her spine. *Safe and sound. Ha. Safe and sound—from Gabriel, from a nightangel who said with easy confidence he was her very own vampire prince and seemed to have found the hidden express lane straight out of the dreams and into the middle of her life?* Why couldn't she believe it? A tiny shudder ran through her.

She was going to go home now. She was going to drink a cup of tea, get into her softest nightshirt, climb into bed, and hide beneath the covers. Under the blankets was as good a place as any to hide from something that could find whatever it meant to discover anyway. "Be brave," he had said to her and she had done her best to do it. For a few minutes here and there she had succeeded. Even Gabriel would have to give her that. But now she was tired of being brave. Her capacity for bravery had been severely taxed in recent weeks, thanks to Gabriel. She could never be a superhero. Lucky for her, she had been tagged a princess instead, whatever that meant. She wasn't going to think about it too hard. She was scared enough already.

She pulled off the parking brake. She turned on the headlights. They flashed back at her from the bumper of the car ahead and she jumped in her seat. She shifted the car into gear. "Goodbye, Gabriel. Thanks for nothing." Her cell phone rang. She leaned over and yanked it out of her bag. If it was Gabriel, she was going to need some smelling salts. She looked at the number. Her date. Perfect. Another reason to use his wireless handheld device. She turned it off and tossed the phone aside. This was one call he was not going to be able to make tonight.

She did not have time to sprint like a frightened deer from her hiding place of steel tucked between steel. Before she could hit the gas, a black Ferrari slid around the corner and came to a hard stop in front of her car, blocking her path. She could see the driver in profile. He turned to look at her. Forest dark eyes delved into bright sky blue. The question in his eyes shot across the gloom as a well-aimed arrow to the mark. *Are you ready, Casey?*

She was not quite done with being brave after all.

If this was what it was like being a princess in the eyes of a nightangel, she was not up for it. This princess gig wasn't as easy as she had always imagined it would be and from what she could tell, the benefits were pretty few and far between. And why did she think there was no way to resign the post now that it had been designated as hers?

Swell. It's the vampire prince and now my coach is probably going to turn into a pumpkin if I don't get going.

"You have a very irritating habit of turning up again after I've already told you goodbye," Casey whispered into the dark interior of her car.

As if in response, he sent a small smile her way. She noticed it was not consoling but more a gentle taunt. He was challenging her to follow through on her decision. Considering he was blocking her in, she didn't have a lot of choices. He was going to continue in this vein until she relented.

Three weeks ago, beneath a tumbling bower of wedding-white roses, he had promised it to her. He had pressed her against a wall of high stone laced thick with wild honeysuckle, waxed-leaved ivy, and trailing rose and given her his vow that this night would come to her as surely as the sun threatened to rise only to set instead. She would find his besieging eyes upon her and his inescapable presence everywhere. And she would be his. *His.* He had sworn it.

It seemed he was not kidding because there he was, staring across the small space between them as though he could drill down to the bottom of her soul and back again in a heartbeat. Casey did not want him to do that. As it was, she was pretty sure he knew she was all about scampering away just a minute before this. Now, she could not move at all. The pounding of her heart increased as his smile faded. Casey prepared herself for what could come next. Kidnapping was high on her list of likely outcomes. A locked car door wasn't going to be an impediment to Gabriel. The good news was he probably did not intend to throw her in the trunk of a car like that. While she was thinking of all the ways this encounter could play out, he did the one thing she had not considered. He pulled away and set her free.

The Ferrari's brake lights were two neon torches in the concrete and metal gloom of the lot. He slowed a moment. He was waiting for her to follow and she'd be damned if she would not. Not after coming this far. Besides, she had a hard time resisting a challenge. That was how she had wound up as an associate attorney in the cold, competitive Phillips & Row when, Ricki was always so quick to point out, she was way too kindhearted to be working in an environment that operated in first-person shooter mode as often as not. That observation was usually followed up by the statement, "Look at that ass, Derek Rider, for example. And you know he's just the tip of the iceberg." And he was. He had been causing her problems since the first day she had walked in the door. But Derek Rider and the law firm of Phillips & Row were blips on the problem radar compared to one nightangel without wings demanding an audience and one mortal, thinking maybe, somehow, it wasn't such a bad idea to at least find out where the wings went.

Tonight, Gabriel would have his way. Tonight, she would follow. Tonight, she would have some answers. She was confident she would not like them but she was still curious to learn what they were. She hoped she wouldn't be traumatized for life but it was difficult to gauge the result of answers from angels. She knew this already from personal experience. It made her want to hear what he had to say all the more.

He was already out of the exit by the time she had fumbled through her bag for her parking stub. The black and white striped barrier fell back into place far away across the lot. *Damn.* The way he came and went was unnerving. She held the ticket tight in her fingers and pulled out like a kid with a brand new learner's permit, wheels screeching against the pavement. She drew up to the wand separating her from this curious night and the nightangel waiting for her within it, lowered her window, and stuck the ticket into the meter. The gate mechanism creaked and the barrier lifted. She pulled through and watched it fall again in the small silver square of rearview mirror; the descending wing of fate closing against her return.

The Ferrari was stopped dead ahead. Its taillights were bright red points of light in the darkness. He revved the motor of his car. She recognized it as a signal to begin; to head out like so many times in the dreams into the unknown together—racing, everything dark, the angel leading the way, and the night so cool and calling. The roar of the motor made her clutch at the steering wheel of her tame BMW. She felt like one of those stupid women in a bad horror flick again just before they got knocked off. The ones she wanted to slap silly for their lack of simple common sense. Why did they do those things? Why did they go where no sensible person would go? And in the depth of the night, half the time. Right into the waiting arms of what was always terrifying. Helpless. Always helpless. And that which waited so overwhelming. But she was not helpless. She even had a weapon. Casey wondered whether mace worked on vampires and then remembered it was sitting in the kitchen junk drawer back home.

Casey considered and tossed aside the idea of fashioning a makeshift weapon out of a canister of breath spray while revving her motor right back at him. She had given him an answer to his call, his challenge, and whatever else he meant to communicate through the primal growl of that powerful engine. She would not be overwhelmed. And she was not the sort to go the helpless route. Gabriel would find that out if he did not know it already.

Lead on, angel.

≪ CHAPTER EIGHTEEN ≫

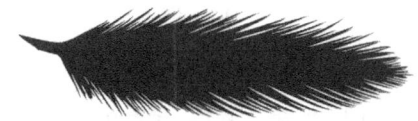

HE PULLED AWAY FROM the curb and began down the road. Casey kept her distance and matched his speed with such precision that it was as though he was tugging her along behind him by some kind of invisible tow line instead of her following after him of her own accord. They curved around to the first light. Green. They went through it. Each light they came to was green. No yellow. No red. Only green. Like so many blazing emerald beacons before the storm. And then there were no more lights. D.C. was twinkling behind them as they crossed the bridge. The waters of the Potomac River were smooth as a pool of licorice cream poured out beneath them.

"I could go for a pack of those black licorice twists right about now," Casey muttered to herself, wishing she had squeezed in dinner before the theater.

They hit the Interstate. Gabriel had picked up speed as soon as the bridge was crossed.

He found an opening in a fast moving swarm of cars and shot into it like a surfer catching a perfect wave. She was impatient to cross after him but she was boxed in. She could no longer see his car. She could not help but think he had done it on purpose.

"Oh, no you don't. You're going to tell me what the hell is going on and you're going to do it tonight. We are done with these damn games."

She felt braver having said all that out loud. And that was good because she thought she knew where he was—up ahead, racing in front of the great roar of an 18-wheeler. Finding her opening, she wrenched the wheel to the right and fell behind the truck. She was coming up on the exit to the Parkway. The truck continued straight down the road and she barely caught the receding headlights of the Ferrari curving down the exit ramp. She shot off the exit after him. Her vision was focused on the Ferrari running rapid and low to the ground and the shadow of Gabriel outlined within it.

They merged onto the GW Parkway. There were stoplights now; each one green just as before. Gabriel did not slow his pace until they came to the fringes of Old Town Alexandria.

Trees gilded with white lights tangled in their branches ran up and down either side of what had turned from the Parkway into North Washington Street. People were still out enjoying the evening, rushing down the cold streets, darting in and out of the restaurants and bars. The pleasant story of their evening was reflected in the glitter and bright shadow of this Alexandria night. But all was not going as well with Casey's evening. There was a new author busy trying to rewrite the direction of her life. Given the intrepid nature of nightangels and their penchant for sudden adventures, she was worried about the way it was going to turn out.

They crossed through the sparkle of Old Town and plunged back onto the dark Parkway. If they kept driving, they would run smack into Mount Vernon. This road was a beautiful stretch but tonight it was nothing more than a path she had to travel if she was ever going to figure out what was happening to her and how to make it stop. By the end of this ride, she could discover she was going crazy without anybody noticing. She'd rather the dream be real, if the alternative was being crazy. Besides, Ricki had told her she didn't think she was crazy. She was relying on Ricki being right on this one.

The brown and white sign that marked the approach of her regular exit came into view. She considered heading home instead of chasing recalcitrant dreams but she pushed past the traitorous feeling. Following something you were afraid to catch up to was not a soothing task.

A silver SUV, coming up on her right side, blocked her view of the Ferrari. As she picked up speed and passed the other vehicle she spied the Ferrari's red tail lights in her rear view mirror. Gabriel had taken the exit and was already halfway down the street. It still took a moment for it to dawn on her where he was going.

He was taking her home.

She roared down to the next exit and turned back onto the Parkway going the other way. Casey's mind began to race. He knew where she lived. He knew her route home and her neighborhood. *Damn*. Of course, he knew what streets she took, what kind of house she had, how she parked her car in the drive just so, and that the porch light would not be on because the bulb had died and she still had not changed it. Something like Gabriel was bound to know all the petty details of her life. She had never considered this propensity of his to know more than he should something to worry about. Now the possibilities of what that could mean in real terms struck her full force.

Gabriel knew a whole lot about her she would prefer he had no idea about. Like, for instance, how for the last three long weeks he was her last conscious thought and his name was the first word to rush whispering through the corridors of her waking mind in the early morning. *He knew.*

She turned left and swung across the Parkway and onto the road that would take her home. He was not at the intersection. He was not at any of the turns she took that brought her closer to her ordinary little corner of suburbia.

The road was the same as always. The houses along it were as inhabited and peaceful as the night before. Electric-bright light pushed against the curtains and shades of each of them and poured out the windows that remained open to the street. The pools of artificial light stuck to the ground in long, white patches. The night that had settled over these familiar images seemed deeper and more looming than usual and the trees in the yards nearer and reaching lower to the roadway than she recalled. Yet, nothing was any different than in a hundred other passings.

She pulled into her driveway and stopped her car with a jerk. She grabbed her purse and coat, and after scanning the area around the car and seeing nothing, slid her feet out onto the cold pavement as though concerned a school of piranhas had taken up residence there. When nothing made a grab at her ankles, she stood behind the shield of the car door watching, listening.

Nothing. No car. No Gabriel. Silence. A somber winter sky. Dark. Dripping with low-slung stars and a sharp sliver of moon. *Dammit, where was he?* What was the point of this little exercise? To show her he knew where she lived? Alright, so he knew where she lived. No big surprise. To see whether she would follow where he led? Well, he knew the answer to that question now. To underline the fact that there was no sanctuary from a nightangel hell-bent on having a word with you? Fine, message received. She did not feel very good about any of this and most of all she disliked the terrible sense of disappointment welling up inside her. That was a bit of a surprise.

Casey slammed the car door closed good and hard. The sound reverberated up and down the street. A dog took up a spell of frantic barking at its echo that was primal and pleasant against the dim suburban night. *I don't care, Gabriel. I'm glad I lost you. Following you was stupid anyway. Why would I want to talk to you? It's ridiculous.* She didn't mean it. Not really. She did not even know why she threw these angry thoughts out against him in her mind. It might be she did it to dispel her own nagging frustration and to chase away the sweet-scented fear that now hugged against her.

It just didn't feel done.

She stood rigid, waiting under the stars. For something. For anything. A noise. A movement. A whisper or stirring that was out of place. A figure walking toward her out of the dense darkness where there had been nothing a moment before. She did not call Gabriel's name. That would be flat-out stupid. Who could know what would happen if she did that?

There sure was a lot of stuff she didn't know right now. For some reason, it made her hungrier than ever for the pack of licorice candies she didn't have.

She did wish they could finish what had been started between them tonight, even if the prospect of such a thing did scare the daylights out of her. She was getting tired of waiting for the nightangel to make his point and be done with it.

Be careful. You might get what you wish for. The age-old warning sounded in her ear like a spiteful taunt. *Yes,* Casey thought. *Yes. Be careful. Be very careful, Casey Sloane, what you wish for, or you just might get it. And what in the world would you do then?*

What indeed?

Another thing to add to the growing list of things she did not know.

If Gabriel were standing there with her, she was sure he would be able to answer that question to their mutual satisfaction. *Where was a know-it-all angel when you needed one?*

On second thought, maybe she wasn't ready for his explanation. At least she was home, a low brick house with a quiet patch of real yard settled in a neighborhood that still held just a drop of character. D.C. was competitive, and expensive, and impersonal—like New York City with a slight Southern accent it could lose on a dime and a penchant for playing politics instead of trading stocks. Her little house in suburbia was an attempt to remedy some of that.

She forced her key into first one and then the other of a double set of locks on the front door and pushed it open. It was darker inside than out on the porch. She reached in and felt for the light switch. If something strong and cold clamped onto her hand from the inky depths of her own living room before she could smack on the lights she was going to be very unhappy.

She flicked on the switch without incident. The room looked all right—safe and empty. She stepped across the threshold and held her breath, listening. She looked around for some sign things were not as they should be; something out of place or perhaps a nightangel lounging about on her living room furniture ready to begin their late-night heart-to-heart, whom she had somehow failed to notice at first glance. But everything was the way she had left it. No lounging angel, with or without wings was there. Not even a very quiet one.

The latest in a line of can't-be-killed houseplants wilting on the coffee table, the magazines and books to the side of the sofa sorted into precarious stacks, the hum of her barren refrigerator, and the steady tick of the clock that hung to the side of the door, all were just as always. She was home. A bright, warm, everyday space. She could see that morning's coffee cup, still on the kitchen counter, from all the way across the living room. The kitchen shutters were half open. Her own figure, and the black void of night hanging over her shoulders, was reflected in the skinny midnight square of kitchen window.

She was still standing on the threshold. She had to admit she was feeling more and more disappointed Gabriel was not loitering outside her door, waiting on her like the obedient dream he should be, so they could get this whole thing over with and she could properly dismiss him from her life. She paused in the chrysanthemum fan of light that stretched from the doorway, listening to the distant traffic and the breeze that had begun to rush through the leafless branches. She let the empty night wrap itself around her. Standing there felt dangerous but it was the closest thing to an engraved invitation she could devise on the spur of the moment. *I'm vulnerable and alone. I'm ready to talk just like you wanted. Come and get me, whatever you are.* He was not doing much in the way of heeding her message because there was still no Gabriel.

It looked as though he was going to be a no-show. The more she thought about the way the snow had fallen in that last daydream, as if it would never stop, and how very dark the angel's wings had grown upon her leaving him there, the more she believed maybe it was all working out for the best. Talking to a vampiric angel in her own living room would not have been like whispering together among the roses in a lilac-skied fantasy world. There would be no way to open her eyes and be done with him or close them tight and shut him out. It was bound to be scary. Casey liked scary two ways—for heightened effect in the dreams or accompanied with butter-drenched popcorn in real life. Considering this was real life and Gabriel was unlikely to be driving around with a popcorn machine and a bunch of scary movies stashed in his car, she was pretty much stuck with the unacceptable straight-out scary option.

She slammed the door behind her. She locked all the locks, like it could keep out the nightangel element in the world. She knew she was kidding herself. He already held the passkey to her life. *That was sure to be very inconvenient.* She leaned back against the door. She was shaken but she was angry too. Her anger upheld her now. She was so close to knowing the answer to all the questions she had been trying hard not to ask. Coming so near Gabriel or whatever it was that bore his features and was walking around like the whole world, or at least one of its inhabitants, was all his for the taking—only to lose that teasing vision on the sedate streets of her own neighborhood—was frustrating.

She kicked off her shoes. She watched them hit against the wall, noting with satisfaction the little black scuffs they left on the white paint. She would be sorry about that in the morning. Right now, they matched her mood. She began to stalk down the hall to her dark bedroom. Good. She was glad it was dark. Maybe he would be there in the gloom waiting for her. Maybe that was where she would find her angel. Then they could have this out. She stiffened. He could be there—another shadow along the wall. She shuddered but she did not stop. She forced herself to walk the length of the hallway. She reached around the doorframe and banged on the bedroom light. Empty.

She let out an exasperated breath. She was alone. She did not know whether that was so great given the stalking nightangel thing, but she couldn't call Ricki about it, so being alone was all she had. She flounced across the room and sat on the edge of the bed. She yanked off her stockings. She could not bring herself to take off the dress because Gabriel had admired her in it.

She gave a weary sigh and crossing to the dresser, studied herself in the large mirror perched on top of it. She had no idea what she had done to merit the attention of a nightangel on the wrong side of the dream or whether there was a way to undo it before Gabriel turned up again. Her experience with nightangels was limited to daydreams. Life was not at all like a daydream and she could not even count on a daydream to be what it should be anymore. That didn't seem right but it wasn't like there was a complaint department for the otherworld she had concocted which could address this for her if she would file the proper complaint form.

Nightangels did not care about complaints anyway. They just explained why you were off base and then you said, "Oh, I see now." And mostly you did. The nightangels had a talent for explaining away things. The creatures of the darkest night telling you how to look on the sunny side of things was kind of nice. Ironic, but nice. And simple. It made everything simple.

She pushed away from the dresser, giving a dismissive toss of her head to her reflection. She headed for the good, honest glare of the bathroom. She leaned over the porcelain edge of the sink and flashed a look of pure disgust into the mirror. She did not think much of Cassandra Sloane at the moment. She had been somewhere she should not have been. She had called out to the very thing she knew she should have left alone. She had reawakened it to her existence beyond the dream when she should have left everything within it thinking her lost to it forever.

Of course, maybe Gabriel would say it did not matter anyway; that all the dreaming or not dreaming in the world could not hold him back or draw him forth because he did what he pleased without any help from some mortal daydreamer. And now, she was not going to have the questionable pleasure of knowing what he would have to say about it. She resented him for that.

She turned on the water, bent low over the basin, and splashed her burning cheeks until the flush subsided. She lifted her hair high on her head and clipping it there, leaned back over the sink. She wet the base of her neck. *Damn, that's cold.* Well, that was how she wanted it. Sobering. Chilling. Like a well-warranted slap in the face. She was her own mean girl now. *Super.* The water spilled between her fingers and ran down the back of her dress, down her shoulders and arms, and onto the floor to form a puddle at her feet. This little pool of water was the closest she was going to come to shedding a tear over lost dreams and wandering angels.

The dress was ruined now. She didn't care. She arched her neck to one side so it lay open and exposed. The way a willing maiden might offer herself up to a vampire in a pulsing fantasy. Casey slid her wet hands along her throat. She thought of Gabriel. She thought of the aching kisses he would have for her if she could find him and tell him even a fraction of what he waited to hear. She thought about what he was, and what she was, and what insanity it was for her to think of him at all—because what Gabriel was could not be right. *And yet, and yet…*

"Will you never learn, Casey? You have to stop this. No more thinking about him. No more dreaming about him. You're done."

Tomorrow she was going to start running, even though she hated running. Tomorrow she might start baking, too. She liked that much better even though she wasn't very good at it. Then she would have to do some more running to make up for eating all that baking, but that might be a good thing. It would keep her busy. She would find other things to do too if she had to; mindless, tiring things. She would populate her life with as many time-consuming activities as necessary to keep thoughts of Gabriel at bay.

She swiped at herself with a fleece bath towel. It didn't do much good. She tossed it on the floor with a shiver, took down her hair, and walked back into the bedroom in her cold, wet dress. She began to rummage through her dresser drawers in search of her coziest nightshirt.

This was all Gabriel's fault. He was playing a game with her she had no way to win. *Rescuing prince, my ass,* Casey thought; anger and fear merging into sudden outrage.

"What do you want, Gabriel?" she said out loud. "What do you want, you arrogant bastard of a dream?" She drew out each word, her voice trembling in anger. "Tell me, Gabriel. Dammit, come here and tell me." She invoked her dreamangel and closed her eyes upon the certainty of the emptiness that would answer back. There was no such thing as a dreamangel or a nightangel. There would never be any vampire resplendent in icy wings; no bloodangels to avoid. Nothing like that of any sort was going to be found anywhere in her small ordinary universe. Vampires did not exist—certainly not vampires with storybook eyes, perilous smiles, and bedazzling wings hanging heavy at their backs. Fragments torn from daydreams did not set out after over imaginative young women in the vast halls of the Kennedy Center, nor did they invade the golden glow of their bedrooms after the chase.

She had just about made her peace with the situation when the air began to stir around her like someone had flipped the ceiling fan above the bed on high and turned the AC to cold front at the same time. Casey's eyes flew open and she found herself staring at her reflection in the mirror.

Behind her stood Gabriel. *Damn.* Another basic vampire myth had just bitten the dust.

Her eyes were fastened on the nightangel in the shimmer of glass. His hands settled on her shoulders and swept down her bare arms to capture her waist as if he meant to do it every day from this moment forward. She did not turn or try to pull away. She had to admit, he was a pretty damn good dream. Even with no wings to be seen, he did know how to make an entrance.

And no matter how much she would like to deny it, she was still all about the dreams in a rebellious little corner of her heart.

≪ CHAPTER NINETEEN ≫

THE GABRIEL OF A thousand shaded daydreams drew her back toward him in one firm, proprietary movement. Hard against soft. Dream against dreamer. He fit himself against her so her breath was his and the pounding of her heart must have echoed in both of their ears. His eyes drank her in as she stood wide-eyed in her wet, black dress, trying to relegate his appearance to nothing more than the hallucinatory aftereffects of too much rolling around on petal-strewn beds with make-believe nightangels when you had sworn off them. She felt like she'd gone on a bender after being in a sort of daydream rehab outpatient program that required total abstinence in order to stay free of nightangel-induced complications.

Where was Dr. Drew when you needed him?

The angel tore his gaze away from her image in the mirror and sought out the smooth cream of her shoulders and neck. He marked the place where they curved together with a single shattering kiss. The power of that kiss rendered her motionless within his hands. *He's not real anyway,* she told herself. She was not going to squander what was a pretty fantastic not-real moment by over-examining it.

She dropped her head back against the nightangel's shoulder instead; her face lifted up and away from him, her neck turned and bared. His cool breath fanned the anticipation that heated her skin. She closed her eyes. She waited. Casey knew the spot where his mouth would touch next. She knew it without looking. He pressed his lips against the sweet spot where her pulse beat so Casey almost cried out and then he rained a brutal storm of soft kisses down upon her. They poured along the places where the damp wisps of hair clung to the nape of her neck, across the heat of her flushed cheeks, against the corners of her open breathless lips—rushing, pausing, traveling forward again. He smoothed her brow with these kisses before releasing another hungry deluge of them along the other side of her neck.

She was soothed and panicked by the frosted, urgent pressure of those lips. She could either scream "stop" and see what happened next, or stay still and silent while he kept making her weak in the knees with this onslaught of kisses. She went with not moving or speaking. She had released herself to the moment. She had given herself over to something that could not be happening anyway.

Soft-eyed vampires, sharp-mouthed angels—these were the things of dreams, not reality.

"It's only a dream." She murmured the sentence out loud, some of her fear melting under the icy sweetness of his kisses on her skin and her own reassuring words.

Her imagining lifted his head. He smiled at her in the mirror with a certain new understanding. Casey produced a small, nervous smile in answer without meaning to smile at all. The exquisite illusion—even more dazzling than in any of her daydreams—buried his face in her sable hair. His mouth was parted and sighing as it brushed against the silk of it. She thought he might speak. She did not want him to speak. Because if he spoke, he would be real. And if he was real, she was so screwed.

"Casey," the vision breathed her name.

She was so totally screwed.

His cold breath moved against her ear and he spoke her name again, in a voice fierce in its tenderness. "Casey, my beautiful dreamer. How I have missed you."

Truly and totally screwed.

A terrible trembling began within the core of her and radiated through her limbs.

"Casey. Why do you shake so? You are safe in my arms." The possessive heaviness of his voice pressed against her heart. He pulled her even tighter to him.

185

"Oh God, you're real." The hard strength of his imprisoning arms around her underlined the truth of her statement. "But you can't be. It's not possible." It was not easy maintaining a state of hard-fought denial when the very thing you were working so hard to deny was standing there, happy as all get out to see you.

"I have always been real, Casey."

Happy and intent on making a point Casey did not want to accept as true. "No, not to me. Never."

His cold mouth speaking each calm, certain word into her ear felt very much like the real thing. "Yes, most especially to you. Always."

"No. It's not true. Please, don't do this. Please, don't be here."

The nightangel still held her fast. Nothing changed. Begging wasn't going so well and it was so humiliating besides. Casey grew silent rather than say "please" even one more time. Asking nicely for a reprieve wasn't doing a drop of good anyway.

"Casey," he said, as if it was the best word in the world and his saying it out loud to her would be enough to silence any future protests on her part regarding the issue of his reality. "Casey." He said it again as though he could not help himself.

Casey did like the way he said her name, as though he wished to say it over and over again without cease. At the same time, it made her more certain he ought to leave without delay. She was sure this was not the desired effect but there was nothing she could do about her reaction.

"I need you to go now. Go away. I'll close my eyes and you disappear."

"I don't think so." He addressed her reflection. "We need to talk."

She watched in fascination as he bent his head and ran his cool mouth along the arched line of her throat.

"Hey, here in Reality-ville, USA that's not talking." She struggled to release herself from the arms wrapped tight around her. How could she think for one instant—being held within the circle of his powerful arms and feeling his cold kisses burn wherever they touched—that he was not real? What an idiot she was and how transparent she had made herself to him. Even if she thought him a vision, a rogue dream made of nothing but her most intriguing imaginings, she should not have allowed herself to submit to his caresses with such obvious desire.

"Do not be afraid."

Now he was talking. And it was typical angel-speak.

186

Of course she was going to be afraid. "I can't help it. Now go away, right now." It was difficult to sound adamant about being released from the tight, protective embrace of an angel when she had been enjoying it so much a moment before.

"I cannot."

This is what she got for daydreaming about nightangels. They always wanted their way. "Why not?"

"I told you. We have to talk."

"I don't want to talk to you. I just want this to stop. I don't want you here."

"Why? In all our time together what have I ever done but love you? When have I ever been anything other to you than your dearest friend?"

They stared at each other in the mirror; both very determined to win the moment. Casey broke eye contact first. Staring down a nightangel was difficult in the best of circumstances. An icy shiver shot through her body and she forced back the dizzy feeling that followed. "How the hell do I know? It wasn't real." She tried to swing around to face him.

He would not release her. He did not seem inclined to leave. "You know." He pressed the words against her cheek.

"What time together?" She stopped her struggle. She met his eyes in the mirror again and this time she refused to look away. "You're nothing but a goddamn dream. None of it ever happened. There has been no time together."

"Wake yourself then, dreamer. And I will be gone—disappeared as if I never existed here or in the dreams. Go ahead. Why do you wait?"

Casey applied all her mental energy to doing just that but nothing she did to send him spinning off to dreamland was having the least effect. All the while she worked to ensure his worldly demise, he held her in the relentless calm of his grip as if he had no confidence in her chances of success. He was more entertained than offended by her determination to toss him back into the prison of her dreams. After a demoralizing interlude of quiet during which she concentrated on a series of heartfelt but ineffectual attempts to dispatch him without so much as a goodbye, he began to speak to her. His voice rubbed like roughened silk against her heart and caused it to flutter in her chest.

"You make such a simple thing so difficult. Why? We come so near and then you turn aside or run away. You put a distance between us and as you do, I hear your sigh—a sigh of relief. I am not sure whether it is relief at escaping me or at avoiding your own feelings. You will tell me which it is, by-and-by. Won't you, Casey?"

His arms unlocked from around her and the urge to flee overcame her. He caught her by the shoulders and spun her around before she could scurry past him. "No more running off, Casey. There's no reason for it, my own. Only safety awaits you in my arms."

Casey knew there was a kind of safety in his arms but the question was, at what price did it come? She did not have time to consider the answer. He was ordering her about again in the manner nightangels like to do that caused her to be angry and beguiled all at once.

"Stand here. I want to speak to you. I want to touch you. I want to look at you as I could never look at you in the dreams. A few moments ago you were willing to allow it."

And he is never going to let me forget it.

"That was then. This is now," Casey shot back. She'd had to say this sort of thing to him a lot lately. She blushed as she remembered what she had allowed him to do in the name of denial and dreams a few minutes before. His eyes filled with heat as he read her thoughts.

"What has changed so much in a span of minutes? Not I. I, Casey, have not changed at all." His hands slid down her bare arms and in their wake there remained the clinging fabric of his touch, as arctic and inescapable as a storm of iron snowflakes knit together into an icy cloth. "You are so beautiful, my own. I do not want to look away. Everything about you is so much more than it could ever be in the dreams. I like the way you feel when I hold you against me. Do you not enjoy it too? Am I not what you expected? Speak to me, Casey. Am I not what you desire?"

She shook her head in disbelief at the materialized vision speaking to her as though she ought to be thrilled by every word he said to her, every question he asked of her, when they were terrifying her instead. She tried to keep him at arm's length and fix him there with her most serious look. "It doesn't matter. I have been confused."

"You have never been confused about your need for me. It is your understanding it, acting on it, giving yourself over to it, that confounds you. You desire me, Casey. Admit it."

"Not at all," she lied. "Besides, I told you, none of it matters anyway."

"But it does matter. All of it."

"No, it doesn't. It doesn't matter because you're not real. You aren't, you know. You can't be." She tried to tug her arms free from his grasp.

"Why not? Why can I not be as real as you?"

"Because you're not." She said it as if that were all the explanation she needed to give and she was being perfectly reasonable. It was very simple after all—he was a figment of the imagination and consequently, he could not be real even if he was standing there, holding onto her as though he was not sure he would ever let her go. Maybe she couldn't explain it to his satisfaction right now but she did not understand how he could not know it anyway. Her poor dreamangel. It felt almost spiteful to tell him but she needed him to know the truth so he would realize there was no place for him but the daydreams and head back there without delay.

Gabriel wasn't impressed with her answer. "Don't I feel real?" Instead of fading back into the dream, his hands tightened around her wrists in two remorseless circles of alabaster ice. "Doesn't my touch feel real to you?"

"Stop it." She tried to shake him loose. "You're hurting me."

"It is not true. I am not hurting you at all. You say that because you think it might cause me to release you. You would like to put something between us again—a piece of furniture, the length of the room, anything at all. As if it would do any good, Casey. It is such a small room and the furniture is flimsy or too heavy to move. The lock on the bathroom will never hold. I stand between you and the bedroom door. There is nothing else, is there?"

He studied her face as her eyes searched the room for a way out, a barrier, a weapon against him. "No, dreamer. No. There is nothing else. Even if you fled, I should catch you. Besides, where could you go? Who could you summon? There is no one to help you in your world. I would assist you, if you would let me, but you will not. You only want to run from me. You are so stubborn, my heart. It is your greatest flaw. You will need to help yourself then, since you turn up your nose at the aid of others. You are on your own, Cassandra, as you wish."

This would have been a good time to scream her head off but she did not. She was a little shocked by that. It did not surprise Gabriel. He took her wrists in one of his hands and traced the tense line of her jaw and the paling curve of her cheekbone with the other—slowly, as if to reassure, and with relentless confidence. The gentleness of his touch threw her off guard. It made her unsure of her own reactions and instincts.

His face came nearer to hers. She could not look away. She was going to fall into those eyes, the forest primeval lit by a distant fire. To walk toward its light and find her warmth at its beckoning flame would be easy to do; she wanted to go there.

Just when she thought she might wind up doing it, the light within those eyes flared and then dimmed. Casey had been released. He began to speak again. The fire had retreated into his voice. It flashed red on his lips before dying down to a soft, burning rush of words.

"You have tried to bar me from your life. You have closed your mind against me. You have deprived yourself of your dreams. You have kept yourself away from me with your work, and your friends, and the mundane details of your life. You latch your windows and bolt your doors. You try never to be alone unless you are behind the sheltering walls of this house or your office. You have attempted to secure every avenue of entry from the intruder that has appeared on your horizon because you do not recognize it is no intruder at all."

His tone grew deeper, more urgent. "It is only me—your own Gabriel, the dreamangel, the nightangel. And now, cautious damsel, careful girl, timid maiden, awakening princess, you begin to understand, I think. I will not be barred. You cannot turn me away or close yourself off from me. You cannot lock me out. There is no place to hide."

Casey's breath caught at the sound of all those names spoken aloud as though they were commonplace. Whether he was real or not, he knew a whole lot more than he should about her and her daydreams and it did not matter to him whether she liked it or not. He was speaking as if it was his right to say whatever he pleased to her and it was her duty to listen—as any good dreamer should—to what the dream had come to tell her face to face.

She would not have been surprised if the room around her melted into the otherworld then, opening itself like an exquisite lady's fan from a bygone era to flutter before her eyes. She wished it would. She might be able to deal with this Gabriel within the confines of the other place. Here, in her own bedroom smack dab in the middle of Alexandria, Virginia, she was sure to run into some problems managing him. Everything around her remained quite solid though. Gabriel did not waver. He went on. She could not keep herself from attending to what he had to say.

"I will always find a path to you, should I choose to search for it. It is the simplest thing in the world. And if you wish to hurry my steps, you need only call. Call me, Casey. That is all you ever need to do."

"I will never call you."

"So you say. How can I believe you when you call me all the time without even knowing it? There are many ways one heart can call to another, especially hearts that are bound together such as ours. Didn't you call me tonight? And didn't I come as you asked?"

All the color ran from her face. The nightangel, or whatever it was that had turned up on her doorstep tonight, noted it as well. "As to the present—be at peace. I will not force you to fall into my arms. But there will be no running off until I say you may go."

Casey did not like the sound of that. He might never dismiss her. On the bright side, crazy was starting to look a little less likely than she would have guessed a few minutes earlier.

"Okay then." Casey switched gears. She could be compliant and non-compliant at the same time. She was an attorney, after all. "You said we need to talk. So talk. This is your chance. Go ahead. Tell me what you have to say. Because after this, I won't think about you anymore. Not ever. I swear it. The daydreams will stop. Every thought of you will stop. You'll have no place to go. You'll dissolve into nothing."

He looked as though he might like to smile. But he did not.

"Go ahead. You think this is funny. Laugh it up." He was making her feel foolish when she wanted to believe she was right.

"I am not laughing, Casey. Not at all."

Casey lowered her eyes so he would not see the fear in them and when she raised them again, they were full of indignation. "Whatever. I don't care because the joke is on you. The bottom line is you can't be real no matter how much you make me think you are. It's just a trick of the mind that has me standing here with you. I'll wake up, or snap out of it, or…something, and then what will you do? I think the answer is nothing. What do you think?" She spoke the question in a defiant whisper. She required an "or something"—and fast.

Relief flooded through her as she considered her own words. *I'm sleeping. That's all.*

If she could get up, she could end this. She must be lying on the bed. If she turned, she would see herself—peaceful, beneath a tangle of cutwork white sheets. The sable halo of her hair spread out across a snowy pillowcase. Her eyelids lowered to shut out the everyday. Her breathing steady and light. The dream upon her. A vision such as one might stumble across in the lush paintings of the Victorian romantics.

The radiant angel leaning close over the dreamer. His wings resting folded and still. The spill of his dark curls falling against the nape of his neck. His face lowered so near the unwary dreamer's that each breath she took was mingled with his. His hand resting on the dreamer's heart; her heart. And the dreamer sinking deeper into the dream that held her tight without her even knowing she was its prisoner.

Casey twisted around. She looked toward the bed, as though she expected to see herself resting on it and the abiding presence of some magnificent pinioned being holding her constrained in her deepening slumber. Her bed was as empty as her list of possible explanations of why she was standing—wide awake, in front of Gabriel—had just become.

She began to retreat as her situation more fully struck her. He allowed her to fall back a step. Then another. And another. Until she began to think it would be much better to remain a captive in the barren center of the room than to find herself pressed helpless against the smooth, white surface of a wall or laid down on the cool, traitorous sheets of her bed. She had not forgotten what good uses Gabriel could put a hard wall or a soft bed.

She stopped. He did the same.

"We should test this theory of yours right now," Gabriel said. "Let's see whether we can snap you out of it, or wake you from this moment altogether. What shall we do? Shall I shake you?" He tightened his hold on her as if that was what he would do if she gave the nod.

"It's not good to shake people," Casey answered. He had already shaken her to the core anyway and it hadn't fixed a thing.

"Shall I pinch you then?" He brushed his fingers across the bare skin of one of her arms.

"No, thanks. I don't want you to pinch me either." She shook his touch off, annoyed.

"Why not? It's a tried and true method to test a dream. Everyone knows that." He touched his fingers to her arm again. "I won't pinch you very hard. A little pinch will do."

"No pinching." Casey drew the two words out as though that would make it more likely he would listen. "None of these ideas is very good, by the way. I would think something like you could do better. Don't you have any less violent solutions?" *What a stupid question.*

"I suppose we could try this instead." His free hand glided down her

192

side to caress the curve of her waist and moved up again to stray across the top of her breasts. His fingers slid along the length of her neck before coming to rest at the trembling curve of her mouth. His lips parted. The razor's edge of his teeth flashed in the smile settling into an insistent bow of pure, deep crimson as he studied her. She stood paralyzed—her breath rising slow and high in her chest, her heart frozen in place—as it faded into something gentler and with nothing of the redness in it which set it apart from the smile of simple mortals.

This was bad. Very bad. A million times worse than a shake or a pinch.

Gabriel was still making his point. "I liked this dress on you in the dream, very much. But I believe I like it better yet here—wet and clinging to your body as it is now. Seeing you standing right in front of me in a small slip of a damp dress and little else is much better than having you held tight under my wings in one of your pretty dreams."

Casey thought about the wings and how nice it would be to lie under them in her damp black dress. Luckily, there were no wings and as much as the dress might please him, it was getting very cold against her skin. Only the places Gabriel's fingers had brushed felt warm. She took that as more a warning to be resolute against him than a temptation to throw caution to the wind. She was sure he would be of the exact opposite opinion but then, she was not about to ask him what he thought so there was no way to tell for certain.

He held her away from him so he could assess her reaction to his touch and what he was saying to her. He took her in with a raw, dilated stare before hiding the hunger in his eyes again but Casey had seen it and it did not improve her state of mind.

"Do not look so startled. Nothing is wrong, my Casey. Do not be so on guard against what you see to be true. Trust yourself. Do you not feel me—the way I am touching you?" He tangled his fingers in her hair before pushing a dark wave away from her face. "The way your body responds to the lightest brush of my hand, the way your heart pounds when I speak to you? Do you think it is not real? Do you not see me standing here? Can you not hear the words I am saying to you?"

He asks a lot of questions for a guy who shouldn't be here at all, Casey thought, wishing she could respond with a resounding no to all of them. He was waiting on her answers and Casey could feel his impatience in his touch. She did not know what to say without giving whatever it was that stood before her more power than it already had, so she remained silent.

His voice grew lower and more insistent for her response. He pulled her a fraction closer and looked down at her with serious eyes. "I, the nightangel Gabriel, am speaking to you, Cassandra; you and no one else in all the world. No other of your kind holds any interest for me—only you, my love. I wish to converse with you—now."

The word "converse" sounded very intimate when it came from Gabriel.

He lifted her chin so her eyes met his. "I am your reality. Look upon me. Speak to me as once you spoke to me in the dreams. Why this waiting? Why this hesitation? How can you not know me?"

More questions. I have some questions too, Mr. I'm-the-Nightangel-Gabriel-and-you-will-swoon-before-me, Casey fumed, averting her eyes. *Like, how can I get rid of you before I get myself in any deeper here?*

Love doesn't conquer all no matter what people say. Falling in love with the wrong person is playing with fire. She'd watched her brother tear his life apart for love. She wasn't going to do the same. Not even for her disarmingly beautiful angel. She knew a damn wildfire when she saw one. There was no way to put something like that out once it took hold.

His finger under her chin moved her look upward again until her eyes were pinned to his. Casey was finding it difficult to open her mouth to speak with him staring with such deep interest into her face. Only the fact that she thought he might be going to kiss her caused her to start talking as though her life depended on it. She knew she had better get right to the point. "I want you to go away. I don't care what you are—fantasy or flesh and blood or—or something else. Whatever it is, it doesn't matter. Nothing can happen between us so just leave."

The nightangel stayed put. "But you invited me here."

"I don't call that an invitation."

"There are all kinds of invitations. Yours will do."

"Is there a way to uninvite you?"

"Not really."

"Will you let go of me?"

"Not yet."

"Fine," Casey said. "Then will you just listen to me?"

"Go ahead, my own. When you speak, it will always please me to listen." Gabriel tilted his head to indicate he was waiting for her to start.

She wondered whether he would be all that happy about listening after he heard what she had to say.

194

❮ CHAPTER TWENTY ❯

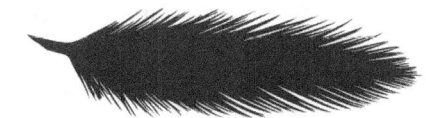

"LOOK. WE'VE HAD OUR little talk and that's nice but I want you to go now. I don't care if you're talking to me when you don't have a desire to speak to any other. I don't give a damn who you say you are. It doesn't make any difference to me. I want you to leave me alone." She shook off his fingers. They settled back at her neck where the pulse beat. She tried to raise her voice but instead, the next words slipped out of her mouth like quiet fugitives. "Get out of my bedroom. Get out of my life. You have no right to be here. Take your hands off me and go."

His fingers grew still but he did not obey. She could have sworn he looked wounded before his features began to harden. Instead of making her sorry for him, it made her more desperate to be rid of him. She did not want a nightangel so determined to have his way standing in her bedroom with her no matter how much he said he had the right to be there.

"Don't you understand? I have no interest in speaking to you about anything beyond your departure. Nothing can happen between us in the real world. Nothing really happened in the dreams." Her blood was banging wildly against the cold weight of his fingertips as she spoke the lie neither of them believed. "Leave now. And stay away. You're not welcome here." *There, that should do something.*

His look iced over. The strange warmth of his fingers drained, then surged. Did anyone ever talk back to him?

"You are my avowed one. How can I be unwelcome here, considering that?"

She did not know what being his avowed one meant but it sounded serious and like something a nightangel would not step away from once it was declared out loud. "Why should I go? Why should I not think we are of the same mind and act on it, no matter what you say now to the contrary? We both know you and I have often wished for this moment to occur between us. Why can we not begin?"

"I have not. I have never—"

"You have as much as pledged yourself to me in your words, in your actions, in your thoughts, in every daydream you have dreamed. Do you think you can deny it now?

He frowned down at her with hard, emerald eyes. "How can you not know? You are my beloved and you shall be with me—not in the dream. That is done. You shall do so here."

Now she was his beloved. It did not sound any less binding than being his avowed one but at least it had a more romantic ring to it and she had a better idea what it meant.

"You have misunderstood something I've done and taken it to mean something it doesn't." Casey was glad she had never spoken the words. All would have been lost then.

"There is no mistake. I am not leaving, beloved. This is no dream and I am no dreamed-of creature you can dismiss at your whim. I did love your dreams though, Casey. I enjoyed every minute I spent with you there. But you know, cautious maiden, they will never be enough in the end. It is time to live in the world together."

"You don't belong here."

"I have a place in this world even if you do not think I ought to have it. Perhaps you are confused because you have known me in the daydreams before you have seen me here. But that does not mean I come from the dreams any more than it means you do."

You couldn't just watch kitten videos or play word games on your smartphone to chill out, could you, Casey? Oh, no. You had to daydream about nightangels. This is your fault.

She wondered where the dreamangel Gabriel's place in the world was and she hoped it was not somewhere in the safety zone of her suburban neighborhood.

"Why should I believe you can live in any world beyond a daydream when I'm not even sure I know what you are?"

"Nightangel, Bloodangel. Vampire. Friend. Champion. Protector." Her visitor ticked off the words like a general calling forth his army. "Not a dream." He paused to let the weight of those last three words sink in. "Is that what you wished to hear from me?"

"No. I'd rather you tell me something a lot less disturbing," she said. Believing him. Not believing him. Intrigued. Appalled.

"You asked me to speak of what I am and I have obliged you."

"Well thanks. I'm sure you're trying to be helpful but what's it all supposed to mean to me?"

She wished instead of answering he would provide her with a FAQ and leave without another word so she could read it at her leisure and find the loophole that would shut the angel down. Angels weren't too big on written explanations though. They liked to tell you things. Sometimes they enjoyed quizzing you later. And they liked contracts—unspoken ones that counted for everything. At least this angel did.

She waited for his wings—fierce and wildly beautiful—to sprout in response to her insolent question but they did not. Casey shook her head. She was surprised at the lack of wings although it was probably best given how provoked this nightangel was beginning to look.

"It means that just as you wanted, the dream is done. There is no need for dreams when the archangel is here in the world with the dreamer."

Oh damn. Maybe she could get assigned to the Seattle office. Seattle was good. Except for the rain. She was not big on too much rain. Maybe L.A. She could do that. Except for the earthquake thing. She was not too hot on that. Why should she have to move to Seattle or L.A. because of him? She would have to hope he leaned toward a D.C. or Maryland address.

He beheld her while she devised this cross-country move as if he could not get enough of her standing there with him even if she was being difficult, as if he saw the potential for all he would have in her and with her and could not wait to begin. He thought to rule her even as he bowed to her. Casey felt it in the way he held her close enough to saturate every fiber of her being with a sense of his desire for her. He was sure that in the end, the outcome would be the one he wished for them.

This intrigued her more than a modern woman should be willing to admit. The idea of putting herself in the angel's hands and yielding to his wishes was both tempting and terrifying.

"What do you want?" She said in a small, hoarse voice instead of disputing the point.

"I want to know you, and for you to come to know me, as we have not done and cannot do in the state of a dream—no matter how beautiful that dream world might be."

"You know me already, don't you? That's what you keep telling me."

He did not respond but he took a step closer to her.

"Answer me. Why don't you answer? If you're what you say, then you must know everything there is to know about me," she said, as if her question would stop him coming any nearer. She was trembling in her damp dress and bare feet with the cold of his hands seeping through her body. She took a step back from him.

"Knowledge is power. You are afraid I know too much and you, not enough. You need not be afraid. I know many things about you; it is true. Little things. Big things. The things you have told me. The things I have observed. Those things I have made it my business to discover. I know what your dreams are made of. I know what you desire and think you can and cannot have. There is more to learn than that."

"What else can there be?" Casey was worried he knew her a whole lot better than she knew herself.

"There is what we could never hope to say and share and do together in a paradise of garden paths and petal-colored skies. I want your love— here. I want you to give it to me of your own volition. I want to love you back—forever and without fail."

I am going to be in deep trouble if he gets even a portion of what he wants. If she was not so busy feeling traumatized by what he had said to her, she would be worried sick about how skilled a nightangel would be at obtaining what it desired when it was walking around in the real world instead of a daydream.

"What about what I want?"

"I believe what you want and what I want are not far apart."

"I don't think so. Not at all. I won't do it," Casey said with a sort of horrified petulance. "You can't make me either." She tore her eyes away from his for an instant but he lowered his face toward hers until she found herself even more trapped in his gaze than before.

He was much less intimidating in the dreams and that was saying something because in the dreams he could be downright formidable when it suited his purposes. And here she had thought she was getting a full dose of fearsome nightangel now and again in the dream. *Wrong.* She had been so wrong.

Gabriel took little notice of anything but the quiver of her lips as she spoke each word. She was infuriated at her obvious display of weakness before him. She tried once more to tear herself from his grip. The temperature of the room was dropping again like a cold snap on a fine fall day and although she could not see them, she felt the stir of frigid wings moving around her.

Talk about a sudden cold spell. She was freezing. What she needed right that very minute was a good, hot cup of cocoa to take the chill off and an express ticket out of town under an untraceable assumed name, Casey thought, as the angel honed in on her lips in a way that promised a whole new level of trouble.

"You must. You will." Gabriel's voice became lower and more intimate. He pressed his hand against her heart. Her trembling subsided and a soothing heat radiated through her. The warmth of the angel's touch was leaps and bounds better than hot cocoa, even if you were to throw whipped cream and marshmallows on top for good measure. With his fingers pressing against her heartbeat, he began to speak again. "I wish to be your love outright as you are mine already. Be with me. I will make you happy. There is little you could wish for I cannot give you, my own."

"You don't have to worry about giving me things. I don't want anything from you. Everything I want, I can get for myself."

"Not everything. I can take you past the ordinary. I will give you the adventure you long for; the freedom you dream about; the contentment that eludes you. Won't you shake off your fear and accept what I am offering, Casey? I would begin if you would take my hand and say you wished it too."

She had to give him points for how extremely hot he was when he got all sincere and forthright. There was nothing like an earnest nightangel in the midst of declaring heartfelt emotions. But it did not matter. Even if she did like the idea of that sort of contentment, she did not see how it could result from investing in a relationship with a creature such as Gabriel, no matter how earnest or hot he was. The injustice of their situation struck her.

He continued. "Give yourself permission to know me in this world. Take a chance on us, Casey."

His speaking grew quieter, his tone more fervent. "Lie with me, Casey. Give yourself to me. I will love you well. I swear it."

Despite her desire to radiate cool disinterest, Casey's eyes grew wide at the thought of sex with the nightangel and the audacity of his suggestion. *Who says things like that?* Casey thought, giving some impromptu consideration to what lying with a nightangel would entail at the same time.

"I require more than the substance of a fantasy to sustain me. This suits me much better."

He looked around as if he was standing in a five star hotel suite instead of a suburban bedroom. He liked real and Casey did not see how she could make that work to her advantage.

"I want the pleasure of your company outside the dreams. And I shall have it, Casey."

Casey was always amazed by how presumptuous a nightangel could be and Gabriel was knocking the ball out of the park tonight. *Pleasure of your company. Right.* "Lie with me" was a hell of a lot more honest take on the scenario he envisioned, she thought while trying without success not to imagine rolling around in bed with her angel like there was no tomorrow. *Of course, she would never do that…*

She was beginning to feel sorry for him. Maybe things that crossed over from dreams did not get how things went in the day-to-day world. She hated to be the one to break it to him but an ordinary mortal and not-ordinary-at-all nightangel were not going to work out in the end in the romance department—or any other department—no matter what he thought. "Don't bank on it. We're not in a dream anymore, you know."

"So you admit that now."

Casey had not meant to admit it because she still was not a hundred percent sure what was going on. It had come out of her mouth though, so maybe he was right and she was leaning more toward real angel-vampire-whatever than dream gone wild, even if she hadn't realized it.

"I guess so, for now at least." *Until I figure out how to toss you out on your ear.*

"Good." He was satisfied with this small bit of progress. Ridiculously satisfied.

"Regarding this relationship thing. Just an FYI. It's not all about you, you know. I'm a piece of the equation too." He smiled like he had an

FYI for her on the tip of his tongue. Casey dreaded hearing what it would be.

"That's true. Let's do the math then. Two can equal one when you do it right."

Casey gave a dramatic sigh. Gabriel providing her a lesson in math was much worse than her giving him one well-intentioned FYI. Not a fair exchange at all.

He continued, his smile fading. "As it is, we both suffer for want of the other. Being your shadow serves a purpose but it is lonely work. And you—you miss me so much you cannot find a way to fill up the emptiness left to you without me. You whispered as much to me in the last dream. Did you forget?"

Casey looked down so she would not have to answer.

"Do not be frightened. You can tell the truth. I mean you no harm."

More angel-speak. If he was a nightangel then he was bound to do her harm, whether purposeful or not. Nightangels were vampires. He said so. And vampires drank blood, probably lots and lots of it. Blood from mortals like her. Flapping those mighty wings around must stir up quite a thirst. "I'm not afraid. I just don't like the way you do your math."

"I am very good at sums, dreamer. And it adds up—you and me together. Casey, don't look like you cannot believe it. Trust in me. Be happy I am here. Give yourself over to what is already between us and rejoice in our future together."

Maybe when creatures from the other side crossed over they became delusional. He could not believe she was going to shift from resistance to being thrilled he had arrived to complicate her life. "There's nothing between us and I'm not starting up anything with you either," she said, rather than telling him he was crazy straight out.

"Too late for that. What's done is done. The bond between us does not exist in one place and not another. This is not our start. We started down this path together long ago. This is our beginning here in this place."

"Even if that were true, it won't last. It can't last. Not here. You have to know that."

"What you and I have, Casey, does not end or fade away. It builds upon itself. It grows stronger. If I thought otherwise, I would never have approached you. Not even in a dream. I am not heartless. I am not careless or cruel."

"But you are scary," she blurted out. *Super scary in a confusing go-ahead-and-throw-me-down-on-the-bed-and-have-your-way-with-me-right-now/oh-damn-why-am-I-even-thinking-that kind of way.*

Unhappiness at her perception of him swept across his features. "I am no monster. At the worst, I am just different from you. And in many ways, Casey Sloane, we are not very different at all."

"Right. Like I believe that one. Excuse me. *Vampire.* Enough said."

"I am amazed at the truths you will not believe and the falsehoods you are so eager to embrace. When did a vampire become a creature of pure darkness in your eyes? It disappoints me that you have not learned all the lessons I have sought to teach to you during our time together. It is fortunate for you I am a patient instructor and you are my favorite student. You must try much harder to understand the things I tell you though. I need to see at least a little progress here. If not, I will have to teach the lessons a different way."

Casey had a feeling a different way meant a way she was not going to like at all.

"I'll take my chances," she answered, resolving to avoid any potential teachable moments. To want the teacher so much and turn from the lesson was ridiculous.

"Do as you must. I believe the outcome will be the same no matter which sort of learner you choose to be."

Casey was getting so steamed about learning lessons from a vampire who was nothing but a dream she pushed back on the question that made her the most uneasy about having him there with her—ever—no matter what he turned out to be. "I find it hard to believe, seeing as how you are some kind of vampire and all, that when things go down the tubes between us, like I think they would in the end if I were ever crazy enough to get involved with you in the first place—which I won't, so don't think I will—everything is going to be just fine."

He raised his eyebrows in feigned shock at so many denials squashed together in one statement and waited to hear what would come next with a gleam in his eyes that spoke more of amusement than annoyance.

"I know it wouldn't be fine. I don't think you'll just smile one of those maddening smiles of yours and wave goodbye. Doesn't getting involved with you have some dangerous possibilities attached to it by default?"

"I will not hurt you. I would never do that."

Oh, alright then, that's all settled. Casey made a little dismissive noise in her throat. Why should she believe him?

"I will always look to your safety, Cassandra Sloane. I will always seek your welfare. It is my greatest duty to you, dreamer."

"If I was looking for a bodyguard that would be a great answer but I'm not, so it isn't."

Something icy and hard brushed against the back of her legs. Casey imagined a cold arc of tremendous wings rising up around her like a fortress. Even though she couldn't actually see the wings exploding into the air where nothing was before, she felt their energy, their presence. She just wished she could get a look at the damn things. Gabriel all in wings was a sight to behold and she was sorry to be deprived of it.

"What I love, I protect. And, Casey, my bespoken, I love you. That love will not change no matter what you do. No harm will ever befall you at my hand. There is your answer and there is my promise."

Bespoken? Aric had said something about that too. *What the hell was that?* Casey wasn't sure but bespoken had a ring to it that left beloved and avowed one in the dust. "That's not much of an answer to my question. You only say it because you think everything will go your way and nothing mine."

"It answers it well enough. It is more of a response than your question deserves. Why are you asking anyway when you insist you will have nothing of me?"

Casey did not have an answer to give him that would not wind up coming out sounding like all the things he wanted her to tell him and she never had. She knew a trick question when she heard one. She remained silent.

"What have I done to earn such sudden distrust from you?"

"Confused me—that's what. I hate that I don't get what's going on here and you think you do."

"Then I will endeavor to erase your confusion. I will make it easy for you. I will tell you what comes next."

"Maybe I'm not interested in knowing what comes next."

The angel however, had some information to impart. Casey would prefer he use the U.S. mail so she could toss his message into her circular file unopened but the nightangel Gabriel, like any proper angel, was dead set on delivering it in person and without delay.

≪ CHAPTER TWENTY-ONE ≫

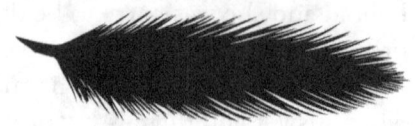

IF HE WERE IN wings now, they would be turning an ashy gray that would grow ember red at the edges before he was done speaking, the kind of burning red that always reflected a deep frustration on his part. Although no wings were in sight, the tone of his voice was smoldering with, what Casey thought, was a barely restrained desire to force her into a state of immediate understanding. Casey did not think such behavior was particularly angelic but then Gabriel was his own kind of angel.

"I fear your lack of understanding comes from a stubbornness to accept the truth rather than a real lack of comprehension. Pay attention, dreamer."

He did not have to be so angry when it was his fault this was happening in the first place, Casey fumed. She did not intend to listen to another word he said. As she had done in the garden, she had already closed her mind to his words.

Casey thought he knew this is what she would choose to do. He was looking at her with the same unwavering glance he had held her with when he had pressed her against the sharp roses growing high and thick on the garden wall within her dreams during their last dispute. She had not come out so well during that argument. But now he was in her world. That had to give her some edge.

As he began speaking, all hopes of prevailing against him began to crumble. If he was a dream, he was convinced enough he was not to still do a lot of damage.

"It's very simple. I have come to claim you. You will keep the promises you made to me—even if unspoken. But not just in the dream, that is not enough. You must keep them here."

How could I not have seen? Casey stifled a groan. In the eyes of the nightangel, the dreams might be a testing ground of possibilities—each one its own unspoken promise waiting to be realized beyond the borders of her daydreams.

"You will love me back—in this world. You will speak the words— all the words—in this world. You will give yourself to me—in this world. We will be as one—here in this world. Nothing else will do. No other outcome is acceptable to me. Soon enough it will be the same for you."

He examined her face to see if perhaps that was the case now that he had spoken so candidly. Casey must have looked as though she was digging in instead of seeing the light because she could sense those invisible wings growing even grayer than before.

His beautiful brow furrowed the smallest bit. "Can I make my intentions plainer? Can I speak my will more bluntly? I wait for you. I cannot wait forever. Still. I wait. Be warned, dreamer of dreams. I grow weary."

At least he had stopped saying "in this world" in that chipped ice tone. She'd be more relieved if she hadn't gotten his message so well— *I'm here. I'm staying. You're mine. Get used to it.*

But she was not going to get used to it. "You can't have what I won't give." Her eyes turned a frosted shade of blue. "And I have nothing I wish to give to you right now."

"Right now," he laughed. "Well put. You mean to give me battle but you shall not win, my own. Your sword has fallen from your hands and your shield shall soon be cast aside as well; you have already ceded the battle to me." The lilt of his laughter cut across the small space between them.

The way he said "my own" as if he really meant it and she really was, if nothing else, exactly that to him no matter how she might argue against it, made her think that maybe to believe anything else was absurd. She had not expected his reaction. Anger, frustration, sadness, furious insistence, any of these she would have expected, but not amusement.

She flushed schoolgirl-pink and then paled again under his indulgent gaze. "No." She shook her head. "It's not true. I'm not yours. I don't belong to anyone except myself."

"Refusing to face the truth does not change it. You carry me in your heart. Don't try to deny it."

"I don't carry you in my heart." She hissed the words at him like a frightened little garden snake caught far out of the protective cover of the high grass. "Nothing could be further from the truth. I could never belong to you or to anyone at all. This is the modern world, sir. Women don't think that way anymore. People don't belong to one another. That only happens in romance novels and the fairytales you read when you're a kid. I'm not yours. I'll never be yours." She hoped he did not know how much she loved fairytales and how many romance novels she had read throughout law school to lighten the pressure of academic life. That would take some of the kick out of her statement to him.

He did not seem to be thinking about fairytales and novels, or her secret pleasure in them. He was concerned with setting the record straight. "You were happy to be mine in the dreams, even if you never spoke of it. You are mine, dreamer, and nothing you can say will change that." He made his pronouncement with a quiet conviction that terrified her.

She was afraid he might be right, that he might know something trapped deep inside her of which she was not yet aware. The possibility that such a thing could be true was damned annoying. Casey would not let it be true because she would not like this insolent dream to be right on such a basic point—and right from the get-go too. She shot a look of out-and-out fury dead into his face. "I guess being a nightangel makes you naturally arrogant."

Gabriel's lovely brow furrowed a fraction more. *Good.* She was on a roll.

"Well, I think you are mine—mine to keep or dismiss as I choose. How about that? And I believe I should dismiss you."

"Yet, you will not." His brow began to clear. Her angry looks pleased him; there was a mocking admiration in his gaze. "Such eyes. You would strike me down with one angry look from them if you could. And so unusual—the different shades of blue they turn depending on your mood. I am captivated anew every time I look into them. What makes you think I will not have such a treasure as you, my beautiful blue-eyed dreamer, for my own?"

Casey had never thought much of her blue eyes. She believed, if

206

anything, they made her look too sweet, too innocent, when she needed to look like she played hardball. *Stupid blue eyes.* "I'm not a thing to be possessed. I told you already, I'm not yours; I'll never be yours."

She wished she had a winter parka at hand and he'd give her a minute to slip it on. This little black dress thing was getting old—and cold. The words he spoke frosted the air and only his hands upon her kept her from shaking in the face of this angel-generated storm front pushing through her room.

"You are being childish, Cassandra. You choose to misunderstand me." He began to walk her back. Step by step. Until her spine was pressed against the rigid spike of a white wrought iron bedpost. "It is difficult not to become annoyed with you. You are always so stubborn, Casey. It is a great trial at times to deal with such a headstrong nature without becoming vexed at its possessor. Can you not see the truth of it? Your dreams have betrayed you. Your heart and body will do the same in time. Surrender to your feelings. They are not wrong."

She concentrated on her answer. She tried to ignore the edge of the bed that cut against her leg. She tried not to think about what would happen if he pushed her down on it. "You can't make me care for you." It was the one thing she could think to say that would give him pause.

"But I have already, haven't I?"

Damn him to hell if he wasn't right, Casey admitted to herself with deepening resentment.

"Well, haven't I?" Gabriel inquired again. "Haven't I made you care for me?"

"No. No. Of course not—" She broke off. *Your dreams have betrayed you. Your dreams have betrayed you.* She flushed and beneath her rising color, undisguised dread was rising faster.

"Surely, I have done that at least. Why not admit it? Tell the truth. It is the truth, is it not? You care for me already." He smiled in the way he had which usually extracted answers from her she had not been prepared to give.

"Care for you?"

"Well, you do, don't you?"

"No, of course not. Well maybe, once in a while. Okay, sometimes. Yes, sort of. God, I don't know. In a way, I guess I do." Casey found herself babbling a series of weakening denials in the face of his encouraging smile. "It doesn't matter anyhow," she declared, as if that could negate everything she had just said.

"No, of course not. Well maybe, once in a while. Okay, sometimes. Yes, sort of. God. I don't know. In a way. I guess I do," he repeated. It sounded absolutely damning the way he lingered over each word like he just had to hear them again even if he had to say them back to her to do it. "What kind of answer is that?" He gave her another fainter smile, as if he knew what she meant anyway.

She thought he might be teasing her. He stared at her in a way that made it evident he was still quite interested in what she would have to say in return. He took his hand from her heart and she began to tremble again. She hated that her body was such a traitor; it revealed everything to him she would not say.

"And no matter what you tell me, Casey, we both know it does matter."

She was going to fall to pieces. Shake apart. Embark upon a fit of hysterics. All before his eerily calm eyes. "I think you are confused."

"Then enlighten me, I entreat you, wise dreamer."

"What you are talking about—"

"You mean about how you already care for me."

"Yes." Casey stammered. "I mean, no." She rushed to correct herself. She took a deep breath. She did not know what the right answer was but she knew he had stepped over the limit of what she could deal with from him and this whole thing had to stop. She had had enough. He had to go before he witnessed a major meltdown.

"Yes or no. You do care."

"Stop saying that. Just listen. What you were talking about. That was the dream. It's all made up. Come on. How could you not know that? You think you're so smart and that you hold all the cards." She let the smug edge of a smile play across her lips. "Well, at least I know the difference between some daydream and real life. It's amazing to me what you've allowed yourself to believe and what you're doing because of it. All in the name of some stupid dreams and some stuff that happened there that wasn't real at all."

His mouth tightened but an indulgent curve touched the edges. He did not argue with her. He waited for her to continue.

Casey was emboldened by his reaction. Maybe he would listen to her now. Maybe he would go before she spun apart. She stood stiff as a soldier and spoke in her most serious tone. "I can't be with you. Not here. Not now. Not ever."

His silence said he did not believe her. Fear crawled through her veins.

What if he would not leave—would never leave? She could not open her world, her life, her heart to something that could sweep away everything she valued with one casual pulse of its wings. Whether he was real or a momentary embodiment of her wildest dreams he was not going to be staying. If she had to wound him to make him stalk off to tend to his injuries in the lilac light of the daydreams, then she would wound him with every word she said.

The angel's eyes were as wide and silent as the empty field of her dreams—waiting for her, waiting for what came next.

She cooled her look and shot her next words at him like they were throwing stars covered in ice. She tossed them at him as hard as she could. "Go away. Get out of here. I could never care for you. I don't want to be with you. I don't know why you think I would." She did not like to lie but what choice did she have?

The angel's fingers tensed against her skin. "As much as you love your dreams, you have to be realistic. Is that it?"

That was one way of putting it. Loving the dreams was like loving the angel. The angel had become the heart of the dream. She wasn't going to clarify that point for him. She wasn't even going to admit it to herself. She shrugged off his question.

An ache brushed across the surface of the nightangel's eyes like a frost icing over bright green grass. Her words had hit their mark.

Her resolve to injure him was swept away by the overpowering need to soften the blow. Why be cruel? Nightangels had feelings too and they were nothing to mess around with. "I apologize if I misled you. I never meant to do that, I swear. This is just a big mistake. I'd undo it if I could. I didn't mean to cause you any pain."

He ought to be turning to go. She ought to be running off and locking all the doors even though it didn't matter. But the angel held her like a prize he had gone to great trouble to secure. He was not releasing her. He was clutching her tighter, drawing her closer. How could she forget—the nightangel had made up his mind and if she had a chance in hell of getting him to change it, there could be no soft words, only hard ones.

Casey pulled as far back from him as he would allow—a fraction and

209

nothing more. "Now go. And don't come back. You aren't welcome here. Are you listening to me?" She gave him her best don't-screw-with-me look.

It was not doing the job because instead of backing off, he dropped a kiss against her frowning lips. *Damn.*

"Yes, I am listening." He touched his fingers to her hair; stroking a stray strand off her brow, resting his fingers in a handful of it. "You are very brave. I believe you would wage war with me if you thought you must. You would do what others more suited for the battle would turn and flee from. And look at you. You stand ready to fight. You steal my breath away, dreamer."

Casey was having trouble breathing herself.

You have no idea of everything you are—everything you can be."

If only angels didn't like talking in riddles so very much. What did he mean? She knew what she was. She was an ordinary woman with no nightangel to worry her outside of her daydreams—at least usually. She knew what she was going to be—a partner at Phillips & Row. That was her goal. *That's enough. That should be enough. It had to be enough.* She shuddered to think what the angel perceived her be-all-you-can-be state in life. It was better not to know.

Casey found it hard not to quake in front of Gabriel. He had the whole angel in charge thing going and he had no intention of listening to her tonight. He was not planning to leave at the moment. She did not know how to send him away. She had tried everything she could think of and none of it had done the trick. Now, she was not sure whether sending him away would keep her safe or turn out to be the biggest mistake of her life. She knew she was being softhearted but she did not want to toss him into oblivion no matter how big of a pain he was being at the moment. He didn't deserve that. "I'm sorry, really sorry," she said. And she was. Sick-at-heart sorry.

"I am full of admiration for you, Casey. I am well aware I am a formidable thing to come upon in any world and yet you confront me here as if you could turn me aside with a few firm words and a stern tone. How easy it is to hold you dear, even when you are being exceedingly foolish. You are all sweetness."

"You're getting it all wrong. I couldn't be less sweet. I'm very un-sweet."

"Un-sweet?" Amusement danced across the curve of his lips before they drew into a serious line again. "Is that so? Yet, you even care about the feelings of something you think may be nothing but a figment of your imagination that has sprung to life and taken a wrong turn."

She hated that the nightangel was so I-just-came-down-from-on-high-to-see-you breathtaking. It made things—like telling him to take a hike back into the daydreams—much more difficult.

He brought his mouth down until he could whisper his next words against her lips. "I will woo you if you wish, like a Victorian virgin, and we shall proceed at a sedate pace though it shall pain me. Or you can fall into my arms tonight without another thought or argument. I will not betray your trust."

She was starting to feel an affinity for Victorian virgins. She was certain he was hoping for the opposite reaction. What else should he think after she had lectured him on what modern women were all about. "You need to go. I can't do what you ask—even if I wanted to do it, which I don't. I'm not afraid to say you scare the living daylights out of me."

That seemed kind of appropriate considering what he was. Maybe that was what he was supposed to do when he was around mortals. She was sure he could not help it. It wasn't like she was mad about it anyway. She just thought he should know because it put a major cramp on any true comfort level developing between them. Yet another reason for him to give up and be on his way.

"If you're what you claim, that fear of you will never change. I could never trust you. I'd be a fool to do that."

"I have given you my promise—my sworn word—you will be safe with me."

"It's not enough. You're a vampire, remember? You told me so. What good is the promise of something like a vampire?"

"I should think you would know the value of my promises already."

Nightangels were always so deadly serious about their promises. When applied outside the dreams, it was bound to lead to worrisome consequences. "I don't care about that. I can't be friends with a vampire—no matter what kind. Not here, anyway. It's crazy and I don't like crazy."

"You want to think it is crazy because you cannot believe you are considering being with me—a nightangel, walking the world—for even an instant. How contrary of you, Casey, as you were willing, eager even, to conduct such a relationship with me for so long in a much more

211

treacherous place than here in the everyday world."

Casey grew pale. She had been stupid in understanding the real power of the dreams but she wasn't quite as foolish in understanding the problems around a relationship with a living, breathing Gabriel no matter how she chose to classify him in the real world.

"Just because I was stupid then doesn't mean I'll be stupid now. You aren't going to happen in my life."

"Yet, here I am."

Yup, there he was. All invisible wings and hidden glory—like the explosive light of the sun burns unseen before the sunrise.

"It won't work. So forget it."

That light shone in his eyes, his smile, heating up his touch. "It can, if you will let it."

"Not likely. I just have to look at you to know the chances are good you'd mess up my life beyond repair if I let you into it here in this world. I don't have time to create utter chaos in my life right now so I can entertain some wayward fantasy. I wish you'd stayed in the dream where you belonged. It was easier."

And I loved it, she thought. *And now it's ruined.*

"Head out. We're done here."

He considered her for a disquieting moment. She considered him right back for an extra beat.

"You will find yourself at my side before too many more nights have passed. In time, you will wonder why you held back from your fate tonight. It is not as hard as you think to take my hand on this side of your dreams. I do not know why you will not at least try."

Casey looked at him as if maybe, he had just rolled back in town after a long break in a mental health facility that hadn't quite served its purpose. "I said we're done here."

His eyes brightened to a shade of green the sky can turn before a tornado. "In time, you will regret every moment you kept yourself from me. It will become clear to you that to be mine is everything you want. For now, I will wait. Call me, Casey. I will answer. Do it soon. If you do not, I will come for you. I will find a way to bring us together again." His mouth moved over the words like the sunset center of a candle flame, fading again to almost ordinary as he finished.

No way, Casey thought, but she did not interrupt him because she wanted to watch his lips form more words in that way he had when he was being adamant. The nightangel could read the directions on an aspirin bottle and it would be mesmerizing.

"Do not wait too long. I begin to tire of this cat and mouse game you have lured me into playing with you. Do not drive me to affect our next meeting. You may not like what I devise. Patience is a virtue but it has its limits, Casey. Three days. Three nights. That is what I can give to you. It is a small piece of forever. I place it in your hand with my promise and this kiss."

Fine, kiss my hand. Make your promises. Big whoop. She did not care what he did as long as he would get the hell out of her bedroom, out of her house, out of her life.

He pulled the fingers of one of her hands open and pressed his cool lips against her skin. This kiss, centered in her palm was seductive, intimate, and possessive. It held a sweetness to it that stung the flesh and heart alike. Nobody had ever kissed any part of her exactly like this. Gabriel took his time in giving it as if he knew that one little act would turn her world upside down forever. And it had. One kiss burnt like a brand of ruby ice into her palm by a nightangel, or whatever the hell he was, was worth more in her estimation than the composite impact of her entire romantic past, such as it now stood. They both knew it was unfair. But it was true. Casey began to tremble worse than before.

The nightangel folded her fingers over the moist trace of his promise, trapping the feeling radiating between them there a moment longer; holding his kiss a willing captive within the quivering prison of her hand. He looked a little shell-shocked and his reaction made her feel the power of his kiss even more.

Okay, so he knew how to explode her universe without much of an effort. *Hurray for him.* She just had to never see him again and all would be well or almost okay. Really, it would be crappy but she could not be hanging out with vampires from dreams no matter what.

"I would be done with patience and waiting. But I see that it is what you require so I shall give it to you."

Casey knew he was annoyed with her. Maybe he thought that in the end, she was more Victorian virgin than modern woman and he would have to go with it or she would become more troublesome. She did not think it was what he expected. She had definitely put a crimp in his plans. She was making him wait. And he did not like to wait. That was too bad because he was going to have to wait until hell froze over.

213

Someone stressing you out, Mr.Big Bad Archangel? Welcome to my world, Casey thought. *Deal with it.*

He gave her a last intense look that spoke of annoyance more than ardor before releasing her. She rubbed her hands against her wrists and for a moment she stood as if he still held her there. He watched her recover herself, then walked away in silence. He turned at the door.

"Goodnight, Cassandra Sloane. Sleep well. When you wake, think of me. Think well on me and what I have said to you tonight. Yesterday was yours but it is already gone. Today is mine as you have seen. Tomorrow shall be ours. Resolve yourself to it. I am your future. I am your fate. I will not be denied. I await you."

What about the Victorian virgin thing? Okay, so she wasn't actually a Victorian virgin but still, if she had wanted to go the Victorian virgin route, shouldn't that mean she would automatically be given more than three days? She was sure it should. "Then you will wait forever," she said, instead of arguing about it.

He did not answer.

"Do you hear me?"

He was leaving.

"Forever. You will wait forever." Alright, maybe she was arguing with him after all.

He paused in the doorway. He turned toward her again and when his eyes had come back to rest on her, she wished she had shut up and let him go. What was she doing, drawing his attention back to her when he was on his way to being gone as she had asked? His fingers tightened against either end of the doorway as if they were the painted edges of the dream. When he spoke his voice was clear and compelling. It leapt across the room and caught hold of her with such force she did not know how she remained standing.

"No, Casey."

She staggered back from the sound of that voice, trying to catch her breath again. It followed after her. She could not block out the echo of it.

"No, my love."

Casey found it hard not to crumble beneath that searing, ethereal voice.

"No, my own." His lips moved like metal heated dangerous red for an instant, parting and meeting again to form each blunt, ember word. "No, my heart." His face was resolute, spectral pale, assured. "Tomorrow never waits."

214

And then he was gone.

When she was certain he had disappeared, she sunk to the floor. She could feel the scraping of his sharp, invisible wings against her stunned heart long past the instant of his departure. *No. Casey.* Each weighted word dropped again and again into that quickly beating place; they saturated the haven Gabriel's daggered pinions had carved within the very center of her being to hold his promise. *No, my love. No, my own. No, my heart.* It caused the strangest ache to grow there—a pure, clear, sweet kind of pain; pulsing, pulsing, pulsing. She was not sure it was going to go away.

Tomorrow never waits. Casey closed her eyes against the echo of his presence. It lingered on; pressing her beneath its wings, lying as his burning kiss upon each shallow breath she took. *Tomorrow never waits.* She looked down at her hand. The shadow of his scarlet kiss stained her flesh. The whisper of his own blood left as a seal upon his vow. *Tomorrow never waits.* She could not take her eyes from it. *Never.*

Gabriel had said "never" and Casey felt with all her heart she would be a fool not to believe him. She wondered whether "never" was negotiable. She dragged herself up off the floor and crept out of her room as though she was on a recon mission. When Gabriel did not jump out from the shadows, she shot down the hall to the kitchen with her plan already formed. She was going to have that cup of tea—even if she did have to throw it into a travel mug—and then she was going to get into her car and drive to Ricki's. She was going to stay there a while—three days to be exact. And maybe a few more after that just to be on the safe side. That way, if she was lucky, she could lay low long enough to not have to find out what *never* meant in the mind of a nightangel set on having his way in the real world.

"Luck, be a lady tonight," Casey implored, knowing very well the odds were already stacked against her. After all, Lady Luck was much more inclined to be interested in helping out Prince Charming than some chick who didn't even know how to play a proper game of poker.

≪ CHAPTER TWENTY-TWO ≫

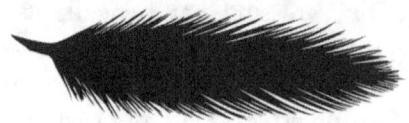

CASEY HELD HER BREATH and hoped that Ed was not going to say the thing she was certain he was going to say next.

"You'll have to meet with the client right away. Can you fit a seven o'clock appointment into your schedule?"

"Tonight?" Casey knew Ed was not asking her a question even if he phrased it as one but the word popped out of her mouth anyway.

"Is that a problem?"

It was more a major inconvenience than a full out problem. Ricki was hell-bent on making sure Casey got her mind off her troubles even if she would not tell Ricki what they were. Ricki had expressed her suspicion that Casey was suffering from some extended form of daydream withdrawal and Casey supposed that was close enough. Ricki's surefire cure was a show at a D.C. club to see a favorite band. Casey agreed to go because she thought the show would be sold out. She was wrong and now the envelope with the tickets was nestled in her purse like one of those chips they give alcoholics in a recovery program. Not going was not an option.

Besides, she was pumped up about it now that the tickets were in her possession. Ricki thought music had a kind of magic to it. She thought maybe it did too. If anything could make her feel better it would be a good dose of earsplitting electric guitar riffs punctuated by pounding drum beats, lyrics she knew by heart, a few drinks, a good friend to keep her company without bugging her with questions she could not answer, and a nice, hard sofa to toss and turn on later without anything running through her head but a favorite song on a hypnotic auto loop. She was going to the concert no matter what.

"No, of course not." Casey began rearranging the evening in her mind.

"I can take the meeting, if Sloane can't manage it." Derek shifted forward in his chair and got that call-on-me-please look that often overtakes the features of rabid overachievers.

Even if she wanted to say no to the meeting, she could not now on general principle. She had no patience with hyper-competitive colleagues. "No, Derek. I've got it." With hundreds of attorneys at the firm, why did she always find herself sitting in a chair next to Derek Rider?

"Good. I assumed you could. Everything's arranged."

Of course it was. "Okay." And the worst part was it was okay. Casey's plans were late enough to accommodate an evening client meeting. Besides, this way she had a shot at crying off on an update meeting with Derek on their pro bono case.

"We should both be there so they can meet the more senior associate on their legal team too. They'll have more confidence they made the right choice that way."

"As confidence-inducing as I am sure the client would find it, your illustrious presence is not necessary for this meeting, Mr. Rider. Casey can handle it. Don't you have enough to do?"

Casey would have been tempted to grin if she did not know Ed talked to Derek that way because he favored him. That Derek and Ed consulted before the meeting and Derek was guaranteed the best parts of whatever legal work the client generated was nothing new.

Swell. More quality time with Derek.

"It's the first meeting. They want to keep it simple. Let's at least let the client *think* their opinion matters with regard to the way we are handling their legal work."

Casey cringed at the implication that the client was going to get screwed on some level by the eminent firm of Phillips & Row. *Talk about vampires. Here they were—at their most litigious and venomous even minus the fangs and fancy supernatural powers.* In fact, their eyes were bright and hungry now. This new client must have the potential to bring big money to the firm. Casey was surprised he did not let Derek start things off if it was that important. As much as she hated to admit it, Derek was more senior than she was. She could tell he was smarting from this perceived slight and it was going to make things worse between them.

"I've arranged the details with their in-house counsel. Everything is set. This is a preliminary meeting before we dive in. Casey, you'll be their first line of contact. Get it right tonight. I want this client happy from the first meeting."

"I still think it would be better if I were present as well," Derek interrupted. "This first meeting will help set the tone for everything that comes after. Does it make sense to just send Sloane here on her own and hope for the best?"

"Are you questioning my judgment?"

Ed hated that. Her stock just went up a few points while Derek's dropped.

For an instant, Derek froze under Ed's glare. Then, trying to mitigate the damage, he explained himself. "I'm just suggesting we give our new client a better sense of the quality of their legal team at Phillips and Row than one junior associate will be capable of establishing."

"Let's start off in the way the client requested, Derek. We've talked strategy already. Leave it," Ed said in his best lord-and-master tone.

Derek fidgeted in his seat as if this was the most difficult thing in the world to sit still for but he obeyed.

"Casey, there's a packet of documents I've left with Jo. Take them with you. You'll want to get those signed. Don't forget." He gave her a pointed look.

She nodded and looked back over her shoulder toward Jo's desk. Jo patted a manila envelope and gave her a there-goes-your-evening wink before she turned back to her computer. Casey was waiting for Ed to dismiss them by beginning some other task and acting like they had gotten sucked back to their desk via some high tech enhanced productivity tool the firm had just invested in. She was not sucked away into thin air, which was somewhat of a relief, but she was not disappointed by Ed. He started scrolling through his email with a vengeance.

Meeting over. Casey began to stand and Derek rose with her.

"One more thing, Casey."

Almost. She settled back into her seat again. Derek followed suit.

"You'll have to go to the client."

218

A client visit was going to make things much tighter. She would have to toss aside good nutrition for yet another evening and indulge in a packet of cheese and peanut butter crackers washed down with a nice cold can of diet cola. Avoiding nightangels did not encourage healthy eating patterns. Still, the realization she could blow off her end of the day meeting with Derek made it worth sacrificing dinner. Nothing was as bad as sitting in Derek's office while he practiced what he thought were partner-like behaviors. If she wasn't the target of it, she might find it amusing instead of depressing to witness. He was going to be a million times worse as a partner than he was as an associate. Then, there would be no stopping his enormous ego.

"Where are they located?" *Please say a metro stop away.*

"Their office is out in the boonies somewhere." The boonies were what Ed called any place not in Washington, D.C. proper.

Now she was going to have to drive out of town and back again. Derek gave her a sly grin, realizing he had dodged the bullet. Grunt work. And out in the burbs or beyond too.

"The client has arranged for a car. Said everybody who goes out there winds up getting lost so I took them up on it. Don't want you driving around in the middle of nowhere and making a wrong turn that causes you to be late." That was Ed, never thoughtful but always practical.

"The meeting shouldn't take long once you get there." Ed turned back to his email. "Well, what are you two doing still sitting here?"

Casey grabbed the envelope from Jo's desk as she escaped the stifling atmosphere of Ed's office.

"Enjoy your errand." Jo smiled.

Yes, Casey the errand girl will get the job done. "Thanks, I will."

They were both aware Derek was standing behind Casey. There would be no small talk today. Casey rolled her eyes at Jo so only she could see and turned to leave. Derek butted shoulders with her as they walked side-by-side down the hall.

"What, Derek?" *Derek was like the bully in high school you thought you'd never have to see once you graduated,* Casey mused. Yet, here he was, camped close by and eager to annoy.

"You drew the short straw. Must be a haul if they're sending a car."

"Yup." Casey was just glad they were not going in the car together.

"Too bad about our scheduled meeting though. We need to stay on track. Can't be falling behind again on the pro bono hours. We could do it after you get back. Then you could brief me on your appointment in the boonies too."

"Sorry. I'm not coming back."

"What? Casey Sloane has got a life after all?"

Barely. Her life was an odd mixture of complicated and boring at the moment. Unsatisfying on every level. "Everyone has a life, Derek." Casey shuddered to think what it could consist of, but even Derek and Ed had a life.

"Well, have fun with that. Rush hour traffic is sure to be a bitch. Hope your life, whatever it is, can wait, and whoever you have to put on hold, isn't too pissed off when you turn up late."

Ricki would be irate if that happened. But it was not going to happen. She was meeting the car at six o'clock that evening in front of the building. Traffic was going to be bad going out of the city no matter where they were headed but coming back it would be much faster. And since there was a car and a driver, she was going to see if she could get door-to-door service right to the club. She'd just go straight home after the concert with Ricki and retrieve her car later. *Problem solved,* she thought with a nod to Derek, as she headed for the safety of her own office.

She had practically lived there for the last three days. Really, she was hiding there. Her work was her fortress. She took full advantage of the barrier it provided against unwanted intrusions. No one roamed the halls of Phillips & Row unless they were supposed to be there. Gabriel could walk around in the world all he wanted. She was not going to be as easy to find as he thought and if found, she was not going to be as easy to get to as he might have assumed.

She was feeling a shade away from cautiously optimistic about ditching the nightangel. Maybe he was more bark than bite. Over the last few days, she had closed off all the avenues she could think of that would allow him access to her. She had been as good as her word to Gabriel. She had not called to him in her dreams—she had shut the daydreams down. She avoided the slightest thought of him. She did not go home at night. She arrived at Ricki's house late and fell into a fitful sleep on her sofa without answering any of Ricki's unasked questions. She did not think she dreamed of him at all. She endured Ricki's frowns and waited.

It seemed to be working so far because there had been no more nightangel encounters.

He had given her three days. She had spent all three of them in this way. Restless nights and long numbing days all running together and Gabriel's words hanging over her head. Day three was his deadline. She had ignored it. She had no idea what was supposed to happen from there but she was on day four and except for having to deal with Derek, it had been uneventful. She did not want to jump the gun, but she was beginning to think the answer to what happens after three days and nights of misery might turn out to be—nothing at all.

∞ ∞ ∞

"Yes. We have the CFR in hard copy. They're over there, to the right of the last carrel, past the stacks." Mira signaled for Casey to wait and coming around the reference desk, marched the associate across the library. A moment later Mira was back at her station and the associate was darting out of the library with three volumes of the Code of Federal Regulations in her hands.

"Don't worry, Jordan. A little regulatory research never hurt anybody," Mira called out to her receding figure. "I have a lunch hour class scheduled on it for next week. I'll send you a meeting notice. I'm bringing cookies. You'll love it."

Jordon nodded and disappeared around the corner.

Well," Mira tapped one carnation-pink nail against her cheek. "I'm sure it *has* hurt someone. It is a little painful. But there's no need to tell that to an associate about to dive into a sea of regulations. Associates have enough problems already. A partnership doesn't come easy."

"You got that right." *And none of the associates she knew had a nightangel to worry about on top of everything else.*

"The CFR is a pretty color this year, don't you think? They kind of stand out on the shelf. But evidently, it's possible to get through three years of law school and one and a half years at Phillips & Row without ever setting eyes on the real thing. Poor Jordan. She just got assigned to work on a new matter and she's got a new partner to please too. You know how Stone loves his regulations and the hard copy in his hands. She'll be back here looking for the Federal Register anytime now. This could be fun."

Casey would have felt sorry for Jordan if her colleague did not make it a habit to ignore the other women associates at the firm. Working for

Stone would be hell and she deserved a little dose of it. Mira must have been thinking the same thing because they were wearing matching smiles. "So, what do you have for me that you couldn't email?" Casey asked. She shook off the petty feelings Phillips & Row seemed to pump into the air until they seeped under the skin.

"This." She handed Casey a sealed manila envelope that held something thick inside. "From your list. It's taking a while to track them all down."

"Thanks." Casey had stuck the small but growing pile of books Mira obtained for her under her bed without even opening the envelopes holding them. She was afraid to look inside and start turning the pages of those books, as though somehow the angel would know she was trying to figure out the puzzle he presented and punish her for it. Maybe she did not really want to know anymore. She was still fanning a small ember of hope she could beat the nightangel at his own game. What if the information she found in those books wiped that hope away like a perfect pair of garnet-red lips blowing out the only tiny source of light left to her? Would she be able to keep up the fight then and try to beat the odds or just surrender to the inevitable? She pictured Gabriel's lips pressing against hers in the dark. *Damn nightangel.*

"I came by your office earlier but you were out."

"I had a meeting with Ed and Derek."

"Derek just stormed past here. Guess it was a good meeting, huh?"

"Kind of hard to say yet."

"Keep me posted." The little nutmeg-colored flecks in Mira's brown eyes grew more vibrant. "And tell me if those books are doing the trick."

"The books. Oh, I don't know. I'll—I'll ask my friend," Casey said, clutching the envelope more tightly against her chest. *Gabriel's right. I'm a horrible liar.*

"Well, I'm curious to know. Make sure to tell you friend those books have due dates too. I don't do late and neither do those libraries. And here, take this too." She grabbed a sheet of pink paper from under the ledge of the desk and it fluttered out of her hands. As she bent to pick it up, Casey noticed the delicate edge of a jet black tattoo peeking out from beneath the bottom of her shirt. *Quite a contrast to all those pearls,* Casey thought, as Mira bobbed up with paper in hand and thrust it at her. "You need to come to my book club. This gives you all the details. We're going out for tapas. You'll love it."

∞ ∞ ∞

Nestled in the dark back seat of a luxurious car complete with stoic driver a few hours later, Casey was feeling just the tiniest bit smug. Ed had run into her as she was leaving the building and gone out with her to meet her ride. Gliding to a stop in front of them like it had its radar set for her arrival, the car was easy to spot. She forced out a thank you when Ed held the car door open for her. "I have the documents," she said, recognizing his act was more concern she was getting this basic thing right than a desire to be a gentleman. God forbid she should forget the documents—like that would happen. *Stupid filing. Stupid me for missing it.* Getting him to recover his confidence in her was going to take months. Maybe longer.

Ed slammed the door and the car slid into the traffic. Everything was going right. Ed was gone. Derek was history for a while. And this meeting could turn out to be a good thing. Her schedule was switched up in a way that was completely unexpected. She would be even more inaccessible. Casey had settled on the idea that when day four was done, her worries were over and everything would go back to normal. And day four was almost over.

She was counting down now. One client meeting. No danger of running into a nightangel in a stuffy business meeting. One concert with a friend. Ricki would not let her believe she saw him there even if he did turn up. One more night at Ricki's. Where she felt safe and sound and hidden away from the world. And then, when she woke up in the morning, she was officially done with day four and worrying about vampires with wings who stepped out of dreams to make all sorts of unreasonable demands as if they were sensible and she should just shut up and get on with it.

Casey stretched out a little and fished her cell phone out of her bag. Being ferried around to a client meeting for a change was kind of nice. The windows were tinted extra dark, the driver was blessedly silent, and there was a privacy window between the front and back seat. This was quite a bump up from a D.C. cab or driving around in rush hour traffic trying to find the place on her own. She could get used to it.

She had no idea where she was going. All she had gotten from Jo was the name of the corporation, NIGHT, Incorporated, a batch of documents, and a reminder to be in front of the building at six. She'd be worried about the name of the corporation but she was practical enough to realize that even a nightangel looking to make trouble couldn't put together a company worth the firm's notice in three days. She had already reviewed the documents. All boilerplate. Perfect. The day was winding down without any unfortunate incidents.

She scrolled through her email with a lighter heart and when she was done, she rested her head against the back of the seat. She thought about day four: the concert—how much fun it was going to be and how lucky it was to have gotten tickets for what was now a sold out show, how horrifyingly uncomfortable Ricki's sofa was when slept on for so many nights running, how unhappy Derek looked that she had an excuse to bail on their meeting, and how Gabriel had not tracked her down and burned another kiss into her hand. And she was glad about all of it.

The backlight on her phone flashed off on her lap. She closed her eyes. The whirl of the wheels accelerated her level of exhaustion. When she opened her eyes again, they had come to a stop along a circular driveway in front of a solitary three-story brick building. A steep set of red brick stairs led up from the wide walkway to a high landing and a set of heavy wooden double doors. Muted lights glowed through a few of the front windows. Heavy black lamp posts with beveled glass lanterns shone like beacons piercing the storm to either side of the base of the steps. No stir of movement came from inside. She checked the time. Five minutes to seven. She looked over her shoulder and saw nothing but a long, dark stretch of private drive and a road beyond devoid of streetlights and traffic. Okay, so lots of businesses had converted historic buildings like this into offices. So what if it was in the middle of nowhere and the tiniest bit creepy? *You're an associate at Phillips & Row. They eat companies like this for breakfast,* Casey reminded herself. *Stop being so jumpy and do what you have to do.*

Casey sat up straight and gathered herself together. She had no time to lose. The faster she got this done, the faster she'd be rocking out with Ricki at the show and putting day four to rest. She thanked the driver and hurried from the car. The building was even more forbidding from the base of the staircase. After fending off the demands of a determined vampire and withstanding Ricki's best attempts to bully answers out of her, this was child's play. She was going to be right on time if she took the stairs at a brisk pace. She squared her shoulders and raced up the long stairway with a resolve to get the job done and get it done fast.

224

She stopped at the top to glance at the small plaque to the side of the door that said NIGHT, Inc. At least she was in the right place. Beneath the sign was a buzzer. She rang it and waited. Nobody came. The wind had kicked up and she was freezing in her more-than-just-a-touch-too-short skirt and quite-a-bit-too-high heels. They were for the evening out that was going to come right after this chore so she was just going to have to freeze. It would be worth it later when she went work-to-play by shedding her crisp suit jacket to reveal a clingy silk spaghetti strap top to compliment the skirt and heels. The buzzer was a frozen circle of metal under her fingertip. She rang it again and then she twisted the little band of golden garden flowers on her finger while trying to discern some small answering sound from behind the door.

"Hello. It's cold out here." Casey breathed out the words in a small, snow-white cloud and watched it float away. She took a few steps back from the door and looked over her shoulder at the car sitting quiet in the drive. The door opened in front of her. The heat pouring out from inside caused her to swing back to greet whoever had turned up to answer the bell and bring her into the warm. They may have taken their time about it but she was cold enough to be grateful anyway and she plastered an overbright smile on her face.

Her smile dropped away like the power grid that had fired it up just went dark. *Where the hell was her client? This better not be her client.* She was staring straight into the nightangel's shadow-green eyes.

Holy deal-breaker. She staggered back in shock and the edge of her stiletto heel caught on the brick. She started to fall backwards and her eyes widened with fear. Not only was she going to kill herself in front of him, she was going to make a fool out of herself while doing it. She gave a little cry of terror. She hadn't believed he would make good on his threat. But he had. And now she couldn't imagine how bad falling down these steps was going to be. But she was going to find out. Day four was coming to a very different end than she had envisioned.

Gabriel's gaze captured hers as she teetered on the edge of the step. His eyes dilated so they were black more than forest green and streaks of cobalt light exploded from their center to twine around her. For a fraction of a second she was upheld when she knew she should be falling. Then, everything rushed ahead. The door slipped from his hand and he stepped forward to catch her in one easy movement, quick as a lightning strike.

"Casey." He said her name through lips that had turned pure scarlet and she felt his concern from the pressure of his touch. She was standing safe on the landing in front of him and he was holding her steady by the shoulders as though she might topple over again without warning. "Casey, are you all right?"

Casey was staring at him and she was not sure she was all right at all. She might not even be breathing. All the air was still stuffed low in her chest. She let it out in a rush as the words he was speaking curled around her like a warm blanket. She couldn't help but look down the steps with a shudder, imagining how awful the fall would have been if he had not caught her.

Of course, it was his fault she almost tumbled down the steep steps in the first place but somehow he was looking at her as though he was her hero and she ought to see him in that light now even if she had not before. It was clear he really liked saving her too. His eyes held a speculative look; he was considering how this unexpected opportunity to act as her rescuer so immediately upon seeing her again might change things up. Casey thought he might have rescuing prince syndrome. He had another thing coming if he was waiting for a thank-you.

"You," she cried instead, as if she was just now figuring out it was Gabriel standing there and the rescue had never occurred. She tore herself away from him in a panic and fled back down the way she had come, cursing her high heels with every step.

Stupid shoes. Why did I wear these to work? They're a hazard. I'm still an inch from killing myself in them, Casey thought as she continued down the stairs at what was close to a treacherous run. She reached the car and grabbed the handle of the limo door only to be arrested there by Gabriel's voice falling over her like a net. She stood stock-still as if he held a gun pointed at her heart and considered what to do next.

"Stop, Casey. Where do you think you are going?" He was following her path down the steps as he spoke. "You have an appointment with me. You have just arrived. Surely you will not leave already. Why, we have not even had a chance to say hello."

She should have put two and two together. Things were going too well for anything other than a trap to open before her. Not a tender trap either but a scary, crappy, totally unfair kind of trap. "No." She squeezed the handle of the rear door and pulled. Locked. She rapped on the rear window. Nothing happened, except her heart began to pound so loud in her ears it drowned out the sound of her hands banging on the glass. "I won't meet with you. I had no idea this had anything to do with you. I'm going right this minute."

"Going? Now? I don't think you will be doing that."

"Well, you're wrong." Why hadn't she agreed when Derek had suggested he come too? Gabriel would not have expected that, and Derek would make him regret ever wanting to do business with Phillips & Row. For once, Derek being his normal pain-in-the-ass self would have been of use to her.

"Hey." She knocked on the window even harder. "Open up."

The driver was on Gabriel's payroll for sure. He kept the car doors locked.

"What do you think Ed Johnson would say about you being responsible for losing a large and steady stream of potential revenue for the firm? Shall we find out?"

Kick her ass, fire her, wreck her career. Casey lowered her head, hearing him but not wanting to believe he was standing there; resolute in not planning to listen to a word he said. "How?" she whispered. "I don't understand how he managed this."

"Come inside and I will tell you all about it." He had come to stand right next to her, as he'd done by the window in the last dream, so that he heard her soft question. She controlled her urge to look toward the speaker of that invitation. If she glanced at him she might do something reckless or sink unconscious to the ground. She did not mean to put herself more at his mercy than she already was. Besides, it was difficult to conduct yourself with even an ounce of outraged dignity when you were out cold at someone's feet. She would not do it.

"No, thank you." She scanned the area, trying to identify their location but there was nothing to help her place it. No landmark. No street sign. She was in the middle of nowhere and she had no idea where that nowhere was. She should have been paying more attention. This did not look good and almost anything would have looked good just then. She had seen this setting in many a scary movie. It never boded well for the person who found herself there.

"That was quite a dramatic entrance, Casey, but I am afraid it is not enough."

"It's going to have to be enough. You can consider it my dramatic exit too." She flashed him an adamant look.

227

He gave her one of those consoling smiles of his. His voice grew gentle. "Are you hurt? I saw you turned your ankle on the steps."

"What?" His concern startled her and his smile made her as angry as she could be considering she was scared out of her mind. A dull pain was pulsing through her ankle but she shook her head. She thought of the angel in the dream resting his hand on that very ankle not too many nights before, like an imprisoning cuff of icy fire that inflamed instead of burned; the two of them lying on a bed of silk and rose petal. She had been held within his wings then and she had been happy for it. She tossed aside the memory.

"You can't do this," she mumbled, struggling to banish the desire for that strong, cold hand to soothe away the ache in her ankle. "I don't have to stay."

"But I have, haven't I? And you do, I think. Are you willing to jeopardize your career for fear of coming inside and meeting with me as arranged? It seems a simple enough thing for you to do. You are already here. I believe you have some papers that require my signature. Tomorrow you will be expected to report on this meeting and produce them. But, of course, it is up to you. You decide, Casey."

The lock on the car door popped up and Casey realized the driver's window was open a slit and he must be listening to the conversation. Instead of opening the car door, she released her hold on the handle. She was of two minds. She wanted to go but what good would it do to go, if he would bring her back to him again and again until she relented? She was sure there was little escape from angels or vampires of any sort once they had set their desires upon you, whatever their intentions. You would give them an audience as they would hardly be denied. She guessed it was best just to do so and get on with things.

Casey could not believe she was considering going inside what looked like a deserted building with this fugitive from some daydream. But she did need those papers signed and she would have to report on the meeting, just as he said. Plus, she was dead set on not losing her job right now. He was never going to let up anyway, no matter what he turned out to be. She saw it in the set of his face—a face even more that of an angel than in the dreams.

"Come along," he said upon seeing her withdraw her hold. "Stop shaking. I won't eat you for dinner, you know."

Maybe, maybe not. That was so not funny, either way, Casey thought, remembering the feel of those resolute rose-red lips pressing against her throat a few nights before.

Casey turned and without a glance in his direction, nodded her assent despite all the reasons she needed to say no. He went ahead of her and as she passed the driver's window she leaned down and whispered into the small opening. "Please don't leave. This won't take long."

As she followed Gabriel back up the steps, she heard the crunch of tires on pavement. She looked back over her shoulder from the top step. The car curved around the circle of the drive and out onto the road like a treacherous black snake disappearing into the dense forest of the night.

Day four was going downhill fast.

≪ CHAPTER TWENTY-THREE ≫

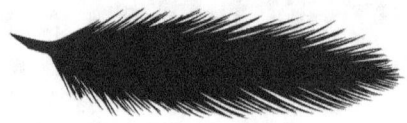

GABRIEL TOOK IN HER desperate glance toward the receding tail lights of the vehicle and held the door open wider. She could either run screaming into the dark, ice-cold night or slip past the nightangel and take her chances with him inside. A blast of wind rushed up the steps and swallowed the flow of warm air spilling out the front door.

No. Tearing off into the desolate night isn't much of an option. Casey thought, shivering. *It's probably better to be warm since this trouble isn't going to leave me alone no matter what I do.* She paused before the threshold anyway as if maybe she could put the meeting off forever by dawdling over the decision.

Drops of freezing white began to flutter down, melting on her skin and catching in her hair. She looked up at the sky in disbelief. Snow was floating down on them like confetti on a celebratory parade. She flashed an accusing look at Gabriel. Somehow, she felt, this could be blamed on him. The snow stopped floating and began falling in a thick shower of ice-edged flakes. She glared down at her stupid high-heeled shoes, then up at his strong hand on the door handle. She lifted her glance until it settled back on his face, half expecting to see him standing there in darkening wings against a snowy landscape. He inclined his head toward the foyer.

It looked toasty in there and at the moment the wind was whipping up her skirt at warp speed. If only her dreaded angel was not standing there as though he was about to usher her into his lair. Casey overcame her terror and slipped past him into the large foyer like a rebellious child who had succumbed to a moment of reason. He followed on her heels, closing and locking the door behind them in one swift motion.

It was too late to change her mind now. *Goodbye, cold. Hello, hot mess of trouble.*

"Come." He turned and crossing the polished wood floor with long noiseless strides, started up a long set of stairs without waiting to see if she followed.

Casey, racing to keep up with him, scrutinized his strong shoulders, still bare of wings, as they climbed the steps to the second level, made their way to the end of a dimly lit hallway, and entered an oversized office that brightened as the nightangel entered.

She could not help but ponder why he was walking around without those wings. Of course, she still was having trouble understanding why he was walking around at all.

He was dressed in a business suit with a white shirt loosened at the neck. Seeing him in business attire was almost as strange as seeing him without his wings. It made him much more real. When he took off his jacket, the effect was complete. He tossed it onto the back of a leather armchair as they passed it. He stepped behind the desk and indicated she take one of the chairs facing it.

Casey stood staring at him with a sense of astonishment tinged with annoyance and more than a drop of panic. He was there, with her, and it shouldn't be happening but it was. The situation she found herself in was worse than anything she could have foreseen, but he looked so good it was difficult to turn away. Her eyes were glued to the outline of the lean, powerful arms that had pulled her away from the edge of the brick staircase. She admired the hard strength of those arms when he held her close in the dreams. If she had not been so scared, she would have liked them out on the landing too. She was not supposed to like things about him though. He was watching her take him in and his lips curved the slightest bit as she tore her eyes away and grew flustered under his stare.

He sat behind the massive desk, motioning again for her to take one of the chairs facing it. She remained standing and looking down, her fingers tightening into a death-grip on her shoulder bag. At least she still had the documents in hand. Ed could rest easy about that. She forced

231

herself to look up again. They stared across at each other with eyes that took in every detail. She really liked looking at her nightangel even if he insisted he was a vampire living in the same world she lived in when he was not supposed to be there at all, and had ditched his beautiful wings when she loved them so much, and was probably going to do something terrible to her by the end of the meeting. He seemed to like looking at her too because his gaze was growing steadier and steadier and his eyes warmer and warmer.

"Do not look so frightened." Gabriel broke the silence. "Take off your coat. Sit down. Let's talk."

Casey kept staring at him while she sorted through possible exit strategies.

"What can I do to make you feel safe in my presence? Tell me." The softest hint of frustration ruffled the calm of his tone.

She set her bag down against the base of the desk. How dare he force her to his side through her greatest defense against him—the insulating power of her work? Her anger emboldened her. She shrugged her coat off, tossed it next to her bag and crossed her arms. "You could try not doing stuff like this. That would be nice."

"I mean you no harm." The calm behind his words began spilling into her senses.

Yeah. Yeah. She was beginning to despise angel-speak. It had so many angles to it. "You need to call back that car. I'm not staying. I told you— I want you to keep away from me and that's what you need to do."

"No, my own, it is not something I need to do. It is something you think I need to do. You must see the difference between the two things. Besides, I have no interest in doing what you request. It does not suit my purposes. I will not keep away. Truly, beloved, I cannot. Ask me something else instead."

"There's nothing else to ask." She began to flounce back and forth before him like a sulky schoolgirl. Her ankle throbbed now with each step. She stopped short and planted herself in front of him, hands on hips. "I've given you—a dream—some kind of entrance into this world."

"Is that it?"

"Yes. And as sorry as I am to have to do it, I have to boot you out again."

"Are you, Casey? Sorry to do it?" he asked, as if her words had surprised and pleased him in one stroke.

232

Casey refused to answer the question. She was not trying to make him happy. She was trying to remove him from her life. "I can make you go away," she said instead.

Maybe the problem was she had been trying to avoid the thought of him here with her instead of embracing the thought of him gone. "I made you up and I can make you disappear just like that." She snapped her fingers in the air. "I know you don't want to believe it because, you're too busy being an arrogant, presuming bastard at the moment but you're my creation, you know, and I'm still the boss of you when all is said and done." She was giddy with disdain.

"Am I?" He smiled. She was amusing him. "Are you?"

"Yes." She was going to wipe that smile off his face with a one-way ticket right back to Dreamland. "All I have to do is erase the idea of you here from my mind and picture you back where you belong—in the dream—and you'll be gone."

"Go ahead then. Why don't you do it?"

"I think I'll do it later, after I'm out of here. You can just anticipate it. Call the car you sent for me back again. I need to leave."

"Oh, Casey, come now. You want me to call you a car before you spirit me back to the safety of your dream world and lock me in there. That's very efficient but a bit unfair. Don't you think I deserve an opportunity to see you expel me from your reality and send me back to the netherworld? It's only just—like the right to a speedy trial. I think you ought to do it now. I want to see this trick of yours."

Did he want her to do it then and there? Okay. She would oblige him with pleasure. She stood still. She pictured an empty chair where he now sat behind the desk and Gabriel fading into the hidden center of her dreams.

Nothing happened. Gabriel remained. He watched her with the detached interest of a spectator. "Perhaps you are not concentrating hard enough."

Damn him. She dug her nails into her palms. She would try again, harder this time. She closed her eyes. She thought of nothing else but pressing him back into the dream and when she opened them again it was done. *Now, that wasn't so hard was it?* She looked across at the empty chair. She was almost disappointed.

"Not quite, Casey." He spoke the words close in her ear and a thrill ricocheted through her, blasting some major holes in her confidence level. He was standing close behind her. He put his hands on her shoulders in a way that said *do not fear me.* His fingers slid down her crossed arms to settle at her wrists so he was holding her in a light embrace that added: *but don't kid yourself, I'm not going anywhere and you don't want me to go anyway.*

He thought she was his already.

He's so wrong about that.

"Do you want to keep trying? You may if you like. I won't stop you. I will wait until you tire of it. It is not going to work though. I am not your creation, you know."

She yanked out of his grasp and he let her go. She backed away from him in one rapid movement, banging the side of her leg against the solid frame of something hard and unyielding as she went. In the morning, there would be a bruise. It would stay there for a week and turn a rainbow of ugly colors before it disappeared. One more injustice to blame on Gabriel. One more way he had caused her unnecessary trouble. She rubbed the offending spot with her hand and glared at him. "I say you are."

"Are you hurt?" He indicated her leg.

Again, with the disarming concern. "I'm fine—just dandy. My damn ankle, my leg—everything. And you are, by the way, my creation no matter what you think."

"I am nothing of the sort. It just seems like that to you. Perspective, my dear Casey, is everything."

Maybe he was right. She was not seeing things the way they were because something in her perspective was off. Had he taken on a power and substance of his own that made her visualization of him unnecessary to his existence? Or was he something else altogether from what she assumed—something that had its own unique existence and had never answered to her at all, as he insisted?

She sank into the chair she had smacked her leg against a moment before. All the wind had gone out of her sails. Everything she thought about him seemed to be wrong and she did not know what else to do but deal with him as he was, very alive and present. She was intimidated by him. She was intrigued somewhere deep down. She was at his mercy and she was flipping back and forth between anger, fear, and the desire to go ahead and surrender to the inevitable.

Instead of sitting back down behind the desk, he deposited himself in the chair beside her.

234

Casey crossed her legs and then uncrossed them again while his gaze lingered on the line of them. She had always been pretty sure he was a leg man and this confirmed it. She straightened and, sliding her feet under the chair, crossed them low at the ankle.

"Show's over."

His gaze shot back up to her face. If she did not know better, she would say the nightangel Gabriel was a little chagrined at being caught in the act of ogling her.

If she started the meeting maybe she could get off the angel's to do list and get on with her evening. "I received a directive from my managing partner to meet with someone from NIGHT, Inc. tonight. Is that person you?"

"Yes, Casey, it looks like it, doesn't it."

She sighed.

The nightangel had the nerve to look like he totally understood. "I know it is a surprise but I hope it is not a disappointment."

She wished she could say it was but something like Gabriel could never disappoint. He could irritate though and she focused on that. "You tricked me into coming here and I bought it. You did a great job setting me up for the fall. Literally."

The color rose and then drained from her face again as she pictured the brick base of the stairs flooded with light from the massive lamps that flanked it and what she would have looked like laid out beneath them. "Hooray for you."

"I am not the one who wore sexy shoes instead of serviceable ones." He stared down at her feet encased in those incredibly expensive, incredibly beautiful shoes.

Casey pressed her feet farther back beneath her chair. "They are not sexy. They're just high."

"Trust me, my charming dreamer, they are sexy."

In truth, the shoes were super sexy. That was why she bought them. They had elicited a kind of primal shoe lust in her that could not be resisted. She saw no reason to admit it to him though. "It wasn't the shoes. It was you."

"I did not push you backwards. You lost your balance. I pulled you back to safety."

"If you call this safety, I guess so. And you wouldn't have had to pull me back if you hadn't startled me like that. You brought me out here

235

under false pretenses. Why wouldn't I be shocked to see you at the door?"

"You are here for a legitimate business reason. You will soon discover the truth of that if you do not believe me now. And it was not my desire to shock or startle you. Things could have unfolded in a different way between us but you would not have it. You are the one who put this all into motion when you did not budge for three days. I told you, Casey, I could not be waiting on you forever. Someone has to take things in hand."

"Well, you didn't waste any time, did you?"

"Why should I? I would be a fool to wait any longer than necessary when a prize such as you awaits me. Thank you for being so punctual."

"You sent a car for me. It's not like I could be late. And I'm not a damn prize."

"A treasure, then."

"Treasure? Try person. I'm a person."

"You can be a person and a treasure too, Casey Sloane."

"Can you be a person and a fake business too? NIGHT, Inc. Nice name for a phony enterprise. What, did it take you—like ten seconds to think that one up? I should have figured it out right away but I never thought you'd be so obvious. Besides, I've been kind of preoccupied."

"With thoughts of me?"

"Yes. And believe me, for the most part they were not happy ones."

He looked as though he was picturing the moment he wrapped his arms around her in her bedroom and she had let him hold and kiss her like he was her own private wildfire and she longed to be set aflame.

Okay, so there had been some semi-happy thoughts but they had slipped into her mind against her will. Besides, she was trying to avoid wildfires at all costs.

"If NIGHT, Inc. was not a real corporation, your firm would never have sent you out to meet with me tonight," he said after a moment.

Casey blushed and lowered her eyes, relieved he had brought the conversation back to safer ground instead of pinning her down on what thoughts were not unhappy with regard to him.

"You know very well the company must have been vetted and you cleared of any possible conflicts of interest before you even set out to this meeting. I imagine it is standard protocol. You, Casey Sloane, are here for a valid business purpose as directed by your managing partner."

Like that was way better news than hearing NIGHT, Inc. was a total fabrication and her visit there a terrible error that could be resolved and forgotten. "And why am I here exactly? So you can hound me into submission tonight in the name of business?"

"Didn't Ed Johnson tell you why?"

"He said I was going to be a primary point of contact for you and part of your legal team at Phillips and Row. He gave me some documents for your signature. I was supposed to show my face here tonight, have a preliminary discussion with you, and come back with everything signed. He didn't say much more. Ed's not the kind of guy who likes a lot of questions once he's told you what to do. I figured I would come here and fill in any details for myself."

"I see."

"Well, I don't. And since I'm here for a meeting, let's have it right now and get it over with. I have plans for tonight and they don't include any extended meetings with you."

"Plans? For tonight? That is unfortunate. I am afraid you may be delayed—seriously delayed."

"No. That can't happen. I have to—"

He interrupted her. "We will finish this talk. I believe everything will become clear to you then. You will see you cannot be going again when you have just gotten here."

Casey did not want to stay. She could feel him starting to wreak havoc with everything she relied on, like her life was a little snow globe he was holding in his hand, ready to turn upside down and shake like crazy. She was not going to stay more than another fifteen minutes. He'd be lucky if he got that. "Give me the details now. I have another appointment after this and I don't have that much more time to give you before I have to leave."

"Another business appointment?"

"It doesn't matter what kind of appointment it is. Whatever you called me here to talk about, you had better talk to me about it now. I'd love to hear why Ed Johnson sent me over here for nothing."

"Not for nothing, Casey. This is not for nothing."

Casey paled. "What's that mean?"

"It's simple, Casey. I have many business interests. This company is one of them. There are some legal issues we choose to address through outside counsel. It's expedient in some cases, as I'm sure you know. We have engaged Phillips and Row for that purpose—with an express request you be part of the legal talent assigned to our work. From now on, you will be involved in the legal affairs of NIGHT, Inc. just as Ed Johnson has indicated to you."

She could think of about a thousand things she would rather do than have any sort of interaction with Gabriel outside the dream but he was making more of this perceived victory over her than he should. She could still walk away. And if she could not, she would find a way to become the invisible component on the legal team assigned to any matters having to do with NIGHT, Inc. after this evening. Derek Rider was going to be ecstatic then, because she was going to let him overshadow her on this case without putting up the tiniest bit of a fight. Letting Derek run some interference for her was just one of the ways she could minimize potential contact with Gabriel in spite of the bogus legal activity he was now generating to get close to her.

She could not resist taunting him with a few facts of life. Obviously, he was clueless about how things worked in the legal world. "Even if I agree to this, it isn't as big a coup as you think. You're not going to be my sole client. And I'll just be one member of your legal team. It's not like I'll be working with you directly on a regular basis. It's amazing how that little thing called email can allow us to communicate when necessary without ever having to see each other face to face. So, nice try but maybe it's time to wake and smell the coffee."

"Smell the coffee, indeed. That's excellent advice. Why don't you take it yourself?"

"Why should I need to do that?"

"You act as if this new assignment is something bad, but you misjudge it. Your career has taken a turn for the better. At least, that's what I believe. You've been a bit distracted lately, I know. And I've heard you have made some mistake of sorts recently. Not on your game for some reason. Now, why would that be?"

Casey was too shocked that he knew about the screw-up she had made at work to deny it had happened.

"This will be your opportunity to redeem yourself. And, of course, it makes both of our lives so much easier because I will be assured you are where I want you to be from now on without any fuss or bother and you can stop trying to avoid the unavoidable and accept that seeing me is going to be an everyday occurrence."

Yeah, that will be a real stress reducer for me and you, alright. She shifted in

238

her seat like she was going to bolt out of there in a panic, despite all the immediate stress reduction he thought she should have gotten from his assertion. Gabriel laid a hand on her arm that was more comforting than restraining and Casey stayed put, soaking in his touch and pretending she was not.

"There is nowhere to go." His voice grew gentle. He was in full angel mode, calming when he should be terrifying.

Casey knew he was right.

He withdrew his hand as he saw the comprehension rise in her eyes. "You will be working directly with me on some urgent legal matters which I believe will suit your experience and background well. Ed Johnson thinks so too. It's a big assignment but I'm told you are not afraid of a little hard work. But I must tell you, Casey, I am not fond of email. I will expect to have you here in person. We will be seeing quite a bit of each other, after all."

Ed Johnson was now officially on her shit list for life.

"I suggest you use in-house counsel instead. You'll find it more cost-effective and efficient."

"As excellent as the company's in-house counsel is, for these matters, I prefer retaining your firm—and you in particular, Cassandra, as part of that package."

"Part of a package? Right. Okay." Casey bit her lip before sitting up ramrod straight in her chair. She was not going to be railroaded. "You're the one dreaming now if you believe I'm going to work for you in any capacity. Do you think I'm crazy?"

"No, not at all, my treasure. I think you many things, most of them admirable, but one of them is not that you are crazy."

"I guess I should be glad that at least you, a dream gone totally haywire, think I'm not nuts. And I am not your treasure."

"I am not a dream, Casey."

"Whatever." She leaned forward and glared at him. "Here's the deal. There are other more senior associates at my firm whom you will find of more use to you than I could ever be. I'm surprised Ed didn't tell you but I guess he couldn't turn down whatever sweet slice of your legal business you dangled in front of him if you got me in the bargain. But I won't be part of this."

Casey did not think she was getting through to the angel. She would lay it out for him. "Listen, this is way it's going to go down. I'll tell Ed

239

that during our meeting tonight we were better able to define the scope of the legal work you require from the firm. In light of our discussion, you directed me to have Ed reassign the work you have lined up for me to one of the more senior legal wizards at our firm without delay. If he calls you to confirm this, you'll tell him how impressed you were with my desire for you to have the perfect fit for your legal needs; how selfless and honest I was in helping you assess your requirements in more detail so they could be best matched to the talents and skills of our excellent legal team. Got it?"

The nightangel was disturbingly silent.

She took a quick breath. "Anyway, I have no idea why Ed told you I could do any work for you at all. I have a full caseload as it is. He must be the one who is crazy." She stood as if preparing to leave.

Gabriel smiled at her in the way he had that meant he was going to say something she was not going to like at all next. "That is a pretty argument, Casey, and spoken with such adamance from such a pretty mouth. I am charmed by you anew with every word you speak."

Oh, brother. Here she was smarting off at him like there was no tomorrow and it was having the exact opposite effect of what she planned. Maybe he was teasing her but it was difficult to tell when his eyes were so dark with desire and his lips had such a hungry edge. She needed to find a way to put the lid back on things. She needed to step it up. She would not fall in with his plans.

"Thanks. Glad you liked it. I believe it will work. I don't care what you think about me, by the way, so stop saying those things." She tried not to dwell on how close she was standing to him and the way he focused on her lips when she spoke.

"Sit down, please."

She remained standing.

He reached across the small space between them and took her hand, examining it for a moment, as if he might pull her toward him with it. He brought it to his lips instead, placed the lightest kiss upon her fingertips, then let if fall from his grasp again. He looked for her reaction.

She was not going to make it easy for him to figure her out.

You're not in the dreams anymore, Prince Charming. Those days are done.

She hid her hands behind her back, her fingers tingling with the power of that kiss. She scrubbed the emotion from her face. She stayed put when everything within her said run. Running would reveal the terrified wonder she felt at being in his presence. He might think terrified wonder was a step in the right direction. She wasn't going to take the chance.

"I like how firmly you spoke to me and the way you looked me in the eye when you were giving me those directives of yours. I am even more confident than before you are right for the job. Yet, what you say makes little actual sense. Do you think I will agree to your suggestion? I want you involved in my legal business matters. No one else will do. Now, sit down, Casey. I will not tell you again. We are not done here. We have not even started yet."

Casey did not like to obey but she sank back into her seat. She did not want him to see how intimidated she felt sitting within such easy reach and she prayed he would not breach the span between them. "Started with what? Oh right, your business matters."

"I don't think you understand, Casey. I am very serious."

"You have no real business for me to conduct. This is just an elaborate lie you concocted to get me to come see you tonight. Well, it worked. Congratulations. How long you can carry on the charade past this meeting is beyond me."

"I needed no lies to get you here. I assure you, Casey, you will find you are going to be working very hard on behalf of NIGHT, Inc. from this evening on. I believe you might even begin to wish there was a little less work to attend to than I have asked be assigned to you."

"This has nothing to do with business. It's a big scam."

"It's not a scam as you will soon come to understand. It's a start, Casey. We must begin somewhere."

"Must we?"

"Yes, my darling. We must."

"Stop it. Don't call me that. What happens if I get up and leave now?"

"I have business to conduct, Casey. You have your marching orders. It seems you must remain."

"What if I go back and say I refuse to work on your legal matters? What then?"

"That would be a bad career move. Don't you think? Your career is important to you. You are such a modern woman. I find that an attractive aspect of your character. Your bright mind and your diligence are a delight. And it suits my purpose in this particular situation, you must admit. Besides, I will settle for no other. I will take my money elsewhere. It will not sit well with the partnership, Casey. I have an impressive portfolio of business I could bring their way. My corporate concerns are many and large. They span far beyond NIGHT, Inc. They are all very successful. Mr. Johnson is well aware of how this little legal project here at NIGHT, Inc. can benefit the bottom line if all goes well."

"Tip of the iceberg?"

"A very big iceberg. Of course, I have a personal interest in the initial selection of any new legal counsel, especially one to whom I intend to give such a significant portion of business—if all goes well. And my interest extends from the partner in charge, down to the associates doing work on behalf of any of my corporations. That is my privilege. I want to work with Mr. Johnson. He has an excellent reputation. And I want to work with you. I have heard good things about you. Some of my contacts have lauded your legal acumen. I suppose you've been told that by now." He paused.

Casey shook her head.

"Mr. Johnson held back part of the story from you. Interesting. He does not like to keep you too happy or too confident, does he?"

Casey frowned. She was beginning to hate Ed instead of just intensely dislike him.

"Do not frown so, Casey. You know, my love, you are much cleverer than he. Take heart. It is rather amusing. It was not a very creative explanation for the basis of my choice to provide to Mr. Johnson. I am sure you, my dreamer, would have devised something much more intriguing. But he swallowed it down without question. Mr. Johnson was not interested in the details either. You and I know details are important but he leans to the bigger picture—mostly money and power, I believe. He thinks you are quite good. Did you know that? He thinks we will be pleased with your work and that of the other attorneys he will be assigning to this initial project, which you will be leading."

"I can't lead—"

"You are the lead because you are the one who will work directly with us. Everything goes through you. Phillips and Row can address their office politics any way they like but this is how it will be because it is the way I wish it."

"And this has already been agreed upon before I came here tonight?"

"Yes." Gabriel's eyes were a soft moss green now and Casey rested in them for a moment while she took in his words. She wished he would sprout some wings while he was giving her all this bad news. She could take some comfort in them as well while she recovered from the devastating power of what that "yes" meant—her, working with Gabriel, with no end in sight and no way out of it.

"You need someone more senior. I am sure you will be happier with that." She could feel his smile. He was so not going to be happier with that.

"I am sure I will be happy with your work, Casey. Ed Johnson says I will be and I believe with regard to this, he is being honest with me. I trust you will oversee everything to my satisfaction because I know you to be diligent and driven. I have given your firm a select piece of legal work. It is a tiny fraction of what I could bring to them. It is large enough to keep several of you busy long-term and provide a reliable stream of billable hours to help fill the firm's coffers. There is the promise of more to come if all goes well—much more. I believe Edward Johnson might have offered you up on a spit if my representative had requested it. I did not require that, of course, so he just agreed to send you here, posthaste and all by yourself. It's best to keep things simple to start. Ed agrees."

Not only was Ed on her shit list for life, he had now risen to the top of it. No wonder he made sure she was safely shipped off to Nowheresville tonight. Casey sunk back into her chair. She was beginning to get a better picture of how well Gabriel had constructed this trap of his and how tangled in it she already was.

"As it is," he went on, "I have asked for little beyond your immediate attention on the matters I bring to the table now. You will be one hundred percent dedicated to this work. You will spend your time offsite, working here with me as I see fit or traveling to various business locations to work with my own people as I require you to do over the course of this assignment.

"I don't get it. Why would Ed agree to this? He knows I can't do it. I have other cases."

"As I understand it, they have already been reassigned."

"What? No. That can't be." Casey's face clouded over. If her cases had already been reassigned, she was trapped. She would not get them back. Everything she banked on as her safety net was gone.

What the hell? My three days are barely clocked in. Now that she thought about it, she was sure Gabriel had known with a certainty this is what it was going to come to and had set the whole elaborate plan into motion from the start. She didn't get how he had done it but she had to admire his efficient use of time and his understanding of what made her tick.

Casey worked for Ed. Her success depended on his goodwill. She could not walk away from her job when she was working towards acquiring the shiny golden ring that was partnership at the illustrious Phillips & Row. "Edward Johnson is a greedy bastard."

"He's a man of business, Casey. You are a means to an end. You should understand that. What else would you expect him to do?"

She did not know what to say. This game was Gabriel's. He had set the rules and conditions before she had been drawn to the board. He was even better at all this in the real world than he had been in the dreams.

"You had better stay and make the best of it. What else can you do?"

What else, indeed? *Checkmate. Well done.* Gabriel was a formidable adversary. She would give him that. But nothing more.

"Don't look so devastated. Perhaps you will like working for me."

Casey raked her fingers through her hair. She did not think so.

"Here." He held out a business card. "Contact our Legal Division Director, Stuart Tanner, tomorrow. He will be available to you anytime you require him and he has been instructed to provide you with whatever information and assistance you need. For now, however, you will be working here with me and only me. Shall we begin then, Cassandra Sloane, Esquire?"

He should have been a goddamn lawyer, too. He would have done well for himself. She took the card from his outstretched hand. She made sure their fingers did not touch.

He thought he had won. His eyes flashed with the certainty of his assumption. He should not be so sure. She did not intend to sit demurely by and make the best of a bad situation. Something must be left for her to do. Some part of the situation must be hers to control. She considered her options. She had so few. Maybe there were none at all and those she'd had up to now were just the ones Gabriel had allowed her for his own well-considered reasons. Where could she go but further into the fine-woven net he had cast about her? It hemmed her in on every side. She took a deep breath. He was right. The battle had fallen to him. All she could do now was try to remain calm and keep a clear head.

"You're very clever. You've left me with no real choice but to comply." *At least for right now.* "Ed has given me an assignment. What more is there to say? We will strive to provide you with the best legal counsel possible." She flashed a brittle smile his way.

244

She hoped he knew how false a thing it was. Sadly, at the moment, the nightangel Gabriel was satisfied with any smile he could get from her and all her pleasure in slighting him was spoiled.

≪ CHAPTER TWENTY-FOUR ≫

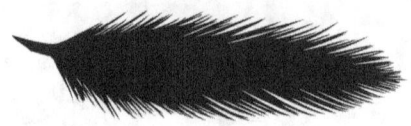

"WE SHOULD BEGIN. COME over here, Casey. I'll show you where you will be working."

Begin. Just begin. That was so like the archangel in the garden. He always thought such things were so easy when they were not easy at all. Here, without his wings, he seemed to hold the same premise to be true. But she could not just begin. This was no garden path to walk. This was real life and she would not go skipping down this route with him.

She remained in her seat. "Fine. We'll begin. Just as long as you understand this is all business. Nothing but business. Stop calling me my darling, my treasure, my own, and all those other terms you insist on using instead of my name, which is Ms. Sloane to you. Anything else is inappropriate to our relationship—a purely business relationship." There were going to be boundaries. She was going to set them right now. She hoped it annoyed the hell out of him.

He looked more astounded by her request than annoyed. "That's a bit formal for the modern work world. As your client, I prefer we be on a first name basis."

"I'd like to keep it as formal as possible, if you don't mind."

His eyes said he did mind, very much. "I suppose I should assume from this you are going to wish to go down the Victorian virgin path when we get to that point," he said, causing her to blush as though she was just that.

Absolutely, Casey thought. *No wait, that's not right. Absolutely not. Damn, that wasn't right either.* She blushed again. "We are not going to get to that point," she told him.

Gabriel drank in her blushes as though she had poured them into a glass one after another and set it down in front of him to savor.

"We'll see. In the meantime, wouldn't you at least like to know my full name?"

"No. It doesn't matter anyway. I don't intend to have a lot of discourse with you. If I start talking, assume it's to you. That way, I don't even need to know." She squashed down her curiosity and her dread. A last name made him more real. Maybe it would summon him more fully forth to haunt the living daylights out of her.

He looked a little taken aback. *Good. Feel the reality.* "Maybe this isn't going to be as much fun as you imagined."

"It's Rule. Gabriel Rule."

Gabriel Rule. It had quite a ring to it. And it was never going to pass her lips.

"We can be friends, Casey, or not, as you dictate. Tell me, how would you like to start this venture? I hope you will say it is as friends."

"Friends? I don't think so. We don't need to be friends." *Did he think she was going to fall into his lap like a ripe plum? Never.*

A subtle darkness moved across his face and then disappeared again. "I do not think you will like it very well if we do not proceed as friends. The choice is, of course, my dear Ms. Sloane, all yours. Please consider well though, as once decided it will be difficult to change course. What shall it be? How shall we proceed?"

"As business associates."

"Friend or foe, Casey?"

Casey did not like either of the alternatives he was proposing. "Isn't there something in between?"

He shook his head. In the dreams his wings would have rattled softly before he settled them tight together with an impatient whisper. They would be growing jet black about now or maybe a dull, cold gray. Casey was glad she could not see them at the moment. If she said "friend", those invisible wings would surely begin to burn with the colors of the roses, the forest, the sky—and if he revealed them to her, she would be entranced and perhaps reconsider her position on ripe fruit and vampire's laps. But she was not going to say that so there was no need to rethink anything.

247

"Work is work. We don't need to be friends to get the job done. I prefer a neutral middle ground."

"Friend or foe? Those are the choices."

"Foe then," she answered with a willful toss of her head so that her dark hair spilled across her shoulders like waves tossed in a sudden storm.

"Very well. So you shall have it, my stubborn Ms. Sloane. Foe it will be then."

The little hairs stood up on the back of her neck. Talk about frying pan to fire. She did not mean to put herself on his enemies list but judging from the hard set of his face, she just had.

She snatched her purse and coat up from where they rested against his desk. Enemy or friend, she needed to go. He had to call the car now or she would never be back downtown in time to meet Ricki. "I have to leave." She stuffed the card in her bag.

"Leave? No, you go nowhere tonight. I told you we would begin this evening and so we shall. You will have to alter your plans."

"I can't. This was supposed to be a meeting—a short one—and nothing else. I'm not staying."

"You were misinformed if that is what you thought. You will be staying. There is work to do. We must begin tonight. Cancel your plans. What are they anyway?"

"It's none of your business." Hoping to soften him, she relented. "I have tickets to a sold out show. Big band. Small venue. I have to go. I have the tickets with me and I'm meeting someone there. I can't stay tonight. Look, I apologize for the inconvenience but I'm afraid you are the one who has been misinformed."

"You misunderstand, Ms. Sloane. This is not a negotiation. You must tell the person you planned to go with you will not be able to make it. Is this a date or an evening out with a friend?"

Was he jealous or curious? She wished she could bring herself to lie just to find out. "Why does that matter?"

"I suppose it doesn't. Either way, work takes precedence for an associate at the firm of Phillips and Row, correct?"

Phillips & Row would make every new associate work that into a needlepoint sampler and hang it on their living room wall if time for hobbies was allowed.

"Can't we start this particular hell tomorrow? Give me the files you want me to review. I'll look them over and come back tomorrow night, the same time or earlier, and give you the whole evening if you want."

It cost Casey something to say she would come back. She did not want to think about what it would be like when the next day arrived and she had to drag herself to his offices. Today, she had not seen it coming. Tomorrow, she would. The idea of turning up on his doorstep, knowing he would be opening the door to her, made her wish she had tumbled down those stairs. Then perhaps some nice team of paramedics would have whisked her away in an ambulance with red flashing lights to the safety of a hospital bed and Gabriel's plans would have been foiled—at least for a little while. It involved pain but Casey could not help but long for the escape from him it would have provided. Of course, it could be he would have just lifted her up from the bottom of the steps and carried her inside, keeping her there until she got all better under his ministrations, whatever they would be. That sounded scarier than falling down the steps or coming back tomorrow.

Her big problem now was the time. She was late. She needed to go to that concert with Ricki. She needed to get away from him before he called her "Ms. Sloane" too many more times tonight in that flame-soft voice cut now with cold steel. The sudden chill under his words made her nervous. He wasn't happy about the not being friends thing. A nightangel who was not happy was not going to be much fun to be around.

"I will want the whole evening tonight and I expect you back earlier tomorrow. Plan to spend all your evenings and nights for that matter, from today on, with me. Here." He gave her a blank sheet of paper and a pen. "Write a note to your friend. It is a friend you were to go with tonight, isn't it?"

Nightangels were way too insightful.

"Yes," Casey snapped. "If you must know, it's a friend."

"I assume it is Ricki? Tell her you will not be able to go tonight. Give me the tickets."

She was disturbed that he mentioned Ricki by name. But it seemed like something a vampire would know even if it didn't call itself a nightangel. Vampires had to be smart and innately a bit stalkerish. Nightangels were downright intrusive. If they decided you were worth their attention, then you had better get used to a general lack of privacy. She had observed this in the dreams and it felt like an exotic form of caring when they did it so she tended to ignore the behavior. The downside was it meant they always knew more than they should. In the real world it was more than a downside; it was flat-out devastating to her general peace of mind.

She hoped he did not notice how she had paled at the mention of Ricki, because the last thing she wanted to do was draw any attention toward her friend. Ricki was the only person on the face of the earth who knew who Gabriel was, even if she didn't believe he existed. She wanted Ricki safe and knowing about Gabriel, whatever it turned out he was, was not the definition of safety. Casey had gotten herself into this trouble somehow. She was not going to allow her best friend to be dragged into it too. Not ever. She turned the conversation away from her friend and back to the need to cut the evening short. "You can't be serious."

"Do I sound as though I am not serious?"

"I need to leave now."

"But you are going to stay for as long as it pleases me to keep you here tonight. Your work rules your life and now, I rule your work. My way will be your way, whether you care for it or not, from this moment on. There is no time for concerts or distractions, Ms. Sloane. There is work to do. Get used to it."

Casey had a look of stunned outrage on her face. The nightangel basked in it for a moment. "The tickets, Ms. Sloane."

She clutched her handbag to her. "Why do you want them?"

"If you give them to me now, I'll get them to her. She is still at work, correct?"

"Yes," Casey stammered. "I'll just call her. Maybe she can meet me somewhere and then I can come back here."

"I do not think so, my little bird. How you would like to fly away right now but I am afraid it is no good. You will not see your friend tonight. Tonight you shall have to make do with seeing me and me alone. Consider it the start of a little tradition between us. Working late. Working hard. All alone here together. Every night. No phone calls. No friends. No disturbances. Just the stubborn maiden and the determined nightangel and nothing else to distract."

Super. Interruption-free quality time with her very own vampiric angel, whether she wanted it or not, stretching way past the evening at hand. Why didn't she think she was going to like day five very much?

"Except all this work you have for me." She was suddenly happy for the work. Work was a good barrier to any trouble. She knew how to employ work to that end.

250

"Yes. But that will be a mutual distraction. Go ahead. Sit down and write a note to your friend. Do it now."

She did not want anything mutual going on between the two of them. Her legs were growing shaky; she sank back down in the chair as he commanded.

"But I don't know the actual street address off the top of my head."

"You don't need to know her full work address. Write the note."

"It would be better if I talked to her."

"It would not be better. Write her the note now. I will take care of the rest." He sat back down behind the desk like he owned the place, which Casey guessed he did.

"I'd rather call," she grumbled.

"And I would rather you did not."

It made her want her own way more. Casey began to reach for the phone but Gabriel caught her by the hand as she lifted it to snatch up the handset. She waited without breathing for him to set her free or pull her closer. She wasn't sure which it would be, which would be better in the long run for both of them. He brushed his thumb across the center of her palm and that touch caused his kiss to burn there again, as red and icy as the night he had first pressed it against her skin. Then, it had felt like an eternal promise. Tonight, it had the quality of a frozen reprimand. "I told you to write the note," he said, his voice stern.

To invoke the power of vampiric kisses like they were stamped upon the mortal heart in indelible red ink was one thing. To talk to her like a mere underling who could be ordered about at whim was quite another.

"I want to call."

"And I told you to write your apologies instead. And that is what you shall do. You work for me now. You will do as I say or you will pay a price. Is this the way you behave toward a valued client? What would Ed Johnson think, I wonder?"

She had no idea what to say in response. They had already agreed between them what Ed was all about. It was unfortunate for her, but it was a perfect garden of possibilities for the nightangel. She could tell already working for Gabriel was going to descend into a nightly battle of wills. She was plenty stubborn but she was not certain, in this case, that would be anywhere near enough to win out.

Her silence satisfied him. He let go of her hand and nodded toward the pen and paper. Casey pulled the paper closer, her palm still tingling from his touch, and began scribbling out her note to Ricki. When it was done she folded it, and taking the tickets out of her bag, gave it all over to him. He looked at the tickets with interest before setting them to one side. Then he opened the note she had scrawled and read it as though he were analyzing every word. She had not expected this. She had written the note for Ricki's eyes alone.

He crumbled it into a little ball and set it aside. He handed her another sheet of paper. "Try again. I do not like the tone of this one."

Casey was dumbstruck. Alright, it was not in a sealed envelope but it was folded up in a way that said, "don't look." She should have scrawled a big "private" across the front of it before giving it to him. This nightangel needed some lessons on basic boundaries in the real world.

"I suggest you stop glaring at that paper and get on with writing your friend."

She did as he said because she could not think what else to do instead. She rewrote the note, softening the tone but still leaving a frustrated edge lying beneath her bland wording she hoped he would not catch but Ricki would. She folded the paper and pushed it across the desk. He opened it as before, read it, looked across the desk at her with undisguised annoyance, crushed it into another tight ball in one fist and laid it next to the first.

"Do you like to play games, Ms. Sloane? Do you really want to play them with me tonight?"

"I'm not trying to play games."

"You will find me a formidable opponent if you continue to challenge me in this childish way. I may choose to play some games with you that you will not enjoy and once I start a game, Ms. Sloane, I do not like to stop until I have won. Do you want to take the chance on starting up such a contest with me just to be contrary?"

"I don't want to play any games with you. I don't even want to be here." She had a feeling any game Gabriel would play with her would wind up in the end with her being the loser and she did not want to know what that would entail.

"Yet, you are. Write it again, the way it ought to be written, and give it to me now so we may dispense with this little roadblock to our evening's work. If I don't like this next version of a simple note to your friend, these tickets will go into the trash. You can explain to your friend later why you could not be bothered to get the tickets to her or let her know you would not be arriving to join her."

Great. Man of business, literary critic, and etiquette police all rolled into one.

He pushed another sheet of paper across the desk to her. She leaned back in her chair as if maybe she would not comply but then she pictured Ricki standing in the cold, waiting for her to arrive with those impossible-to-get tickets, and thought better of it. She yanked the sheet closer and picked up the pen again. She went with short and sweet for this version and left out the hostile undertones aimed at the creature watching her write as though he could read the flurry of conflicting emotions behind every stroke of pen on paper.

Transparency was not what she wanted at the moment. Not with him. Not with Ricki either.

Casey stared down at her unfinished note. Even if she could tell her the truth, she wouldn't. She wanted Ricki insulated from Gabriel and everything he represented. She was in trouble. Ricki did not need to be in trouble too. If Casey could not go, then the note was a much better way to duck uncomfortable questions from her friend. Trying to explain the mess she had gotten herself into without explaining it at all would be impossible over the phone, especially under the watchful eyes of Gabriel Rule.

If Ricki was angry enough at being abandoned at the last minute and getting a couriered note with two tickets stuffed inside instead of a hurried phone call wreathed in desperate apologies and a promise to show up late with money for band merchandise and drinks, they would not speak for a few days and Casey might never have to explain.

Suddenly, the note felt like a reprieve and the words started to flow.

Ricki—I can't go to the concert. Sorry about the last minute notice and this note instead of a call. I'm in a meeting with a new client and this was the only way I could get you the tickets. For some reason, Ed said I could put in hours right away, as in—tonight. The client expects me to stay, so I'm going to need to do that. You understand how it is. Tickets are enclosed. It's going to be an amazing concert. Find someone else to go in my place and don't worry about me—just have fun. If you're not too mad, buy me a t-shirt. I'll pay you back. You don't owe me anything for the tickets.

Case

She did not bother to fold the note this time. She handed it across the table and waited for him to look it over.

"This will do," he said. He folded the tickets in it and put it all into an envelope. "Address it. Just write her name and the name of the firm. I'll take care of the rest."

She did as he said, trying hard not to look like she begrudged it as much as she did. Casey was not worried about Ricki finding someone else to join her at the concert. She was concerned that she had cleared away the one thing standing between her and an unpredictable evening alone with something so inexplicable that it was looking more and more like it had to be the real deal.

"Now, wait here and try not to get into any trouble." His eyes traveled around the room and settled back on her with a satisfied gleam that said he was confident it was impossible for her to do anything troublesome even if she tried. She really was trapped like a little bird in a cage and the door had just shut tight with a firm clang. "Can you do that?"

She nodded her assent, making sure their eyes did not meet. She needed to get out of this but she had no idea how she would do it. In lieu of escape she would embrace avoidance. When he left, she began to take the room in from her seat. The office was large and well appointed. A rectangular wooden conference table and four chairs were placed off to one side of the room with a laptop hooked up so whoever worked at it would be in constant view from the desk the nightangel had already claimed as his.

He was so going to stick her at that table. "The better to scrutinize you, my dear," she imagined him saying, while pointing ominously to her assigned workspace.

A comfortable seating area with a large leather sofa, elegant chairs, and long coffee table dominated the main area of the office. Original pieces of art hung over the sofa and his desk. If she were more knowledgeable about artwork, Casey was sure she would recognize them and be impressed.

When Gabriel came back a short time later she did not look up. Looking up meant they would begin, and when nightangels begin something they tend to do it with a vengeance. Casey did not think she would ever be ready to begin anything with Gabriel outside her beautiful dreams. So she kept her gaze focused on the toes of her shoes and refused to acknowledge his return.

Instead of speaking, he said nothing. The silence grew heavier and heavier. She concentrated on the thrumming ache in her ankle instead of the uncomfortable weight of his stare until all the air seemed pressed from her lungs. She was compelled to lift her eyes again to meet his just to be able to breathe. He did not smile or speak when their gaze met. Okay, now she was officially intimidated. She was not used to such hard looks from Gabriel and being the beneficiary of them gave her an inkling of why vampires, by whatever name they liked to call themselves, had the reputation for being such intense, imposing creatures.

She would admit without hesitation she liked the amenable angel in the dreams better than the coming-to-you-live-and-up-to-no-good-from-somewhere-in-Northern-Virginia nightangel demanding her attention now. This Gabriel was not very accommodating at all. If he wanted to win her regard, he was going about it in a strange way. They continued to stare at each other until her gaze fluttered down to her shoes again.

"That ankle."

She did not need to look back up at him to know he was indicating the one she had twisted on the steps.

"It needs ice." As soon as the words were spoken, the nightangel was on one knee before her, reaching out to test how badly injured her ankle was.

"It needs nothing." The scent of roses spun around her and her skin buzzed at the nearness of his fingertips.

She meant to push aside his hand before those fingers could rest on her skin but she could not react fast enough and the haughty words she meant to speak caught in her throat. His fingers were cool and gentle where they touched just as she knew they would be. The certainty of his power over her at that moment immobilized Casey. She could not resist him and so she grew still like a little deer in the bush, waiting for the lion to walk past without settling its attention too fully upon it. So far, that strategy was not working very well. She had his complete attention whether she wished for it or not.

He wrapped his fingers around the ankle in question and a cold, soothing sensation began to sweep away the pain. He glanced up into her face to gauge her state. For all his talk about being enemies and nothing else because that was how she would have it, he looked an awful lot as though he wanted to be her friend more than anything in the world. And she could not have that. Not with him. Friendship with the nightangel would be a slippery slope. It didn't take a genius to recognize that friendship with a vampire of any sort would be too dangerous to consider. When she studied him, though, despite the sickening fear that welled up inside her as she thought about what Gabriel being there with her could mean, she wished with all her heart there was a way to do it. Gabriel was a very good friend in the dreams. Good friends were rare commodities in any setting. And he was a good friend who knew how to kiss her nearly senseless, too. That was a rare quality to stumble upon in the normal course of life as well. Nobody she had ever met could do that—except Gabriel. And there was no way she was going to let that count for anything.

His fingers continued to caress her ankle while she considered how dangerous he was and how a nightangel would kiss in the real world versus the dreams. She abandoned these thoughts when he began to slide his hand up and down the injured area in a way that shot alarming little sparks of desire through her. He was watching her as if there was something in his skin against hers that was going to smash down the wall between them any second now.

Yeah, he was going to be a standout kisser in the real world too. Not that she planned to verify that assumption. If he thought his touch was going to heal her fear like it was healing the pulsing pain in her ankle, he was wrong. She pushed aside his hand and sprang up. "I just want to get to work and get this done."

"Over there then." He indicated the conference table and the laptop as he rose along with her. "That's where I want you." His voice was all business again and he was the one in command. The subtle warmth in his eyes had frosted over. He was still standing very close to her. Personal space was going to be an issue with him.

Casey's heart did a flip. Her ankle, however, felt much better.

≪ CHAPTER TWENTY-FIVE ≫

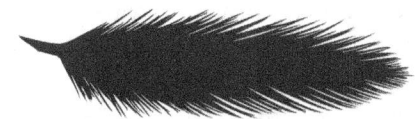

"OKAY," CASEY SAID, GIVING the desk and the angel a dismissive look.

"But first, come here." He walked back to the desk and sitting down behind it, waited in silence until she stood in front of him again.

No, the angel was not much for being dismissed. She saw it in the hard set of his jaw.

She was expecting an edict. Instead, he pulled open a drawer and produced a huge stack of files. "You will review all of this. You need to familiarize yourself with the contents of these files by tomorrow evening. You can do that after you leave for the night. Right now, I want you to do something a little different so I can gauge your business mind instead of your legal acumen. You will be researching some companies we are considering as potential acquisitions. You will get their financials, provide me a comparison in a spreadsheet format, research their background, market performance, competitors, projections, and find out if they have any troubles, including legal troubles, we should know about. Be prepared to discuss all of this with me by the end of the evening." He tossed a file at her. "All the information is here."

Casey stood firm in spite of this clear dismissal. "First, you need to review and sign the paperwork I brought for you."

"Ah yes, the paperwork waiting for my signature. Give it to me. I'll look it over while you get busy."

A sarcastic or flat-out obscene response was on the tip of her tongue but he looked even more severe behind the span of that heavy wood desk than when he had walked back in the room a short time before and she lost her nerve. Why be a total smart-ass to something that could maybe drink you up for dinner? This wasn't a daydream where she could be insolent and brush it off with a teasing little smile. *Not at all.*

She hoped if he required dinner, he had indulged himself already.

Casey yanked the envelope with the documents out of her bag and laid it in front of him on the desk. "You don't need me to do this research. It's busy work to keep me here. I'd rather discuss these documents with you and answer any questions you may have about them instead of wasting time on trumped up projects."

"So you shall. If I require any such explanations. But not now. Now, you shall do the work I requested. Frankly, whether it is trumped up or not does not matter. You will get your billable hours. I don't see why you look so unhappy. I thought you liked research. You have told me so many times."

Now, he was quoting things she had told him in the privacy of her own daydreams to justify his actions. *This could be the tip of a sizable iceberg,* Casey thought. *And it's the second one this evening. Thank goodness I'm not floating along on the Titanic. Of course, maybe I am. He'd just rescue me if we started sinking. I couldn't take another rescue tonight.*

"I meant legal research and this is business research. And besides, this isn't real research. This is made-up research."

"It's going to be a late night as it is, Ms. Sloane. I hardly think you ought to be standing here arguing with me, your client, about the merits of a request I have made of you. Instead, I suggest you just get started."

Get started. That was "just begin" in another form. He was playing with her and she was going to have to let him do it. She needed those papers signed and she noticed he had set the envelope to the side of his desk without opening it.

"I'm not arguing. I just don't see why you can't sign the documents I gave you right now."

He laid his hand on the envelope but made no move to open it. "You'll have my signature on them by the night's end if you do as I say without too much more argument. Otherwise—"

Casey did not like the idea of any sort of "otherwise" cropping up.

She could not afford another misstep at work. She wondered when the end of the night would come. A late night by a vampire's standards was bound to be late indeed and the idea of how very alone she was going to be with this adamant nightangel filled her with apprehension. She went over to the table and sat in front of the laptop set up there.

"I don't have a MBA. I'm not some kind of analyst or a librarian. I'm an attorney."

"You know how to do basic business research and analysis. Do it."

"I don't normally—"

"Do it, now."

"I'm just telling you something you ought to know before we get started."

"Ms. Sloane. You can begin or you can go home now with the papers unsigned. Which will it be?"

"What an arrogant ass," she whispered to herself in injured tones.

"What did you say?" Gabriel lifted his head to stare across the room at her.

If she had any illusions about how well he could monitor her from where he sat, they were swept away by the look of irritation on his face. Everything she did and said could be plainly discerned from his desk. Sitting there was like being under surveillance in some spy thriller without having all the wardrobe changes available to that chick in Alias.

"Answer me. What did you say?"

"Nothing." The chick in Alias would have said "nothing" too. Maybe she should change careers. The wardrobe perks were tempting. And think of all the paperwork she could escape.

"Consider that the last nothing of the night."

She shook her head in disbelief and flipped open the folder he had given her as though she did not consider his statement worth a response. Probably CIA operatives—even those with the most gorgeous wardrobes—got stuck with paperwork too and she was nearly having palpitations just being an attorney to this totally annoying angel. The more she paged through the file, the more outraged she became that he believed she should meekly accede to his wishes when he was keeping her there against her will.

"This is bullshit. What a bastard." Casey could not help but mumble these last angry thoughts under her breath, so strong was her desire to rebel against his unexpected hold over her and so ill-used did she feel already.

"I am being generous, Ms. Sloane. Lose the attitude and do it now or the evening is bound to grow very unpleasant and you shall leave here without these papers in hand. Do I make myself clear?"

"Yes." Casey sighed, and without further comment, began as he directed. Thanks to Mira, and the recent online session on advanced news and business research she had arranged for her to take right in her office, she did know how to proceed with confidence. Somewhere, Mira was painting her nails a new shade of pink with a beatific smile on her face, knowing she had helped others avoid the always looming potential for research disaster without missing a beat.

She started with her preferred online research system, throwing in her password, and jumping right into her project. She was digging out the SEC filings, checking for negative news, looking for pertinent case law, searching a host of business directories and trade publications for background information, and checking public records and court dockets. She found the latest financials and began to load them into a spreadsheet. Gabriel had still not touched the envelope. He was watching her progress with unwavering interest.

She paused, staring at the screen and trying to look as though she was thinking hard when, in fact, she was trying to push down her anxiety over having her actions monitored with such meticulous care. She needed to focus but he was making that a challenge.

"Is there a problem?" Gabriel asked, noting the sudden pause in her work.

"No," she snapped. *No problem except you.*

"Are you done then?"

"Done? No. No, of course not." *And you are a really big problem.*

"Then why have you stopped?"

"I haven't stopped. I'm thinking."

"Is that what you are doing?"

"Yes, it is. And I need a cup of coffee or tea. Please?" She tacked on the last word as a hasty afterthought and even she had to admit it sounded a little hostile.

"There is no coffee or tea."

"Okay. What about soda then?"

"I'm afraid not, Ms. Sloane."

"Bottled water?"

Gabriel shook his head no.

"You're a pretty poor host if you don't mind me saying so."

"Why should I supply you with refreshments and cosset you? You have made it very clear you are no friend of mine."

"So, if I said 'friend', I'd be swilling down a diet soda right now?"

"You said 'foe', so the point is moot."

"I didn't think that would mean I'd be deprived of the basic amenities of the workplace. I suppose there's no food here either."

"Not a crumb."

"What if I'm hungry?" Food was the last thing on her mind but she wanted to make him lay out exactly how rude he was going to be to her just because she didn't want to be best buddies.

"Then you shall stay hungry. I am not in the habit of indulging enemies."

"Fine. I don't want to be your friend or drink your coffee anyway."

Casey was beginning to feel much mistreated by this Gabriel. "What about tap water? You do have tap water, don't you?" She could not keep the sarcasm out of her voice. She had seen the wet bar in the corner. Maybe he was going to tell her he had no glasses but they were stacked right there beside the sink so then again, maybe she was safe.

"Tap water? Certainly, it's right there. Help yourself."

Casey did not say a word. She got up, poured a glass of water, put it down with an adamant little bang on the table so some of the water almost spilled, and started back on her work without another glance toward him.

"You are not very good at listening, Ms. Sloane. I told you to drop the attitude but it seems you cannot."

Casey kept on working as if he was not speaking to her.

"Come here, Ms. Sloane, right now."

"What?" The sharp edge to his tone made her jump in her seat but she stayed put.

"You heard me. Print what you have now. It will come out at this printer. I want to see what you have done so far."

Oh crap. She let the water sit without taking a sip, wishing she had not slammed the glass down on the desk. It had stirred him to give her the sort of attention she did not want from him. She saved her document and printed it before going to stand sulky and quiet before him.

He glanced up at her. "Sit down." He was looking at the numbers on the sheets in front of him with a furrow in his brow. A sick, nervous thrill ran through her as he perused her work for errors. "I gave you a simple task, yet it looks as if you have done a poor job of it so far. There is something wrong with these numbers. I hope you did not do it on purpose. Did you?"

"No, I would never do something like that. I don't understand. What's wrong with it?" Casey was embarrassed. As much as she did not want to be there doing this work for him, she did have an innate desire to do it well on general principle.

He tossed the pages at her. "Go back and figure it out and don't take long about it. I have other things for you to do tonight besides this basic task. This is well within your capabilities. I expect you to get it right this time. And I will need to see more than some numbers in a spreadsheet."

Casey felt foolish. She had no idea what the mistake could be or why he would not point it out to her. She scooped up the papers from where they had landed on the desk and held them away from her between two fingers as if they were tainted. Her hands were shaking and she knew without looking at him that he saw it. She began to head back to the conference table but his voice stopped her progress.

"And Ms. Sloane," he called.

The way he spoke her name caused a thin whisper of dread to travel through her. She turned around, wishing she did not have to acknowledge him but knowing she must. She clutched the papers tight so they did not flutter from her fingers.

"Don't ever hand me something like that again. I will not tolerate sloppy work from anyone—especially not from you."

'I wasn't done with it,' she felt like crying out. The nightangel was being so unjust. Half her work was sitting in an open document, waiting to be reviewed and organized in a nice report format in order to satisfy his fabricated requirement for a summary of her research.

She sat down again. She wanted a drink of water but she could not bear to bring the glass to her mouth. Her throat constricted. She struggled to hold back tears made up of equal parts shock, fear, shame, hurt, and anger. She could feel his eyes on her across the room but she ignored him. *Don't cry. Don't cry. Don't cry. Damn.* A heavy tear, then a second one dropped onto the keyboard.

She pretended this had not occurred. It did not help.

She had rubbed the genie right out of the bottle by the force of those two betraying teardrops. She did not have to look to know Gabriel Rule now loomed over her. His presence crackled beside her in the most alarming way. She was chilled to the bone by the fact that he was standing so near her when a second before she was sure he had been sitting in a chair across the room staring at her like there was no tomorrow. He was going to have to stop indulging that propensity of his to arrive when and how he pleased but she was not going to tell him so tonight. It would probably only make him do it more just to drive her crazy. She began to review the figures in front of her as if her life depended on it.

"I am going to leave you here while I take care of a few things downstairs. I hope you use the time wisely because I will want to hear a summary of your findings upon my return. I'll require a written report as well—error-free, please."

"Okay." As scary as it was to have him in the room with her, it was even more frightening to be alone there. She hid her shaking hands in her lap.

"Okay then," he whispered close in her ear. "Don't let me keep you from your work."

Don't let the door hit you on the ass on the way out, she thought. She knew better than to indulge in smarting off to him at this point, however, as much as it would have pleased her to do it. She was not going to give him one more reason to toy with her tonight.

Casey looked at the clock on the computer. She could not let him walk out of there for who knew how long without an argument when it was well after ten thirty now. "Wait. Before you go anywhere, I want to know how long you expect me to stay."

"Until we have finished, of course." He was looking down at the keyboard where the two fat teardrops were still evident on the black keys, assessing her in profile.

Casey gritted her teeth and tried to answer with a calm she did not feel. "I wasn't prepared to stay this late. I never had dinner and I'm not feeling very well for some reason."

"Some reason? Ms. Sloane, at least give me a little credit here. I feel confident I am the reason. You do not like being here alone with me so late into the night. But you must resolve to become used to it for this is to be your constant fate, thanks to Phillips and Row. I appreciate the full value of the law now more than ever before."

And she appreciated it a little less. For the first time in her legal career, her work had become her prison instead of her sanctuary.

263

She believed him when he said they were all alone together. The house was as silent as a snowdrift. Being alone with him was scary-movie scary and she was feeling very much like the girl who got her ticket punched before the opening credits had stopped rolling. She took a small, ragged breath and said in her bravest voice, "I would appreciate it if you let me finish this tomorrow and go home now. It's close to eleven. Isn't that late enough for one night?"

"What, Ms. Sloane. Is it past your bedtime?"

"It's unreasonable of you to ask me to stay any longer tonight. I'm going to have a full day tomorrow and you want me back in the evening. I need to get some rest if I am going to be of any use to you."

Gabriel was remarkably unimpressed. "I am certain you are made of sterner stuff than that. There is work to be completed before you may leave for the evening. You have hours in front of you. Go wash your face in the bathroom over there if you must. Freshen your glass of water if you like. Then get right back to the task at hand. Well?"

He was still staring down at those two telling teardrops and she'd be damned if she would give him any more to gloat over.

"Alright," Casey's said in a faint voice, realizing he expected an answer from her before he would leave her be. Being alone had to be better than having an angel glowering down at her, even if there were no angry wings stirring the air while he was doing it.

After the door clicked shut behind him, she got up, pitched the water back into the sink, and put the glass back on the bar. She went into the bathroom and silently scolded herself for being such a coward tonight with Gabriel to keep the tears from falling. She knew if they did she would never get them to stop before he was back in the room with her again and that would be too humiliating.

She dampened her hands and pressed them against her flushed cheeks. Then she returned to the computer, wiped off the keyboard with her skirt, and went over all the numbers until she found the error to which he had been referring. Two column headings had been transposed. That's what she got for fiddling with the format to make it extra pretty and wow him with her mad computer skills. How he had noticed it, she had no idea. He was sharp. Well, of course he was. The whole thing was a set up. He knew about the businesses in question already. He was testing her. She was also certain he was looking for a mistake, something to nail her on right from the get-go, to make sure she was giving the proper amount of consideration to how much better it was to be Casey than Ms. Sloane when working with Gabriel Rule.

Casey saved the document and printed it out again. She took it out of the printer and stared down at it. She did not like to admit it but she had been sloppy just as he had said. Although, she did not think it was very kind of him to be so blunt about it. Fortunately, Mira had not witnessed this failure or she'd be pointing her to a spreadsheet basics class.

After a while, it became clear he was not coming right back. Casey began to explore the room. She crossed to the door and gave the handle a turn. Locked. She let go and drew herself back against the wall like a silent movie heroine who had just figured out all was not well and she was in real peril even if she had not spied the railroad track and the rope yet. Something about knowing she was locked in terrified her at a whole new level.

She was beginning to think perhaps she was in dire trouble that went beyond the dire trouble she had imagined she was in upon first following Gabriel inside. The hour was late and he did not seem inclined to let her leave. What if she did everything he said and at the end, he would not let her go anyway. Maybe he was planning on locking her in some room at the end of the night, only letting her out the next evening to do more made-up work and depriving her of everything but tap water until she caved in to all his demands. That would be bad because she was not going to say any of the things he was waiting on her to say and maybe that meant she was doomed to death by tap water and black looks.

Now she was freaking herself out.

She went back to where her purse rested beside her chair and pulled out her cell phone. She was going to call someone, maybe Ricki, maybe 911. She needed to put out the call for somebody to get her out of there.

It did not take long to discover there was no cell phone reception to be had. She walked the phone around every inch of the room. A tug at one of the drapes revealed there was no window behind it. *No windows. Locked door.* She did not like that at all. In a final effort to locate cell reception, she took off her shoes and stood on the sofa and a series of chairs—still nothing. Casey rushed over to the laptop he had provided her. She tried to bring up her email account but she found the service blocked. A hostile network message popped up stating such access was a network violation that would be reported to the network administrator. Social sites and even an instant message window yielded the same result.

Great. He was sure to have something to say to her about all these attempts to communicate with the outside world. She was confident he had an email about these infractions in his mailbox already. Heart sinking, Casey scurried over to his desk. His computer was locked along with every desk drawer. Except for the manila envelope she had given him, the desk was bare. She lifted the receiver of the phone to her ear with a sense of willful rebellion.

You're not here and I'm picking up the phone. What are you going to do about what you don't know?

She almost dropped it when she heard a voice very much like Gabriel's on the line. She set it back down with a shaking hand and raced to her seat. Gabriel entered a moment later, looking from her to the desk and back again while she tried to be a study in industrious innocence.

"Done?"

"Yes."

"Print it out and bring it here to me."

She did as she was told, meeting him in the center of the room.

He looked it over and thrust it back at her. "Next time, give it to me this way from the start. I do not have time to double-check your work for errors." His voice was as hard as the curve of the gray stone window that looked over the fragile garden of her daydreams. "Now, you may have your wish. The car is here, put that on my desk and take your envelope back. You'll find all the documents are inside and signed just as I promised. Gather up the files I gave you as well and then I'll take you downstairs to meet your ride."

Casey nodded. She was exhausted and happy to know she would soon be free of him. Best of all, not only had she been spared providing him with any verbal presentation of her research findings as he had mentioned he was expecting earlier, it looked as though he was not going to keep her prisoner in some dismal room or make her drink any tap water tonight.

She did as he said; making a show of checking the documents for his signature even though she knew they would be in perfect order. She was pleased when she glimpsed a small frown cross his face. Gabriel had always been very good at keeping his word and she did not expect that to change now but there was no reason for him to know it. She shoved the envelope into her bag, threw on her coat, and grabbed the heavy stack of files. He was right next to her, watching every move as if storing it for

266

further analysis after she departed.

When they got to the door he spun her around and pressed her up against it with a restraining hand at her shoulder. His eyes darkened as his wings had when she had made him particularly frustrated in the dreams. "By the way, next time I tell you not to do something—like not use the phone—you will be more obedient and not disregard my wishes as you did a few minutes ago. Do you understand me, Cassandra Sloane?"

"Okay," she croaked. The blood rose in her cheeks. "I won't."

"Won't what?"

"I won't do something like that again." A frightened little sob escaped her. Couldn't he just let her go home now? Didn't he see she had had enough for one night?

This small sign of weakness emboldened him. "Tell me, I'm curious, am I real enough for you now?"

His face was close to hers but there was nothing friendly or that spoke of desire in its expression. She felt threatened more than beguiled. "Speak, Ms. Sloane. Am I a dream or have you been mistaken in your assertion of that fact to me earlier this evening?" He took her chin in his one hand and turned her face up toward his. "Real or not? Tell me this moment or perhaps I will not send you home quite yet. I will know your answer before you leave me tonight so you had best speak it to me now."

She twisted her head aside as if somehow that could diminish the pure terror she was feeling at his proximity and touch; the unwieldy stack of files almost slipping from her trembling hands. "Real," she squeaked in a tiny voice.

"What? I can hardly hear what you said. Tell me again."

Even when there were no wings to be seen, it was always "tell me" with this angel.

"Real," she said, her voice getting more steel to it, now more than willing to concede the point she had been so adamant to withhold from him when she had first arrived, since if nothing else, at least she had come to feel the truth of that one fact from the events of the evening. She was relieved to have figured something out for all her troubles with this Gabriel. "I think you are real."

"Exactly right," he said. His voice grew the slightest bit softer but upon glancing up Casey could notice no difference in the hard set of his face.

"Now, please, please, let me go home." She was begging but she was too weary to care anymore for pretending to be braver than she was.

"You have gained a little more good sense in the last few hours. I had almost despaired of it. I expect you to continue in that direction, Ms. Sloane. Don't disappoint me. I dislike being disappointed and I especially dislike it in all matters in which you are concerned in any way." He let her go as abruptly as he had taken hold of her and proceeded to bring her down to the waiting car without another word.

Casey followed a few steps behind him the whole way; juggling the bulky stack of folders in her arms and wishing she could pitch the pile of them at his head instead of carrying them out with her to be reviewed with great diligence before the next evening.

In the back seat of the car, the smoked glass acting as a shield between her and the driver, she began to sob as soon as the car turned from the drive onto the deserted road; all her outrage, fear, and confusion spilling out of her in an outpouring of hot tears. She did so nonstop until the car arrived at her doorstep and she scurried out of the vehicle to escape into the safety of her small suburban house for at least a few precious hours of rest before facing the renewed demands of Phillips & Row and its new client, NIGHT, Inc.

Once she had locked herself up tight inside, Casey changed into a faded nightgown with a picture of Alice in Wonderland looking up into a tree at a disappearing Cheshire cat and with a relieved sigh, sank under the warm weight of the down comforter she had pulled up to her chin. The true depth of her problems was as difficult to discern as the form of the clever cat grinning away like it knew lots of things Alice did not. Gabriel smiled at her that way tonight. She did not like that smile at all.

Stupid cat, Casey thought. *Stupid Alice.*

The evening had been long and exhausting, and Casey realized with a pang that she was not even going to have an overpriced band t-shirt to show for it in the morning.

"I was dying to go to that concert." Casey sighed. "Stupid angel," she groused. She was surely in a big pile of trouble. "Stupid me." She gave the covers a fierce tug and dropped into sleep as fast as Alice fell down, down, down into the dark, deep depths of the rabbit hole.

And she was glad to do it.

≪ CHAPTER TWENTY-SIX ≫

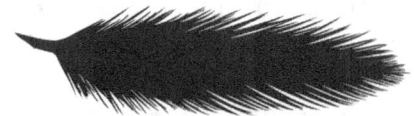

CASEY SLID INTO THE back seat of the car that sat, motor idling, in her driveway the way it had every night for the last two weeks. As usual, her arms were full of files and she was mumbling small curses about how it would be nice, damn nice, if the nightangel Gabriel, would get up to speed on the whole technology thing. Hadn't he heard of the concept of digitizing?

Casey thought he had, and that the company possessed a state-of-the-art document management system, from which someone was busy printing copies of the documents and whole files Gabriel deemed necessary every day so he could set them like a prison sentence on his desk each evening. He loved handing her heavy stacks of folders, a few times entire boxes, brimming with documents for her review just before he spoke the four words she currently cherished above all others: "The car is here." She did not know whether to love the car and driver or hate the car and driver. It depended upon whether she was coming or going.

The car was always waiting for her in her driveway at the appointed time. The driver never lifted his head to look her way from under the brim of the peaked cap he wore pulled down low over his eyes as she came along the drive. The windows were so smoke-dark she could not make out his features as she passed him anyway. She knew it was not Gabriel because Gabriel was always waiting at the other side. Even if he could have pulled something like that off, she was still sure it was not the nightangel because the driver was not much for curb-side service, something Casey believed Gabriel would not be able to resist out of some kind of ingrained chivalry he could not shake off.

The driver never got out of the vehicle or made any gesture of acknowledgment to her as she approached. Maybe he thought she would argue about going if he got out to open the door for her and then he would have to wrestle her into the car, creating a scene that might not go unnoticed in her quiet neighborhood. Maybe the deal was that she had to deliver herself into the car for the whole thing to unfold in the correct manner. She didn't know and she didn't care. She did not bother to look his way anymore. She proceeded with the business of pushing down the dread creeping up her spine at the sight of the car that would ferry her to the nightangel's doorstep and rushed down the driveway to get in the car before she could change her mind.

Tonight she marched down the drive at an impressive speed, given how much she had to carry. She yanked open the back door, threw the box of files in, and flung herself into the seat after it. She buckled up like she was in for the ride of her life although the driver took the car down the roads to NIGHT, Inc. every night as though the pavement beneath the rushing wheels was smooth as silk and they were sailing past the landscape instead of driving. The sensation was soothing but disorienting and Casey kept her eyes away from the blur of scenery flashing past the heavily tinted windows to minimize the effect.

It was Saturday night and she should be stretched out on her sofa in something comfy watching all the TV shows stacking up on her DVR while eating pizza or carryout Chinese food. She would give a lot to be curled up under a cozy blanket with the light of the TV flickering like a warm little fire in front of her. But she was trapped in what was beginning to feel like an extended state of indentured servitude with no end in sight that did not require giving the nightangel his way. She was still feeling a big *hell no* on that point so here she was heading back to face him again as if it was exactly what she should be doing until she came to her senses or something else happened. She worried a lot about that something else.

"Good evening, Miss." The driver had a voice like sugar cane frozen solid—sweet and hard. He greeted her with the same words every night as she settled into the back seat. His voice drifting through a small opening in the glass that separated driver from passenger, made her feel like a prisoner being transported under heavy guard.

Good evening, Miss, my ass, Casey fumed to herself. Her usual reply was the single word "right." Tonight, she went with a variation in honor of the weekend. "Yeah, it's another fabulous Saturday night for me." *Enough with the socializing.* She picked up a folder from the pile in the box beside her and began going through it.

Casey was well aware that right now she was pretty much hating everyone whether they deserved it or not. She had not spoken to Ricki since the night she had sent off the concert tickets to her without the requisite phone call to go with them. She figured Ricki had a right to be mad at her but now Casey was beginning to feel annoyed at Ricki in turn. Didn't Ricki notice how lost to the world she was?

The driver had not earned any special exemption either. He had to know something shady was going on but he drove her to hell and back again each night anyway. He had asked her during every ride home if she was well, if she needed anything, if he could help—this much was true. But that was probably because she had developed the troublesome habit of crying in soft, outraged little sobs on the return trip and he felt obliged to at least try to act concerned. The point was he still drove the car back and forth with her in it anyway. And so, she pretended she did not hear his questions. He never pressed her past those. At least he gave her that small courtesy.

She had decided right away not to waste any time trying to figure out where she went every night, as she had to go anyway wherever it was. She spent the time traveling there in feverish preparation for another evening with Gabriel, though it seemed a losing battle.

Casey had discovered that telling an angel you would prefer being enemies to being friends had some unfortunate consequences in the workplace. For one thing, angels were very good at handing you a heaping helping of whatever you ordered up. And they expected you to clean your plate. Casey was starting to think she should have read the menu better. If only it had allowed for substitutions she'd have never chosen so poorly in the first place. Being Ms. Sloane instead of Casey had its price, and it was a heavy one.

Casey flipped the folder in her lap closed. She powered up her phone and let the cascade of text messages from Ricki float in front of her tired eyes. The string of texts between them comforted and irritated Casey in turns; she treasured them. Ricki's words were some kind of absolute proof that the normal world was still there—even though she wasn't seeing much of it these days—and all she had to do was pick up the phone and get yelled at by her best friend to grab hold of it again.

She read them over starting from the top as she did every night on the ride to NIGHT, Inc. as a sort of restorative tonic she could drink down before diving into a flurry of preparations for the daunting evening ahead.

A courier. Really? You're not getting any t-shirt.

I'm home and you're not here. Where are you?

WHERE ARE YOU?

??????????????

We are going to have words tomorrow.

But they had not had words because Casey was unavailable to exchange them with Ricki—except by text—something that would never satisfy her friend.

These first texts were the worst because Casey knew from them that she was going to have to avoid Ricki at all costs until the battle with Gabriel was behind her. The problem with this approach was that Ricki was having none of it and Gabriel was no more ready to call a cease fire now than at the moment she first spoke the word "foe" to him. Her life was getting more complicated by the day.

She scanned the next few texts. Here their exchange skipped down either side of the screen in alternating colors like fighting words encased in bright bubble gum. They had not begun until after a morning and afternoon of silence on both their parts.

Ricki had fired off the next message. *You said you were camping out on my sofa all week. You didn't think I'd be worried?*

Casey understood that not answering a text message from Ricki was a hazardous business and she stood on the dangerous edge of unanswered text message number six in a 24-hour period. She had texted back and waited for the remonstrations to begin. *Said a few days not week. Just wanted to sleep in my own bed last night. Sofa not exactly comfortable.*

You should have let me know. And I warned you about the sofa.

Fell asleep. Figured you wouldn't expect me.

Wrong. What if you were in an accident or something?

I guess that would have been a better excuse for not calling but falling asleep is all I got.

Not enough.

Okay, mom. From now on I'll check in if I am going to be in past curfew.
We are so going to have words tonight.
I'm working so you're going to have to text them to me.

She looked the texts over one more time as though maybe that would be enough to erase the dispute between them, erase the night when everything started going so wrong, erase the steep steps that led up to NIGHT, Inc. and the menacing angel who waited at the top of them. But it wasn't enough. Nothing she could do would be enough to make any of her angel-related troubles disappear.

Her phone gave a cheerful chirp. Casey, thinking about all the things she would change if she had a time machine and could go back and make a few adjustments, was so startled by this noisy interruption that the phone almost fell from her hands.

She frowned down at the screen. She was okay reading past messages. She really didn't want any new ones. *Like she was going to get off that easy.*

A text message from Ricki lit up the screen, waiting to be answered. *Your stuff is still over here. When are you going to come get it?*

Casey could almost imagine it tapping its little text toes, counting down the seconds of delay until her response. *Not tonight.*

When? More toe tapping.

Let you know.

We're still going to have words. Doesn't matter how long you put it off.

I know.

Ricki's ringtone sliced through the air. Casey stared down at the phone as the picture of Ricki and Casey, heads mashed together and big smiles plastered on their faces filled the screen. Ricki was upping the ante but Casey wasn't sitting down at the table. They were not having words tonight as much as it would please Ricki to do it.

Casey rejected the call. That was a kind of word, wasn't it? A nice no-nonsense goodbye spoken via the push of a button.

Enough said, she told the phone with a wink.

No doubt, Ricki Lee Harrington would have some of her own words to provide in answer to having her call rejected if only Casey would give her an opening to start talking.

Maybe, by the time that happened she'd have a better chance of holding her own. She was getting a lot of practice in the fine art of verbal sparring these days, thanks to the uncompromising nightangel Gabriel.

Casey looked down at the display and her fingers hesitated over the keypad. She wanted to call Ricki but what was there to say that could be spoken out loud? Did she want to dig a deeper hole for herself? Was she available to patch things up anyway? She tossed the phone back in her bag and turned to the nightangel's papers with a defeated sigh. *Oh, yeah. He was a damn vampire alright. Sucking away her life hour by hour, day and night.*

"Is everything alright tonight, Miss?"

The driver was changing his tactics, starting the questions on the ride over instead of the ride back. *Smart move.* The chance of getting an answer out of her with any success when she was sobbing her eyes out on the ride home was next to zero. Maybe he had figured that out.

"No, not really. It's okay, though. I'm fine."

"It doesn't seem okay and no offense, but you do not seem fine. May I help you in some way?"

She laughed a weary, bitter little laugh. "I don't think anyone can help me. I got myself into this and I'm the only one who can get myself out of it. I just haven't figured out how to do that yet. The way it's going, I'm starting to wonder if I ever will." Why had she told him this last part, her greatest worry, when she did not want to tell him a single thing?

"Are you in danger, Miss? Shall I call the police?"

Call the cops. That was a good one. Casey started laughing at the idea of this and that laugh morphed into something alarmingly like a small fit of hysterics. The driver was quiet until the giddy gasps accompanied with some sniffling and breathless sobs tapered off. She took the linen handkerchief the driver offered through the opening in the window and wiped at her eyes. She blew her nose in a very un-princess-like manner. Aric had been so wrong about that princess stuff. She balled the handkerchief up and tossed it in her purse. She was pretty sure he would want her to keep it. "No. Please, don't do that. No need for any sort of intervention here."

What were the police against something like Gabriel anyway? Besides, what in the world could she say? *My boss is a vampire I met in a daydream. He's making me work for him and he's being so mean. There are no diet sodas in the place. No snack machine. No coffee. He frowns at me all the time and keeps me up way past my bedtime. He calls me "Ms. Sloane" for goodness' sake. Please give him a serious talking to and tell him to let up.*

Like that wouldn't say crazy with a big C. They'd probably arrest her for prank calling 911. And the angel would have to come bail her out. He wouldn't like that. She was supposed to be locked up with him.

"Maybe it would be best, though. I'm concerned about you. You seem frightened."

Now you want to help. What would have been helpful was if you hadn't driven off and left me standing there with a damn nightangel that first evening. "It wouldn't be best. No police."

"Then, tell me what's wrong and maybe I can be of assistance."

Casey wished she had never said a word. What if he told Gabriel she had spoken to him about her situation? Nightangels were private creatures and would not let such an indiscretion go without taking some action to resolve it. Who knew what that would entail? Especially with the nightangel in such a severe mood.

"No. No. I'm not afraid of anything. There's nothing wrong."

"You do not seem like a young lady who is enjoying life. Something is wrong, no matter what you say. I wish you would tell me what it is."

"I may not be enjoying life right now but that doesn't mean something is wrong. And even if there was something wrong, there's nothing you could do to help so just forget it. You've been happily shuttling me back and forth so far. Keep doing your job."

Okay, so she was a little bitter. Casey yanked her iPod out of her bag and stuck her earbuds in without bothering to turn it on. She had just given him the universal signal for "don't bug me."

The driver rapped on the window between them. He was either not up on his universal signals or did not care about them.

She yanked the earbuds back out again. "What?" She did not try to hide the exasperation in her voice.

"You are afraid of him. Why?"

Casey looked down at the iPod. She supposed it was too late to turn it on now. She dropped it back into her purse and answered the driver instead. She felt a desperate need to shut him down before she said something she should not. She did not trust the driver or his questions. "I don't know what makes you say that. I'm not afraid of anyone. I'm not feeling well. That's all." To make her point, she yanked the soggy handkerchief back out of her purse and gave her nose another adamant blow to keep from crying in earnest again.

Now, she was dodging the driver too. She wished everyone would let her be.

"You can talk to me if you want. In my line of work I hear many things. Nothing you say will shock me. Besides, I have been told I'm a good listener. Maybe you need someone to talk to right now."

She did indeed but there was no one she could go to or trust. She had said too much once to Ricki and that hadn't turned out to be such a great idea. She did not plan on ever telling anyone about her recent troubles again. No one would believe her if she did. Even Ricki didn't really believe her. The truth of it was, thanks to the nightangel, she had begun to live an isolated life and whether she liked it or not, she would have to keep it that way until she wiggled her way out of this difficult situation. The problem was she was at Gabriel's mercy and he was not interested in giving her any breaks or cutting her any deals. That merciful angel thing was a total crock as far as Casey was concerned.

"I can't talk to you. I have all this work to do. Thanks for your concern, though," Casey said. She turned her attention to the documents piled beside her until they arrived at the offices of NIGHT, Incorporated.

The very individual responsible for all her current misery handed her out of the car as if she was indeed his treasure and her worth was beyond estimation before giving her a cold look that said just the opposite and walking her inside. "Why are you dressed like that?" Gabriel asked as they headed to the upstairs office.

"Like what?"

"You know very well what I mean."

Casey did. She was dressing like a modern Vestal Virgin and she was doing it on purpose. She had purchased some new suits and shoes so unattractive it pained her to put them on and pretend they were what she liked in clothing and footwear. "I have no idea what you mean." She had become a study in dowdy—closed-toed flats, formless suits, prim blouses, dark hose, hardly any makeup, and tonight she had yanked her hair up into a tight bun because she knew he admired her hair and wanted to deny him that pleasure.

"It is as though you are trying to disappear into the woodwork."

"I'm dressed in a businesslike manner."

"You were dressed in a businesslike manner the first night you came to me. Now, well I do not see the use in this camouflaging of your beauty. I see it anyway, no matter how you try to hide it from me."

Right. Well, he was not enjoying the view as much as before and this made Casey smile. The nightangel did not look as amused. He sat down at his desk and stared at her while she settled in at the conference table. If there was an Olympic medal for staring, Gabriel would be the gold-medal winner.

She was willing to endure his stare with a happy heart because she interpreted it as a sure sign her wardrobe choices had resulted in a small coup in the subtle battle in progress between them. When it did not stop, she began to rethink the level of her little victory. She pulled a pair of reading glasses out of her purse and put them on to up the ante. "What? What are you looking at?" She pushed the glasses up on her nose and matched his stare.

"You. With your hair up like a librarian or a schoolmarm. And now, the glasses too."

Casey's hand fluttered to the tight little bun and she gave it a satisfied pat. She was going for prim and proper and she took it she had hit the mark well enough. "I don't think there are such things as schoolmarms anymore and for your information, one of the librarians at Phillips and Row sets the standard at the firm for hotness with a brain attached."

"Does she now? And does she wear her hair in a bun like that too?"

"Not that I've seen."

"Well, my dear Ms. Sloane, my apologies to your female librarian friend, but I don't care what the other women at the firm of Phillips and Row are about. My interest is limited to you." His stare deepened and Casey struggled not to squirm in her seat.

"Your hair looks lovely down but this style provides me a much better view of your beautiful neck. I'd be a fool to complain about that." Casey gasped and as she let her breath out again, Gabriel spoke his next words into her ear. "Perhaps, you are dressing to please me after all."

"Maybe you presume more than you should." Casey pulled the pins out of the smooth bun as fast as her trembling hands could find them and shook out her hair. She was going to think about the strategic use of hairstyles as a tool for setting the tone in a different light from now on.

She pulled off her glasses and turned her head to glare at him but he was not there. *That was just not right*, Casey thought, alarm racing through her as she glanced around and behind her before looking ahead again. It did not help her mood to see him sitting at his desk as if he had never left it, observing her bewilderment with the smallest hint of amused satisfaction curving the sharp red line of his lips.

∞ ∞ ∞

By the time Gabriel led her out to the car in the early hours of the morning, Casey was desperate for someone to talk to for a few minutes. A good listener who could hear enough of her dilemma to soothe her frazzled nerves but not enough to cause either of them any unnecessary problems if the root of all her current troubles should discover such a discussion had occurred. She did not want the driver to suffer Gabriel's displeasure on her behalf. It would be nice to talk to someone though. She was tired of feeling so alone in the world. Her options for companionship beyond her angel were limited. She had nothing to say to him and even if she did, it would be impossible. He was all ruffled feathers and injured feelings at the moment.

Even Ricki seemed to have abandoned her except for a few spurts of scolding text messages—and these were becoming less and less frequent as the weeks passed. She did not know how to heal the rift between them without betraying her situation with Gabriel in the process. She did not have the energy to tell the sort of white lies that would be needed to keep things in hand with such an inquisitive friend. She was off Ricki's special no-daydream diet in a way neither of them could ever have foreseen.

No good would come from telling Ricki something like that. She would think Casey was not trying hard enough to set Gabriel to rest in the dreams. But she had tried her ass off and there he was walking right beside her anyway as though he could sip her up with a straw if he had half a mind to do it. He would not though. He had other plans for her and they all involved her shouting some form of "yes" to the very rooftops.

The driver, however, did not have any unrealistic expectations about her. At least if she did not count the part about how he expected her to get into the car, where it sat waiting for her in her driveway every night, without a fight. His offer to provide a sympathetic ear had taken root in her mind as the evening had worn on. It had not escaped her notice that when he spoke to her earlier that evening she had felt calmer and more cared for than she did throughout any other part of her day, although it was just a few words offered up without any proper response from her in return.

Of course, considering what her average day was like at the moment, that might not be that remarkable, but still—it was refreshing and she

278

appreciated it more than the driver would ever know. That sweet but solemn voice drifting back past the glass between driver and passenger made her want to answer his soft-spoken questions. Or at least a few of them. That voice belonged on late-night radio, soothing the soul and burning up the airwaves without trying. He would make a fortune and the world would be a little less troubled for it.

At the moment, the driver was sitting in the dark car and Gabriel was handing her into the back seat just as he handed her out when she arrived. These were the solitary glimmers of graciousness she received from him each night. In the dreams, he would have followed this action by brushing his lips against her hand settled in his and she would have smiled and blushed like a schoolgirl. A bout of kissing might have ensued. But this was no dream and she yanked her hand out of his as though his touch was toxic. He nodded then, as if she only behaved in the disappointing manner he expected and for now, he was willing to let pass.

Casey would have felt ashamed if she was not so furious and frightened all at once. Even as miserable as he was making her each and every night she spent in his presence, it was difficult to be cruel to him in this ewww-you-have-cooties kind of way. First, realistically speaking, no good could ever come from pissing off a nightangel. Second, she could not look at him without recalling the gentle angel walking hand in hand beside her along the garden paths of her dreams.

But then, just when she was starting to feel a bit guilty about how she refused to give him even the smallest chance to prove himself in this world, he stared into her eyes as if he had won the game between them already and it was only a matter of time before she admitted it so they could get on with things. His look said he was going to enjoy the moment she provided him that admission with every fiber of his being.

That look was her saving grace. It allowed her to toss aside her guilt and fight another day. The rules applied to both sides. No good ever comes from pissing off a mortal woman, either. Even a nightangel fresh out of a perfectly beautiful daydream ought to know something as simple as that.

And it was Gabriel Rule's own damn fault if he didn't.

≪ CHAPTER TWENTY-SEVEN ≫

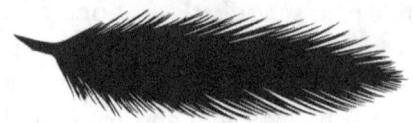

CASEY TOOK A BIG gulp of her grande, extra hot, extra caramel drizzle, skim caramel macchiato gone cold. She was going to need more coffee before the afternoon was done. She'd need a jumbo thermos of it if she was going to make it through another evening under Gabriel's watchful gaze without cracking around the edges from sheer exhaustion. He put the D in damn demanding without a single please or thank you to soften the blow.

She was paying a semi-wistful visit to her office at Phillips & Row to gather up a few files and make sure no one had been presumptuous enough to squat there for the fantastic airshaft view that was the privilege to which she had ascended at her level of seniority in the associate ranks. She saw no evidence to make her think anyone had been in her office. No crumbs, soda can or coffee cup rings, random post-it notes, or adjustments to the layout of her desktop or the height of her chair.

Derek had been low-key during the initial follow-up meeting in Ed's office about how the NIGHT, Inc. workload was going to be distributed between them. Ed was happy, so Derek concurred as a matter of momentary self-preservation. The calm did not last. Casey soon began to understand just how much Derek believed she was thwarting his ambitions when it had been revealed she, and only she, would be in direct communication with the client, and that, in fact, she would be based at the client site until further notice. The way things were going, Casey thought, until further notice would be about the same time hell froze over.

Normally, being stuck at a client site was the last thing any associate would want, but in this case it resulted in her having more authority than Derek where NIGHT, Inc. was concerned. As much as she saw it as a dubious honor at best, NIGHT, Inc. had developed a golden status in Derek's mind and the passage of time increased Derek's discontent. Consequently, Casey was not surprised to be entertaining a very unpleasant Derek Rider in her office when she did not remember inviting him to stop by.

Casey was shoving folders into her briefcase and listening to Derek's statements about how to handle such an important new client at the same time. She had learned anything that allowed her to decrease the level of eye contact she had to make while talking to him was well worth the effort of doing. She continued with her labors while he worked up to the major bone of contention in his mind—how their responsibilities with regard to NIGHT, Inc. should be switched around. Casey should be doing whatever drudge work he threw her way while he spent quality time with the client setting them up to throw all their business the firm's way.

If Derek knew how fast she'd offload everything to do with NIGHT, Inc. to him if it were possible, he would faint from excitement. She would love to turn him over to the nightangel so she could get a little R&R but no such luck. Gabriel wanted Casey—and Casey alone—isolated with him out at this off-the-grid NIGHT, Inc. office each evening. Derek did not like Casey having anything he could not turn down as beneath him before she took it on. She had tried to downplay it, make it sound small and ordinary, but he was smart enough to know something favored Casey in the equation. He wanted it too.

Gabriel would squash him like a bug and Casey was thinking about whether he would use a fly swatter or his thumb when Derek's voice broke in on her reverie. "I don't understand, Sloane. What can you do there you couldn't do here much better?"

Let's see. Casey considered the question. *I know. I could spend every night locked up in an empty building in the middle of nowhere with a nightangel who is feeling exceedingly thwarted and really not liking it very much. That would be one thing.*

Casey kept her eyes focused on her files. "Ask Ed. He sent me and he's told me to continue until the client says there's no more need for me to show up there every day." Casey chugged down more coffee to hide a satisfied little smirk. Derek was not going to go back and pester Ed on this. Ed had reached his saturation point with Derek's whining and Derek realized it. That's why he was complaining to her instead.

"I can understand the client wanting someone on-site, but why does that mean I should be getting assigned work by you? It's insane."

Casey could not agree more.

"This is all turned around." He was at her elbow now and his annoyance radiated across the small space between them.

"Maybe, but that's how Ed set it up with the client so that's what we're doing." The one good thing that had come out of the situation was seeing Derek so beside himself with envy over what he saw as some kind of professional coup. If he knew the depths of her misery, he'd be positively ebullient. As it was, he was green with envy and an envious Derek was a malicious, irksome Derek.

"You need to find a way to fix this, Casey. I should be taking the lead, not you." He touched her arm and let his fingers linger there. "How can I help you, if you don't help me?"

"I can't help you and I can't help what the client wants. And don't worry about helping me out. I can take care of myself." Except with Gabriel, who was dismantling with slow, methodical precision, every defense she could think of to keep him at arm's length.

"Come on, Sloane. Don't be like that. Let me help you out."

"You can help me out by not touching me again." Derek's creep factor was off the charts.

Casey did not have time to file a sexual harassment complaint against Derek. The last woman who did that wound up jobless and friendless while the firm closed ranks around the guilty-as-sin Derek as though he was the injured party. Casey figured it would be an uphill battle and why fight it when working for Gabriel took her out of Derek's reach while providing her an opportunity to annoy him without any real effort. Why, she had even been assigned pro bono work she could do solo instead of in tandem with Derek, in spite of his arguments about the problems it would create. Derek had been teamed with some poor first-year, a male first-year who thought a great deal of himself. Tales of regular pissing matches between them had already begun drifting through the office. Casey pitied the hapless recipient of their efforts.

"You need to learn to cooperate with your colleagues, Sloane. You're too competitive. Learn to be nice and you'll get further around here. For starters, you should be more helpful about NIGHT, Inc."

"It's out of my hands, Derek. I'm just trying to be a good team player. That's what you need to be, too. You know how Ed feels about teamwork at Phillips and Row." She escaped to the window, adjusting the blinds and craning her neck to see whether the sky was bright blue or darkening. She had a car to meet at her house by 6:00 PM and she was not going to be late because Derek couldn't bear not having his basic rights trampled on by the powers that be at NIGHT, Inc. just like Casey.

"This is not going to fly."

Casey thought of the nightangel's wings and how all-powerful he could look with them spread full out behind him. "Seems like it's flying fine to me."

"I don't think you know your place in the universe of things."

How right you are, Casey thought. *I'm slaving away for some vampiric angel that should not exist in the world. I'm going to have to go do it again tonight even though I am exhausted and beyond terrified. In the meantime, you'll continue steamrolling your way through life with no unpleasant consequences and will be in bed by a reasonable hour so you can create more misery for everyone you come across tomorrow. Something is out of place here. But it's not anything you think, Derek Rider.* "Maybe not, but the universe is spinning along, doing what it wants anyway. I'm just hanging on for dear life and doing the best I can."

"So what—now you waltz out of here and set up at the client's private offices for a working dinner and some gold stars?" Derek believed a private setting was a privileged setting and he disliked not being asked to the party.

"Not quite."

"Sounds pretty cozy to me, Casey."

Casey snapped shut her briefcase, torn between riotous laughter and crying her eyes out. She settled for sprinting out the door instead. She was missing the gentle dreamangel she had found in her daydreams in exact proportion to how much she despised the unyielding nightangel who had found her in the world. Being that they were one and the same, it was a sure recipe for doubling all her troubles.

"You can rest easy, Derek," she said with a halfhearted laugh over her shoulder. "It's not cozy. I won't get dinner. And there are no gold stars or other incentives involved."

∞ ∞ ∞

She had one last stop to make before she raced out the door. She headed for the library and her secret weapon against Gabriel Rule. As usual, Mira was entertaining the attentions of some lovelorn first-year associate who had more chance of getting a partnership on the spot than a date with the research superstar of the firm. Mira tilted her head so the sharp line of her chocolate-brown hair cut across her cheek and fell back to reveal her face like a curtain being pulled across the stage when she spied Casey walking up to the reference desk. She dismissed the associate with a nod and the words, "If you don't call me to ask about my progress, you'll have it in your email in less than an hour. If you do, you might not see it until tomorrow." He rushed off into the bowels of Phillips & Row as if she'd slap him if he stayed put.

Casey gave her a broad smile. "Nice. You train them well."

"Yes. You have to be firm with the young ones."

"So, what have you got for me?"

"This. It's the last of those books. I would have dropped it by your office but I saw Derek in there with you. He loves to know everybody's business. Especially yours, Casey. Whatever is going on with this NIGHT, Inc. thing is making him crazy. Well, crazier. He'd never stop asking you what was in the envelope."

"You're probably right. Why rile him up?"

"Exactly. Besides, you," Mira toyed with the pearl necklace at her throat with cherry blossom pink nails and stared hard at Casey, "and your friend, have a right to your privacy."

"I guess that's true," Casey said, wishing she could let Mira in on her secret. She'd probably be able to research the hell out of nightangels if she could set her free on it. "This is it then?"

"I do have this." She glanced up at Casey with a hopeful look as she handed her a book. "I knew you'd be too busy to go out and buy it right now but maybe this way you'll come."

"Come?" Casey asked, turning over the book in her hands. It had one of those covers that would have made her itch to buy the book if she'd run across it in one of her bookstore runs.

"To my book club. Remember, we've talked about it before. I'm giving you my copy of the book we're going to discuss. I've already read it. Several times." Her dark eyes twinkled. "It'll be fun."

284

"It sounds great but I don't think I'll be able to do that. I'm working late every night."

"It's on Saturday. And we're meeting at this new tapas bar in Arlington. They serve eight kinds of sangria."

Casey would love to talk about books over several glasses of sangria but Gabriel stole every minute of her free time. "Believe me, Mira, I'd love to but I don't see how I can fit it in."

"You need to do something for your mind that doesn't have to do with work. Besides, you'll like my friends, and they want to meet you."

"Maybe a future meeting, Mira. Right now, I'm working on Saturdays and Sundays, too."

"NIGHT, Inc. a lot to handle?"

"You could say that." *And a lot more. But that would be so not smart.*

"I heard you're working with the head of the organization. Is that true?"

"Where'd you hear that?"

"Derek told Richard. They're working on some pro bono case together. And Richard told me. He needs conversation starters. That was a pretty good one. So what's that like?"

Great. It's just great. "Nothing exciting. Standard stuff," Casey said, concentrating on the book cover instead of looking at Mira. *She was a crap liar alright.*

"That so? I heard this company is kind of mysterious and so is the man who runs it. You got anything to say about that?"

Not a thing. "Nope. If that's what Derek's saying, he's got it wrong. I gotta go." She was halfway out the door before she realized she still had the book club read in her hand.

"Keep it." Mira called out. "The hero is tortured and extremely hot. The author writes like Austen on a bender. You'll love it."

∞ ∞ ∞

A drive home and a quick change of clothes later, she was sitting in the quiet back seat of the car Gabriel sent for her every evening like a visible summons on wheels. Casey had switched her text message alert sound from a chime to chirp but it still startled her when it rang out in the plush silence that surrounded her. She wasn't getting many texts these days but those she did get were from Ricki.

Ricki's irate texts had gone from a flood to a trickle over the last few weeks. Casey did not think it meant Ricki had stopped being angry at her. It just meant she was storing everything up to hash out face to face or in one incredibly painful phone call.

We need to talk. This had become Ricki's war cry.

"No we don't." She could feel the driver's eyes land on her as she said the words out loud. So what if she was talking to herself. Who else did she have to talk to?

Can't. Working. She punched the two words into the text message box and tapped send. "Well, I am kind of working," Casey mumbled. Maybe heading to work counted as a work activity in this situation.

You need to come get your stuff.

Casey knew Ricki didn't care about the few things she had left at her place. She wanted her to come over there so they could clear the air and get things back to normal. She'd give anything for normal, anything to watch Ricki Lee moving through life like a whirlwind and occasionally dragging her along for the ride. It could be very entertaining—but it wasn't going to happen at the moment. She had enough excitement in her life right now anyway. In Gabriel, she had found someone who could outdo Ricki on every level with regard to the whirlwind thing. Gabriel kept life from getting boring too but on a whole new—and pretty much intolerable—level. She wasn't enjoying it much but at least she could count on him not to insist she discount what she saw with her own two eyes as Ricki did. That had gotten her into a lot of trouble in the end. And it wasn't even the end yet; it was more like the beginning or the middle.

Can't now. Stick it in a bag in your closet and I'll get it when I can.

I've got your tablet.

She really needed her tablet. She was reading three books at once on it and it bugged the hell out of her not to be able to finish them. Not that she had time to read these days anyway.

That's okay.

I can bring everything by your house later.

I won't be there.

Then your office now. Can be there in 30.

Not there now. She needed Ricki to step away from her sudden desire to deliver things to her doorstep.

Where the hell are you then?

At client site. Well, she was almost at the client site.

Ok. I'll bring it there. Where is it?

Have to kill you if I tell you that. Casey planted a little smiley face after that statement.

WHERE? Ricki hated smiley faces.

Sorry. She couldn't help adding another smiley face. *Can't be entertaining guests here. High level of intolerance for disruptions.*

Really? Receiving a package is a disruption? Ricki was not used to so much push back from Casey and her outrage was leaking through the edges of her questions.

No but receiving you there with or without a package will be one.

WHY?

You're naturally disruptive. I say that in love.

WE NEED TO TALK.

Can't talk there so forget it.

SOON. Don't care where. Nobody is that busy.

We can talk but can't promise it will be soon. And I am that busy.

Giving you the benefit of the doubt here you are trying to save your ass at work and that's what this is all about.

Okay. Thanks.

But something is not right.

Smart Ricki, Casey thought. *Everything is fine,* she texted back.

Don't think I don't know that's BS.

Right. Whatever you say.

And we are going to have words. Many words. Some will not be nice. I say that in love.

Ricki was dying to have her words with Casey. Casey swung between desperately wanting them too and appreciating the wall her difficult angel had provided for her to hide behind until Ricki could focus a chunk of her ire back on opposing counsel in some of her upcoming cases.

Of course. Looking forward to that.

Makes two of us.

Casey missed the hell out of Ricki but she wasn't relishing their next encounter. She wondered if she could buy her way out of this with a couple orders of that lobster ravioli in pink sauce Ricki was addicted to if it was accompanied with a remorseful apology, extra heavy on the remorse. Ricki liked to judge and then forgive. If Casey took this approach, Ricki would do both quickly, their argument would be put behind them with a proper post-fight hug, and they could focus on having a nice dinner to celebrate getting back to friendship as usual.

287

Gotta go. Casey stabbed the letters into the keypad and powered the phone down without waiting for Ricki's response. Said in love or not, she was sure whatever Ricki would have answered would include some of her best not-nice words and Casey could do without them tonight.

≪ CHAPTER TWENTY-EIGHT ≫

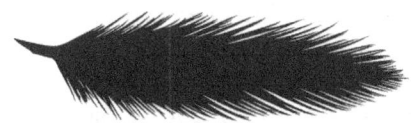

CASEY TURNED TO THE pile of folders she had placed on the seat beside her and dug in. She was going over documents as if somehow that was going to save her ass just like Ricki said, though she knew by now it would not. Still, she did it. Gabriel could turn her inside out with one displeased look and she did not want to earn any more than necessary by being unprepared.

She had already answered the driver's eternal question, "And how are you tonight, Miss?" She had tried to be pleasant when she responded because she was starting to think he had a real interest in her answer.

It seemed that was not enough because now that she was done texting back and forth to her irate best friend, he fired a question at her. "You never answered me the other night. Will you answer now?"

Casey looked up from her papers with a frustrated little sigh. *Crap.* He was like one of those dogged TV detectives who, without any evident effort, pried all the answers from the people trying hardest to give them the slip. And while he was doing it, he drove the car so that it felt as though it was flying across the ground at warp speed instead of bumping along at an everyday pace. She was impressed with his driving skills but that didn't mean she wanted to answer any of his questions. She sensed he was studying her in the rear view mirror to gauge her mood before continuing. She was sure her anxiety was written across her face.

"You are afraid of him, aren't you?" His tone was gentle but the expectation she would answer him this time ran through it like a rod of steel.

Casey wished she was still engrossed in her text message quarrel with Ricki. He had left her alone while she was doing that—but then, maybe that was just because she was talking to herself while texting.

"Answer, Miss."

He demanded her response with such authority Casey found herself spitting it out before she had time to frame her response in the proper light. "A little," Casey admitted. *Oh, damn.* If she had texted him the answer, she wouldn't have made that mistake. She could have shut down the exchange with a tap of the finger. But they were talking to each other through the gray glass and that wasn't an option.

"Just a little?"

"Maybe more than a little." *Double damn.* That was not the answer she meant to give. She was a better lawyer than that. Gabriel was destroying her brain cells with this nonstop exercise of *will* versus *won't* they were engaged in. *Okay, sue me; I'm afraid of a vampire. Like you could do better,* Casey thought, starting to fume at the injustice of it all.

"Then it might help to talk to someone. Besides, you have to stop crying at some point, don't you think, Miss?"

She thought it would help too and she had been thinking it more and more since he had first suggested it to her. She could not bring herself to do it, though. Casey did not want him to think she was a complete loser who didn't have a friend in the world. "I'm not crying."

"But you have been crying. Quite a lot. And that is just here in the back seat of this limousine. That leads me to believe you will be crying again sooner than either of us would like to think because you are in the back seat of this limo quite a bit."

"I'm sorry I'm such a big crybaby. If I'd known I was disturbing you, I would have stopped it right away." She despised her recent propensity to get all weepy just because her life was a hopeless, irredeemable wreck. Being exhausted, terrified, and attracted with every molecule of her being to the perpetrator of her misery, had that sort of effect on her.

"Now, you know that is not what I said, Miss."

Casey was embarrassed by her flash of sullenness. He was only being honest. She was a sad, friendless mess right now and if she had a brain in her head she would tell the driver what he wanted to know. Maybe he would see something in it she did not and she could extricate herself from this nightmare. "Are you going to report our conversation to him?"

"Are you going to say anything that would ethically require it?"

"Like what?" Casey asked.

"I don't know—like revealing trade secrets, providing insider trading information, confessing a secret murder plot?"

"No." Casey found herself giggling at his statement. Maybe it was the secret murder plot. She had not laughed out loud in weeks and it felt good. "I don't think so."

"Then you need have no fear of speaking to me. What is said here will stay here."

"You must be from Vegas," Casey quipped. This time the driver laughed. She appreciated his sincerity and the way his laugh embodied an honest respect for her flash of levity during what was obviously a difficult time for her.

"No, but now that we have established some ground rules, why not talk to me?"

Casey's urge to talk to the driver was beginning to overwhelm her fear of saying something to him she should not. He had a nice laugh—like sunlight splitting the clouds. His sense of humor lifted her spirits. And he wasn't ordering her about like the nightangel or acting all offended like her best friend was because she couldn't go to some stupid concert. Casey let out a deep breath and gave a truthful answer. "Because he might get angry about it and he's already not thrilled with me. I don't want to stir up any more problems between us."

"Why would he be angry about that?"

Casey cringed. Already she was saying the wrong thing. "He likes it best when I'm too busy to talk to anyone except him. He has to know I haven't talked to a soul since all this started—except for a few people at work," Casey said, thinking about her hasty conversations with co-workers. "And I don't think that counts much."

"But you have friends, I am sure. Even being so busy, you must talk to them."

"My best friend is mad at me right now and the feeling is starting to be mutual. We haven't spoken lately."

"I'm sure that's difficult."

"It's not that bad. We're in texting mode right now. Believe me, it's better that way."

"How can that be better than sitting down with your friend and making things right?"

"I have something to sort out first and she doesn't understand the meaning of none-of-your-business. The two don't mix well. It's easier to dodge her questions in a text than in person."

"So who do you talk to until you can solve that problem of yours and the two of you can mend your fences?"

"Nobody, I guess. She's the person I talk to when anything is worth talking about. I spend a lot of time working. There's not much time left over for a social life and I'm not big on a bunch of casual friendships anyway."

"One good friend is worth a host of others."

"True," Casey said, thinking of the angel in the dream instead of Ricki, as she ought to be doing.

"You and your friend sound very close."

"We are."

"What could make her so angry with you that the two of you would not speak for what—a few weeks now?"

"I guess it has been weeks." Casey gave a heavy sigh as the reality of that sunk in. *Weeks.* That was a long time between best friends. "It was that first evening I went to NIGHT, Inc. You remember—when you left me there all alone after I asked you to wait."

"I remember, Miss. Unfortunately, I had a previous directive."

"I bet you did."

"And you weren't all alone. I left you there safe and sound with Mr. Rule."

"Really. Well, I'm glad you have so much faith in Mr. Rule's good intentions."

"If I didn't, Miss, I would not have driven away that night." He ignored Casey's belligerent "phfft" of disbelief and brought the topic back to Ricki. "But you were telling me what happened with your friend."

Casey wanted to ask him why he had such confidence in Gabriel Rule beyond the fact that he was paying his wages but she didn't want to risk hearing anything good about the nightangel. She answered the driver's question instead. "I was supposed to go to a concert with her. I had to blow it off because *he* said I had to stay—we had work to do, it couldn't wait. *He* didn't care what I had planned." Casey figured the driver would get who the *he* in question was.

The driver made no comment on the way she accentuated each "he" as if she was poking a pin into it. "Skipping a concert was that significant?"

"Yes. It was a big deal. She has this thing about doing what you say you're going to do and following through on promises. He wouldn't even let me call her. I had to write a note."

"You blame Mr. Rule for this falling out between you and your friend."

"You bet. I suppose I should get used to it. This type of thing is going to be par for the course. I should have seen it coming from the beginning. I suppose he can't help himself. It's just natural he's going to cause problems for me. We are never going to be on the same page and we're both going to have to accept that. Except, he's never going to accept it."

The driver pondered this for a moment. "I asked you last night, Miss, if he is a dangerous person. You said it didn't matter but I would like to know the answer because I think it does."

He said this as if she had a choice about answering. Casey knew the bottom line was he was going to get her answer or keep asking until she said something that satisfied him on this point.

She was not sure what the right answer was. She had no idea what the driver would do if she said his employer was the devil and she needed immediate delivering. She imagined the driver would say, "I see," then deliver her express, no extra charge and without any more conversation, straight to NIGHT, Inc. But there were no devils here, just a vampire with a wicked set of wings and a serious sense of entitlement. Casey felt safe enough to give an honest response.

"I guess so, in a way. Like I said, it doesn't matter. It's too complicated to explain. It's just who he is, his nature. It seems like he must be dangerous by default."

"By that standard, everybody could be a little dangerous. Especially if we did not trust them or found ourselves suddenly at their mercy while not in their good graces."

"Maybe," Casey conceded. "I mean he's not a mobster, or serial killer, or drug lord or anything. He's not slapping me around or something crazy like that. He's just very intimidating, that's all. It scares me half to death sometimes being in the same room with him. And I have to go face him every night anyhow and pretend he doesn't scare me at all."

"It sounds as though you are being very brave."

"Brave. Me? No. He'd laugh to hear you say that. He knows I'm shaking in my boots. And he's turning the screws more and more—like maybe that will hurry me along. It's hard not to fall apart on the spot when he does it but so far I've held it together. I don't know how much longer I can do that."

"Why don't you stop going?"

"He's outsmarted me, that's why. I'm in a no-win situation. I have to go or I'll lose my job. If I do, maybe I'll never get another. I can't afford not to go. I'm a lawyer, by the way—just so you don't think this is about something else. I'm still paying my law school loans. I have a house, and car, and other bills that need paying like everyone else does."

"Of course, Miss. So I thought with all those legal files and boxes coming home with you every night and back again." His smile traveled through the glass.

"Yeah, it's like a gym membership, a speed reading course, and sitting in the front row of a law school class all rolled into one." She almost smiled herself for a minute.

"It's a difficult situation for you. I'm sorry you have to suffer through it."

And Casey believed he was. For the first time in weeks, someone got her without wanting to use that information to suit their own agenda. His compassion was melting her reserve.

"Yes. It is difficult." Casey did not want to think about how very difficult it was. When she considered the fresh trials that came with each evening spent in the presence of the clever angel, she felt like Alice, swimming through a sea of her own tears. And they were worthless anyhow. They never washed away the edge of hurt, shock, and anger she was feeling. She suspected she could cry her eyes out all over again right then and there anyway. And she could not do that. They were about to pull into the gates to NIGHT, Inc. and she'd be damned if she would give Gabriel the satisfaction of seeing her teary before their evening battle had even begun. "I'm sorry. I can't talk about this anymore."

The conversation was officially over. She had a moment left to steel herself for an entire evening in the middle of nowhere with a despotic nightangel and no help to be had for it beyond her own resolve to be as difficult as possible. As though that would wear out her welcome—as hostile as it was—or make him irritated enough at her to send her packing.

Ah, there he was—the very nightangel in question, waiting for her at

---

the base of the steps like he was checking her in to a detention center and did not want her sneaking off somewhere before he could turn the key and lock her inside. For someone who was so set on treating her as his enemy, he sure liked to have her around.

He opened the door when the car came to a stop as if he could not help himself from performing this small courtesy to her even as he denied her so many others. Casey always mumbled a thank-you as though it was squeezed out of her. Their eyes locked for a moment of assessment after these two acts as if maybe, by some miracle, one or the other had decided to capitulate rather than go on like this for another night. So far, that had not panned out for either of them.

She trudged up the steps after him, slipped through the door, and watched him bolt them in against the night before turning to lead the way to the upstairs office.

"There's soda and bottled water in the mini fridge under the bar," he told her after she had settled in.

Amazing. What would be next, instant coffee, soup packets, a microwave and individual microwavable snacks? An ice machine? "I know. You told me already, remember. And I told you that you shouldn't bother with it because I wasn't going to drink any." Since the tap water incident, Casey had not asked him for a drink of anything again.

"There's nothing wrong with any of it, if that's what you think."

"I'm sure you don't have to drug me to take advantage of me. After all, you're taking advantage of me right now, aren't you?"

"And how is that?"

"By pretty much kidnapping me anew every night and forcing me to come here and work for you against my will. It is against my will, you know."

"How could I forget something you feel obliged to point out to me at every conceivable opportunity, Ms. Sloane? This is not a prison. I am not your warden. If you wish to go, go. Go right now."

"Like I could do that."

"You can do anything you like, Cassandra Sloane. You could even choose to rethink your stance with regard to me and how we relate here in this world together."

"You mean the friend or foe thing."

"Yes. You could change your mind about that."

"And everything would be wonderful between us just like that?"

"Better than it has been over the last few weeks. What do you have to lose?"

Casey believed she had everything to lose. She shook her head no.

Gabriel had the look of someone who was not used to being thwarted but had decided to tolerate it for the moment to prove his goodwill.

"I don't want your sodas, bottled waters, or second chances to bend myself to your will. I don't want to be friends because you think that's what we should be. I want to be left alone to go about my business like before you turned up. I want my freedom—from you. I hate this. And I hate the way you're putting me through all this hell to get your way. I hope you know it's all for nothing."

The angel was starting to look rather cross. She continued anyway. "You can make me show up here but you can't change my heart."

"No, I can't do that. But then, neither can you. You can choose not to listen to it for a while but you cannot change it."

Now it was her turn to look annoyed. Casey was desperate for an ice-cold shot of caffeine to keep her from sinking into a state of exhausted compliance. After all, he had a point. Denying it was wearing her out.

"Alright. I'll tell you what. I'll take a damn soda. But I'm paying you for it."

She yanked a dollar out of her purse, set it on the edge of the table, and grabbed an ice cold diet cola out of the refrigerator. She flipped the top and began drinking it down in front of him because it took her somewhere he could not go—poolside on a hot summer day, blanket on a sun-drenched beach. The panic receded and her energy bumped up. This wasn't just diet cola, it was diet cola with lime. Her favorite. If little bottles of creamy coffee beverages started turning up in that fridge, she'd be hard pressed to keep resisting him. Fortunately, it did not look as if he knew about these twist-top miracles of caffeinated convenience or how addicted she was to coffee drinks with mocha or caramel in the name.

"You don't need to pay me."

"Yeah, I do."

"Casey."

"Ms. Sloane, please. And I do need to pay you."

He pushed the dollar back across the table.

"Fine. Don't take the dollar. I won't take the soda." In reality, it was too late for that because she had taken the soda and swallowed half of it down already. She turned around and dumped the rest of it out in the sink in a show of belated resolve.

She thought she heard him sigh.

"Very well, Ms. Sloane. If you change your mind though, please help yourself. You don't need to pay me. Consider it part of your compensation."

Even the partnership of Phillips & Row would not have the audacity to suggest a couple cans of soda in a mini fridge were some delightful perk. Casey could have burst out laughing but the nightangel seemed to be taking this very seriously.

"I'd rather you install a soda machine and give me Saturdays and Sundays off."

"Let's see how this works first."

"I can drink all the icy beverages in the world and it won't change a thing between us."

"Are you so sure?" He flashed a glance her way that was all heat and honey. She was smart enough to get what that meant beyond the initial weak in-the-knees sensation it produced. In it, she glimpsed everything he wanted and she did not. He was not going to be carving "Casey + Gabriel 4EVER" dead center of an arrow-pierced heart in some tree trunk for her to admire anytime soon. No matter what he thought. He might as well stop smiling and settle in for the fight.

"Yes, I'm sure."

"Then I suppose I will have to find something else that will do the trick."

Casey hated to consider where that line of thinking would lead him. "Good luck on that. I think you'll find me extremely uncooperative."

"Not even you can be difficult forever."

"I can try."

"So you choose to continue on this path? You want to further pursue this little war between us?"

"I see no alternative."

"You know, dreamer, I would think at this stage, you would begin to open your eyes at least a bit to all the choices you could make where you and I are concerned. Why don't you take advantage of this short cease-fire while you can? It is not too late for us to be friends and put these cat-and-mouse games aside. You are no good at them."

"That's because I don't want to play these stupid games with you in the first place. Why don't you get it? I don't want to have anything to do with you. I wouldn't be here if you weren't forcing me to do it. I don't see how that can satisfy."

"It does not satisfy." His voice was tinged with hunger.

His lips turned the kind of red that made her want to kiss him and then run for the hills. Casey did not believe there were any hills to run for however, so that was a no-go. Even if she did kiss him, it wouldn't fix anything. No matter how much he thought they could make it work, there was no way to fit a vampire into her life. At some point he was going to bite and it was all she could do not to make a scene the last time she had blood drawn at the doctor's office. She would be a bad girlfriend for even the most patient vampire. And Gabriel was the nightangel sort of vampire—not a patient lot at all. Although, Casey had noticed he liked to think he was.

"It's not going to satisfy and it's not going to be more than what it is right now. Why don't you give this up and be done with it?"

"Because, I am a nightangel. And that's not what nightangels do. Do you know what we do, Cassandra Sloane?" His eyes were dark with disappointment and renewed determination.

She met his glance and shook her head no because she was afraid to say anything that might incite him to demonstrate what that would be. He took a step closer to her and catching her hand in his, pressed a bitter-cold kiss into her palm. The hurt beneath the suppressed desire of his kiss stung her. All the prior kisses echoed up from within it like so many seals upon a bond. Every one of them said, "You are mine." This one said, "You are more unkind than you will ever know."

They both looked down at her hand still held in his.

"We keep our promises."

He didn't have to sound so damn virtuous about it, Casey thought.

He took the dollar from the table, folded it in half and put it in his breast pocket as if they were not done with this particular dollar bill yet and he meant to hold on to it until they were. "So then, it is still foe?"

"Yes, it is still foe. My answer is not going to change. Don't ask me again, please."

"Certainly not." His voice was as brisk as a winter wind pushing through the treetops in the dark woods at the edge of the dreams; always a precursor of something coming down the pike, something unexpected and dangerous too.

Casey was startled by the edge of pain that chilled his words. A shiver ran through her. Her refusal wounded him and Casey would be feeling guilty about it if she did not want him to walk away from her so badly. Gabriel was looking at her in a way that said, "You ain't seen nothin' yet." And Casey gave him a "back at you" glare that looked braver than it really was. She was well aware an injured nightangel was going to be a doubly determined nightangel and she was only making things worse. That impression was confirmed by his next words.

"It seems we must be back to business as usual, my darling foe." And the way he lingered over the word "foe" left no room for doubt about what a pain it was going to be to be designated as such by the nightangel Gabriel. He was staring at her again. He was going to do that for the rest of the night.

Casey disliked being stared at by Gabriel a great deal. She could not tell whether he was taking in everything she was because he liked it so darn much or just the opposite. Even worse, she did not know which she would prefer.

She was certain of one thing. If he continued to look at her in that daunting way and spoke the awful words "document production" at the same time, all would be lost.

≪ CHAPTER TWENTY-NINE ≫

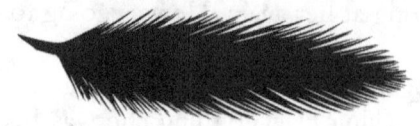

OH, YES, IT WAS still so definitely foe. She had never understood how down-to-the-bone exhausting and profoundly distressing being someone's beloved enemy could be.

Gabriel was bringing her down to the car later and later every night. She was past weary and he knew it. Not only that, he was happy she was pretty much dead on her feet. He was turning those screws alright. *Tell me. Tell me. Tell me.* It vibrated from every corner of the night. But Casey kept her mouth shut. She was in no mood for such dangerous disclosures. Besides, she had someone else to talk to now.

The night had been a trying one and she realized, as she headed down to the car with Gabriel brooding by her side, it was the promise of the drive home that brought her through every evening intact. The ride there and back home was now the one time in her day when she felt a modicum of security and comfort. The driver was her sole contact with the outside world besides the standard work interactions. Talking to him gave her a lifeline. She had grabbed hold of it and did not mean to let go. And so far, the driver was okay with that.

Gabriel waited until she got into the back seat and then leaned in to give her a last unsettling look. His face was stern and he did not say goodnight. It seemed vampire princes did not feel obligated to lay on the charm when their chosen one was being all uncooperative. She fumbled

with her files and her seat belt; anything to avoid that look. *Close the door.*
Close the door. Close the door. She chanted the words in her head and waited
for him to send her home.

The chanting was not helping though. He still had the un-charming
thing going at full blast. He stood staring in at her until she figured he'd
never stop if she didn't say something. "Well, goodnight," she mumbled.

He did not wish her goodnight back but he closed the door and that
was good enough in Casey's book. He struck the side of the car twice
before he stepped back to watch the vehicle pull away. He did this every
night and Casey dreaded that look he gave before the door closed on her
each evening more than anything that had gone on between them earlier.
She gave a little shudder as though she was shaking off everything that
had hung over her throughout the course of the hours she had spent
inside the NIGHT, Inc. building with Gabriel Rule.

"Good evening, Miss," the driver said in a deep voice that was
comforting without striving to be. It drifted back like a cool ocean breeze
as she settled the files around her. "Still in one piece, I see," he added
after they had taken the turn out of the driveway.

"Barely," Casey whispered, feeling as though a brief crying jag would
be in order but not having the energy to accomplish such a feat. A small
smile crossed her face instead at his comment and that surprised her.

"Are you hungry? I can drive through a fast food place and get you
something. I imagine that in the midst of such unsettling circumstances,
you are not eating as you should."

"I can't do anything right these days—eat, sleep, think straight—
nothing. Someday soon, you'll be able to skip taking me here and drive
me straight to the emergency room. Maybe they'll put me in a nice bed,
drug me up, and give me a doctor's note to get me out of work for a day
or two. Maybe if I'm unconscious, he'll believe I'm not slacking if I
require a few hours off to eat and sleep. Of course, maybe not. He's
unpredictable these days. I never know what he'll throw at me next,
except he expects to see me here every night. That's the one thing he's
very set on."

"You knew him before all of this started?"

Casey had not seen this question coming. "I don't know whether I
did or not."

"That's a strange answer, Miss. Most people would know one way or
another."

"Most people are luckier than I am. They don't have to worry about their lives being complicated by things that can't be reasonably explained even if they have a really good imagination."

"So, things are complicated and every night you go to see the author of all these complications with a heavy heart."

"You got it."

"And you expect this to continue for a while?" He took her deep sigh as an answer. "Then, perhaps we should find a way to set all right between you two before things go too much further. Hospitalization is an expensive resolution to any problem and besides, you do not seem the sort to enjoy a dramatic intervention unless a happy ending is ensured."

The driver sure has my number, Casey thought. *I do love a good happily-ever-after.*

"Perhaps you should tell me what went wrong in the first place."

He thought he could help her fix it as easily as if it were a flat tire. A small smile pushed up through her distress at the idea of it. "Well," she answered, "it's like you said. I find myself at his mercy but not in his good graces."

"Were you ever in his good graces? Once we understand this, we will be in a better position to judge your options."

Now he thought she had options. She answered as if she thought so too, although nothing seemed less possible. "Oh, yes. Before? Always. At least, I think I was." Her voice sounded sad instead of careless as she had intended.

"What happened to change that, if I may ask?"

"I guess I did something dumb."

"How dumb?"

The driver did not mince words. Casey appreciated that, though it stung a bit.

Yeah. Hey, I'm a dumb ass when it comes to Gabriel Rule. Deal with it. I have to. "You were supposed to say, 'I'm sure that's not true, Miss' or something along those lines."

"Now why should I do that when you have provided me an honest assessment of the situation and yourself within it? And so succinctly, too."

"It's just polite."

"Are you looking for polite words or a swift resolution to your problem? Since I imagine you are in great need of that resolution, we ought not to waste time pretending things aren't what they are. We can get somewhere with an honest discussion."

302

Oh, now he is all practical. What happened to all that 'if I may ask' and 'Miss' stuff? She figured she'd better continue with all the honesty even though it was painful. It did not look as if she had much choice anyway. "Pretty darn dumb."

Casey would have left it at that but the silence from the front seat demanded more. The weight of it pulled the exact explanation of pretty darn dumb out of her mouth and into the air between them in quick order. "I made him angry but that's not the bad part. The bad part is, I think I really hurt him. Oh, crap. I know I did." She was feeling guilty about it when she would have much preferred to feel glad instead.

Was it possible she had done that? Casey paused to consider the nightangel's feelings without considering her own first for a change. She preferred her version of the distressing turn of events so well that this was difficult to do. Gabriel had his perspective on her and the way everything was playing out between them but Casey did not think it would be a very good idea to consider it too thoroughly. It would give him more leverage over her than he already had.

"It happened on the first night I went to see him here and I've kind of expanded on it since then. I'm not always good about knowing when to give it a rest. And I've never known him to do anything halfheartedly. We make quite the pair. I don't know how it can result in any good. It's mostly his fault but I'm sure I've done my share of damage."

No. Wait a minute. I have to be the wounded party here—the real wounded party. Don't I? Not the nightangel with his 'Ms. Sloane' this and 'Ms. Sloane' that.

She pictured Gabriel's beautiful face and the way it looked each night before he sent her back home again. He did not look wounded. He looked emboldened. He was waiting for her to fall before him in this battle of wills. He expected to win. And if she had caught flashes of something else fly across his face when she said or did something even she thought was not very nice at all? Casey reminded herself in those moments it was what he deserved for making her so miserable.

"So you can see the problem right there. I don't know how it got out of hand so fast but it did. There's no way to repair it now anyway so what does it matter? It's done and everything is ruined."

"I doubt that's true. You said there was a time when you were in his good graces. That is always an indicator things could go back in the other direction given the right level of attention to approach and effort." His voice reflected his conviction.

She had found a champion and coach all in one.

"I don't think it can go back to the way it was before. Things are too different. I don't see a fix for it. He hates me now." Her voice cracked. She did not want him to hate her.

"Hate is a strong word. His actions, as you describe them, don't reek of hate—just strong emotion."

"I'm pretty sure it's hate. If you saw the way he behaved toward me—you'd see why it's hard to believe anything else."

"And what about your emotions? Do you hate him?"

"No." She did not and that surprised her.

"That's something at least," the driver said in a dry tone. "And you did say he never hated you before."

"I would have sworn to it. I mean, he's been mad at me before, I'm sure, but we had no hating going on between us ever. I could have never imagined it happening. I thought he really—" She stopped herself. "I thought he cared about me. I thought we were—" Casey struggled to find a word to describe what they were that made it sound as innocuous as possible. "I thought we were friends. I relied on that and I guess I shouldn't have."

"Why should you not have relied on it? We should rely on our friends. And it sounds as though you had a true attachment to each other."

"I guess it's what I should have expected all along. He was a sort of virtual friend. You know, like someone you meet on the web. That's a minefield. I felt I knew him well but given how everything is going on this side of things, I'm not so sure about that anymore. Maybe I didn't know him at all." Casey heaved a dismal sigh. She hated thinking the nightangel was anything but what he had always been in the dreams.

"I should have known better than to put my faith in something so impossible. Nothing could ever be that good. Nobody could ever be that perfect." Her tone had grown bitter. It seemed to her the angel had used the daydreams as his own little online dating site. She ought to have made him fill out forms, do some paperwork, get a background check and present it to her.

"What made you do it then?"

"I liked him," Casey said. *That was the understatement of the year.* "I liked him so much." *And that would be the second biggest understatement of the year.* To think you could not like something as wondrous as a nightangel was unrealistic. Or that was what she had believed until she had come upon her angel on the flip side of the daydreams. She was not finding it so difficult to dislike Gabriel Rule.

"So why see it as impossible? It doesn't sound impossible." He interrupted her thoughts.

"Long-distance relationships never work out," Casey responded.

"Is that so? Strange. Your relationship sounds as though it was working out fine."

"Well, it's not working out fine anymore."

"And when did that change—from fine to not fine—happen?"

"The moment he turned up here."

"Just like that? Why the sudden turnabout? You enjoyed his company before."

"Haven't you heard about the hazards of meeting people on the web and such? They seem fine there—and then they turn up at your door with a hatchet or something."

"That does sound dangerous. Did he turn up at your house with a hatchet, Miss?"

"No. He did not." An edge of embarrassment crept into her tone. *It would have provided me a little more clarity if he had,* she thought. "He changed the context of the relationship, that's all," Casey said stiffly, as if that explained the whole problem.

The driver did not seem to think so because he asked another question. "How?"

"By just showing up, that's how."

"What, Miss? Without even a by-your-leave?"

Casey was pretty sure he was mocking her. Worse, she could almost hear Rane's teasing voice call across the void. "Princess, is that fair?"

I am not acting like a damn princess, she told herself.

She rushed to explain. She couldn't stand the idea of the driver falling off her dwindling list of friends. "He had an obligation to tell me. I hadn't thought I'd run into him here. He lived ...so far away. I kind of liked it like that. Then he shows up—out of nowhere, without us agreeing to it beforehand—and making a lot of assumptions about how things are going to be with us. He's forgetting I have a say, too."

"Maybe he thinks you did have your say. Are you telling me that you never talked about him coming to see you or your feelings for each other? I'd find that unusual given how close you say you two were." The driver had teased out the flaw in her argument and laid it out for her to consider. He was waiting for her answer.

"Not exactly." She was starting to feel defensive. "And even if that's true, he should have gotten the message his presence was not required at this time after all and left. But no, he has to have his way—he has to stay and prove his point. He's so stubborn."

"Unlike you. You're not stubborn at all, I am sure."

"I'm not all that stubborn."

"Yet, you deliver yourself to his doorstep each evening as much because he summons you as that you will not allow him to win the day."

"Don't start with me. I thought you were on my side." Casey gave a little laugh and shrugged. The driver did have her pegged. "Besides, seriously, I need my job. That means I have to do this."

The driver was quiet for a moment, as if he wanted to give both of them time to consider her explanation. Casey shuffled the papers around on the seat beside her until he began speaking again and when he did, his voice held a knowing smile deep within it. He was thinking it was as much about prevailing as about holding on to her job for Casey. Casey thought he might ask her what would happen if she changed course and allowed Gabriel to win the day. But he did not. She was glad because then she would have to think about that and if she did, she wasn't sure what she would do anymore.

She was on a kind of you-can't-make-me autopilot. Her heels were dug in and she was not allowing herself to consider alternatives. She did want to prevail, though she no longer believed prevailing would bring her what she wanted. Especially because what she wanted was what she could not have—Gabriel in the real world without all the troublesome issues attached to his being a vampire and much worse somehow, she was sure, a vampire with an impressive set of wings to his credit.

The driver's next question pulled her back before she had a chance to examine some of her premises too closely. "Think hard now. You are sure there was nothing that would have led him to believe you might like to see him here; nothing to make him believe he is right to stand his ground with you? Nothing at all?"

Just every moment they had ever spent in the dreams together which maybe did count a little. "I don't know why he thought because we had the long-distance thing going that meant there could ever be more than that. He just did. And now there's no way to avoid him. I keep telling him this won't work and he should give it up, go. But he stays." Casey's voice trailed off on this last point. "Why won't he listen?"

"Maybe he doesn't believe you. Did you give him a reason not to believe you?"

Casey could not think of a good answer for that because she sure wasn't going to say yes and she couldn't say no without it being a lie. "He doesn't quite get the word 'no' in certain contexts. He believes he knows best. I'll give it to him—sometimes he does. Not this time though. He shouldn't assume things. It's arrogant."

"It doesn't sound like you are giving him much of a chance, considering your friendship. Why is that, Miss?"

Was there an accusation under that question that she was not being fair? "The timing's not right." Casey gave her head a willful little toss in the darkness.

"Life rushes by. It is not always what we were expecting. Maybe you should forget about the timing and accept the moment as it comes to you. Perhaps it has been brought to you for a reason and you are more ready for it than you understand. Maybe, Miss, it is good enough for now."

Everyone thinks I am ready. Hey, I am not ready, Casey fumed in silence. *There were more reasons anyway.* "It's not just that. It's a lot more than timing. He's complicated. The whole thing is complicated. I'm not sure I'll ever be prepared to see him standing in front of me. I mean, excuse me, have you met him?"

"Yes," the driver said. "I have met him."

"And what did you think?" Casey was curious to hear his impression.

"It seems to me he is a man who understands the world around him, what he wants there, and how to get it. He does not care for unnecessary delays."

"That's one way to put it."

His smile radiated through the darkened glass, warming her mood. The driver had Gabriel pegged too.

"You do not want to give him his way. It does not seem fair to you."

"It isn't fair."

"Maybe, Miss, it is fair enough for the moment."

Did the adamant vampire waiting on her to arrive so he could put her through the wringer think this whole thing was unfair too; that she was the source of the injustice instead of him. Maybe what she was unprepared for was to be wrong about him. Because what would happen then?

"My life is total shit right now because of him and I've lost a best friend too. If he wasn't in my face every night, I could just miss him. Instead, I have to deal with him—not being like I knew him to be. I hate that."

"There was something special between you and that sort of thing may change but it doesn't just evaporate."

Casey hesitated. If she stopped talking now, she would feel safer for a moment but she would be stuck where she was with Gabriel until she broke. Because deep down, she knew she was going to be the one who broke. Nightangels did not break. Nightangels stood firm. Yet, she would keep fighting him unless she could sort out how to get around it. She needed some good counsel and the driver seemed willing to give it, so she decided she'd keep talking.

She took a deep breath and let it out in a slow stream like steam from a kettle. "Yes. At least that's what I've always thought. We liked each other—a lot. I could tell him anything and he always got me. Even when I was being difficult, he got me." Casey grinned. "He appreciated me for who I am."

"That's worth something."

"Yes, it is." *Probably everything right there in a nutshell.* And then, there were the kisses on top of it. They were awfully good. Unfortunately, there was the vampiric angel thing going on as well. And the whole stepped-out-of-a-dream problem had not gone away either.

Her grin evaporated when she considered how very little she was making him smile now. "He's—fascinating. I've never met anyone else like him." Casey gazed out the smoky window at the rushing nothingness pressing against the glass. "Right now, though, he's just obnoxious."

"Do you believe he is finding you equally annoying, Miss?" He said "Miss" like a tutor trying to draw the student to think harder on the question being put to them—encouraging, no-nonsense, and already in possession of the answer himself.

"I hope so. It's my current goal in life. Do you have any ideas about how I could up the annoyance factor? Maybe he'll throw up his hands and let it go. I could waltz off and never have to see him again."

"Is that what you really want?"

He asked way too many thoughtful questions.

Well of course not, Casey thought. *I just said how damn remarkable he was.* "Miss?"

But it's what I should want because going down impossible paths with impossible beings is not wise—or safe. And although safety was probably already a lost cause, Casey longed to be wise with regard to the nightangel Gabriel.

"I don't know what it is I should want anymore."

"It sounds like something worth trying to sort out, Miss, despite the annoyance factor. Fascinating is difficult to find in this world."

≪ CHAPTER THIRTY ≫

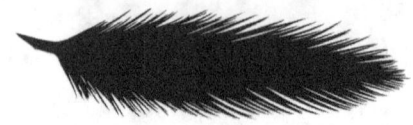

FASCINATING WAS FLAT-OUT TROUBLE, Casey had figured out way too late with the nightangel. "Even if I wanted to sort it out, it's not that easy. It's like I'm in the driver's seat of a barely street-legal sports utility vehicle. I don't know how I got behind the wheel but there I am. I'm trapped in this powerful machine and it's rolling along like it has a mind of its own. I'm trying to stop it but I don't know how to put on the brakes. It should be like driving any other vehicle but it's not." Casey flung her hands up like she was lifting them from an imaginary steering wheel. "And now, to make matters worse, somehow I've gotten off the main road. Nothing is working right. There's no GPS. All I want is to get back on the highway and to the place where everything is normal again. But I can't figure out how to slow it down, or turn it around, or find where I was before all of this started. It's like I've forgotten how to drive and navigate. I'm all turned around. I don't know how to handle this out-of-control situation."

"I'd say you're doing a fine job handling it. The problem is you're slow on the uptake. That may be a frustration to you and your employer but it's not a sin."

Casey made a huffy sound and, pressing back against the seat, folded her arms across her chest. "I am not slow on the uptake. I'm cautious."

"Is that it?"

She wished the driver were less astute. She was trying to lie to herself and he was compelling her to come clean.

"Maybe you're not supposed to go back to the place where everything was the way it always was before. Maybe you're driving toward a new road up ahead somewhere. You have to go forward to find it. And when you do, you are going to realize it's where you need to be. You will see putting on the brakes, turning around, or finding a place that does not work for you anymore would have been a catastrophe and finding this new path is what mattered. Why don't you keep your foot on the gas and find out what happens?"

Throwing caution to the wind was not her idea of a resolution but the driver was appealing to that little piece of her that craved adventure and was more curious than she believed she ought to be. "That would be nice, but where does it go?" Casey protested.

"Perhaps you should not worry about that yet. Maybe you should find this new road and go from there. It must go someplace more pleasant than your current evening destination."

"I bet you're right about that." She would find it easy to identify a place better than that—visiting the dentist for a root canal every night might meet the requirements if only she did not fear getting stuck with needles so much. Maybe she had hit on the one thing that beat out a visit to the secluded NIGHT, Inc. office for last place in the world she wanted to be. That was somewhat of a relief but she hated the dentist's office so much it was hardly saying anything. "However, I don't see how that's going to happen." Casey leaned forward. "Do you?"

"You said you think he hates you but you do not hate him. Why not hate him?"

"I don't think I can. I should though. He's been a total bastard to me. Sorry if that sounds harsh, I know he signs your paycheck, but it's the truth. I just want him to cut it out." She could not keep the outrage from her voice.

"If that's the way you feel, isn't it possible he has not gone from liking to hating you just like that either, no matter how it seems? Go back to the start. How did you upset him?"

Casey was embarrassed to say what she had told Gabriel. She justified it a bit first. "He gave me this ultimatum. I'm not good with ultimatums, you have to understand. Well, I kind of told him—in the heat of the moment—I'd rather not be friends."

"Ah."

Casey felt that small acknowledgment demanded details because as it stood, she sounded like the wrongdoer in the situation and that was just—well, that was just wrong. Gabriel was at fault for pressing her to make a choice. The driver remained silent, waiting for more. Casey plunged in and began to lay out the evils done to her by Gabriel Rule.

"I realize it doesn't sound very nice of me or even reasonable but you don't know the whole story. I mean, he puts my job at hazard and he rearranges my life so I'm at his beck and call. Then he stands there, calm, cool, and collected, and says, like it's nothing at all, 'And hey, let's be friends while we're at it'. And I'm just supposed to fall in with his plans? No way."

"Aren't you curious to know what being his friend would be like?"

Oh, the curious thing again. How did he know how very curious she was about Gabriel Rule and how he could fit into her world? Because she was. The kind of curious that killed a cat or two. "I wouldn't use that word. You have no idea how complicated it would be."

"Because he's complicated."

"Right. It's complicated. He's complicated. Maybe I'm complicated too. And now he's so impatient when before he was so understanding," Casey said with deep frustration.

"Does he see it as being impatient?"

"No. He thinks he's being the most patient person in the world. He's always telling me about how damn patient he is over all this. 'I am being patient, Ms. Sloane.'" Casey mimicked Gabriel's tone.

"And you don't think so?" The driver was laughing at her peevish imitation.

"I don't see it but it's not like I can tell him so. I think he's confusing patience before with patience now, like it's one straight line from A to B or like because he's run the race once, I ought to give him the medal he earned again."

"That's not your take on it though."

She detected a note of surprise in his tone. "No. This is here. He has to start over again and earn his medal from scratch. Or maybe not quite but still, come on. How presumptuous and egotistic can you get? I mean, how did he even get into the race?"

"Frankly, Miss, not many men would be willing to do what you are suggesting."

"Really?" Casey was stunned.

"Really," the driver said, like it was just common sense.

"Would you?" Casey was a little less sure of her stance now.

A small scoff escaped him. "Not for a second."

"Oh." Casey's voice reflected her astonishment. She blushed in the darkness.

"I am not sure it has so much to do with presumption or ego, Miss, but with the reality of having given part of his heart away to you already. How can you expect him to start over with you when you are holding part of what he has to give in your hands as if it does not exist? It doesn't seem very fair or even realistic, does it?"

Was she the villain here? "I guess that's true. I hadn't thought about it that way. Maybe he thinks all he's doing is moving things forward from where we were before. He sees our mutual happiness, where I see nothing but problems. Maybe I lack vision. Crap."

She leaned forward and pressed her head close to the window between them as though she was kneeling in a dark confessional whispering her sins to her confessor. "I didn't say I'll take the foe option right off—that's the thing. I said I wanted it to be all business, but that wouldn't do for him. It was friend or foe and nothing in between. I mean, is that reasonable?"

"Perhaps he thought it would be easier to choose friend if the alternative was something less neutral."

"Well, I couldn't give it to him because everything was going his way, and I hate feeling I have no control or choice in a matter. My entire life is in a shambles and he is the person responsible for it. I wasn't feeling so friendly toward him. So you see, when he said my choice was between friend and foe and that was it, I got angry and said—"

"You said 'foe'. And he took you at your word."

"Very much so. And he's been hell on wheels ever since. And it's a shame because I think deep down he's not the sort of person he's being right now. He's always been so kind." Casey was overcome with a small bout of sobbing.

"Being someone's foe is much more than not being friends, Miss."

"I know that, thank you. Mr. Rule is working hard every night to drive home that point."

"Maybe you are both a little stubborn in your own right."

"Maybe." She rubbed at her eyes. She pressed her knees into the back

313

of the seat and leaned closer so her mouth was as near to the opening in the window as possible and she could whisper. "There's more."

"I thought as much. Perhaps it is best you tell me all then."

She might as well. She didn't have any answers. She thought maybe the driver did. "He did ask me if I would change my mind, after the first few days. And the way he said it made me believe for a second he hated the fight between us with all his heart. But then I thought maybe I was wrong, so I told him I was fine going on being his foe forever and not to ask me again. I wish I hadn't said it because, when I did, his expression changed."

Casey had never seen the nightangel look quite like that before. That look was stuck in her mind like a snapshot she couldn't find a way to erase from her camera.

"First, he looked sad. I should have taken it back right then and told him what a lie it was but I couldn't bring myself to admit it. Then the sadness was replaced with resolve. I knew right away I'd unleashed a whole new pile of trouble onto myself." Casey paused, feeling sorry for herself and Gabriel Rule in turns.

"Has he asked again?"

"Yes but I shut him down. I guess I haven't wanted to come to an understanding; I haven't been interested in seeing things from his side. I've wanted my way no matter what the cost. That's funny because five minutes ago I would have told you it was the other way around."

"When you're trying so hard not to see anything but what you want to see, it's easy to lose perspective, Miss."

It wasn't that easy. I've put some effort into it, Casey thought. "You must not think very much of me after hearing this. I'm not proud of myself for doing it. I'm not a mean person but I was mean to him in those moments and maybe all along at every step without realizing I was doing it."

"Don't be so hard on yourself. People make mistakes."

"I wish I would not have made these ones. They escalated things. Now, I don't know how to stop it."

"Would you like to make a different choice about the friend or foe question?"

Casey had thought about this a hundred times but had put the idea aside. She did not think the angel would go for it. "It's too late. He's already asked and I've already refused. I've turned away every peace offering he's directed my way too. Why should he ask again?"

"Peace offerings? What do you mean? What were they?"

"Diet colas. He put them in this little fridge for me after a dispute we had about tap water."

"Interesting."

She couldn't see why that would be so interesting, but maybe arguments about tap water were rather unusual. More likely what he meant by interesting was—*you've done a great job screwing this up but I can't say so because I need to get the rest of the story out of you first.*

"That's it?"

Casey forced herself to continue. "And the roses. He left them on my desk. And believe me when I say they are not any old roses. He went to trouble over them."

The driver considered these diverse olive branches as if he might be about to say something very wise about them. Casey did not give him a chance to comment on them or her. "I bring my own soda now and ignore the ones he has set out for me. And the roses—" Here, she took a deep steadying breath.

"Go on." The driver's voice was stern when it had been neutral a moment before.

"I...I threw them away right in front of him."

"My impression is this is not something you would normally do."

She did not know how the driver had determined that about her but he was right. Again. "It's not. I hated to do it but I couldn't let him think he was getting to me."

"But he was—getting to you?"

Casey did not answer because the answer was so dangerous to her peace of mind she did not want to voice it. "When he left the room, I got the roses out of the trash and put them in a crystal ice bucket sitting on the counter behind me; then I ignored them," Casey said instead. "We didn't talk about it after but I think we both felt better. And I was glad, though I'm not sure it's a good thing for him to feel better about anything concerning me. Since then, he leaves another flower on the desk every day like some kind of scented time bomb. I stick it in the ice bucket with the others like that will diffuse it. Then I ignore them too. And I never thank him. You think he would know to stop but nothing I do fazes him. I'm going to need another ice bucket soon if he won't cut it out."

"You look at them though?"

"Actually," Casey said in a conspiratorial voice, "it's impossible to ignore them. They're…magical. Those astonishing flowers remind me of the kind and considerate person I knew him to be before he became such a pain. It's a relief to have a reminder of that in plain sight. Not that I'd ever tell him that. It would be much better if he didn't leave them for me. If they're from where I think, he shouldn't be bringing them here and I shouldn't be enjoying them."

The driver ignored her commentary on the flowers and focused on the practical aspect of what they represented. "Roses indicate love, not hate. You could have taken it as a sincere peace offering. You could still take it as a sincere peace offering."

"Maybe. But if that's a peace offering, he isn't doing a very good job of being peaceful with me afterwards. At first, I figured there would be a kind of built in safety net in being his foe. As long as I'm his foe, I thought, I can keep him at arm's length while I figure out what to make of things. But it hasn't worked out that way. There's a kind of up-close intimacy to being on someone's shit list when you have to see them every day."

"I imagine so." The edge of a smile deepened the driver's voice. She amused him.

"Yeah, it's pretty bad. I miss being friends. I just don't know how to get things back on track in a way I'm comfortable with and he'll accept as enough."

"Why don't you ask him if you can change your mind and choose friend instead of foe with some caveats. You've had some time to think about it, and he has, too. From what you've told me he has made some good faith efforts to rectify things between you. You've chosen to ignore them. I'm not judging your actions. I'm simply pointing out that perhaps he doesn't like the current situation any better than you do."

"I don't know. He seems to be enjoying himself. Maybe he'll say no. What if he steps it up? I'll have a nervous breakdown if he does that."

"What if he accepts and this awful weight is lifted off your shoulders. Most people don't like to be at war with those they care about. It sounds as if he cares about you even though it doesn't feel like it right now. If not, how do you explain all those roses? And let's not forget the diet colas."

"You're definitely laughing at me now."

"No, Miss. Not at all. But you mentioned these things in particular, so they must be worth some consideration."

"Now I know you're making fun of me. And it's not diet cola. It's diet cola with lime."

"I'm afraid he knows you too well, Miss. If you continue this battle, he will surely best you. You may as well seek to resolve it without further delay."

It was not that simple. As much as she might like to befriend Gabriel in the real world, there were some basic issues with a supernatural boss-slash-friend-slash-kind-of-more.

"Look, even if he did say okay and agree with all my relationship rules and regulations, it still opens the door to tons of other problems." As difficult as the status quo was, Casey had already moved on to the next reason to avoid fixing things.

"Like what?"

"Like being in a relationship with him that is not virtual. We're from such different worlds. What if we don't mesh like before? What if we can't overcome our differences? What if it doesn't work and it blows up in our faces? I know that must be the only logical outcome."

"Why not think beyond logical outcomes? There's more to life than logic alone."

"I'm being realistic. Look what's happening now. Mr. Rule and I are not exactly enjoying each other's company."

"Right now you are foes. And you told me you made that choice, not him."

"He made me pick foe."

"Did he?"

"Yes. Well, kind of." The driver's silence caused her to modify her statement. "Okay. Not exactly. But it felt like he did. And it feels like he's still making me pick foe."

"You want to be realistic, so be realistic. You picked it, Miss. You're picking it every night when you walk in there. And it sounds like Mr. Rule is not one to walk away from the battle without giving it his all—especially when he has such a powerful interest in the outcome."

Casey could barely catch her breath thinking about why she should say "no" to the angel at every turn and why she didn't want to ever let go of him. "I don't know what to do with him or myself at the moment. I don't know if I can be with him right now—or ever. I want him to go but I can't stand the idea of him being gone now that he's here. I want it to be done so I can get back to business as usual but I'm worried I'll die of boredom if everything ever went back the way it was before." Casey took a sharp breath. "How did this happen? Things used to be so much easier."

The car slid through the dense night like a knife through a slice of rich chocolate cake. Casey wanted to learn how to drive this way. Was there some trick to it that the driver would teach her if she asked? The way he drove made her feel calm, soothed, safe.

"You're making things more difficult than they need to be. Why don't you take the problems as they come instead of anticipating them all at once? After all, you said you were friends before and the world didn't fall apart, did it?"

"Well, it was a different situation. It felt safer."

"Nothing in life is totally safe, Miss."

That was an understatement considering her situation.

"Well, I thought I was more in control and that made everything easier."

"And were you, really?"

"No." *Of course not.*

"Maybe you are clinging to an illusion and choosing safety is no choice at all. Maybe for you the true danger lies in taking what seems like the safe route."

"Maybe you're right. Anything has to be better than this daily hell. Maybe I will look back and realize I was at an impasse without knowing it and his arrival here set me free from it."

The problem was how to accomplish this simple task when it did not feel so very simple at all. She could not take much more, so it had better be soon. For the first time in weeks, Casey's mind was clear. She realized what she wanted to do and she thought maybe there was a way she could do it. She had to summon up enough courage to override her fear. She needed to set aside her stubborn resolution to ban wayward dreamangels, and bossy vampires, and nightangels without wings from her life just because she didn't know what to do with them at the moment. She needed to set aside the impact of her brother's actions—his despair, his anger, his loss—and not make it her tragedy too. He had walked away from everything, everyone. She didn't know what had really happened. And he wasn't there to tell her. Yet, without realizing it, she was living her life, making her decisions, based on what he'd done wrong instead of what she'd done right. Ricki would say "I told you so," if she only knew. She'd have loved saying that. It would have softened some of the other words she was waiting to say to Casey.

Casey did not feel quite so much like crying now. The driver was pulling up to the drive-through window of a brightly lit fast food joint.

"What do you want, Miss? Shall you pick or should I order something for you?"

"I don't want anything."

"We'll order something anyway since we are already driving through." His words were so sensible and his tone so pleasant she could not bring herself to argue about it.

"A coffee, then."

"No. Food, Miss. Not coffee."

"Okay," she capitulated. "A cheeseburger, please, and a coffee."

"How about the sandwich and an orange juice?"

"I suppose. Since I guess I'm not getting my coffee."

"It's very late for coffee, Miss. How will you sleep?"

Good question. She was developing a sudden craving for a large order of French fries to go with the cheeseburger. Of all the times for her appetite to kick in. "And some fries, too," Casey amended her order. "Not the small side but the big one, if you don't mind."

"Not at all. It's my pleasure."

He passed the food back to her a few moments later. She ate it with a hunger she had no idea she was holding in check until the request for the fries had popped out of her mouth.

"I'll pay you back," she said, after she had finished inhaling every last morsel.

"Consider it my treat," said the driver. "How was it?"

"Good. Really good. It's already gone. I guess I was hungry after all. Thanks." Casey gave a small, contented sigh. Fast food had never tasted so good. She would have asked him to drive through all over again for one of those apple turnovers if he would have added even a small cup of coffee to the order. But he was probably right about the coffee.

She leaned back in her seat without another word instead. She was thinking about what the driver said, and remarking to herself maybe there was a way out of the seemingly inescapable trap into which she had fallen, and gauging her odds of whipping up the nerve to speak to Gabriel when she saw the next opportunity to discuss the idea about switching sides—from foe to friend with a few little rules attached.

The driver was as good as a guardian angel. And that was lucky for her since she didn't seem to have a real one ready to step up to the plate and run some non-guardian-angel interference for her. The driver had led her to answers and given her hope when no one else could help.

How ironic was it the driver had never told her his name, never asked for hers? Yet, she felt closer to him than anyone else she knew. Next to Ricki, who wasn't talking to her, and Gabriel, who was hell on wheels when he wasn't walking around in her daydreams, the driver might be her very best friend in the world. Casey did not feel too bad about that. A friend was a friend and right now, she needed one. And she appreciated the way he said "Miss" as if she was someone special, not because Gabriel thought so but because he did.

She closed her eyes and when she opened them again the car was sitting in her driveway and the driver was repeating her name, "Casey, Casey, Casey," in increasingly louder tones in an effort to rouse her. The driver did know her name after all.

Casey sat up and yawned. She hated to get out of the back seat of the car and go into the house. She'd just enjoyed the most peaceful few minutes of sleep she'd had in weeks. She did not feel as fresh as the morning dew or anything but she did feel better. Gabriel thought he had plugged up all the avenues to any support network that could help her with her nightangel problem but he had not. He had given her the driver, and the driver had given her some hope when all seemed darkest. She was glad she knew the driver.

"Will you tell me your name?" She was feeling guilty about not knowing that when he was springing for cheeseburgers and fries and listening to her problems.

"Just call me Amicus," the driver said.

Casey raised an eyebrow at that but went with it. "Well, Amicus, maybe pretty soon we can stop meeting like this," she said, stifling another yawn. "And then we may both get some well-deserved rest. Although you'll be out of a job—at least this one."

"And is that going to happen by tomorrow night?"

"No way."

"I'll be happy to lose my current assignment with Mr. Rule if it is because the two of you have settled your differences. Until then, I'll be waiting right here for you each night."

"Goodbye then," Casey said, gathering her files and dragging herself out of the car. How long was it going to take to face her fears surrounding Gabriel Rule? It was difficult to say. Gabriel Rule was making her life a living hell but if he wasn't doing that, who knew what he would be up to next where she was concerned. Even setting that aside, when you are a foe and nothing else, finding the perfect moment to be something less hostile instead was not going to be easy. Gabriel had told her so from the first moment but she had chosen not to listen. Listening was not one of her strong suits, especially when it involved someone telling her what to do when she did not want to do it, so she cut herself some slack on the guilt trip.

"See you tomorrow, Miss," the driver said as she shut the car door.

She might be a dreamer but Amicus was a realist. And he was right. At least for the moment, he had a guaranteed passenger and she had an employer who knew plenty of games to play with her until she got tired of losing.

≪ CHAPTER THIRTY-ONE ≫

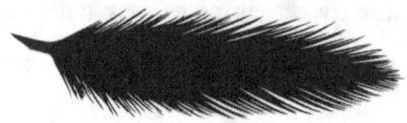

CASEY JUMPED UP FROM her uncomfortable non-ergonomic chair as if she had been stung. Gabriel was beside her before the scream left her mouth. "Something jumped on me. It's not on me, is it?" She swiped at her clothes and backed away from the desk like she had become motorized. "Well, is it?"

Gabriel responded to her panicked question by stepping in front of her and stopping her where she stood while assessing her from head to toe in one look that might have stripped her bare if it were a little less controlled.

"No." Her fear of creepy crawly things overcame her modesty. "You can't just look. You need to really check."

Gabriel stepped closer and began running his hands quickly up and down her clothing with a brushing motion that had a heat to it that just about fried Casey's circuits.

"It's not on you," he assured her.

"It better not be in my hair. Is it in my hair?" Casey switched to banging at her hair. "Please tell me it's not in my hair."

"Stop." He caught her hands in his and brought them down to her sides. The firm tone of his voice combined with the cool heat of his hands over hers made Casey keep them glued where he had placed them when she would have preferred wringing them together in distress.

Gabriel slid his fingers into the sea of dark waves framing her face and Casey froze. He began to carefully comb through the silky strands with a slow precision that felt intimate instead of methodical. He stared into her face as though he had just won the lottery but Casey didn't care because she really needed to make sure that damn bug wasn't nesting in her hair like in some horror movie. He might be enjoying the moment way too much but at least he was being thorough. "There's nothing there," he said, smoothing her hair back into place with calming strokes that rippled through her like moonlight on a summer lake.

It was those green eyes, always pulling her in, pulling her closer.

"Okay, then. What are you doing?" She tore her gaze away to look back toward her abandoned workspace. "You have to find it. You have to get rid of it."

Casey wasn't sure what it was exactly but whatever it was, it had to go. A bug was a bug and except for ladybugs and fireflies, she hated bugs. Especially ones that could launch themselves at her without warning. Her mood was not enhanced by the way the angel's touch was tearing away at her resolve to pretend she could live without him.

Gabriel's fingers continued their soothing motion for another instant and then he turned back to her workstation. Pushing her chair aside, he scooped something up from the floor beside it. He held it cupped in his hands. "I've captured your villain."

"Very funny."

"Do you want to see it? Maybe say hello? It's just a cricket."

"I don't care what it is and no, I don't want to see it. It might hop on me or—"

"He is an active little fellow." The angel interrupted her as he peered into the dark center of his hands held together in a makeshift bug prison.

"Or something," Casey finished, glaring at his cupped hands.

"Or something? That sounds serious. Worse than simple hopping. We'd have to check you all over again from top to bottom if he got loose and made a beeline for you." The angel's voice was serious but his mouth quirked up in the corner when he got to the checking her out all over again part.

"Just get it out of here," she ordered.

But Gabriel was already walking out of the room.

Casey followed behind, intrigued. The terrifying bloodangel, Gabriel, was taking his small captive somewhere and Casey was curious to see where that would be.

They went down the hall. Down the stairs. Out the front door. She lingered at the top of the landing, watching. The nightangel sprinted down the long, blood red brick steps and deposited the cricket in the bushes.

Casey took a step nearer to the edge, her arms wrapped around herself to ward off the cold and the strange shivery feeling that came from her close encounter with the large black cricket overlaid with the desire invoked by just looking at the angel a little too long. Now, she cast caution to the wind and gave in to her desire to stare at the angel full out. He was well worth a good case of the shivers.

She liked that he put the cricket in the garden, liked the way he looked up and smiled at her over this small, sudden adventure, liked the way he did everything—even the things she didn't like—with infinite care.

She liked the way the night got brighter when he stood in it too; the way he changed the whole world just by being in it. The air shimmered around Gabriel as he started back up the stairs. The brightness of the stars in the cold, cloudless sky glinted in his eyes. A look of concern crossed his face. Then he was standing right in front of her—all green shining eyes and dark hidden wings. The starlight receded from his eyes and the wind that had tousled his hair as he approached twisted around her and then grew quiet.

"We need to go inside." The night darkened again like he had hit some invisible switch on the way out of a room. He ushered her in with a hand placed firmly at the small of her back and her shivers turned to tingles.

She'd avoided his touch for weeks and now he had his hands all over her. And she'd started it by commanding him to pat her down and run his fingers through her hair because of some bug. He had only done what she'd told him to do. He was only taking his cue from her.

"You're cold. Come with me." He dropped his hand from her back but the warm sensation remained. It made her want him to touch her again. Make her warm all over. She had to stop that train from leaving the station. This touching thing was going to stop as quickly as it started.

He was right. She was cold. She wasn't sure how coming with him was going to warm her up but she walked beside him towards the back of the first floor anyway. She saw the answer as they entered an oversized room that was a modern mix of meeting and reading room. On one side of the wall was a gas fireplace flanked by two overstuffed chairs. Gabriel directed her to sit in one of them. "I'm going to make you some tea." He disappeared across the hall where Casey imagined there was a full kitchen in perfect working order complete with the requisite tea kettle and mugs for tea and coffee.

She settled into the chair closest to the door and leaned forward to study the violet and blue flames burning from a long bed of sparkly broken glass. She felt warmer already.

She glanced around the place. The angel had been holding out on her. At least, that was what she was guessing given the in-use feel to the room. When he chose to abandon her to work and think on her choices in that lonely upstairs office in utter silence, Gabriel was doing who knew what in the comfort of this wide-open and perfectly lovely space.

She'd be hanging out here too if she had a choice. She loved everything about it. The old-school high ceilings. The polished hardwood floors covered with jewel-toned oriental rugs. The wall of books that swept along one wall from top to bottom even if it did have a huge flat screen embedded into the center of it. Casey had a sudden desire to switch the TV on and start watching all the shows she'd been missing recently because of Gabriel and then find a sturdy library ladder so she could discover what titles were hidden on those top shelves, but she stayed seated and examined the showy orchid that graced the center of the table instead, glad to see Gabriel wasn't just focused on contraband flowers from the dreams. This orchid wasn't a grocery store variety orchid. The flowers had an unusual pattern and coloring she'd never seen before. Of course, it was thriving under Gabriel's care while even the hardiest of houseplants was sure to perish in her hands.

"Beautiful," she murmured, running a finger along the delicate edge of a petal so that it quivered. "Lucky you're with him. Don't let him take you upstairs. I'd knock you off without meaning to in no time if I start taking care of you. Even philodendrons aren't safe with me."

To one side of the table was a chess board, game in progress. On the other was an arsenal of high-end technology—tablet, open laptop, and smart phone resting on top of a spread of papers and files she didn't recognize. Gabriel was much more comfortable with technology than he was willing to concede to her. *And tonight he's going to hand me another big box of paper files. He's so definitely screwing with me.* She lifted a piece from the chess board and plunked it down again a few squares away. "Check, you troublesome angel."

"That's not check. But almost." The nightangel leaned over her shoulder and his voice vibrated through her. He pushed the piece ahead to another square. "Try this move instead."

He stepped over to the chair across from hers and sat forward as if he was ready to continue the game. "I can teach you if you like."

The color burned in her face. Ricki had taught her how to play—just barely. Now, she wished she'd paid more attention.

"I kind of know the basics already."

Gabriel looked at the board and a smile slid into his eyes. "Chess is a complicated game. There's much to learn if you're going to win at it."

Maybe I don't want to win, Casey thought, frowning down at the board.

Gabriel smiled at her full out now, like in the dreams—when everything was right between them.

Then again, maybe I do. Of course I do. He knows I won't be happy until I have a decent chance of beating him at it. He had tapped right into her competitive streak. He admired her desire to excel and that was a relief to Casey. The real world men she knew weren't too hot about it. "I'm surprised you don't put it on the nightly itinerary."

"I could if you believe it would help us make a little progress here."

"You're all about progress, aren't you? You're like the cruise director on one of those ancient galley ships. Put your shoulders into it and let's sing a happy song, boys."

"Progress is required. Singing is not."

"That's lucky for you. I can't sing to save my life. You're the only one with the voice of an angel walking around here."

Casey lowered her eyes, which had been pinned on the nightangel throughout this discussion. *Dang it.* The last thing she needed to do was let him in on the fact that his voice made her feel like he was dragging her around on a gleaming cloud while they were talking.

"I like your voice too. So about the chess," Gabriel said, his glorious voice lowering just enough to call her eyes back to his.

"Well, you've already got me here. You may as well stuff one more fun activity into the evening. What's next? Role playing? Team building exercises?"

"No. I don't have any unrealistic expectations. Just chess."

"Just chess, huh? Well, that's all I need—another thing to worry about prepping for every day."

"No need for preparation. It would be on the job training."

"Who doesn't love that?"

"It could be a nice break in the evening. You might win. And don't forget the no-singing part."

"Yeah, that's the deal breaker on my side." Casey rose abruptly and Gabriel did the same. She drifted over to the massive worktable, curious about the array of papers, open volumes piled one upon the other, and rolls of oversized documents stacked to one side like firewood. "That was nice, what you did with the cricket."

"I had to do it. If you'd got to him first, he would have been done for. Admit it. You'd have smacked him with something. Probably one of those very serviceable shoes you're wearing."

The angel was absolutely right. Casey's glance jumped from the documents she'd been trying to casually study down to her kitten heels. As she had so often told the angels, she was no damn kitten. She hated her shoes. She'd give a lot to be wearing some beautiful peep-toe high heels but for the purposes of bug killing and staving off the interested stares of nightangels who enjoyed looking at her legs, these shoes were the ticket.

"He was jumping around. It's the kiss of death with me and bugs. If you hop, it's over. No bug is going to fling themselves on me and live to tell the tale. I'm not saying I'm proud of it. But seriously, he was terrifying."

"Lucky I was there then. I saved you from a guilty conscience and that tiny monster from total annihilation."

Casey pictured herself dancing around insisting the angel lay his hands all over her in the quest for one small cricket and how prompt his compliance to her demand had been and she began to laugh. "It was pretty funny wasn't it? For a minute there, I just went crazy. And the funniest part was I think maybe you liked me better that way. You were certainly getting more action from me. Oh, no, I can't believe I said that. Forget I said that."

Gabriel's eyes sparkled like fireworks were being set off somewhere deep inside them. "If I'd known that one little cricket could get us to talking like this, I would have brought in a whole jar and set them free the first night you came here."

She was laughing so hard at the thought of her hopping around in the middle of a batch of crickets like that would be a great conversation starter, at the thought of crazy Casey being easier for the angel to deal with than regular Casey who showed up on his doorstep each night, the tears started forming at the corners of her eyes and her sides started to ache.

"I was so scared of him," she said, wiping at her eyes, "I forgot to be scared of you."

He was laughing with her and when she looked up from where she was bent half over gasping for air, his smile cut through the barrier of her most desperate fears like the first rays of sunlight pierce the darkest moment of the night.

"That's good."

She wasn't sure that was good. Maybe she wanted to be afraid of him so she wouldn't have to wade through all the anxious feelings that swirled around her when she thought about her, with Gabriel, here. Maybe she needed to be afraid of him to keep from falling into a new life with Gabriel she wasn't ready to live yet.

"I don't want you to be scared of me." His voice was a verdant field, stretching calm and peaceful between them, calling her to trust in the words drifting across it.

"Well, maybe I do want it. Maybe I need it."

"No. You don't need it. Step forward and meet me in the place you are ready to stand. Where is that? Almost anyplace will do to start. I can be accommodating."

Even Casey knew she couldn't keep this up forever. Not when the angel was standing in front of her reminding her of how much she missed this Gabriel. The one who knew how to crack open her heart with a smile. The one who probably was already being amazingly accommodating for a nightangel waiting on getting his way—even if she couldn't quite see it.

The driver would advise her to stop dragging her feet. That this was the moment to take things in hand and ask the nightangel about the friend or foe thing.

"I think…"

"Yes."

"I think we should…"

He brought his face closer and the fire in his green eyes engulfed her. She felt swept up, swept away.

"Tell me."

Tell me. He had to lead with that. Casey stepped back. She had meant to ask him something. That was all. Not tell him something. Telling him something was more difficult. Not in the game plan right now.

"I think we should go upstairs now."

The playful light fled Gabriel's eyes. "Casey."

She shook her head. She turned without waiting to hear what he had to say and bolted out of the room, along the lower corridor, up the stairs, down the upstairs hall. The whistle of the tea kettle screaming behind her like the siren on a cop car fell silent as she entered into the office. She planted herself at her desk without even looking for additional crickets.

Maybe she did have a real reason to be afraid of him when she could not conceive a way to make even a small part of what he wanted her to tell him work while still keeping her life the way she wanted it. A life that was safe and secure, without the inevitable tragedy being with a nightangel would surely bring in the end.

Because mismatched relationships like Gabriel was so set on them entering into would always end. Wouldn't they? And she'd be standing in the embers while he soared away without a backward look when it did. Her brother had shown her the result of misplaced love. And as far as she could tell he wasn't even standing around in the ashes. He was just gone. Maybe her brother was nothing but a coward who ran away from problems when he should stand and fight for what he loved. It's not like she could ask him what the hell happened.

She had thought she knew what lesson her brother's mistakes and disappearance taught, thought it underlined why she was right for refusing the angel entrance into her life and why Gabriel was wrong for wanting something from her here in the first place. Now, she wasn't sure it had anything to do with her relationship with Gabriel at all.

She should have asked Gabriel about it when she was downstairs basking in the light of those warm green eyes. He could have helped her sort it out without advocating too much for his own position. He was good like that. At least he used to be. Now it was too late. Her fear overcame her desire for peace between them. Her anxiety shivered through her body and she craved the safe harbor of her indecision even if it resulted in pain for both of them.

The air sizzled with the sudden presence of the angel. "Fear makes us do things we wish we wouldn't do and not do things we wish we would," Gabriel said, placing a mug of steaming tea by the keyboard. She could smell the citrus. Earl Grey—her favorite.

It's what I have right now, she thought. *All I have. And I think it really stinks, too.* "Thank you for the tea," she said in a strained voice, not turning to look at him.

"You're welcome, Ms. Sloane."

The sharp edge to his polite words was a proclamation of renewed battle hammered into the wall she had flung back up against him. They were going to continue on until she conquered her fear or he got tired of waiting on her to come around. And he never seemed to tire so it looked like she was going to have to find a way to grapple with her fears whether she cared to do it or not.

"Drink up."

Listening to his voice didn't make her feel so much like he was tugging her around on a cloud anymore, unless it was a storm cloud. Her heart contracted. Was it possible she had just made things worse between them?

She didn't think she was going to tell the driver about any of this. She really wanted to get home and hide under the covers for a few hours and he'd probably insist she march right back inside instead and tell the damn nightangel something even if it wasn't everything he wanted to hear.

Telling Gabriel anything at all had become the hardest thing she had ever done.

And the sad part was she hadn't even started to do it yet.

≪ CHAPTER THIRTY-TWO ≫

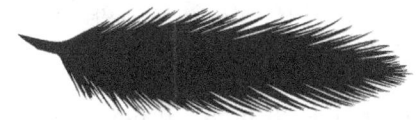

AS SOON AS THE nightangel left the room, Casey heaved a sigh of relief. She leapt up and retrieved the vase of flowers from where it sat behind her on the sidebar. She had no idea how he could have done it but she was pretty sure the bouquet was entirely composed of lush otherworldly roses. Not one of them had faded, and they smelled like the dream. Something inside her gave a visceral twang every time she laid eyes on them. That twang might have emanated from her heart or something located south of it that was just as opinionated about Gabriel. She wouldn't be surprised if it was caused by both at once. Whatever it was, it would not be silenced. It really wanted Gabriel Rule and was not willing to stop wanting him no matter how much she reasoned with herself.

She gave the flowers a sniff and the scent of everything she had forced herself to stop dreaming about exploded around her in an idyllic flash before dissipating again. He was so good at calling her to him without speaking a word and she was beginning to think maybe it wouldn't be as dire as she first thought to answer that call and venture a few steps closer to befriending a vampiric angel in this world, if that vampiric angel was Gabriel. She had played her conversation with the driver through in her head over and over but she could never bring herself to broach the topic of friend or foe with the beautiful and formidable angel breathing down her neck as though it was his solemn duty, and if he did it hard enough and often enough she would see where her duty lay as well.

Fear stopped her cold each time she thought maybe she could speak up, so there was silence between them most of the time. *That was best.* She walked across the room with purposeful strides, and plopped the flowers on the coffee table on the other side of the room, nearer to his desk than hers. "You smell them for a while," she said to Gabriel, even though he was not there to hear her. He'd get the message when he saw them.

The good thing about all of the time Gabriel required she spend alone with him in the quiet upstairs office of NIGHT, Inc. was that her billable hours were through the roof. The long hours had begun to wear on Casey. At home, she struggled to sleep, although she was exhausted. She could not stop her mind from racing each time she lay down. She slid from weary to wearier each night as her high-handed angel put her through her paces as though he was a ringmaster and she was his favorite center ring act. She'd be damned if she'd let him see it, though.

But weary she was and weary she stayed. She knew it made her a little stupid and she sought to remedy it with caffeine derived from the cans of diet cola she stashed in her purse each day before leaving home, and by reminding herself he had his eye on her and not in an isn't-she-perfectly-amazing sort of way. She could not appear inattentive or she would pay a price. His expectation that evening was that they would be discussing the details of an important contract he wanted her to review with him. If she could read it over once more without feeling as though she had not absorbed a word of what it said, she would be happy.

When Gabriel left the room, he sometimes did so for hours, and he had indicated this would be the case tonight. She found herself drawn to the large leather sofa in his absence. Maybe if she changed where she was sitting, she could concentrate. If he were in the room, she would have stayed glued to the workstation that had become hers—a place from which his glance rarely left her except to return again with unnerving regularity.

Sometimes she thought she saw him looking at her the way the dreamangel had done when he supposed she did not notice, as though she was the most beautiful thing he had ever happened upon in his entire existence and he could not help but stare at her for the wonder of it. If she looked up to confirm this, she saw nothing of it and was left to speculate on whether she had imagined the warmth of that look falling on her from the evergreen eyes of this colder, harder Gabriel or she had caught him out.

Casey sat on the sofa with the papers in hand. When he left her, she missed him, yet when he arrived back, she was filled with anxiety. She did not want to camp there too long in case he should reappear and think she was not preparing for their meeting as she ought. What would it hurt to lie down for one moment to rest her burning eyes? Wouldn't it help her concentrate on the fine points of the contract he meant to go over with her if she could take a five minute break? *Shut your eyes. You can't sleep at home, so there's no way you're going to fall asleep here.* She could lie there for a few minutes and she would feel more refreshed. He never had to know she was not planted at her desk rereading the same lines over and over again in the hopes of retaining their meaning. Casey sighed. She laid her head against the arm of the sofa and closed her eyes.

How strange. The garden at dusk was so peaceful but she had no idea how she had come upon it. She was sure that a moment before she was sitting on Gabriel's leather sofa trying to prepare for their next meeting. Now she was looking down at the roses and the pathways from the nightangel's keep. She breathed in the scent. The smell of that garden in full bloom was like heaven. She could hear Gabriel but she could not bring herself to turn toward the angel.

She stood, suspended in motion, gazing down at the roses. She continued to listen for his voice, as it had that sweetness to it that it had always held in the dreams. And as she did, she began to realize he was standing right next to her, whispering in her ear.

"Casey. My poor, Casey," he said, as though his heart was breaking for her. "I hate to see you like this. I despise being the author of one ounce of your fear or the smallest teardrop that falls from your eyes. I dislike seeing you so distraught, but you have said you would be my foe and so I must let you go down that path until you realize you wish to turn from it." He paused, waiting, but she said nothing.

His cool breath feathered her hair as he began to speak his next words close in her ear. "Do not make me continue with this conflict. I am loath to do it, my own, for in my heart I am always your friend. Won't you release us from this battle?"

His voice was soft, anguished. The echo of it spiked the air. The angel was waiting for her answer again. His ice-blue wings began to curve in a possessive arc around her; their cold, dangerous protection shutting out her fear.

Casey wished she could bring herself to answer because now was the time for the friend or foe talk if there was ever one but she could not stir.

The nightangel's words began to flow to every side of her again—like a building stream of whispering water rushing around a little stone that would soon be dislodged and swept up in the tide. "I swear to you, Casey, I am your Gabriel. The one you love even if you fear to reveal it to me. I understand. It will come in time. Trust in me now. Take the leap. Just jump. It is not so far to go—a step or two. My hand is there for you. I will not let you fall. I will never let you fall."

He was smoothing back her hair and his touch was snowy cold. She moaned at the cool pleasure of it and how it soothed her tired head.

The angel growled out a sigh that reflected his readiness to calm away her every worry forever if she would allow it. "Start toward me and it will be done. You will look back and see it was nothing to have worried over. Do it soon, my own. Aren't you weary of this yet?"

She wished she could press her lips against his hand in thanks for the small, unexpected comfort of his fingers caressing her skin but she stood as if in a stupor and let her perfectly beautiful nightangel touch her as he pleased without any response to him. The gentle pressure of his hand swept against her cheeks like he was wiping away every tear she had cried over the past few weeks—first one side, then the other. His scorching kiss followed in the wake of that touch. Didn't he realize she wanted to relent but did not know how to do it?

In the garden, a ragged snow began to fall in sharp, white angles until everything was gone except his touch and the echo of his words. She could not move from where she found herself. She rested in ringing emptiness laced and bound with the angel's touch until something pulled her from it with a start.

"Ms. Sloane."

Her eyes opened wide. Her angel did not look very interested in chasing all her cares away like he had a moment ago.

Gabriel was sitting on the edge of the coffee table by the sofa, shaking her awake. "Napping on the job? Get up, Ms. Sloane. I'm interested in your explanation. Now."

Casey was so shocked to find him in front of her and herself prone on the sofa she slipped off the cushions and landed at his feet, banging her knees soundly on the hardwood floor in the process. The papers scattered everywhere.

"Is this how you work when I leave you?" He glared down at her.

An angry nightangel asking questions she did not want to answer was not a happy sight. Casey kicked into apology mode in an attempt to damper down the potential for any avenging angel behavior on Gabriel's part. She could not do it with any grace because there was no way to get around the fact she was sleeping on the job and had, no doubt, been doing so for some time very happily. Did he ever rest or did he just go about his business with the relentless calm of the preternatural being? She began babbling her excuses. "I'm sorry. I'm really tired. I must have fallen asleep for a minute."

His frown deepened. She tried to gather the pages up, feeling foolish and wishing she was not wedged between the sofa and Gabriel, not sitting at his feet, not looking like such a total idiot.

"Well, it's a minute too much."

"I don't think you understand how exhausted I am. These are late hours and I'm having trouble sleeping."

"Are you being paid to sleep while you are here?"

"No, of course not." Casey stumbled over her words as she struggled to pick up the last of the scattered pages of her document.

"What do you do with your days, anyway?" He sounded sincerely curious.

"More work for you," she said in a soft voice infused with a mutinous undertone.

"Learn to manage your time more wisely and perhaps you will have time to sleep when you are not at work."

"I'm sorry. It won't happen again," she mumbled; anything to stop this conversation.

"I certainly hope not," he went on, not appeased by her apology or assurance. "Where is the report you were supposed to finish while I stepped out?"

Report? She'd gotten so tied up in reviewing the contract and taking an unscheduled nap that she'd forgotten all about that. Casey flushed pink and bounced up, untidy pile of papers in hand, like a slightly dazed pop up toy suddenly sprung from the box by a mischievous hand. She rushed around the far side of the coffee table toward the center of the room in an effort to avoid moving past the nightangel. She could not be so close to him when he was sure to begin berating her as soon as she admitted the report was still undone.

Anticipating her desire to escape, he came around the near side of the table and stepped in front of her so she had to halt in her path. "Well? Where is it?"

"I didn't finish it," she admitted. She tried not to hang her head like a criminal. "I forgot. I don't know how it happened. I'm sorry."

"Another thing to be sorry about. You are full of sorrys and poor excuses tonight. Wake yourself up and get back to work, Ms. Sloane. Just get it done and get it done now."

She wanted to say "screw you," but somehow something very different came out of her mouth. "I'm trying to do my best job for you." She wished she could take the words back as soon as they were said. They sounded childish and left her feeling more vulnerable than ever.

"Are you? Well, that's a bit of a shock, Ms. Sloane. If this is what you call your best job, I can only imagine what those who do not get that level of service from you may expect. Frankly, from what I have seen, it's not good enough all around. You make mistakes, you don't keep up with the work you are given, you tremble when you stand in front of me and shoot me hateful looks when you think I don't see, you are insolent and slow to speak in turns, and now I find you napping instead of doing the work you should have been about. I thought your career meant something to you and you would bring something more to the table than what you have. I find myself disappointed in this expectation."

The blood ran out of her face. "I'm sorry you see it that way," she said, and she was. Yet, it was nothing more than another "sorry" to him. She'd given him so many tonight; maybe he could take a few of them and practice apologizing for a change. He might be a nightangel from the other side but that was no reason to behave as if he was a law unto himself and did not owe her the slightest courtesy.

He was being harsh and rude, and Casey hated that because she did not think it was his way. None of it synced up with the vampire prince in the dreams. *The stupid friend or foe thing was the problem*, Casey thought. He was going to make her live by her words until she chose to tell him she wanted something else instead.

Tell me. It was what the nightangel demanded at every step and each time she acquiesced she was pretty sure all it did was provide him the opportunity to queue up the next request. Gabriel had a long list of things he thought she ought to tell him.

His insistence made it easy for Casey to justify her silence because telling the angel must be very important or he would not want it so much. That didn't mean it was easy. Or that she particularly wanted to stay silent any more—at least not with regard to the friend or foe matter.

Being enemies with a nightangel was the pits. As he predicted, the consequences for her choice were very unpleasant and hard to renegotiate. As much as she was all about making him unhappy enough with her to cut her loose, she was ashamed he was not satisfied with her work when she spent every waking hour of her day trying to excel amid an impossible set of circumstances. Deep down, she did not think Gabriel would lose interest in her through her efforts to push him aside. He was supposed to loosen his hold enough to pine away for her like any decent thwarted lover would. And he was supposed to go back and do all that pining away in the dreams. Was he tiring of her already? Casey found she did not like the idea as much as she would have thought.

What stung her most was while he might be speaking with little thought to her dignity or feelings, there was a kernel of truth to his assertions. She was so routinely distressed and overwrought that it could not be anywhere near her best work, no matter how much she strove to make it so. He had to know it. He was creating the situation in which she was forced to work and it was not conducive to top quality legal performance, only plain day-to-day survival skills.

If she were being honest, she would have to agree what he said had more truth in it than she wanted to admit about not just the quality of her work but the attitude she brought to it. She had not been able to snuff out her desire to strike back at him through secret, angry glances and little acts of insolence. She did not think he noticed them most of the time. When he did, she was glad to cause him some pain.

"You're right. I don't work well under this kind of pressure. I've never experienced anything like it before and maybe I haven't coped well with it. I apologize if you felt I was being rude or insolent. It's not the way I usually behave. No matter what you think, I have tried to do the best I could for you in the midst of a difficult situation."

"I had been led to believe that lawyers from the firm of Phillips and Row were brave warriors. I thought nothing could faze the likes of such fierce legal counsel. Yet, you crumble under my words and look like a fearful child instead of a competent professional woman when I cast as little as a stern glance or severe word your way. Mr. Johnson would be in a state of despair if he was witness to such weakness in one of his up-and-coming associates. I believe, Ms. Sloane, you would have an immediate fall from grace from which you would never recover."

Ed Johnson would pee his pants if he ever got a dose of the nightangel in a state of even mild displeasure. Casey believed with all her heart that even if she was barely standing up before him, she was still standing and that counted for more than he was giving her credit at the moment.

Casey glanced at the roses on the table and thought about throwing them out all over again to spite him. She wanted to do something childish to show him the difference between what he was calling her and what she really was.

"A true foe would toss them in my face," Gabriel said, glancing at the roses.

Casey did not respond. She did not want to throw the flowers or anything else. She just wanted an escape from the nightangel's hard words.

"Go ahead. Pitch them at me. You say you are my foe. You take pains to be at odds with me. Show me how much you hate me. Why don't you?"

Casey looked at the jewel-colored roses and shook her head no. "I'm conflicted. Besides, I don't throw things."

"Except flowers in the trash," the nightangel pointed out in a cool, reasonable voice.

"I pulled them out again," Casey answered, matching his tone.

The angel raised a dark eyebrow. "Why? Why did you do that?"

"I don't know," Casey said.

Taking her by the upper arms, he pulled her a fraction closer. He looked as though he was an inch from shaking it out of her. "Yes, you do. Tell me why. Why?"

"It's so confusing—you here, everything that is happening now. I'm not sure what is best to do."

"No. That's not it. There's something else," he said.

Casey felt as though he was intent on shoving her over some invisible line so she would just tell him—tell him everything. *Tell him, dammit.* Her own brain was screaming it. She thought about the way she had begun to fall backwards down the steep blood-red bricks stairs that led to NIGHT,

Inc. and the angel. They were standing face to face and deeply at odds as much at that moment as they were now. She remembered how afraid she had been when he had opened the door between them, how she had lost her balance in an instant, and how sure she was that she was done for. She had been so certain about falling into a world of pain. But Gabriel did not let it happen. That he had not allowed her to tumble off the landing was of critical importance—not only in that almost-could-have-killed-herself moment but right now. Still, she resisted thinking about what her rescue at his hands signified then, now, and for her future.

"What are you waiting for?"

A whisper of accusation blended with the scent of roses curled across the room. "He's your angel. He's your angel. Don't you know him?"

She did not want encouragement from some flowers that should not be sitting around on tabletops in the real world. She wanted a way to elude the moment.

"I'm not brave," Casey breathed. "I can't do what you want."

Gabriel stared at her until her knees began to tremble beneath her. He shook his head. "In the dreams, you were someone different. You were never afraid of a challenge. You never fell apart under the pressure of the moment. You never did your best job without it being good. What happened to that Casey Sloane? I liked her much better. I wonder now who that was because it does not seem to be you."

An edge of something very much like scorn in his voice cut Casey to the quick. Maybe he had hit his cutoff point for being the ever-patient bloodangel. He reached over and shoved the hair that hung in her face behind her ears with hard fingers. "Stop hiding from me. Do you think you can veil yourself from me behind that curtain of hair? I want to see your face when I talk to you. All of it."

A sense of overwhelming defeat washed over her. Like a tired swimmer pulled out too far by a riptide and unable to swim to shore, she felt the fight go out of her. What else was left to do but go under? She pushed his hands away and shoved her hair back around her face again. "I guess I'm not that person then. Maybe I never was. I don't think I know her anymore myself. Sometimes, I wish I'd never known her at all. She's been nothing but trouble for me," Casey said, her heart sinking under the weight of his contemptuous words, hating that he wanted to see her face while he spoke them at her.

She turned away from him and walked to the bathroom. She left the door open and she washed her face with a calm violence, stripping every stitch of makeup from it, dampening her hair, and yanking it back behind her ears again as he had done but more severely. She drifted back past him then without a glance, as if some light of hope that had been burning low within her until then had been snuffed out and all she had left was the dark. She did not cry. Why bother? She felt dead inside.

She sat staring at the computer. Suddenly, nothing mattered much to her anymore. She had resigned herself to something painful but inescapable. That something was the nightangel in all his unyielding glory. Of course, she was a disappointment to him. Wasn't it inevitable?

She could feel his eyes on her. Finally, she looked up toward him, sitting back at his desk, and said, "You asked what happened to that girl you knew in the dream. I'll tell you, Gabriel, if you really want to know."

She had not spoken his name in his presence once since he had arrived in her world and it felt dangerous saying it out loud; as if she was opening a door she could never shut again. She had now acknowledged the vampire in a way that, though small, gave him a sense of legitimacy in her eyes that was both tangible and irrefutable to both of them. She knew it was one of the things he wanted from her and now, it did not even matter that she was giving it to him.

She dragged herself up from the undertow of the latest sickening wave of emptiness rushing over her and continued. The girl in the dream deserved at least that much from her. "I'll tell you because she would want you to know. You frightened her away, Gabriel, and I doubt she is going to make another appearance again anytime soon because you know what—you are not the Gabriel she knew in the dreams either. He was kind, and good, and caring. You haven't shown me an ounce of that since I got here, unless you count bringing in some cans of soda and throwing them in a mini fridge. And I hardly think that counts." The quiver in her voice disappeared beneath her indignation. She crossed her arms across her chest.

The angel was chagrined. "You seem to like those particular sodas. You bring them in with you every night. I thought you would be pleased."

Casey shook her head.

"And there were flowers," he said, as if somehow, she might have forgotten about them.

Yeah, there were flowers alright. Flowers that shouldn't be there any more than he should be. Casey glared over at them. They were almost glowing with unnatural color and if she crossed the room and leaned over them right then, she wouldn't have been surprised if they said right out loud, "stop whining and get with the program." The flowers all loved Gabriel from what Casey could tell. Their colors grew more brilliant and their scent sweeter whenever he arrived in the garden within the dream. It didn't seem fair, considering the flowers belonged to her daydream world and as such, should have been all about her.

"You were using them as a weapon to make me submit to your will."

"That is not true."

Casey waved away the explanation he was about to make with one airy gesture of her hand. "The Gabriel in the dream would never do that. He would know damn well none of that would compensate for what he was doing every night to make things as hard as possible for me."

"It's what you wanted. You said foe." He was very matter-of-fact about the reason for her misery. She had made the choice.

Casey ignored him even though there was some underlying truth to what he said. She had declared them to be foes. Over and over again. In everything she did and said. She never gave him a chance to be something else to her and he had tried. Casey considered some of his efforts pitiful but maybe he thought he had to start somewhere. The truth was that he had opened the door to something different, something better, between them many times and she had slammed it shut again, whiplash fast. He frightened her down to the bone sometimes. Why could something as smart as a nightangel not get that?

"The Gabriel in the dreams would never have taken me up on it. He would have found another way. He would have understood me better."

"He understands you perfectly. It is you who do not understand him. If you did, all of this would have been unnecessary."

Casey knew there was no other way that would have brought them as nicely to the moment they were standing in—on the brink of a real dialogue between extraordinary and ordinary, as if that was the norm—with such inevitability. Casey was now feeling inclined to admit her world might just include insistent vampires, lately cloaked in wings, as well as ordinary mortal beings of the sort she represented. Every time she thought about what he was, all the courage drained out of her. And she was angry with him too that he would attempt what she would not—to bridge two worlds and go after happiness with no qualms, no second-thoughts. And, it seemed, with no consideration for what she wanted.

"He was something wonderful and special." Pleasure at her statement flashed in his eyes. "You're just terrifying and have a power over me I can't fight against without hurting myself in the process. He would have done anything to make me happy, but you—you would do anything to break me apart."

Her accusation stung him. The light left his eyes and they darkened to the color of deepest forest shadow.

"Casey," he breathed. "I never meant to—"

She stared into his face in a way that said she didn't care what he meant to do. "That girl in the dream, Casey Sloane—she's scared to death of you. And she has good reason for it. Look how you've treated me. What would that promise for her should she dare reveal herself? I don't think she should do it. Maybe she's gone for good. It would serve you right; her too for getting herself into this mess in the first place. Maybe she never really existed."

Her heart sank as she said this. Everything she loved seemed lost, yet she was still looking straight into its eyes like there was a chance for her to have it after all. It required some response to the standard demand, "tell me." That was clear. Telling him, however, was a big step. She did not know if she could take it; if she should take it. Giving a vampire entrance into your life was something Casey had to think was dangerous. Who could know what would spring from that small action?

Casey wondered if all she had to do was step aside and let Gabriel go from there.

They assessed each other in silence. His eyes grew a darker shade of green, like pine boughs mixed with smoke, before turning the pure fresh shade of new leaves in the spring. Casey tried not to admire them. "She exists. She is not gone," Gabriel said, finally.

"How do you know?"

"Because I know my dreamer when I see her, and I am looking at her right now."

Casey brought her hands to her face as if to shield herself from the intimate knowledge such a statement indicated and said nothing in return.

"Let me talk to her for a moment—the girl in the dreams. She might be of help to us. She is right here after all. She has been right here all along—very quiet, trying to be invisible. As if I would not see her. As if that would be possible."

She hesitated. "Why do you think it would help?"

"Because she always wished things well in the end. Her eternal optimism is one of her most endearing characteristics. Besides, she is a good friend of mine and I miss her."

Casey nodded her assent. He allowed the silence to build until her words began to explode like small flowers pushing up from beneath a late spring snow; a surprising burst of soft, passionate revelations opening before him. "Why should I show myself to you anyway—like I did in the dreams? Why should I make myself vulnerable to something that has done nothing but fill me with dread every night? Do you think what has gone on between us here is encouragement for me to step forward with an open heart? How have you been my friend here?"

"You should not be afraid of me." He turned his chair toward her as he spoke, leaning forward to gauge her reaction to his statement more completely. "All is not as you imagine."

"How can you say that?"

"I wished to be your friend from the start—the way I have ever been—but even though you knew me well, dreamer, you ran from me each time I approached. I tried to signal you a thousand subtle ways there was hope and all it would take was one word from you. You refused to understand me. Up to this very evening—you have refused to understand me. And when I did speak to you of my heart, you did not seem to care at all. You pushed me away. You did not give yourself a chance to see if I was whom I said and what that really meant to you. You never allowed me to show you the least kindness. You refused every conciliatory action I laid before you as if I were beneath contempt and not worthy of knowing in this world."

Casey blushed. Maybe she shouldn't have said anything about the damn sodas. Maybe she shouldn't have tossed the exquisite flowers into the trash like she was at some summer basketball camp and all that mattered was making the point. Casting aside his gifts was petty and she was not usually petty. And it wasn't even practical because she loved diet colas, yet here she was hauling her own cans of it in her handbag every night so she could reject his small act of hospitality. And there was no way she had ever figured out to get flowers delivered straight from her dreams to her doorstep. Gabriel had done it though—because he knew how much she loved those flowers—and she never gave them a glance until she was sure he could not see her pleasure in them.

Pretending to scorn someone all the time was difficult when every secret look their way made you want them more. Living a dream had been a lot of fun. Living a lie, not so much.

≪ CHAPTER THIRTY-THREE ≫

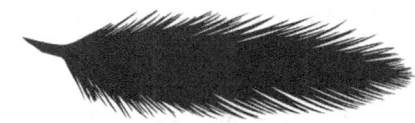

"THAT'S NOT WHAT I think. Not at all." Casey was appalled he should believe such a thing. "What else did you expect? I was shocked as hell to find you here—and scared. I was scared. I hardly had time to process your arrival before I discovered I was your sudden prisoner. I hated that."

"You are only a prisoner of your own fear and denial. You could have left if you wished at any time."

"No, I couldn't. You know I couldn't," Casey protested. *Maybe vampiric angels thought everybody was essentially born yesterday. She was not, however.*

"You are wrong about that."

"That's how it felt. I tried to hide behind a wall of business so I could think what to do but soon things got so out of hand I couldn't think at all. I could only come and go every night."

"Better to keep you safe by my side every night while we sort things out than leave you to wander through your daily life pretending you don't believe nightangels really exist. Who knows what ill-considered ways you might undertake to prove your point?"

"So that's what you're after—my safety and well-being?"

"You could say that."

"I'm not sure you're doing as good a job as you think."

"I'm doing a better job than you understand."

"Here's what I understand—you want things I can't give you."

"Don't you mean 'won't give me'? I've asked you for nothing not already there between us. I just begged the favor of having it in the real world. Is that so difficult?"

"Obviously, yes it is."

His eyes captured hers. "You have wished it so, too. Do you think I never heard you call out to me across the void between the dream and the world? Would you deny it?"

Yes, I would. I would deny it to hell and back again if I thought there was the smallest smidge of a chance you would believe me. Since she was sure he would not, she slipped around it by giving a semi-explanation. It was probably best not to admit too much calling forth of vampire princes into the real world, especially when the vampire prince was standing right in front of you, large as life.

"It's a bigger step for me to take than you think to flip everything over from the dream to the world just like that." Casey was glad they were talking as though she had stepped out of the dreams and onto his carpet to provide all the explanations Ms. Sloane, trying so hard to escape him, ignore him, hate his guts, or at least stop wanting him anyway, had not been able to speak until now.

Gabriel was pleased to have found a way to discuss everything they had not been able to speak about before, and he continued the conversation in this vein. "I could not let you run forever. The step you are afraid to take is not as big as you imagine, dreamer. You should trust me. You should know my heart. After all," he said, his voice free of any trace of reproach, "you crush it under your heel every day now for weeks as if it is nothing to you."

Casey's eyes widened. "I didn't mean to do that. I had no idea. I don't like feeling I'm not in control. You should know that about me."

The sudden warmth surfacing in his eyes said he did know that very well. "You are more in control than you realize. If not, do you think we would be going through these endless nights of conflict together? I would have something different between us than this tedious game that boils over into battle without cease." He examined her face for some sign she would too. "Why do you continue in it?"

Casey pulled her eyes away from him for a moment to rally her nerve. She thought about what the driver had said to her in those few moments of quiet clarity she had in the course of her recent days. She raised her eyes back to the nightangel's and she found herself really looking at Gabriel for the first time since he had appeared within her world in the way she had done in her dreams. He was ridiculously beautiful.

She could be brave, couldn't she? She could be calm—for a moment or two, couldn't she? Her dreamangel had come to her without wings in this place but he was still her angel. He was still listening to her with the same rapt attention he had always done when she spoke from the heart what was difficult for her to say. She'd been waiting for an opening to push the reset button. And here it was. The time to start talking was now.

"I thought I was playing it safe but now I've begun to understand sometimes choosing safety is no choice at all. I've begun to realize the true danger to me is in taking what seems like the safe route because maybe it's really not in the end. I'd like to reconsider my answer to you— the confident Casey in the dreams, the confused Casey who turns up here every night— if you'd let me."

Gabriel gave her an encouraging nod. Casey figured he was expecting her to finally tell him something worth hearing and he didn't want to say anything that would stop her doing it.

The question is," Casey paused and took a soft, ragged breath. "Do you have a Get Out of Jail Free card on you?"

"Yes, of course." He leaned further forward in his chair and his voice melted over her as he spoke like a warm wave pushing up through a frozen ocean. It dragged her up from the deep, drowning sorrow that had pulled her down within its cold depths and thrust her back to shore again. "You handed it to me yourself while the game was well underway. I have kept it with me since then in case you wished to put it to better use. Come here," he said without making it sound like a demand, "and you may have it from me for the both of you, my beautiful dreamer, my cautious Ms. Sloane."

"A two for one deal? What's the catch?"

"No catch. You may take it or leave it. But you must do one or the other now." Gabriel stood and pulled a folded dollar bill from his breast pocket. He laid it on the table.

Of course she must. Casey looked at the dollar, certain it was the one she had given him in exchange for slugging down half a can of soda and pouring the other half of his small peace offering down the sink, and a shocked laugh escaped her. She got up and walked with a determined step over to the desk.

Gabriel's demeanor was just as in the garden, when she had gone looking for him and finally came upon him—beckoning, inviting, impatient for her to cross the space between them. Casey dropped her eyes as she came closer. The intensity of everything the nightangel was by his very nature was much too much to stare in the face at the moment. She could barely keep her legs moving forward as it was. She stopped right in front of him and with shaky fingers, reached across to claim the reprieve being offered to her.

Her fingertips touched his where they rested on the bill. That small touch of flesh to flesh released her from all her qualms about going forward. A warming fire shot from the nightangel's heart straight through into hers as if an unquenchable flame had been ignited between them by the quick strike of a match. Suddenly, she wanted that stupid dollar bill from him more than anything she had ever wanted in her life. His fingers caressed hers and her desire to be at peace with him overrode all her pride, anger, and fear of what the future would hold when it contained the presence of a nightangel in her life who wasn't in a constant tug-of-war with her. How bad could that be? It had to be better than all this. Besides, it was a two-for-one deal, and she liked a good bargain. She snatched it from the table and clutched it in her hand.

Casey thought Gabriel looked very relieved to be rid of that particular dollar.

"That was close," she said, flustered, not sure what would come next.

"Indeed," Gabriel agreed, not making things any clearer.

"Looks like I just busted out of jail. And, lucky me, I've got a dollar to spare now." She was nervous in a whole new way, standing there in front of him without the safety of the battle between them. "Don't I get something if I pass Go?"

"Roll the dice and let's find out." He moved to pull her away from the desk and closer to him. That small act pushed aside any uncertainty as to what her current direction should be. She threw herself into the nightangel's arms with a little cry. Judging from how tight he held her, he was satisfied with her decisive action. For a minute, they stood pressed close together. Casey was shocked by what she had done. Gabriel was intent on savoring the moment without asking for something more.

Casey guessed this cost him something. And that made her trust him—at least for the moment. She burrowed deeper into his arms so he would know it. She buried any thoughts about how smart it was to be cuddling with a creature of the night because for the first time—maybe in her whole life—she felt safe. Because, after all, who was going to screw with you when you had a dangerous, preternatural beau looking out for you whether you liked it or not.

Casey pulled away a bit. "I know you might not think it right now but I am that Casey Sloane—the same one you've always known."

"I know, my love. I would never mistake my dreamer. And you, I do not believe you would mistake your dreamangel either. And I, Casey Sloane," he said, gathering her close again and speaking the words against the dark silk of her hair, "I am still the same Gabriel you have always known as well."

She buried her head in his shirt until she could steady her breathing and then pushed against his chest with enough force that he reluctantly released her. "I have to know right now—is it true you are so unhappy with me and the work I have done for you? I can't stand thinking it." A shiver of anxiety ran through her while she waited to hear what he would have to say about Casey, the attorney, versus Casey, the dreamer.

"I have not put you in the best situation for optimum performance. It's part of the problem with having a foe. Foes do not want to make things easy or see you succeed. And you have been adamant over these weeks—it was foe at every juncture."

True enough. She had radiated foe in everything she had said and done during her hours at Night, Inc. with Gabriel Rule.

"I made sure there was no way you could accomplish anything I set out for you to do very well or within the time constraints I gave you. What purpose would it have served to do otherwise?"

On one hand, Casey was relieved by this piece of information. No wonder she was working so hard without making the progress needed. There was nothing wrong with her legal acumen. She hadn't suddenly become a sub-par attorney. Then, all she had suffered over the last weeks courtesy of the nightangel Gabriel crept back into her mind. Anger percolated up inside her. "Are you kidding me?"

The nightangel cocked a dark eyebrow and stared back down at her. "I only sought to speed you on the path to peace between us in everything I did."

He ran a soothing hand across her hot, pale face. The tenderness of his fingers moving against her skin was making it impossible for her to think of why she should be holding on to her anger but she clung to it like a security blanket. "You're very resourceful. There must have been another way to make that happen besides all this."

"Not that would bring us together with such ease every night without fail while we came to an understanding. Look at how you have come to my call with so little argument to sit before me for so many hours. And if you were not always as pleasant as I would have liked, it was a small enough price to pay to have you here, safe and sound, with me, every evening bringing us closer to this moment."

"Frankly, I think it was a pretty rotten thing to do."

He nodded his agreement but shrugged. "I am sorry, my dreamer. It was not my original plan. I thought you would say 'friend' that first night."

Casey scoffed. "You got that wrong, didn't you?"

"Yes, I did. You surprised me. When you said no to our friendship, my intention was to accept your request at face value, so you would understand what a mistake it was and rethink it. It was not my desire, however. My desire has always lain in a very different place. I would prefer to make you nothing but happy and I believe I can do it if you will let me."

She let out a sigh that teetered between forgiving and resigned.

"Even knowing your propensity for out-and-out stubbornness, I did not expect it would take you so long to turn about. I think you should forgive me for my miscalculation. After all, my own, who could have believed anyone would be quite as obstinate as you have proved to be over the last few weeks?"

Like he wasn't?

"So I'm stubborn sometimes. That doesn't excuse everything on your part. You didn't make it all up, did you?" She spoke the words with rising horror. "Everything you had me do wasn't just to drive me crazy, was it?" She could not stand knowing the whole thing had been an elaborate fabrication meant to do nothing but confound her.

"Everything I have had you do has been legitimate work."

Casey continued to stare at him, waiting for more.

"The timeline and workload were compressed. You have gotten more done than I would ever have imagined you would be able to do under such difficult circumstances."

"Is that supposed to make me happy? Because I'm not feeling too happy right now."

Gabriel leaned his face closer to hers in that way he had that made all the thoughts fly out of her head. "What are you feeling then?" He signaled for her to speak with an inclination of his head that told Casey he was curious to hear her answer.

"Mad. I'm feeling mad at you for putting me through so much torment to get your way," she said, trying to sound as stern as she could manage under such scrutiny. "Really mad. And don't say it was about me too. You wanted to win. And you did."

"It was not about winning. It was never about winning. It was about beginning." There was the solemn angel again, intent on making sure she understood the message he had delivered to her.

"That's fine but I don't think you played fair."

Gabriel sighed in an appreciative way—as if he understood just how she must feel.

"And now, you can't just say 'sorry' and expect it to be enough."

"Making you comfortable would have drawn out our misery. You would have been content to linger in this limbo for longer than even the most patient angel or obstinate mortal could tolerate. Maybe you should be thanking me."

He was such a smartass sometimes. It shouldn't be funny but it was. Casey had to bite her lip to keep from laughing. He gave a teasing tug to a strand of her hair before pushing it back from her face. "What can I do to set it right?"

Casey hesitated for a moment, as if considering whether any resolution was possible. An exquisite furrow of his pale brow caused her to give up this paltry attempt at revenge before she got any satisfaction from it. "We could do it over."

"And how would we do that?" He sounded intrigued and a drop concerned, like Ricky Ricardo might be upon hearing Lucy say, "I have a wonderful idea."

"You know. Start fresh. Like in one of the dreams when something didn't work the first time and we did it over to get it right."

Understanding curved his reddening lips. "Shall we do better this time around?"

"Jury's out," Casey said, unwilling to allow him to think he had won with so little effort. She shook her head at her flawed reasoning. Like this had been so easy.

He was silent and his eyes turned serious. She wasn't in any position to overplay her hand. She loved everything about the nightangel in the dream. She loved everything about him so much she was afraid her whole life would be empty forever without him. And Gabriel Rule might have shown her a different side of the angel in the dreams, but he was never anything but the nightangel Gabriel in the end. Casey was captivated by every aspect of the nightangel—even those aspects she wasn't so thrilled about right now. She didn't want to risk losing him again in a childish bid to satisfy her wounded sensibilities.

"Well, what do you think? Worth a try?" She stared down at the glint of metal flowers circling her finger while he considered.

"Yes, if it is what you really wish." He was searching her face, watching her toy with the ring.

"I do."

He looked relieved. Now, he was on the receiving end of a bargain and he was smart enough to know it. "You're sure?"

Was he testing her level of desire or considering withdrawing his agreement to continue? Casey had no idea but an eagerness to proceed overcame her. She was not going to work one more night for some tyrannical vampire who wanted nothing from her but business and law when before his desire for her lay in areas so much more interesting, even if they were totally out of the question in the real world. She'd have to think about that later. She didn't give a damn at the moment about all the good reasons she should never consider it. She pushed him further away from her and stared into his face with a clear expectancy of his beginning the process without delay. "I do wish it."

"Very well, you shall have it as you wish," he said, very much in the manner of a vampire prince making a decree. He was definitely game for starting over.

"Who should start?" Casey concentrated on twisting the golden ring of flowers circling her finger like she was pacing a garden path they frequented in the dreams. "Will you?"

"Yes. I will start," the nightangel said in a soft, honey-sweet voice.

"Go ahead, then. Ask me again. Say, 'What shall it be?' Hurry up," she said in a tight whisper.

He took her hands in his. The blood heated in her veins. She saw in his face he felt it too. She held still and waited, as though her whole world hung in the balance. And Casey thought, deep down, maybe it did.

The angel spoke the question without hesitation, just as she requested. And his voice was a summons as much as a question. "Foe or friend, Ms. Sloane?" He smiled at her impatience but his eyes were serious. "What shall it be?" He was calling. But he was leaving it to her, to answer or not. He was gazing into her face with unmistakable interest. He wanted her to tell him how it would be between them. He wanted her answer to fill the air between them with a new certainty.

Of course he did. And she would. Tonight, she would tell the nightangel what he waited to hear without any hesitation.

"Friend," she said. "I choose friend." She said it in a rush, as if she must hurry or lose her chance.

He paused and Casey's heart stood still. Now she was the one waiting on him to tell her something she'd set her heart on hearing. Casey did not miss the irony of this but she didn't dwell on it either because the nightangel was about to speak. She understood her angel better now than a moment before. It was a scary, lonely place to stand in—this waiting place—even if you thought you knew what the answer would be in the end. She had made him stand there a long time. The nightangel Gabriel wasn't lying when he said he was being patient—he really had been patient; a million times more patient than she was feeling now that she was standing in his shoes.

His lips grew deep scarlet and his eyes turned the color of the deep woods when shot through with moonlight—bright and dark at the same time.

"Very well. Then so it will be, Casey. May I call you Casey, Ms. Sloane?"

"Yes," she said, struggling not to stammer out her response. "Yes, please. I can't stand hearing another 'Ms. Sloane' come out of your mouth."

"Fair enough. Casey it will be and nothing else. And you will call me Gabriel."

That was going to be hard when she had been calling him so many other names under her breath, none of them very polite, for weeks. "Okay. I can do that."

He looked expectantly at her, waiting for more. His hunger to hear his name cross her lips again was just as it had been in the dreams—powerful and humbling. It made her rush to correct herself. "I—I can do that, Gabriel."

"I like the way you say my name, Casey. Thank you, my dreamer, for

353

the gift of speaking it here instead of just there."

"Speaking of here and there, I have a few rules, for here versus there before we go any further."

"Rules? Already?"

"That's right."

"Strange. You are all about rules and caution here but in the dreams you broke so many rules and so often too that I began to wonder if there were any real rules at all."

"There were rules in the dreams—lots of them," Casey protested, thinking about every moment she had ever spent breaking the rules with the nightangel. She cast her eyes down.

"Yes, my own." His voice drew her eyes back to his. "But so many of them were unspoken. Yet, I suppose you decreed an adequate number aloud to cause me distress enough. Now that I think upon it, I am surprised you do not have a whole list for me, already written out."

Her mind was racing as she thought about all the possible contingencies she would have to guard against through the careful use of rules when it came to this nightangel. As Gabriel had surmised, her list was growing in leaps and bounds and they had only stopped the foe thing for a few minutes. "Maybe later. The big rule is that for now, we're friends and nothing else." She ignored his frown. "Do you understand what I'm saying?"

"It will do—for now." His indulgent gaze grew brighter, deeper; it poured over her like a refreshing summer rain after a long, hot day. She could get very used to that look. "I hope you understand I will have some rules of my own. And," Gabriel added as if it was something hardly worth the mention, "let's not forget. Ours are not the only rules."

Casey gave him a questioning look. "Whose rules are you talking about?"

"Aric and Rane will have some rules as well."

"Aric and Rane?" Casey repeated. *Oh, hell, no. He did not just say that.* Distress wiped the smile from her face and she began to push away from him.

"But maybe I am wrong." Gabriel said in a soothing voice, pulling her closer. "Do not worry."

No band of nightangels was going to be tromping through her life. *One nightangel was plenty, thank you.* "You had better be wrong."

"I am usually right about everything though," the nightangel said, as if that was a perfectly acceptable thing to say about oneself. "But we shall see."

Casey did not like the sound of that. In her experience with the nightangels, "we shall see" meant what you do not want to happen is so going to happen more quickly than you could ever imagine and you aren't going to be able to do a darn thing about it.

Gabriel pulled away enough to give her a playful smile and a surge of relief flowed through her. Was her nightangel teasing her?

"Oh, I get it. You're joking." She hoped with all her heart he was joking. He looked as if he might be joking. With vampires, it was hard to tell—even when they called themselves nightangels and you had seen the wings that proved they weren't kidding; wings so unspeakably magnificent they could freeze you in your tracks. "Very funny."

Aric and Rane. Like that could happen. Gabriel was standing there with her and no one else. No angels of any sort had stepped out of the daydream to yell "surprise" and revel in her reaction. Besides, she found it hard to believe Aric and Rane would be able to resist turning up if they had broken free and were wandering around in the world. Not after her last encounter with them deep inside that final terrifying daydream when they had refused to give her a true goodbye. That was then and there. This was here and now. And so far, she had come across this one solitary nightangel and nothing else.

That was good. Really good. She was barely okay with one nightangel at the moment, and even that had been a battle.

She let out a relieved sigh. The angel breathed it in with a satisfied look.

"Oh, by the way, don't make the assumption I'm still going to be working for you after tonight."

"Don't make the assumption you won't be."

"Let me guess. You expect the work situation to stand as is."

"I believe you will find your work conditions much improved."

Of course. Casey could guess what a nightangel meant by a statement like that. "So what are you saying? I still have a job if I continue to work with you?"

"You, Casey, have a secure place on NIGHT, Inc.'s legal team. I hope that is where you will decide to stay. I mean to do my best to keep you content there. After all, I have put a lot of time and energy into training you up."

He had invested weeks into making her work a living hell. She wasn't one bit sorry for him. Mostly, he was happy enough to do it. "But I work for Phillips and Row."

"Phillips and Row wants you here at NIGHT, Inc., working under my direction. And that means, for all intents and purposes, you work for me."

She crossed her arms and pursed her lips together in a way that said she did not like his answer one bit and meant to argue about it. "What if I don't want to work for you?" She needed to understand right from the beginning how he meant this to go.

"I suppose you will lose your job or at least set yourself back on the partnership track—most likely forever. But that doesn't mean I will stop you from quitting."

"You'll just make sure I feel the full force of my decision."

"Decisions have consequences."

"But you don't think it matters. You don't think I'm really going to quit no matter what the provocation, do you?"

"Given these last few weeks, I'd be a fool to assume anything. Go ahead, Cassandra Sloane, Esquire. Decide away."

Casey tried her hardest to glare at him. Instead, she found herself concentrating on the little glints of warm light sparkling in the evergreen depths of his eyes. "Right. But remember those consequences. Well, that works well for you, anyway."

"Some choices are not easy. Be that as it may, you have always had a choice."

"That's very comforting," Casey said, her voice heavy with sarcasm. He was still holding her captive via the job but he would let her go if she was set on leaving. She believed him when he said so. It was something— not a very heartening something but it was somewhat reassuring. She hadn't believed until that moment she had any choice at all.

Of course, Gabriel knew how to frame a choice to his best advantage. Casey understood from the friend or foe conflict that the nightangel was into providing choices weighted toward his desired outcome. And it was likely quite against his nature to make things easy. And he probably believed with all his heart he was doing it for the best.

Casey wasn't thrilled about any of these things but she got her nightangel's intent pretty well and it could be a hell of a lot worse.

"I would never take your ability to choose away from you."

"Now you're sweet-talking me."

Gabriel had the grace to smile. "It's the truth. Never doubt it. So what do you intend to do now that everything is in your hands?"

"Tell you what I want if I am even going to consider staying on," Casey said, turning serious.

"What do you want, my darling friend?"

"I want to keep the driver. I don't plan on driving around in the middle of nowhere in the dead of night just because you like to work late." He opened his mouth to respond but Casey cut him off. "And about weekends, I want them off. I don't think you get the normal and reasonable business hour thing. Not even in the way Phillips and Row interprets it, which is pretty much in the vein of all work and no play is A-OK."

The nightangel's smile poured over her again, like a pitcher of hot fudge drizzled over a scoop of vanilla ice cream. She melted a little. "For now, the driver will remain part of the package. Finding this particular office of NIGHT, Inc. tends to be troublesome but he knows the way very well."

"Yes, he certainly does."

"And, he is quite dependable." He smiled again. He was killing her with those smiles.

"Yeah," Casey agreed. "That too."

Yes. He was dependable. He was the most dependable thing in all the change that had been thrust upon her in recent weeks. And he gave excellent advice. With her Gabriel Rule problem under control for the time being, maybe the driver could turn his attention to providing her some tips on how to resolve things with Ricki next.

Casey was delighted Gabriel had not handed her a set of driving directions and canceled the one comforting aspect of her nightangel-constructed life-crisis now that she wasn't going to be arriving under a sort of mobile house arrest anymore. Gabriel was full of surprises. She had learned this was not always such a good thing but tonight it was working for her.

"But you are working weekends," he said. "Every one of them."

That was more like it. This answer did not surprise her at all. Casey shrugged. *Guess you can't get normal from a nightangel.* "Okay. Except this one. I want this one off. All three days of it. And I want them to myself."

"Three days? Why three?"

"Federal holiday. You're in D.C. now. We take our federal holidays very seriously. I suggest you do the same."

Gabriel Rule looked as though he was going to take everything that involved her very seriously whether she liked it or not. Casey thought that might be good and it might be bad. What it would never be is ordinary. She liked that idea enough to set aside most of her qualms about embarking on a real this-side-of-things relationship and take at least a step or two forward into the unknown. She was sick of ordinary. She wanted extraordinary. And that was something Gabriel could bring with a vengeance.

Gabriel was grasping her by her arms and his thumbs were making little circle motions on her skin that were inciting her to at least consider some rash acts. In the dreams, she would have let him continue but they were not in the dreams anymore. "You need to stop that," she said. "You're making me kind of dizzy and stuff." The stuff part was what worried her most.

He stopped and her head slowed its spinning. Casey already knew Gabriel was going to be good at everything and this was going to be a blessing and a curse in equal measure.

Her gaze fluttered up to his. Right now he was giving her request to be out of his sight for an entire holiday weekend the kind of consideration that made Casey's rebellious streak come dangerously close to surfacing. *It was just three days. He had better not say no. That was not going to fly.* Her protests already arose in her throat. Her desire to maintain the hard-fought peace between them was all that kept her from saying she would take the days no matter what he thought. Being in Gabriel's good graces again was nice—nicer than she would ever admit.

Besides, what would she tell the driver? She'd blown everything by getting into a skirmish over one stupid three-day weekend? She did not believe she would want to admit something like that to Amicus through the smokescreen of gray glass that separated them on their drives—not after all his wise counsel.

And she could see by the way Gabriel was looking at her, he did not want to be parted from her now that she had agreed to accept him— even if just to a small degree—into her world. She sensed he would pine for her over those three days. Nobody had ever pined for her in her life.

If he knew of her inner struggle, he made no sign. His eyes were dark with concentration as he considered her request. "Under these new, happier circumstances, I'd prefer you here, with me, but you may take the time, my own, since you are so set on having it. What will you do with the three days?"

Three whole days—all hers. The possibilities were endless. Then her practical side took over. "Sleep," she answered.

"Sleep." The angel leaned in and spoke the word back feather-soft against her mouth. A surge of desire hit her like a bolt of sugared lightning. He lifted his mouth away from hers again. "And what about daydreaming. Will you be doing any of that?"

"Not a chance." *Not a snowball's chance in hell. Daydreaming was off the list of allowable pastimes.* "No dreaming whatsoever. At least, not if I can help it," Casey replied.

Gabriel brought her right hand to his lips and pressed a melting kiss upon it. The velvet sound of the roses murmuring with pleasure at this turn of events grew louder. They were hopelessly romantic. She could not be annoyed at them for it when they were so elated on her behalf.

It was all very plain. Dreams and the things that come and go within them could never be managed. *Even the roses know that. Deep down, even I know that,* Casey admitted as the cool sweetness of the angel's kiss flooded her senses.

Judging from the power even this one small kiss held right then and there in the real world, Casey feared the nightangel knew it most of all.

About the Author

MARIE MICHELLE COLEMAN lives in the Washington D.C. area. She believes in the power of a compelling dream, the therapeutic merits of loud music, and the benefits of always being in the middle of reading a good book. She grows roses in her garden but no matter how hard she tries, they don't look anything like the ones in Casey Sloane's daydreams.

Visit her website at www.mariemichellecoleman.com to explore Casey's world in pictures, check out playlists for **Bespoken,** and more. Follow Marie on Twitter @M_M_Coleman and find her on Pinterest at www.pinterest.com/MarieMColeman.

www.ingramcontent.com/pod-product-compliance
Lightning Source LLC
Chambersburg PA
CBHW071209250626
47159CB00001B/263